THE APES OF WRATH

Tachyon Publications
1459 18th Street #139
San Francisco, CA 94107

Series Editor: Jacob Weisman
Project Editor: Jill Roberts

ISBN 10: 1-61696-085-X
ISBN 13: 978-1-61696-085-8

Printed in the United States by Worzalla
First Edition: 2013

9 8 7 6 5 4 3 2 1

Other books by Richard Klaw

Anthologies (as editor):

Modern Perversity
Creature Features
Weird Business (with Joe R. Lansdale)
The Wild West Show
The Big Bigfoot Book
Rayguns over Texas (forthcoming)

Books (as Rick Klaw):

Geek Confidential: Echoes from the 21st Century

For Mom,

Who'd have thunk it'd all lead to this?

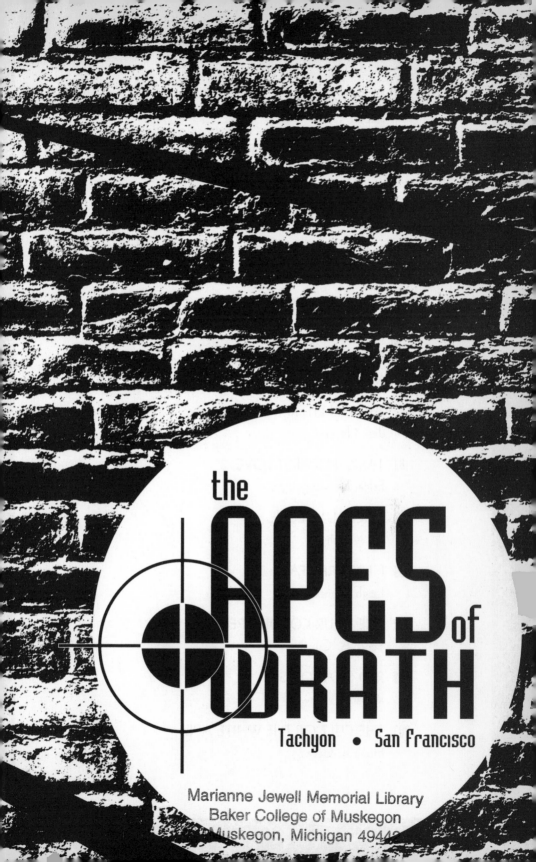

the APES of WRATH

Tachyon • San Francisco

FOREWORD

Rupert Wyatt

Consider the following characteristics of the most majestic of great apes: the mountain gorilla—

> The dominant silverback generally determines the movements of his group, leading it to appropriate feeding sites throughout the year. He also mediates conflicts within the group and protects it from external threats. When the group is attacked by humans, leopards, or other gorillas, the silverback will protect them even at the cost of his own life. He is the center of attention during rest sessions, and young animals frequently stay close to him and include him in their games. If a mother dies or leaves the group, the silverback is usually the one who looks after her abandoned offspring, even allowing them to sleep in his nest. Experienced silverbacks are even capable of removing poachers' snares from the hands or feet of their group members.[1]

---

[1]   http://en.wikipedia.org/wiki/Mountain_gorilla

You read this and one thing is clear: gorillas survive and prosper in a stable, cohesive, and nurturing environment that's held together by a protective and resourceful leader. In short, their society represents the ideal human society: they are a mirror of our best selves.

And then there's the chimpanzee—

> Adult chimpanzees, particularly males, can be very aggressive. They are highly territorial and are known to kill other chimps. Chimpanzees also engage in targeted hunting of lower order primates such as the red Colobus and bush babies, and use the meat from these kills as a "social tool" within their community.[2]

Sound familiar?

Of course, it would be unfair to paint chimps with such a broad brush. Their aggressive traits belie many other far more sociable habits. (For example they are known to share food, form coalitions, and even adopt young from outside groups.) Humans don't hold the monopoly on contradiction. And that's precisely why we're fascinated by our closest cousins, and *The Planet of the Apes* mythology exploits that fascination to the fullest. It presents the notion that we are not the only sentient creatures on Earth, capable of both good will and savage instinct. Like us, apes are a contradiction.

So that being the case, then what is to stop the apes taking over?

Our bodies and histories are so similar—and we share nearly all of our genes.

They are far stronger and faster than us.

And they require little from their habitat save cover, food, and water.

Put it this way: I wouldn't want to meet an angry ape in a dark

---

2   http://en.wikipedia.org/wiki/Chimpanzee#Behavior

alley. There's a reason why there's no "Planet of the Dogs" or "Planet of the Owls."

But then as much as the idea may be abhorrent to our more intellectual and urbane selves, would it be so bad to climb that tree in the back garden or do away with a knife and fork for just one meal time? As an ex-ape myself, I'm often tempted.

And if you can get behind that, then let's take it a step further— what would it be like to share the planet with another species that "talked back"? What if the closeness between humans and apes spilled over to be an absolute sameness?

This is the core question we should always be asking ourselves: What gives humans the right to dominate the planet? What are our obligations and what would happen if we were not the only game in town?

I have always wondered what an ape would say to his human counterpart were they ever to debate the hierarchy of the two species; if an ape could challenge his human counterpart to alpha status, using the power of speech to argue his point. Perhaps it might go something like this...

Has any ape ever torn the glands from a living man to graft them upon another ape for the sake of a brief and unnatural extension of that ape's life?

Was Torquemada an ape?

Was Adolf Hitler an ape?

Has it been necessary to found a society for the protection of ape children?

Are all the wars between apes or men?

Was poison gas an ape invention or a human one?

Could you ever mention the word cruelty in the presence of an ape without blushing?

Are you not what we've always been: the cruelest of all animals?

That is one point of view, a critical and anti-human argument that supports animal rights.

As its director, I made *Rise of the Planet of the Apes* a film ABOUT animal rights. And here's the reason why. We were telling the story from the apes' point of view.

Apes are our protagonists, and therefore I had to somehow make a film that required its human audience to root for a different species against our very own. And remember, we weren't telling a story that played out in isolation, but rather a global shift in hierarchy—The demise of our civilization and the dawn of a new alpha species: The Rise of the Ape.

How is it possible to do that? Surely that goes against every survival instinct we have. Why would we cheer and applaud the sight of our civilization being wiped off the face of the Earth?

The answer: Empathy.

That the film has been so successful and embraced by so many different age groups and backgrounds is testament to one of the greatest of all human qualities.

And that is why we are the alpha of our planet.

We are not the devil. We are humane; imaginative; creative; communicative; forgiving; caring; and nurturing.

As individuals we have it in us to achieve extraordinary things, even though as a group we are so often prone to falling prey to the darker aspects of our nature. All of this is encapsulated in the pages of this book. It's why we need great leaders to show us the right path. And in these unsettled times of environmental destruction, species decline, human overpopulation, water shortage, social and economic revolution, it is all the more crucial we look for those selfless leaders and follow them through thick and thin. If we do so, our future knows no bounds.

We have much to learn from the silverback.

Rupert Wyatt
April 2012

A BRIEF INTRODUCTION

Richard Klaw

Simians, especially the great apes, play an integral, vital role in our culture and in our collective unconscious. These creatures represent a part of humanity that must remain hidden. They can be both savage and gentle. They are much like man but they are not men. With their humanlike appearance and behaviors, it's easy to see what Darwin saw. As humanity's closest relation, how could apes not fascinate?

From Shakespeare's *Tempest* to Swift's *Gulliver's Travels* to James Fenimore Cooper's *The Monikins* to Edgar Allan Poe's "Murders in the Rue Morgue" through the twentieth-century tales of Edgar Rice Burroughs, Max Brand, Earle Stanley Gardner, L. Sprague de Camp, Wyndham Lewis, Rudyard Kipling, Franz Kafka, Gaston Leroux, C. S. Lewis, Michael Crichton, Pierre Boulle, Bernard Malamud, Pat Murphy, and countless others, simians infuse the literary playground. Similar influences abound in other media, especially film, as typified with the popular and culturally significant movies such as *King Kong*, *The Planet of the Apes* series, *Mighty Joe Young*, and the numerous Tarzan incarnations.

Surprisingly, given the simian's influential role in popular culture, only one previous anthology of ape fiction exists. Published in 1978 by Corgi, *The Rivals of King Kong* collected eight reprinted stories, two originals, and an excerpt from one of H. Rider Haggard's Allan Quatermain books. Editor Michel Parry contributed the introduction and checklist of simian cinema. The difficult-to-locate collectible paperback original commands a ridiculous price ranging from $30–$200.

John DeNardo, producer of the Hugo Award-winning website SF Signal, asked me to contribute to his popular Mind Meld series. This confluence of thoughts by science fiction writers, artists, editors, and critics ponders topics and themes of interest to fans of the genre. The subject this time ("If you could publish a short fiction anthology containing up to twenty-five previously published sf/f/h stories, which stories would it include and why?") enabled me to elaborate on one of the least understood and appreciated subgenres of fantastic fiction. I listed twenty-one stories all featuring apes by some of the biggest names in literature. It was a short jump to assembling this very book.

From that original list, I kept thirteen tales and added four more. The talented Gio Clairval supplied fresh translations for the Flaubert and Kafka contributions. Then using Ann and Jeff VanderMeer's extraordinary primer/anthology *Steampunk* as a template, I recruited fellow ape aficionados Scott A. Cupp, Mark Finn, and Jess Nevins to help me uncover the breadth of apes in pop culture and explore the simian's place in literature, comics, and film. Rupert Wyatt's marvelous foreword and the extraordinary Alex Solis cover round out this unique volume.

Despite the quality of the stories within, the authors are, at times, sadly the victims of the shallow and ignorant societal views of their time. Rather than preclude several otherwise excellent tales, I decided to include the unabridged versions, offensive beliefs and comments intact.

A brief note on the difference between apes and monkeys: While both are primates, apes do not have tails. Apes also tend to be larger and have bigger brains. Gorillas, chimpanzees, orangutans, gibbons, and even humans are classified as apes, while baboons, marmosets, and macaques are monkeys.

THE APE-BOX AFFAIR

James P. Blaylock

Arguably the first American-penned steampunk story, Blaylock's inventive tale about the panic after an orangutan-piloted flying ship crash lands in St. James Park incorporates H. G. Wells and Jules Verne by way of *The Three Stooges* and *Monty Python*.

A good deal of controversy arose late in the last century over what has been referred to by the more livid newspapers as "The Horror in St. James Park" or "The Ape-Box Affair." Even these thirty years later, a few people remember that little intrigue, though most would change the subject rather abruptly if you broached it, and many are still unaware of the relation, or rather the lack of relation, between the actual ape-box and the spacecraft that plunked down in the Park's duck pond.

The memoirs of Professor Langdon St. Ives, however, which passed into my hands after the poor man's odd disappearance, pretty clearly implicate him in the affair. His own orang-outang, I'll swear it, and the so-called Hooded Alien are one and the same creature. There is little logical connection, however, between that creature and "the thing in the box" which has since also fallen my way, and is nothing more than a clockwork child's toy. The ape puppet in that box, I find after a handy bit of detective work, was modeled after the heralded "Moko the Educated Ape" which toured with a Bulgarian Gypsy fair and which later became the central motif of the mysterious Robert Service sonnet, "The Headliner and the Breadliner." That the ape in the box became linked to St. Ives's shaven orang-outang is a matter of the wildest coincidence—a coincidence that generated a chain of activities no less strange or incredible. This then is the tale, and though the story is embellished here and there for the sake of dramatic realism, it is entirely factual in the main.

Professor St. Ives was a brilliant scientist, and the history books might some day acknowledge his full worth. But for the Chingford Tower fracas, and one or two other rather trivial affairs, he would be heralded by the Academy, instead of considered a sort of interesting lunatic.

His first delvings into the art of space travel were those which generated the St. James Park matter, and they occurred on, or better yet, were culminated in 1892 early in the morning of July 2. St. Ives's spacecraft was ball-shaped and large enough for one occupant; and because it was the first of a series of such crafts, that occupant was to be one Newton, a trained orang-outang who had only to push the right series of buttons when spacebound to motivate a magnetic homing device designed to reverse the craft's direction and set it about a homeward course. The ape's head was shaven to allow for the snug fitting of a sort of golden conical cap which emitted a meager electrical charge, sufficient only to induce a very mild sleep. It was of great importance that the ape remain docile while in flight, a condition which, as we shall see, was not maintained. The ape was also fitted with a pair of silver, magnetic-soled boots to affix him firmly to the deck of the ship; they would impede his movements in case he became restive, or, as is the problem with space travel, in case the forces of gravity should diminish.

Finally, St. Ives connected a spring-driven mechanism in a silver-colored box which puffed forth successive jets of oxygenated gas produced by the interaction of a concentrated chlorophyll solution with compressed helium—this combination producing the necessary atmosphere in the closed quarters of the ship.

The great scientist, after securing the ape to his chair and winding the chlorophyll box, launched the ship from the rear yard of his residence and laboratory in Harrogate. He watched the thing careen south through the starry early-morning sky. It was at that point, his craft a pinpoint of light on the horizon, that St. Ives was stricken with the awful realization that he had neglected to fill the ape's food dispenser, a fact which would not have been of consequence except that the ape was to receive half a score of greengage plums as a reward for pushing the several buttons which would affect the gyro and reverse the course of the ship. The creature's behavior once he ascertained that he had, in effect, been cheated of his greengages was unpredictable. There was nothing to be done, however, but for St. Ives to crawl wearily in to bed and hope for the best.

Several weeks previous to the launching of the craft (pardon the digression here; its pertinence will soon become apparent) a Bulgarian Gypsy caravan had set up a bit of a carnival in Chelsea, where they sold the usual salves and potions and such rot, as well as providing entertainments. Now, Wilfred Keeble was a toymaker who lived on Whitehall above the Old Shades and who, though not entirely daft, was eccentric. He was also the unloved brother of Winnifred Keeble, newly monied wife of Lord Placer. To be a bit more precise, he was loved well enough by his sister, but his brother-in-law couldn't abide him. Lord Placer had little time for the antics of his wife's lowlife relative, and even less for carnivals or circuses of gypsies. His daughter Olivia, therefore, sneaked away and cajoled her Uncle Wilfred into taking her to the gypsy carnival.

Keeble assented, having little use himself for Lord Placer's august stuffiness, and off they went to the carnival, which proved to be a rather pale affair, aside from the antics of Moko the Educated Ape. Actually, as far as Keeble was concerned, the ape itself was nothing much, being trained merely to sit in a great chair and puff on a cigar while seeming to pore over a copy of the *Times* which, more often than not, it held upside down or sideways or chewed at or tore up or gibbered over.

Olivia was fascinated by the creature and flew home begging her father for a pet ape, an idea which not only sent a thrill of horror and disgust up Lord Placer's spine, but which caused him to confound his brother-in-law and everything connected with him for having had such a damnable effect on his daughter. Olivia, her hopes dashed by her father's ape loathing, confided her grief to Uncle Wilfred who, although he knew that the gift of a real ape would generate conflicts best not thought about, could see no harm in fashioning a toy ape.

He set about in earnest to create such a thing and, in a matter of weeks, came up with one of those clockwork, key-crank jack-in-the-boxes. It was a silver cube painted with vivid circus depictions; when wound tightly, a comical ape got up as a mandarin and with whirling eyes would spring out and shout a snatch of verse. Wilfred Keeble was pretty thoroughly pleased with the thing, but he knew that it would be folly to go visiting his brother-in-law's house with such a wild and unlikely gift, in the light of Lord Placer's hatred of such things. There was a boy downstairs, a Jack Owlesby, who liked to earn a shilling here and there, and so Keeble called him up and, wrapping the box in paper and dashing off a quick note, sent Jack out into the early morning air two and six richer for having agreed to deliver the gift. Having sat up all night to finish the thing, Keeble crawled wearily into bed at, it seems, nearly the same hour that Langdon St. Ives did the same after launching his spacecraft.

Three people—two indigent gentlemen who seemed sea-captainish in a devastated sort of way, and a shrunken fellow with a yellow cloth cap who was somehow responsible for the chairs scattered about the green—were active in St. James Park that morning; at least those are the only three whose testimony was later officially transcribed. According to the *Times* report, these chaps, at about 7:00 AM, saw, as one of them stated, "a great fiery thing come sailing along like a bloody flying head"—an adequate enough description of St. Ives's ship which, gone amok, came plunging into the south end of the Park's duck pond.

This visitation of a silver orb from space would, in itself, have been sufficient to send an entire park full of people shouting into the city, but, to the three in the park, it seemed weak tea indeed when an alien-seeming beast sailed out on impact through the sprung hatch, a bald-headed but otherwise hairy creature with a sort of golden dunce cap, woefully small, perched atop his head. Later, one of the panhandlers, a gentleman named Hornby, babbled some rubbish about a pair of flaming stilts, but the other two agreed that the thing wore high-topped silver boots, and, to a man, they remarked of an "infernal machine" which the thing carried daintily between his outstretched hands like a delicate balloon as it fled into Westminster.

There was, of course, an immediate hue and cry, responded to by two constables and a handful of sleepy and disheveled Horse Guards who raced about skeptically between the witnesses while poor Newton, St. Ives's orang-outang, fuddled and hungry, disappeared into the city. At least three journalists appeared within half an hour's time and were soon hotfooting it away quick as you please with the tale of the alien ship, the star beast, and the peculiar and infernal machine.

Newton had begun to grow restless somewhere over Yorkshire, just as the professor had supposed he would. Now all of this is a matter of conjecture, but logic would point with a stiffish finger toward the probability that the electronic cap atop the ape's head either refused to function or functioned incorrectly, for Newton had commenced his antics within minutes of takeoff. There were reports, in fact, of an erratic glowing sphere zigging through the sky above Long Bennington that same morning, an indication that Newton, irate, was pretty thoroughly giving the controls the once-over. One can only suppose that the beast, anticipating a handful of plums, began stabbing away at the crucial buttons unaffected, as he must have been, by the cap. That it took a bit longer for him to run thoroughly amok indicates the extent of his trust in St. Ives. The professor, in his papers, reports that the control panel itself was finally dashed to bits and the chlorophyll-atmosphere box torn cleanly from the side of the cabin. Such devastation couldn't have been undertaken before the craft was approaching Greater London; probably it occurred above South Mimms, where the ship was observed by the populace to be losing altitude. This marked the beginning of the plunge into London.

Although the creature had sorted through the controls rather handily, those first plum buttons, luckily for him, activated at least partially St. Ives's gyro homing device. Had the beast been satisfied and held off on further mayhem, he would quite possibly have found himself settling back down in Harrogate at St. Ives's laboratory. As it was, the reversing power of the craft was enough finally to promote, if not a gentle landing, at least one which, taking into account the cushion of water involved, was not fatal to poor Newton.

Jack Owlesby, meanwhile, ambled along down Whitehall, grasping the box containing Keeble's ape contraption and anticipating a meeting with Keeble's niece whom he had admired more than once. He was, apparently, a good enough lad, as we'll see, and had been, coincidentally enough, mixed in with Langdon St. Ives himself some little time ago in another of St. Ives's scientific shenanigans.

Anyway, because of his sense of duty and the anticipation of actually speaking to Olivia, he popped right along for the space of five minutes before realizing that he could hardly go pounding away on Lord Placer's door at such an inhuman hour of the morning. He'd best, thought he, sort of angle up around the square and down The Mall to the park to kill a bit of time. A commotion of some nature and a shouting lot of people drew him naturally along and, as would have happened to anyone in a like case, he went craning away across the road, unconscious of a wagon of considerable size which was gathering speed some few feet off his starboard side. A horn blasted, Jack leapt forward with a shout, clutching his parcel, and a brougham, unseen behind the wagon, plowed over him like an express, the driver cursing and flailing his arms.

The long and the short of it is that Jack's box, or rather Keeble's box, set immediate sail and bounced along unhurt into a park thicket ignored by onlookers who, quite rightly, rushed to poor Jack's aid.

The boy was stunned, but soon regained his senses and, although knocked about a good bit, suffered no real damages. The mishaps of a boy, however, weren't consequential enough to hold the attention of the crowd, not even of the Lord Mayor, who was in the fateful brougham. He had been roused out of an early morning bed by the reports of dangerous aliens and inexplicable mechanical contrivances. He rather fancied the idea of a smoke and a chat and perhaps a pint of bitter later in the day with these alien chaps and so organized a "delegation," as he called it, to ride out and welcome them.

He was far more concerned with the saddening report that the thing had taken flight to the south than with the silver sphere that bobbed in the pond. The ship had been towed to shore, but as yet no one had ventured to climb inside for fear of the unknown—an unfortunate and decisive hesitation, since a thorough examination would certainly have enabled an astute observer to determine its origin.

It was to young Jack's credit that, after he had recovered from the collision, he spent only a moment or so at the edge of the pond with the other spectators before becoming thoroughly concerned over the loss of the box. The letter from Keeble to Olivia lay yet within his coat, but the box seemed to have vanished like a magician's coin. He went so far as to stroll nonchalantly across the road again, reenacting, as they say, the scene of the crime or, in this case, the accident. He pitched imaginary boxes skyward and then clumped about through bushes and across lawns, thoroughly confounded by the disappearance. Had he known the truth, he'd have given up the search and gone about his business, or what was left of it, but he had been lying senseless when old grizzled Hornby, questioned and released by the constables, saw Jack's parcel crash down some few feet from him as he sat brooding in the bushes. In Hornby's circles one didn't look a gift horse in the fabled mouth, not for long anyway, and he had the string yanked off and the wrapper torn free in a nonce.

Now you or I would have been puzzled by the box, silvery and golden as it was and with bright pictures daubed on in paint and a mysterious crank beneath, but Hornby was positively aghast. He'd seen such a thing that morning in the hands of a creature who, he still insisted, raged along in his wizard's cap on burning stilts. He dared not fiddle with it in light of all that, and yet he couldn't just pop out of the bushes waving it about either. This was a fair catch and, no doubt, a very valuable one. Why such a box should sail out of the skies was a poser, but this was clearly a day tailor-made for such occurrences. He scuttled away under cover of the thick greenery until clear of the mobbed pond area, then took to his heels and headed down toward Westminster with the vague idea of finding a pawnbroker who had heard of the alien threat and would be willing to purchase such an unlikely item.

Jack, then, searched in vain, for the box he'd been entrusted with had been spirited away. His odd behavior, however, soon drew the attention of the constabulary who, suspicious of the very trees, asked him what he was about. He explained that he'd been given a metallic looking box, and a very wonderful box at that, and had been instructed to deliver it across town. The nature of the box, he admitted, was unknown to him for he'd glimpsed it only briefly. He suspected, though, that it was a toy of some nature.

"A toy is it, that we have here!" shouted Inspector Marleybone of Scotland Yard. "And who, me lad, was it gave you this toy?"

"Mister Keeble, sir, of Whitehall," said Jack very innocently and knowing nothing of a similar box which, taken to be some hideous device, was a subject of hot controversy. Here were boxes springing up like the children of Noah, and it took no longer than a moment or two before two police wagons were rattling away, one to ferret out this mysterious Keeble, in league, like as not, with aliens, and one to inquire after Lord Placer down near the Tate Gallery. Jack, as well as a dozen policemen, were left to continue futilely scouring the grounds.

Somehow Newton had managed, by luck or stealth, to slip across Victoria Street and fall in among the greengrocers and clothing sellers along Old Pye. Either they were fairly used to peculiar chaps in that section of town and so took no special notice of him, or else Newton, wittily, clung to the alleys and shadows and generally laid low, as they say. This latter possibility is most likely the case, for Newton would have been as puzzled and frightened of London as had he actually been an alien; orang-outangs, being naturally shy and contemplative beasts, would, if given the choice, spurn the company of men. The incident, however, that set the whole brouhaha going afresh was sparked by a wooden fruit cart loaded, unfortunately, with nothing other than greengage plums.

Here was a poor woman, tired, I suppose, and at only eight o'clock or so in the morning, with her cart of fresh plums and two odious children. She set up along the curb, outside a bakery. As fortune would have it, she was an altogether kindly sort, and she towed her children in to buy a two-penny loaf, leaving her cart for the briefest of moments.

She returned, munching a slab of warm bread, in time to see the famished Newton, his greengages come round at last, hoeing into handfuls of the yellowy fruit. As the *Times* has the story, the ape was hideously covered with slime and juice, and, although the information is suspect, he took to hallooing in a resonant voice and to waving the box like a cudgel above his head. The good woman responded with shouts and "a call to Him above in this hour of dreadful things."

As I see it, Newton reacted altogether logically. Cheated of his greengages once, he had no stomach to be dealt with in such a manner again. He grasped the tongue of the cart, anchored his machine firmly in among the plums, and loped off down Old Pye Street toward St. Ann's.

Jack Owlesby searched as thoroughly as was sensible—more thoroughly perhaps, for, as I said, he was prompted and accompanied by the authorities, and as soon as the crowd in the park got wind of the possible presence of "a machine," they too savaged the bushes, surged up and down the road behind the Horse Guards, and tramped about Duck Island until the constables were forced to shout threats and finally give up their own search. The crowd thinned shortly thereafter, when a white-coated, bespectacled fellow hailing from the Museum came down and threw a tarpaulin over the floating ship.

Jack was at odds, blaming himself for the loss, but mystified and frustrated over its disappearance. There seemed to be only one option—to deliver the letter to young Olivia and then return the two and six to Mr. Keeble upon returning to the Old Shades. He set out, then, to do just that.

Inspector Marleybone was in an itch to get to the bottom of this invasion, as it were, which had so far been nothing more than the lunatic arrival of a single alien who had since fled. Wild reports of flaming engines and howling, menacing giants were becoming tiresome. But, though rumors have always been the bane of the authorities, they seem to be meat and drink to the populace, and here was no exception. Bold headlines of "Martian Invasion" and "St. James Horror" had the common man in a state, and it may as well have been a bank holiday in London by 9:00 that morning. A fresh but grossly overblown account of the plum-cart incident reached poor Marleybone at about the time he arrived back at the Yard, just as he had begun toying with the idea that there had been no starship, nor hairy alien nor dread engine, and that all had been a nightmarish product of the oysters and Spanish wine he'd enjoyed the night before. But here were fresh accounts, and the populace honing kitchen knives, and a thoroughly befuddled Wilfred Keeble without his cap, being ushered in by two very serious constables.

Keeble, who normally liked the idea of romance and grand adventure, didn't at all like the real thing, and was a bit groggy from lack of sleep in the bargain. He listened, puzzled, to Marleybone's questions, which seemed, of course, madness. There was no reference, at first, to strange metallic boxes, but only to suspected dealings with alien space invaders and to Marleybone's certainty that Keeble was responsible, almost single-handedly, for the mobs which, shouting and clanking in their curiosity, came surging up and down the road at intervals on their way to gaze at the covered ball in the pond, and to search for whatever wonderful prizes had rained on London from the heavens.

Keeble pleaded his own ignorance and innocence and insisted that he was a toy-maker who knew little of invasions, and would have nothing to do with such things had he the opportunity. Marleybone was wary but tired, and his spirits fell another notch when Lord Placer, his own eyes glazed from a night of brandy and cards at the club, stormed in in a rage.

Although it was all very well to ballyrag Keeble, it was another thing entirely with Lord Placer, and so the inspector, with an affected smile, began to explain that Keeble seemed to be mixed into the alien affair, and that a certain metallic box, thought to be a threatening device of some nature or another, had been intercepted, then lost, en route from Keeble to Lord Placer. It wasn't strictly the truth, and Marleybone kicked himself for not having taken Jack Owlesby in tow so that he'd at least have someone to point the accusatory finger at. Lord Placer, although knowing even less at this point than did his brother-in-law (who, at the mention of a silver box, saw a glimmer of light at the end of the tunnel), was fairly sure he could explain the fracas away even so. Wilfred Keeble, he stated, was clearly a madman, a raving lunatic who, with his devices and fables, was attempting to drive the city mad for the sake of company. It was a clear go as far as Lord P. could determine, and although it did not lessen the horror of being dragged from a warm bed and charged as an alien invader, it was at least good to have such a simple explanation. Lunacy, Lord Placer held, was the impetus behind almost everything, especially his brother-in-law's actions, whether real or supposed.

Finally Marleybone did the sensible thing, and let the two go, wondering why in the devil he'd called them in in the first place. Although he believed for the most part Keeble's references to a jack-in-the-box, he was even more convinced of Lord Placer's hypothesis of general lunacy. He accompanied Lord Placer to his coach, apologizing profusely for the entire business. Lord P. grunted and agreed, as the horses clopped away, to contact Scotland Yard in the event that the mysterious machine should, by some twist of insane fate, show up at his door.

Lady Placer, the former Miss Keeble, met her husband as he dragged in from the coach, mumbling curses about her brother. If anyone in the family had, as the poet said, "gone round the bend," it was Winnifred, who was slow-witted as a toothpick. She was, however, tolerant of her brother, and couldn't altogether fathom her husband's dislike of him, although she set great store in old Placer's opinions, and thus often found herself in a muddle over the contrary promptings of her heart and mind. She listened, then, with great curiosity to Lord Placer's confused story of the rumored invasion, the monster in the park, and his own suspected connection with the affair, which was entirely on account of her damned brother's rumminess.

Winnifred, having heard the shouting newsboys, knew something was in the air, and was mystified to find that her own husband and brother were mixed up in it. She was thoroughly awash when her husband stumbled away to bed, but was not overly worried, for confusion was one of the humours she felt near to and was comfortable with. She did wonder, however, at the fact that Lord Placer was involved in such weird doings, and she debated whether her daughter should be sent away, perhaps to her aunt's home near Dover, until the threat was past. Then it struck her that she wasn't at all sure what the threat was, and that spaceships might land in Dover as well as London, and also that, at any rate, her husband probably wasn't in league with these aliens after all. She wandered out to her veranda to look at a magazine. It was about then, I'd calculate, that the weary Marleybone got wind of the plum business and headed streetward again, this time in the company of the Lord Mayor's delegation.

It's not to be thought that, while Scotland Yard was grilling its suspects, Newton and Jack Owlesby and, of course, old Hornby who was about town with one of the two devices, stood idle. Newton, in fact, set out in earnest to enhance his already ballooning reputation. After making off with the plum cart, he found himself unpursued, and deep into Westminster, heading, little did he know, toward Horseferry Road. It's folly for a historian in such a case to do other than conjecture, but it seems to me that, sated with plums but still ravenous, as you or I might be sated with sweets while desiring something more substantial, he sighted a melon cart wending its way toward the greengrocers along Old Pye. Newton moored his craft in an alley, his box rooted in the midst of the plums, and hastened after the melon man, who was anything but pleased with the ape's appearance. He'd as yet heard nothing of the alien threat, and so took Newton to be an uncommonly ugly and bizarrely dressed thief. Hauling a riding crop from a peg on the side of the cart, the melon man laid about him with a will, cracking away at the perplexed orang-outang with wonderful determination, and shouting the while for a constable.

Newton, aghast, and taking advantage of his natural jungle agility, attempted to clamber up a wrought-iron pole which supported a striped canvas awning. His weight, of course, required a stout tree rather than a precariously moored pole, and the entire business gave way, entangling the ape in the freed canvas. The grocer pursued his attack, the ruckus having drawn quite a crowd, many of whom recognized the ape as a space invader, and several of whom took the trailing canvas, which had become impaled on the end of Newton's conical cap, to be some sort of Arab headgear. That, to be sure, explains the several accounts of alien-Mohammedan conspiracies which found their way into the papers. References to an assault by the invader against the melon man are unproven and, I think, utterly false.

When Newton fled, followed by the mob, he found his plum cart as he had left it—except for the box, which had disappeared.

Jack Owlesby hadn't walked more than a half mile, still glum as a herring over Keeble's misplaced trust, when, strictly by chance, he glanced up an alley off St. Ann's and saw a plum cart lying unattended therein. The startling thing was that, as you can guess, an odd metallic box was nestled in among the plums. Jack drew near and determined, on the strength of the improbability of any other explanation, that the box was his own, or, rather, Olivia's. He had seen the thing only briefly before it had been wrapped, so his putting the gypsy touch to it can be rationalized, and even applauded. Because he had no desire to encounter whoever stole the thing, he set out immediately, supposing himself to have patched up a ruinous morning.

Old Hornby had not been as fortunate as had Jack. His conviction that the box was extra-terrestrial was scoffed at by several pawnbrokers who, seeming vaguely interested in the prize, attempted to co-erce Hornby to hand it over to them for inspection. Sly Hornby realized that these usurious merchants were in league to swindle him, and he grew ever more protective of the thing as he, too, worked his way south. His natural curiosity drew him toward a clamoring mob which pursued some unseen thing.

It seemed to Hornby as if he "sniffed aliens" in the air and, as far as it goes, he was correct. He also assumed, this time incorrectly, that some profit was still to be had from these aliens, and so, swiftly and cunningly, he left the mob on Monck Street, set off through the alleys, and popped out at about the point that Horseferry winds around the mouth of Regency Street, head-on into the racing Newton who, canvas headgear and all, was outdistancing the crowd. Hornby was heard to shout, "Hey there," or "You there," or some such, before being bowled over, the ape snatching Hornby's treasured box away as it swept past, thinking it, undoubtedly, the box that had been purloined in the alley.

Jack Owlesby, meanwhile, arrived at Lord Placer's door and was admitted through the rear entrance by the butler, an affable sort who wandered off to drum up Miss Olivia at Jack's insistence. Lord Placer, hearing from the butler that a boy stood in the hall with a box for Olivia, charged into Jack's presence in a fit of determination. He'd played the fool for too long, or so he thought, and he intended to dig to the root of the business. He was well into the hall when he realized that he was dressed in his nightshirt and cap, a pointed cloth affair, and wore his pointy-toed silk house slippers which were, he knew, ridiculous. His rage overcame his propriety, and, of course, this was only an errand boy, not a friend from the club, so he burst along and jerked the box away from an amazed Jack Owlesby.

"Here we have it!" he shouted, examining the thing.

"Yes, sir," said Jack. "If you please, sir, this is meant for your daughter and was sent by Mr. Keeble."

"Keeble has a hand in everything, it seems," cried Lord Placer, still brandishing the box as if it were a great diamond in which he was searching for flaws. "What's this bloody crank, boy? Some hideous apparatus, I'd warrant."

"I'm sure I don't know, sir," replied Jack diplomatically, hoping that Olivia would appear and smooth things out. He was sure that Lord Placer, who seemed more or less mad, would ruin the thing.

Casting caution to the winds, Lord Placer whirled away at the crank while peering into a funnel-like tube that protruded from the end. His teeth were set and he feared nothing, not even that this was, as he had been led to believe, one of the infernal machines rampant in the city. Amid puffings and whirrings and a tiny momentary tinkling sound, a jet of bright chlorophyll-green helium gas shot from the tube, covering Lord Placer's face and hair with a fine, lime-colored mist.

A howl of outrage issued from Lord Placer's mouth, now hanging open in disbelief. It was an uncanny howl, like that of moaning elf, for the gaseous mixture, for a reason known only to those who delve into the scientific mysteries, had a dismal effect on his vocal cords, an effect not unnoticed by Lord P., who thought himself poisoned and leapt toward the rear door. Winnifred, having heard an indecipherable shriek while lounging on the veranda, was met by Olivia, fresh from a stroll in the rose garden, and the two of them were astounded to see a capering figure of lunacy, eyes awhirl in a green face, come bellowing with an elvish voice into the yard, carrying a spouting device.

Winnifred's worst fears had come to pass. Here was her husband, or so it seemed, gone amok and in a weird disguise. Lady Placer, in a gesture of utter bewilderment, clapped a hand to her mouth and slumped backward onto the lawn. Olivia was no less perplexed, to be sure, but her concern over her mother took precedence over the mystery that confronted her, and she stooped to her aid. Lady Placer was a stout-hearted soul, however, and she was up in a moment. "It's your father," she gasped in a voice that sounded as if it knew strange truths, "go to him, but beware."

Olivia was dumbfounded, but she left her mother in the care of the butler, and launched out in the company of Jack Owlesby (who was, by then, at least as confused as the rest of the company) in pursuit of her father, who was loping some two blocks ahead and still carrying the box.

It was at this point that the odd thing occurred. Newton, having lost the crowd, still swung along down Regency past stupefied onlookers. He rounded onto Bessborough and crossed John Islip Road, when he saw coming toward him a kindred soul. Here then came Lord Placer in his own pointed cap and with his own machine, rollicking along at an impressive clip. Now apes, as you know, are more intelligent in their way than are dogs, and it's not surprising that Newton, harried through London, saw at once that Lord Placer was an ally. So, with an ape's curiosity, he sped alongside for the space of a half block down toward Vauxhal Bridge, from which Lord Placer intended to throw himself into the river in hopes of diluting the odious solution he'd been doused with. Why he felt it necessary to bathe in the Thames is a mystery until we consider what the psychologists say—that a man in such an addled state might well follow his initial whims, even though careful contemplation would instruct him otherwise.

Inspector Marleybone, the Lord Mayor, and the delegation whipped along in their brougham in the wake of the mob. As is usual in such confusion, many of those out on the chase knew little or nothing of that which they pursued. Rumors of the alien invasion were rampant but often scoffed at, and secondary rumors concerning the march of Islam, and even that the walls of Colney Hatch had somehow burst and released a horde of loonies, were at least as prevalent. Marleybone blanched at the sight of clubs and hay forks, and the Lord Mayor, aghast that London would visit such a riot on the heads of emissaries from another planet, demanded that Marleybone put a stop to the rout; but such a thing was, of course, impossible and they gave off any effort at quelling the mob, and concentrated simply on winning through to the fore and restraining things as best they could. This necessitated, unfortunately, taking a bit of a roundabout route which promoted several dead-ends and a near collision with a milk wagon, but finally they came through, careening around the corner of Bessborough and Grosvenor and sighting the two odd companions hotly pursued by a throng that stretched from the Palace to Millbank. Here they reined in.

The Lord Mayor was unsure as to exactly what course of action to take, considering the size and activity of the crowd and the ghastly duo of cavorting box-carriers that approached. If anyone remembers Jeremy Pike, otherwise Lord Bastable, who served as Lord Mayor from '89 almost until the war, you'll recall that, as the poet said, he had a heart stout and brave, and a rather remarkable speech prepared for the most monstrous audience he was likely to encounter.

So the Lord Mayor, with Marleybone at his heels, strode into the road and held up his hands, palms forward, in that symbolic gesture which is universally taken to mean "halt." It is absurd to think that there is any significance to the fact that Newton responded correctly to the signal, despite the suggestion of two noted astronomers, because their theory—the literal universality of hand gestures—lies in Newton's other-worldliness, which, as we know, is a case of mistaken identity. Anyway, the pair of fugitives halted in flight, I believe, because it was at that point, when presented with the delegation, that Lord Placer's eyes ceased to revolve like tops and it looked as if he were "coming around." He was still very much in some nature of psychological shock, as would anyone be if thrown into a like circumstance, but he was keen-witted enough to see that here was the end of the proverbial line. As Lord Placer slowed to a stop, so did Newton, himself happy, I've little doubt, to give up the chase.

The mob caught up with the ambassadorial party in a matter of moments, and there was a great deal of tree climbing and shoulder hoisting and neck craning as the people of London pressed in along the Thames. Marleybone gazed suspiciously at Lord Placer for the space of a minute before being struck with the pop-eyed realization of the gentleman's identity

"Ha!" shouted the Inspector, reaching into his coat for a pair of manacles. Lord Placer, sputtering, proffered his box to the delegation, but a spurt of green fume and the tick of a timing device prompted a cry of, "The devil!" from Marleybone and, "The Infernal Machine!" from a score of people on the inner perimeter of the crowd, and everyone pressed back, fearing a detonation, and threatening a panic. Another burst of green, however, seemed to indicate that the device had miscarried somehow, and a smattering of catcalls and hoots erupted from the mob.

Lord Placer, at this point, recovered fully. He tugged his cloth cap low over his eyes and winked hugely several times at Olivia as she pushed through to be by his side. Olivia took the winks to be some sort of spasm and cried out, but Jack Owlesby, good lad he, slipped Lord P. a wink of his own, and very decorously tugged Olivia aside and whispered at her. Her father made no effort to rub away the chlorophyllic mask.

The Lord Mayor stepped up, and with a ceremonious bow took the glittering aerator from Lord Placer's outstretched hands. He held the thing aloft, convinced that it was some rare gift, no doubt incomprehensible to an earthling. He trifled with the crank. As another poof of green shot forth, the crowd broke into applause and began stamping about in glee.

"Londoners!" the Lord Mayor bawled, removing his hat. "This is indeed a momentous occasion." The crowd applauded heartily at this and, like as not, prompted Newton, who stood bewildered, to offer the Lord Mayor his own curiously wrought box.

A bit perturbed at the interruption but eager, on the other hand, to parley with this hairy beast who, it was apparent, hailed from the stars, old Bastable graciously accepted the gift. It was unlike the first box, and the designs drawn upon the outside, although weird, seemed to be of curiously garbed animals: hippos with toupees and carrying Gladstone bags, elephants riding in ridiculously small dog-carts, great toads in clam-shell trousers and Leibnitz caps, and all manner of like things. Seeing no other explanation, the Lord Mayor naturally assumed that such finery might be common on an alien star, and with a flourish of his right arm, as if he were daubing the final colors onto a canvas, he set in to give this second box a crank-up.

The crowd waited, breathless. Even those too far removed from the scene to have a view of it seemed to know from the very condition of the atmosphere that what is generally referred to as "a moment in history" was about to occur. Poor Hornby, his feet aching from a morning of activity, gaped on the inner fringe of the circle of onlookers, as Lord Placer, perhaps the only one among the multitude who dared move, edged away toward the embankment.

There was the ratchet click of a gear and spring being turned tighter and tighter until, with a snap that jarred the silence, the top of the box flew open and a tiny ape, singularly clad in a golden robe and, of all things, a night cap not at all unlike Lord Placer's, shot skyward, hung bobbing in mid-air, and, in a piping voice called out Herodotus's cryptic and immortal line: "Fear not, Athenian stranger, because of this marvel!" After uttering the final syllable the ape, as if by magic, popped down into the box, pulling the lid shut after him.

The Lord Mayor stared at Marleybone in frank disbelief, both men awestruck, when Lord Placer, his brass having given out and each new incident compounding his woe, broke for the stairs that led to the causeway below the embankment and sailed like billy-o in the direction of home. About half the mob, eager again for the chase, sallied out in pursuit. When their prey was lost momentarily from view, Jack Owlesby, in a stroke of genius, shouted, "There goes the blighter!" and led the mob around the medical college, thus allowing for Lord Placer's eventual escape. Marleybone and the Lord Mayor collared Newton, who looked likely to bolt, and were confronted by two out-of-breath constables who reported nothing less than the theft of the spacecraft by a white-coated and bearded fellow in spectacles, ostensibly from the museum, who carried official-looking papers. After towing Newton into the brougham, the delegation swept away up Millbank to Horseferry, lapped round behind Westminster Hospital and flew north back across Victoria without realizing that they were chasing phantoms, that they hadn't an earthly idea as to the identity or the whereabouts of the mysterious thief.

The Lord Mayor pulled his folded speech from his coat pocket and squinted at it through his pince-nez a couple of times, pretty clearly worked up over not having been able to utilize it. Marleybone was in a foul humor, having had his fill of everything that didn't gurgle when tipped upside down. Newton somehow had gotten hold of the jack-in-the-box and, to the annoyance of his companions, was popping the thing off regularly. It had to have been at the crossing of Great George and Abingdon that a dog-cart containing a tall, gaunt gentleman wearing a Tamerlane beret and with an evident false nose plunged alongside and kept pace with the brougham. To the astonishment of the delegation, Newton (a powerful beast) burst the door from its hinges, leapt out running onto the roadway, and clambered in beside Falsenose, whereupon the dog-cart howled away east toward Lambeth Bridge.

The thing was done in an instant. The alien was gone, the infernal machine was gone, the ship, likewise, had vanished, and by the time the driver of the brougham could fathom the cacophony of alarms from within his coach, turn, and pursue a course toward the river, the dog-cart was nowhere to be seen.

A thorough search of the Victoria Embankment yielded an abandoned, rented dog-cart and a putty nose, but nothing else save, perhaps, for a modicum of relief for all involved. As we all know, the papers milked the crisis for days, but the absence of any tangible evidence took the wind from their sails, and the incident of "The Ape-Box Affair" took its place alongside the other great unexplained mysteries, and was, in the course of time, forgotten.

How Langdon St. Ives (for it was he with the putty nose), his man Hasbro (who masterminded the retrieval of the floating ship), and Newton the orang-outang wended their way homeward is another, by no means slack, story. Suffice it to say that all three and their craft passed out of Lambeth Reach and down the Thames to the sea aboard a hired coal barge, from whence they made a rather amazing journey to the bay of Humber and then overland to Harrogate.

This little account, then, incomplete as it is, clears up some mysteries—mysteries that the principals of the case took some pains, finally, to ignore. But Lord Placer, poor fellow, is dead these three years, Marleybone has retired to the sea-side, and Lord Bastable... well, we are all aware of his amazing disappearance after the so-called "cataleptic transference" which followed his post-war sojourn in Lourdes. What became of Jack Owlesby's pursuit of Olivia I can't say, nor can I determine whether Keeble hazarded the making of yet another amazing device for his plucky niece, who was the very Gibraltar of her family in the months that followed the tumult.

So this history, I hope, will cause no one embarrassment, and may satisfy the curiosities of those who recall "The Horror in St. James Park." I apologize if, by the revelation of causes and effects, what was once marvelous and inexplicable slides down a rung or two into the realm of the commonplace; but such explication is the charge of the historian—a charge I hope to have executed with candor.

THE MURDERS
IN THE RUE MORGUE
Edgar Allan Poe

Poe's classic tale introduced the first true detective in fiction, C. Auguste Dupin.
Called upon to solve the brutal murder of two women, Dupin discovers a hair at the
murder scene that does not appear to be human.

> What song the Syrens sang, or what name Achilles
> assumed when he bid himself among women, although
> puzzling questions, are not beyond all conjecture.
> — Sir Thomas Browne, *Urn Burial*

The mental features discoursed of as the analytical, are, in themselves, but little susceptible of analysis. We appreciate them only in
their effects. We know of them, among other things, that they are
always to their possessor, when inordinately possessed, a source of
the liveliest enjoyment. As the strong man exults in his physical
ability, delighting in such exercises as call his muscles into action,
so glories the analyst in that moral activity which *disentangles*. He
derives pleasure from even the most trivial occupations bringing his
talent into play. He is fond of enigmas, of conundrums, hieroglyph-
ics; exhibiting in his solutions of each a degree of acumen which
appears to the ordinary apprehension praeternatural. His results,

brought about by the very soul and essence of method, have, in truth, the whole air of intuition.

The faculty of re-solution is possibly much invigorated by mathematical study, and especially by that highest branch of it which, unjustly, and merely on account of its retrograde operations, has been called, as if *par excellence,* analysis. Yet to calculate is not in itself to analyze. A chess-player, for example, does the one, without effort at the other. It follows that the game of chess, in its effects upon mental character, is greatly misunderstood. I am not now writing a treatise, but simply prefacing a somewhat peculiar narrative by observations very much at random; I will, therefore, take occasion to assert that the higher powers of the reflective intellect are more decidedly and more usefully tasked by the unostentatious game of draughts than by all the elaborate frivolity of chess. In this latter, where the pieces have different and *bizarre* motions, with various and variable values, what is only complex, is mistaken (a not unusual error) for what is profound. The *attention* is here called powerfully into play. If it flag for an instant, an oversight is committed, resulting in injury or defeat. The possible moves being not only manifold, but involute, the chances of such oversights are multiplied; and in nine cases out of ten, it is the more concentrative rather than the more acute player who conquers. In draughts, on the contrary, where the moves are unique and have but little variation, the probabilities of inadvertence are diminished, and the mere attention being left comparatively unemployed, what advantages are obtained by either party are obtained by superior acumen. To be less abstract, let us suppose a game of draughts where the pieces are reduced to four kings, and where, of course, no oversight is to be expected. It is obvious that here the victory can be decided (the players being at all equal) only by some *recherché* movement, the result of some strong exertion of the intellect. Deprived of ordinary resources, the analyst throws himself into the spirit of his opponent, identifies himself therewith, and not unfrequently sees thus, at a glance, the sole methods (sometimes indeed absurdly simple ones) by which he may seduce into error or hurry into miscalculation.

Whist has long been known for its influence upon what is termed the calculating power; and men of the highest order of intellect have been known to take an apparently unaccountable delight in it, while eschewing chess as frivolous. Beyond doubt there is nothing of a similar nature so greatly tasking the faculty of analysis. The best chess-player in Christendom *may* be little more than the best player of chess; but proficiency in whist implies a capacity for success in all these more important undertakings where mind struggles with mind. When I say proficiency, I mean that perfection in the game which includes a comprehension of *all* the sources whence legitimate advantage may be derived. These are not only manifold, but multiform, and lie frequently among recesses of thought altogether inaccessible to the ordinary understanding. To observe attentively is to remember distinctly; and, so far, the concentrative chess-player will do very well at whist; while the rules of Hoyle (themselves based upon the mere mechanism of the game) are sufficiently and generally comprehensible. Thus to have a retentive memory, and proceed by "the book" are points commonly regarded as the sum total of good playing. But it is in matters beyond the limits of mere rule that the skill of the analyst is evinced. He makes, in silence, a host of observations and inferences. So, perhaps, do his companions; and the difference in the extent of the information obtained, lies not so much in the validity of the inference as in the quality of the observation. The necessary knowledge is that of *what* to observe. Our player confines himself not at all; nor, because the game is the object, does he reject deductions from things external to the game. He examines the countenance of his partners, comparing it carefully with that of each of his opponents. He considers the mode of assorting the cards in each hand; often counting trump by trump, and honor by honor, through the glances bestowed by their holders upon each. He notes every variation of face as the play progresses, gathering a fund of thought from the differences in the expression of certainty, of surprise, of triumph, or chagrin. From the manner of gathering up a trick he judges whether the person taking it can make another in the suit. He recognizes what is played through feint, by the manner with which it is thrown upon the table. A casual or inadvertent word; the accidental dropping or turning of a card, with the accompanying anxiety or carelessness in regard to its concealment; the counting of the tricks, with the order of their arrangement; embarrassment, hesitation, eagerness, or trepidation—all afford, to his apparently intuitive perception, indications of the true state of affairs. The first two or three rounds having been played, he is in full possession of the contents of each hand, and thenceforward puts down his cards with as absolute a precision of purpose as if the rest of the party had turned outward the faces of their own.

The analytical power should not be confounded with simple ingenuity; for while the analyst is necessarily ingenious, the ingenious man is often remarkably incapable of analysis. The constructive or combining power, by which ingenuity is usually manifested, and to which the phrenologists (I believe erroneously) have assigned a separate organ, supposing it a primitive faculty, has been so frequently seen in those whose intellect bordered otherwise upon idiocy, as to have attracted general observation among writers on morals. Between ingenuity and the analytic ability there exists a difference far greater, indeed, than that between the fancy and the imagination, but of a character very strictly analogous. It will be found, in fact, that the ingenious are always fanciful, and the truly imaginative never otherwise than analytic.

The narrative which follows will appear to the reader somewhat in the light of a commentary upon the propositions just advanced.

Residing in Paris during the spring and part of the summer of 18—, I there became acquainted with a Monsieur C. Auguste Dupin. This young gentleman was of an excellent, indeed of an illustrious family, but, by a variety of untoward events, had been reduced to such poverty that the energy of his character succumbed beneath it, and he ceased to bestir himself in this world, or to care for the retrieval of his fortunes. By courtesy of his creditors, there still remained in his possession a small remnant of his patrimony; and, upon the income arising from this, he managed, by means of a rigorous economy, to procure the necessities of life, without troubling himself about its superfluities. Books, indeed, were his sole luxuries, and in Paris these are easily obtained.

Our first meeting was at an obscure library in the Rue Montmartre, where the accident of our both being in search of the same very rare and very remarkable volume, brought us into closer communion. We saw each other again and again. I was deeply interested in the little family history which he detailed to me with all that candor which a Frenchman indulges whenever mere self is the theme. I was astonished, too, at the vast extent of his reading; and, above all, I felt my soul enkindled within me by the wild fervor, and the vivid freshness of his imagination. Seeking in Paris the objects I then sought, I felt that the society of such a man would be to me a treasure beyond price; and this feeling I frankly confided to him. It was at length arranged that we should live together during my stay in the city; and as my worldly circumstances were somewhat less embarrassed than his own, I was permitted to be at the expense of renting, and furnishing in a style which suited the rather fantastic gloom of our common temper, a time-eaten and grotesque mansion, long deserted through superstitions into which we did not inquire, and tottering to its fall in a retired and desolate portion of the Faubourg St. Germain.

Had the routine of our life at this place been known to the world, we should have been regarded as madmen—although, perhaps, as madmen of a harmless nature. Our seclusion was perfect. We admitted no visitors. Indeed the locality of our retirement had been carefully kept a secret from my own former associates; and it had been many years since Dupin had ceased to know or be known in Paris. We existed within ourselves alone.

It was a freak of fancy in my friend (for what else shall I call it?) to be enamored of the night for her own sake; and into this *bizarrerie,* as into all his others, I quietly fell; giving myself up to his wild whims with a perfect *abandon.* The sable divinity would not herself dwell with us always; but we could counterfeit her presence. At the first dawn of the morning we closed all the massy shutters of our old building; lighted a couple of tapers which, strongly perfumed, threw out only the ghastliest and feeblest of rays. By the aid of these we then busied our souls in dreams—reading, writing, or conversing, until warned by the clock of the advent of the true Darkness. Then we sallied forth into the streets, arm in arm, continuing the topics of the day, or roaming far and wide until a late hour, seeking, amid the wild lights and shadows of the populous city, that infinity of mental excitement which quiet observation can afford.

At such times I could not help remarking and admiring (although from his rich ideality I had been prepared to expect it) a peculiar analytic ability in Dupin. He seemed, too, to take an eager delight in its exercise—if not exactly in its display—and did not hesitate to confess the pleasure thus derived. He boasted to me, with a low chuckling laugh, that most men, in respect to himself, wore windows in their bosoms, and was wont to follow up such assertions by direct and very startling proofs of his intimate knowledge of my own. His manner at these moments was frigid and abstract; his eyes were vacant in expression; while his voice, usually a rich tenor, rose into a treble which would have sounded petulant but for the deliberateness and entire distinctness of this enunciation. Observing him in these moods I often dwelt meditatively upon the old philosophy of the Bi-Part Soul, and amused myself with the fancy of a double Dupin—the creative and the resolvent.

Let it not be supposed, from what I have just said, that I am detailing any mystery, or penning any romance. What I have described in the Frenchman was merely the result of an excited, or perhaps of a diseased, intelligence. But of the character of his remarks at the periods in question an example will best convey the idea.

We were strolling one night down a long dirty street, in the vicinity of the Palais Royal. Being both, apparently, occupied with thought, neither of us had spoken a syllable for fifteen minutes at least. All at once Dupin broke forth with these words:

"He is a very little fellow, that's true, and would do better for the *Théâtre des Variétés.*"

"There can be no doubt of that," I replied, unwittingly, and not at first observing (so much had I been absorbed in reflection) the extraordinary manner in which the speaker had chimed in with my meditations. In an instant afterward I recollected myself, and my astonishment was profound.

"Dupin," said I, gravely, "this is beyond my comprehension. I do not hesitate to say that I am amazed, and can scarcely credit my senses. How was it possible you should know I was thinking of—?" Here I paused, to ascertain beyond a doubt whether he really knew of whom I thought.

"—of Chantilly," said he, "why do you pause? You were remarking to yourself that his diminutive figure unfitted him for tragedy."

This was precisely what had formed the subject of my reflections. Chantilly was a *quondam* cobbler of the Rue St. Denis, who, becoming stage-mad, had attempted the *rôle* of Xerxes, in Crébillon's tragedy so called, and been notoriously Pasquinaded for his pains.

"Tell me, for Heaven's sake," I exclaimed, "the method—if method there is—by which you have been enabled to fathom my soul in this matter." In fact, I was even more startled than I would have been willing to express.

"It was the fruiterer," replied my friend, "who brought you to the conclusion that the mender of soles was not of sufficient height for Xerxes *et id genus omne.*"

"The fruiterer!—you astonish me—I know no fruiterer whomsoever."

"The man who ran up against you as we entered the street—it may have been fifteen minutes ago."

I now remember that, in fact, a fruiterer, carrying upon his head a large basket of apples, had nearly thrown me down, by accident, as we paused from the Rue C—— into the thoroughfare where we stood; but what this had to do with Chantilly I could not possibly understand.

There was not a particle of *charlâtanerie* about Dupin. "I will explain," he said, "and that you may comprehend all clearly, we will first retrace the course of your meditations, from the moment in which I spoke to you until that of the *rencontre* with the fruiterer in question. The larger links of the chain run thus—Chantilly, Orion, Dr. Nichols, Epicurus, Stereotomy, the street stones, the fruiterer."

There are few persons who have not, at some period of their lives, amused themselves in retracing the steps by which particular conclusions of their own minds have been attained. The occupation is often full of interest; and he who attempts it for the first time is astonished by the apparently illimitable distance and incoherence between the starting-point and the goal. What, then, must have been my amazement, when I heard the Frenchman speak what he had just spoken, and when I could not help acknowledging that he spoke the truth. He continued:

"We had been talking of horses, if I remember aright, just before leaving the Rue C——. This was the last subject we discussed. As we crossed into this street, a fruiterer, with a large basket upon his head, brushing quickly past us, thrust you upon a pile of paving-stones collected at a spot where the causeway is undergoing repair. You stepped upon one of the loose fragments, slipped, slightly strained your ankle, appeared vexed or sulky, muttered a few words, turned to look at the pile, and then proceeded in silence. I was not particularly attentive to what you did; but observation has become with me, of late, a species of necessity.

"You kept your eyes upon the ground—glancing, with a petulant expression, at the holes and ruts in the pavement (so that I saw you were still thinking of the stones), until we reached the little alley called Lamartine, which has been paved, by way of experiment, with the overlapping and riveted blocks. Here your countenance brightened up, and, perceiving your lips move, I could not doubt that you murmured the word 'stereotomy,' a term very affectedly applied to this species of pavement. I knew that you could not say to yourself 'stereotomy' without being brought to think of atomies, and thus of the theories of Epicurus; and since, when we discussed this subject not very long ago, I mentioned to you how singularly, yet with how little notice, the vague guesses of that noble Greek had met with confirmation in the late nebular cosmogony, I felt that you could not avoid casting your eyes upward to the great *nebula* in Orion, and I certainly expected that you would do so. You did look up; and I was now assured that I correctly followed your steps. But in that bitter *tirade* upon Chantilly, which appeared in yesterday's *'Musée,'* the satirist, making some disgraceful allusions to the cobbler's change of name upon assuming the buskin, quoted a Latin line about which we have often conversed. I mean the line

Perdidit antiquum litera prima sonum.

I had told you that this was in reference to Orion, formerly written Urion; and, from certain pungencies connected with this explanation, I was aware that you could not have forgotten it. It was clear, therefore, that you would not fail to combine the two ideas of Orion and Chantilly. That you did combine them I saw by the character of the smile which passed over your lips. You thought of the poor cobbler's immolation. So far, you had been stooping in your gait; but now I saw you draw yourself up to your full height. I was then sure that you reflected upon the diminutive figure of Chantilly. At this point I interrupted your meditations to remark that as, in fact, he was a very little fellow—that Chantilly—he would not do better at the *Théâtre des Variétés.*"

Not long after this, we were looking over an evening edition of the "Gazette des Tribunaux," when the following paragraphs arrested our attention.

"EXTRAORDINARY MURDERS.—This morning, about three o'clock,

the inhabitants of the Quartier St. Roch were roused from sleep by a succession of terrific shrieks, issuing, apparently, from the fourth story of a house in the Rue Morgue, known to be in the sole occupancy of one Madame L'Espanaye, and her daughter, Mademoiselle Camille L'Espanaye. After some delay, occasioned by a fruitless attempt to procure admission in the usual manner, the gateway was broken in with a crowbar, and eight or ten of the neighbors entered, accompanied by two *gendarmes*. By this time the cries had ceased; but, as the party rushed up the first flight of stairs, two or more rough voices, in angry contention, were distinguished, and seemed to proceed from the upper part of the house. As the second landing was reached, these sounds, also, had ceased, and everything remained perfectly quiet. The party spread themselves, and hurried from room to room. Upon arriving at a large back chamber in the fourth story (the door of which, being found locked, with the key inside, was forced open), a spectacle presented itself which struck every one present not less with horror than with astonishment.

"The apartment was in the wildest disorder—the furniture broken and thrown about in all directions. There was only one bedstead; and from this the bed had been removed, and thrown into the middle of the floor. On the chair lay a razor, besmeared with blood. On the hearth were two or three long and thick tresses of gray human hair, also dabbled with blood, and seeming to have been pulled out by the roots. Upon the floor were found four Napoleons, an ear-ring of topaz, three large silver spoons, three smaller of *métal d'Alger*, and two bags, containing nearly four thousand francs in gold. The drawers of a *bureau*, which stood in one corner, were open, and had been, apparently, rifled, although many articles still remained in them. A small iron safe was discovered under the bed (not under the bedstead). It was open, with the key still in the door. It had no contents beyond a few old letters, and other papers of little consequence.

"Of Madame L'Espanaye no traces were here seen; but an unusual quantity of soot being observed in the fire-place, a search was made in the chimney, and (horrible to relate!) the corpse of the daughter, head downward, was dragged therefrom; it having been thus forced up the narrow aperture for a considerable distance. The body was quite warm. Upon examining it, many excoriations were perceived, no doubt occasioned by the violence with which it had been thrust up and disengaged. Upon the face were many severe scratches, and, upon the throat, dark bruises, and deep indentations of finger nails, as if the deceased had been throttled to death.

"After a thorough investigation of every portion of the house without farther discovery, the party made its way into a small paved yard in the rear of the building, where lay the corpse of the old lady, with her throat so entirely cut that, upon an attempt to raise her, the head fell off. The body, as well as the head, was fearfully mutilated—the former so much so as scarcely to retain any semblance of humanity.

"To this horrible mystery there is not as yet, we believe, the slightest clew."

The next day's paper had these additional particulars:

"*The Tragedy in the Rue Morgue.* Many individuals have been examined in relation to this most extraordinary and frightful affair," [the word '*affaire*' has not yet, in France, that levity of import which it conveys with us] "but nothing whatever has transpired to throw light upon it. We give below all the material testimony elicited.

"*Pauline Dubourg,* laundress, deposes that she has known both the deceased for three years, having washed for them during that period. The old lady and her daughter seemed on good terms—very affectionate toward each other. They were excellent pay. Could not speak in regard to their mode or means of living. Believe that Madame L. told fortunes for a living. Was reputed to have money put by. Never met any person in the house when she called for the clothes or took them home. Was sure that they had no servant in employ. There appeared to be no furniture in any part of the building except in the fourth story.

"*Pierre Moreau*, tobacconist, deposes that he has been in the habit of selling small quantities of tobacco and snuff to Madam L'Espanaye for nearly four years. Was born in the neighborhood, and has always resided there. The deceased and her daughter had occupied the house in which the corpses were found, for more than six years. It was formerly occupied by a jeweller, who under-let the upper rooms to various persons. The house was the property of Madame L. She became dissatisfied with the abuse of the premises by her tenant, and moved into them herself, refusing to let any portion. The old lady was childish. Witness had seen the daughter some five or six times during the six years. The two lived an exceedingly retired life—were reputed to have money. Had heard it said among the neighbors that Madame L. told fortunes—did not believe it. Had never seen any person enter the door except the old lady and her daughter, a porter once or twice, and a physician some eight or ten times.

"Many other persons, neighbors, gave evidence to the same effect. No one was spoken of as frequenting the house. It was not known whether there were any living connections of Madame L. and her daughter. The shutters of the front windows were seldom opened. Those in the rear were always closed, with the exception of the large back room, fourth story. The house was a good house—not very old.

"*Isidore Muset, gendarme*, deposes that he was called to the house about three o'clock in the morning, and found some twenty or thirty persons at the gateway, endeavoring to gain admittance. Forced it open, at length, with a bayonet—not with a crowbar. Had but little difficulty in getting it open, on account of its being a double or folding gate, and bolted neither at bottom nor top. The shrieks were continued until the gate was forced—and then suddenly ceased. They seemed to be screams of some person (or persons) in great agony—were loud and drawn out, not short and quick. Witness led the way up stairs. Upon reaching the first landing, heard two voices in loud and angry contention—the one a gruff voice, the other much shriller—a very strange voice. Could distinguish some words of the former, which was that of a Frenchman. Was positive that it was not a woman's voice. Could distinguish the words '*sacré*' and '*diable*.' The shrill voice was that of a foreigner. Could not be sure whether it was the voice of a man or of a woman. Could not make out what was said but believed the language to be Spanish. The state of the room and of the bodies was described by this witness as we described them yesterday.

"*Henri Duval*, a neighbor, and by trade a silver-smith, deposes that he was one of the party who first entered the house. Corroborates the testimony of Muset in general. As soon as they forced an entrance, they reclosed the door, to keep out the crowd, which collected very fast, notwithstanding the lateness of the hour. The shrill voice, this witness thinks, was that of an Italian. Was certain it was not French. Could not be sure that it was a man's voice. It might have been a woman's. Was not acquainted with the Italian language. Could not distinguish the words, but was convinced by the intonation that the speaker was an Italian. Knew Madame L. and her daughter. Had conversed with both frequently. Was sure that the shrill voice was not that of either of the deceased.

"———— *Odenheimer, restauranteur.* This witness volunteered his testimony. Not speaking French, was examined through an interpreter. Is a native of Amsterdam. Was passing the house at the time of the shrieks. They lasted for several minutes—probably ten. They were long and loud—very awful and distressing. Was one of those who entered the building. Corroborated the previous evidence in every respect but one. Was sure that the shrill voice was that of a man—of a Frenchman. Could not distinguish the words uttered. They were loud and quick—unequal—spoken apparently in fear as well as in anger. The voice was harsh—not so much shrill as harsh. Could not call it a shrill voice. The gruff voice said repeatedly, '*sacré*,' '*diable*,' and once '*mon Dieu*.'

"*Jules Mignaud*, banker, of the firm of Mignaud et Fils, Rue Deloraine. Is the elder Mignaud. Madame L'Espanaye had some property.

Had opened an account with his banking house in the spring of the year —— (eight years previously). Made frequent deposits in small sums. Had checked for nothing until the third day before her death, when she took out in person the sum of 4000 francs. This sum was paid in gold, and a clerk sent home with the money.

"*Adolphe Le Bon*, clerk to Mignaud et Fils, deposes that on the day in question, about noon, he accompanied Madame L'Espanaye to her residence with the 4000 francs, put up in two bags. Upon the door being opened, Mademoiselle L. appeared and took from his hands one of the bags, while the old lady relieved him of the other. He then bowed and departed. Did not see any person in the street at the time. It is a by-street—very lonely.

"*William Bird*, tailor, deposes that he was one of the party who entered the house. Is an Englishman. Has lived in Paris two years. Was one of the first to ascend the stairs. Heard the voices in contention. The gruff voice was that of a Frenchman. Could make out several words, but cannot now remember all. Heard distinctly '*sacré*' and '*mon Dieu.*' There was a sound at the moment as if of several persons struggling—a scraping and scuffling sound. The shrill voice was very loud—louder than the gruff one. Is sure that it was not the voice of an Englishman. Appeared to be that of a German. Might have been a woman's voice. Does not understand German.

"Four of the above-named witnesses, being recalled, deposed that the door of the chamber in which was found the body of Mademoiselle L. was locked on the inside when the party reached it. Every thing was perfectly silent—no groans or noises of any kind. Upon forcing the door no person was seen. The windows, both of the back and front room, were down and firmly fastened from within. A door between the two rooms was closed but not locked. The door leading from the front room into the passage was locked, with the key on the inside. A small room in the front of the house, on the fourth story, at the head of the passage, was open, the door being ajar. This room was crowded with old beds, boxes, and so forth. These were carefully removed and searched. There was not an inch of any portion of the house which was not carefully searched. Sweeps were sent up and down the chimneys. The house was a four-story one, with garrets (*mansardes*). A trap-door on the roof was nailed down very securely—did not appear to have been opened for years. The time elapsing between the hearing of the voices in contention and the breaking open of the room door was variously stated by the witnesses. Some made it as short as three minutes—some as long as five. The door was opened with difficulty.

"*Alfonzo Garcio*, undertaker, deposes that he resides in the Rue Morgue. Is a native of Spain. Was one of the party who entered the house. Did not proceed up stairs. Is nervous, and was apprehensive of the consequences of agitation. Heard the voices in contention. The gruff voice was that of a Frenchman. Could not distinguish what was said. The shrill voice was that of an Englishman—is sure of this. Does not understand the English language, but judges by the intonation.

"*Alberto Montani*, confectioner, deposes that he was among the first to ascend the stairs. Heard the voices in question. The gruff voice was that of a Frenchman. Distinguished several words. The speaker appeared to be expostulating. Could not make out the words of the shrill voice. Spoke quick and unevenly. Thinks it is the voice of a Russian. Corroborates the general testimony. Is an Italian. Never conversed with a native of Russia.

"Several witnesses, recalled, here testified that the chimneys of all the rooms of the fourth story were too narrow to admit the passage of a human being. By 'sweeps' were meant cylindrical sweeping-brushes, such as are employed by those who clean chimneys. These brushes were passed up and down every flue in the house. There is no back passage by which any one could have descended while the party proceeded up stairs. The body of Mademoiselle L'Espanaye was so firmly wedged in the chimney that it could not be got down until four or five of the party united their strength.

"*Paul Dumas*, physician, deposes that he was called to view the bodies about daybreak. They were both then lying on the sacking of the bedstead in the chamber where Mademoiselle L. was found. The corpse of the young lady was much bruised and excoriated. The fact that it had been thrust up the chimney would sufficiently account for these appearances. The throat was greatly chafed. There were several deep scratches just below the chin, together with a series of livid spots which were evidently the impressions of fingers. The face was fearfully discolored, and the eyeballs protruded. The tongue had been partially bitten through. A large bruise was discovered upon the pit of the stomach, produced, apparently, by the pressure of a knee. In the opinion of M. Dumas, Mademoiselle L'Espanaye had been throttled to death by some person or persons unknown. The corpse of the mother was horribly mutilated. All the bones of the right leg and arm were more or less shattered. The left *tibia* much splintered, as well as all the ribs of the left side. Whole body dreadfully bruised and discolored. It was not possible to say how the injuries had been inflicted. A heavy club of wood, or a broad bar of iron—a chair—any large, heavy, and obtuse weapon would have produced such results, if wielded by the hands of a very powerful man. No woman could have inflicted the blows with any weapon. The head of the deceased, when seen by witness, was entirely separated from the body, and was also greatly shattered. The throat had evidently been cut with some very sharp instrument—probably with a razor.

"*Alexandre Etienne,* surgeon, was called with M. Dumas to view the bodies. Corroborated the testimony, and the opinions of M. Dumas.

"Nothing farther of importance was elicited, although several other persons were examined. A murder so mysterious, and so perplexing in all its particulars, was never before committed in Paris—if indeed a murder had been committed at all. The police are entirely at fault—an unusual occurrence in affairs of this nature. There is not, however, the shadow of a clew apparent."

The evening edition of the paper stated that the greatest excitement still continued in the Quartier St. Roch—that the premises in question had been carefully re-searched, and fresh examinations of witnesses instituted, but all to no purpose. A postscript, however, mentioned that Adolphe Le Bon had been arrested and imprisoned—although nothing appeared to criminate him beyond the facts already detailed.

Dupin seemed singularly interested in the progress of this affair— at least so I judged from his manner, for he made no comments. It was only after the announcement that Le Bon had been imprisoned, that he asked me my opinion respecting the murders.

I could merely agree with all Paris in considering them an insoluble mystery. I saw no means by which it would be possible to trace the murderer.

"We must not judge of the means," said Dupin, "by this shell of an examination. The Parisian police, so much extolled for *acumen,* are cunning, but no more. There is no method in their proceedings, beyond the method of the moment. They make a vast parade of measures; but, not unfrequently, these are so ill-adapted to the objects proposed, as to put us in mind of Monsieur Jourdain's calling for his *robe-de-chambre—pour mieux entendre la musique.* The results attained by them are not unfrequently surprising, but for the most part, are brought about by simple diligence and activity. When these qualities are unavailing, their schemes fail. Vidocq, for example, was a good guesser, and a persevering man. But, without educated thought, he erred continually by the very intensity of his investigations. He impaired his vision by holding the object too close. He might see, perhaps, one or two points with unusual clearness, but in so doing he, necessarily, lost sight of the matter as a whole. Thus there is such a thing as being too profound. Truth is not always in a well. In fact, as regards the more important knowledge, I do believe that she is invariably superficial. The depth lies in the valleys where we seek her, and not upon the mountain-tops where she is found. The modes and sources of this kind of error are well typified in the contemplation of the heavenly bodies. To look at a star by glances—to view it in a side-long way, by turning toward it the exterior portions of the retina (more susceptible of feeble impressions of light than the interior), is to behold the star distinctly—is to have the best appreciation of its lustre—a lustre which grows dim just in proportion as we turn our vision *fully* upon it. A greater number of rays actually fall upon the eye in the latter case, but in the former, there is the more refined capacity for comprehension. By undue profundity we perplex and enfeeble thought; and it is possible to make even Venus herself vanish from the firmament by a scrutiny too sustained, too concentrated, or too direct.

"As for these murders, let us enter into some examinations for ourselves, before we make up an opinion respecting them. An inquiry will afford us amusement," [I thought this an odd term, so applied, but said nothing] "and besides, Le Bon once rendered me a service for which I am not ungrateful. We will go and see the premises with our own eyes. I know G——, the Prefect of Police, and shall have no difficulty in obtaining the necessary permission."

The permission was obtained, and we proceeded at once to the Rue Morgue. This is one of those miserable thoroughfares which intervene between the Rue Richelieu and the Rue St. Roch. It was late in the afternoon when we reached it, as this quarter is at a great distance from that in which we resided. The house was readily found; for there were still many persons gazing up at the closed shutters, with an objectless curiosity, from the opposite side of the way. It was an ordinary Parisian house, with a gateway, on one side of which was glazed watch-box, with a sliding panel in the window, indicating a *loge de concierge*. Before going in we walked up the street, turned down an alley, and then, again turning, passed in the rear of the building—Dupin, meanwhile, examining the whole neighborhood, as well as the house, with a minuteness of attention for which I could see no possible object.

Retracing our steps we came again to the front of the dwelling, rang, and, having shown our credentials, were admitted by the agents in charge. We went up stairs—into the chamber where the body of Mademoiselle L'Espanaye had been found, and where both the deceased still lay. The disorders of the room had, as usual, been suffered to exist. I saw nothing beyond what had been stated in the "Gazette des Tribunaux." Dupin scrutinized everything—not excepting the bodies of the victims. We then went into the other rooms, and into the yard; a *gendarme* accompanying us throughout. The examination occupied us until dark, when we took our departure. On our way home my companion stepped in for a moment at the office of one of the daily papers.

I have said that the whims of my friend were manifold, and that *Je les ménagais*—for this phrase there is no English equivalent. It was his humor, now, to decline all conversation on the subject of the murder, until about noon the next day. He then asked me, suddenly, if I had observed anything peculiar at the scene of the atrocity.

There was something in his manner of emphasizing the word "peculiar," which caused me to shudder, without knowing why.

"No, nothing *peculiar*," I said; "nothing more, at least, than we both saw stated in the paper."

"The 'Gazette,'" he replied, "has not entered, I fear, into the unusual horror of the thing. But dismiss the idle opinions of this print. It appears to me that this mystery is considered insoluble, for the very reason which should cause it to be regarded as easy of solution—I mean for the *outré* character of its features. The police are confounded by the seeming absence of motive—not for the murder itself—but for the atrocity of the murder. They are puzzled, too, by the seeming impossibility of reconciling the voices heard in contention, with the facts that no one was discovered upstairs but the assassinated Mademoiselle L'Espanaye, and that there were no means of egress without the notice of the party ascending. The wild disorder of the room; the corpse thrust, with the head downward, up the chimney; the frightful mutilation of the body of the old lady; these considerations, with those just mentioned, and others which I need not mention, have sufficed to paralyze the powers, by putting completely at fault the boasted acumen, of the government agents.

They have fallen into the gross but common error of confounding the unusual with the abstruse. But it is by these deviations from the plane of the ordinary, that reason feels its way, if at all, in its search for the true. In investigations such as we are now pursuing, it should not be so much asked 'what has occurred,' as 'what has occurred that has never occurred before.' In fact, the facility with which I shall arrive, or have arrived, at the solution of this mystery, is in the direct ratio of its apparent insolubility in the eyes of the police."

I stared at the speaker in mute astonishment.

"I am now awaiting," continued he, looking toward the door of our apartment—"I am now awaiting a person who, although perhaps not the perpetrator of these butcheries, must have been in some measure implicated in their perpetration. Of the worst portion of the crimes committed, it is probable that he is innocent. I hope that I am right in this supposition; for upon it I build my expectation of reading the entire riddle. I look for the man here—in this room— every moment. It is true that he may not arrive; but the probability is that he will. Should he come, it will be necessary to detain him. Here are pistols; and we both know how to use them when occasion demands their use."

I took the pistols, scarcely knowing what I did, or believing what I heard, while Dupin went on, very much as if in a soliloquy. I have already spoken of his abstract manner at such times. His discourse was addressed to myself; but his voice, although by no means loud, had that intonation which is commonly employed in speaking to some one at a great distance. His eyes, vacant in expression, regarded only the wall.

"That the voices heard in contention," he said, "by the party upon the stairs, were not the voices of the women themselves, was fully proved by the evidence. This relieves us of all doubt upon the question whether the old lady could have first destroyed the daughter, and afterward have committed suicide. I speak of this point chiefly for the sake of method; for the strength of Madame L'Espanaye would have been utterly unequal to the task of thrusting her daughter's corpse up the chimney as it was found; and the nature of the wounds upon her own person entirely precludes the idea of self-destruction. Murder, then, has been committed by some third party; and the voices of this third party were those heard in contention. Let me now advert—not to the whole testimony respecting these voices—but to what was *peculiar* in that testimony. Did you observe anything peculiar about it?"

I remarked that, while all the witnesses agreed in supposing the gruff voice to be that of a Frenchman, there was much disagreement in regard to the shrill, or, as one individual termed it, the harsh voice.

"That was the evidence itself," said Dupin, "but it was not the peculiarity of the evidence. You have observed nothing distinctive. Yet there *was* something to be observed. The witnesses, as you remarked, agreed about the gruff voice; they were here unanimous. But in regard to the shrill voice, the peculiarity is—not that they disagreed—but that, while an Italian, an Englishman, a Spaniard, a Hollander, and a Frenchman attempted to describe it, each one spoke of it as that *of a foreigner.* Each is sure that it was not the voice of one of his own countrymen. Each likens it—not to the voice of an individual of any nation with whose language he is conversant—but the converse. The Frenchman supposes it is the voice of a Spaniard, and 'might have distinguished some words *had he been acquainted with the Spanish.'* The Dutchman maintains it to have been that of a Frenchman; but we find it stated that '*not understanding French this witness was examined through an interpreter.*' The Englishman thinks it the voice of a German, and '*does not understand German.*' The Spaniard 'is sure' that it was that of an Englishman, but 'judges by the intonation' altogether, '*as he has no knowledge of the English.*' The Italian believes it the voice of a Russian, but '*has never conversed with a native of Russia.*' A second Frenchman differs, moreover, with the first, and is positive that the voice was that of an Italian; but, '*not being cognizant of that tongue*', is, like the Spaniard, 'convinced by the intonation.' Now, how strangely unusual must that voice have really been, about which such testimony as this *could* have been elicited! —in whose *tones*, even, denizens of the five great divisions of Europe could recognize nothing familiar! You will say that it might have been the voice of an Asiatic—of an African. Neither Asiatics nor Africans abound in Paris; but, without denying the inference, I will now merely call your attention to three points. The voice is termed by one witness 'harsh rather than shrill.' It is represented by two others to have been 'quick and *unequal.*' No words—no sounds resembling words—were by any witness mentioned as distinguishable.

"I know not," continued Dupin, "what impression I may have made, so far, upon your own understanding; but I do not hesitate to say that legitimate deductions even from this portion of the testimony—the portion respecting the gruff and shrill voices— are in themselves sufficient to engender a suspicion which should give direction to all farther progress in the investigation of the mystery. I said 'legitimate deductions'; but my meaning is not thus fully expressed. I designed to imply that the deductions are the *sole* proper ones, and that the suspicion arises *inevitably* from them as the single result. What the suspicion is, however, I will not say just yet. I merely wish you to bear in mind that, with myself, it was sufficiently forcible to give a definite form—a certain tendency—to my inquiries in the chamber.

"Let us now transport ourselves, in fancy, to this chamber. What shall we first seek here? The means of egress employed by the murderers. It is not too much to say that neither of us believe in praeternatural events. Madame and Mademoiselle L'Espanaye were not destroyed by spirits. The doers of the deed were material and escaped materially. Then how? Fortunately there is but one mode of reasoning upon the point, and that mode *must* lead us to a definite decision. Let us examine, each by each, the possible means of egress. It is clear that the assassins were in the room where Mademoiselle L'Espanaye was found, or at least in the room adjoining, when the party ascended the stairs. It is, then, only from these two apartments that we have to seek issues. The police have laid bare the floors, the ceiling, and the masonry of the walls, in every direction. No *secret* issues could have escaped their vigilance. But, not trusting to *their* eyes, I examined with my own. There were, then, no secret issues. Both doors leading from the rooms into the passage were securely locked, with the keys inside. Let us turn to the chimneys. These, although of ordinary width for some eight or ten feet above the hearths, will not admit, throughout their extent, the body of a large cat. The impossibility of egress, by means already stated, being thus absolute, we are reduced to the windows. Through those of the front room no one could have escaped without notice from the crowd in the street. The murderers *must* have passed, then, through those of the back room. Now, brought to this conclusion in so unequivocal a manner as we are, it is not our part, as reasoners, to reject it on account of apparent impossibilities. It is only left for us to prove that these apparent 'impossibilities' are, in reality, not such.

"There are two windows in the chamber. One of them is unobstructed by furniture, and is wholly visible. The lower portion of the other is hidden from view by the head of the unwieldy bedstead which is thrust close up against it. The former was found securely fastened from within. It resisted the utmost force of those who endeavored to raise it. A large gimlet-hole had been pierced in its frame to the left, and a very stout nail was found fitted therein, nearly to the head. Upon examining the other window, a similar nail was seen similarly fitted in it; and a vigorous attempt to raise this sash failed also. The police were now entirely satisfied that egress had not been in these directions. And, *therefore*, it was thought a matter of supererogation to withdraw the nails and open the windows.

"My own examination was somewhat more particular, and was so for the reason I have just given—because here it was, I knew, that all apparent impossibilities must be proved to be not such in reality.

"I proceeded to think thus—*à posteriori*. The murderers *did* escape from one of these windows. This being so, they could not have refastened the sashes from the inside, as they *were* found fastened—the consideration which put a stop, through its obviousness, to the scrutiny of the police in this quarter. Yet the sashes were fastened. They *must*, then, have the power of fastening themselves. There was no escape from this conclusion. I stepped to the unobstructed casement, withdrew the nail with some difficulty, and attempted to raise the sash. It resisted all my efforts, as I had anticipated. A concealed spring must, I now knew, exist; and this corroboration of my idea convinced me that my premises, at least, were correct, however mysterious still appeared the circumstances attending the nails. A careful search soon brought to light the hidden spring. I pressed it, and, satisfied with the discovery, forbore to upraise the sash.

"I now replaced the nail and regarded it attentively. A person passing out through this window might have reclosed it, and the spring would have caught—but the nail could not have been replaced. The conclusion was plain, and again narrowed in the field of my investigations. The assassins *must* have escaped through the other window. Supposing, then, the springs upon each sash to be the same, as was probable, there *must* be found a difference between the nails, or at least between the modes of their fixture. Getting upon the sacking of the bedstead, I looked over the head-board minutely at the second casement. Passing my hand down behind the board, I readily discovered and pressed the spring, which was, as I had supposed, identical in character with its neighbor. I now looked at the nail. It was as stout as the other, and apparently fitted in the same manner—driven in nearly up to the head.

"You will say that I was puzzled; but, if you think so, you must have misunderstood the nature of the inductions. To use a sporting phrase, I had not been once 'at fault.' The scent had never for an instant been lost. There was no flaw in any link in the chain. I had traced the secret to its ultimate result,—and that result was *the nail*. It had, I say, in every respect, the appearance of its fellow in the other window; but this fact was an absolute nullity (conclusive as it might seem to be) when compared with the consideration that here, at this point, terminated the clew. 'There must be something wrong,' I said, 'about the nail.' I touched it; and the head, with about a quarter of an inch of the shank, came off in my fingers. The rest of the shank was in the gimlet-hole, where it had been broken off. The fracture was an old one (for its edges were incrusted with rust), and had apparently been accomplished by the blow of a hammer, which had partially imbedded, in the top of the bottom sash, the head portion of the nail. I now carefully replaced this head portion in the indentation whence I had taken it, and the resemblance to a perfect nail was complete—the fissure was invisible. Pressing the spring, I gently raised the sash for a few inches; the head went up with it, remaining firm in its bed. I closed the window, and the semblance of the whole nail was again perfect.

"This riddle, so far, was now unriddled. The assassin had escaped through the window which looked upon the bed. Dropping of its own accord upon his exit (or perhaps purposely closed), it had become fastened by the spring; and it was the retention of this spring which had been mistaken by the police for that of the nail, —farther inquiry being thus considered unnecessary.

"The next question is that of the mode of descent. Upon this point I had been satisfied in my walk with you around the building. About five feet and a half from the casement in question there runs a lightning-rod. From this rod it would have been impossible for any one to reach to the window itself, to say nothing of entering it. I observed, however, that the shutters of the fourth story were of the peculiar kind called by Parisian carpenters *ferrades*—a kind rarely employed at the present day, but frequently seen upon very old mansions at Lyons and Bordeaux. They are in the form of an ordinary door (a single, not a folding door), except that the lower half is latticed or worked in open trellis—thus affording an excellent hold for the hands. In the present instance these shutters are fully three feet and a half broad. When we saw them from the rear of the house, they were both about half open—that is to say they stood off at right angles from the wall. It is probable that the police, as well as myself, examined the back of the tenement; but, if so, in looking at these *ferrades* in the line of their breadth (as they must have done), they did not perceive the great breadth itself, or, at all events, failed to take it into due consideration. In fact, having once satisfied themselves that no egress could have been made in this quarter, they would naturally bestow here a very cursory examination. It was clear to me, however, that the shutter belonging to the window at the head of the bed, would, if swung fully back to the wall, reach to within two feet of the lightning-rod. It was also evident that, by exertion of a very unusual degree of activity and courage, an entrance into the window, from the rod, might have been thus effected. —By reaching to the distance of two feet and a half (we now suppose the shutter open to its whole extent) a robber might have taken a firm grasp upon the trellis-work. Letting go, then, his hold upon the rod, placing his feet securely against the wall, and springing boldly from it, he might have swung the shutter so as to close it, and, if we imagine the window open at the time, might even have swung himself into the room.

"I wish you to bear especially in mind that I have spoken of a *very* unusual degree of activity as requisite to success in so hazardous and so difficult a feat. It is my design to show you first, that the thing might possibly have been accomplished:—but, secondly and *chiefly,* I wish to impress upon your understanding the *very extraordinary*— the almost praeternatural character of that agility which could have accomplished it.

"You will say, no doubt, using the language of the law, that to make out my case, I should rather undervalue than insist upon a full estimation of the activity required in this matter. This may be the practice in the law, but it is not the usage of reason. My ultimate object is only the truth. My immediate purpose is to lead you to place in juxtaposition, that *very unusual* activity of which I have just spoken, with that *very peculiar* shrill (or harsh) and *unequal* voice, about whose nationality no two persons could be found to agree, and in whose utterance no syllabification could be detected."

At these words a vague and half-formed conception of the meaning of Dupin flitted over in my mind. I seemed to be upon the verge of comprehension, without power to comprehend—as men, at times, find themselves upon the brink of remembrance, without being able, in the end, to remember. My friend went on with his discourse.

"You will see," he said, "that I have shifted the question from the mode of egress to that of ingress. It was my design to convey the idea that both were effected in the same manner, at the same point. Let us now revert to the interior of the room. Let us survey the appearances here. The drawers of the bureau, it is said, had been rifled, although many articles of apparel still remained within them. The conclusion here is absurd. It is a mere guess—a very silly one—and no more. How are we to know that the articles found in the drawers were not all these drawers had originally contained? Madame L'Espanaye and her daughter lived an exceedingly retired life—saw no company—seldom went out—had little use for the numerous changes of habiliment. Those found were at least of as good quality as any likely to be possessed by these ladies. If a thief had taken any, why did he not take the best—why did he not take all? In a word, why did he abandon four thousand francs in gold to encumber himself with a bundle of linen? The gold *was* abandoned. Nearly the whole sum mentioned by Monsieur Mignaud, the banker, was discovered, in bags, upon the floor. I wish you therefore, to discard from your thoughts the blundering idea of *motive*, engendered in the brains of the police by that portion of the evidence which speaks of money delivered at the door of the house. Coincidences ten times as remarkable as this (the delivery of the money, and murder committed within these days upon the party receiving it), happen to all of us every hour of our lives, without attracting even momentary notice. Coincidences, in general, are great stumbling-blocks in the way of that class of thinkers who have been educated to know nothing of the theory of probabilities—that theory to which the most glorious objects of human research are indebted for the most glorious of illustration. In the present instance, had the gold been gone, the fact of its delivery three days before would have formed something more than a coincidence. It would have been corroborative of this idea of motive. But, under the real circumstances of the case, if we are to suppose gold the motive of this outrage, we must also imagine the perpetrator so vacillating an idiot as to have abandoned his gold and his motive altogether.

"Keeping now steadily in mind the points to which I have drawn your attention—that peculiar voice, that unusual agility, and that startling absence of motive in a murder so singularly atrocious as this—let us glance at the butchery itself. Here is a woman strangled to death by manual strength, and thrust up a chimney head downward. Ordinary assassins employ no such mode of murder as this. Least of all, do they thus dispose of the murdered. In this manner of thrusting the corpse up the chimney, you will admit that there was something *excessively outré*—something altogether irreconcilable with our common notions of human action, even when we suppose the actors the most depraved of men. Think, too, how great must have been that strength which could have thrust the body *up* such an aperture so forcibly that the united vigor of several persons was found barely sufficient to drag it *down!*

"Turn, now, to other indications of the employment of a vigor most marvellous. On the hearth were thick tresses—very thick tresses—of gray human hair. These had been torn out by the roots. You are aware of the great force necessary in tearing thus from the head even twenty or thirty hairs together. You saw the locks in question as well as myself. Their roots (a hideous sight!) were clotted with fragments of the flesh of the scalp—sure tokens of the prodigious power which had been exerted in uprooting perhaps half a million of hairs at a time. The throat of the old lady was not merely cut, but the head absolutely severed from the body: the instrument was a mere razor. I wish you also to look at the *brutal* ferocity of these deeds. Of the bruises upon the body of Madame L'Espanaye I do not speak. Monsieur Dumas, and his worthy coadjutor Monsieur Etienne, have pronounced that they were inflicted by some obtuse instrument; and so far these gentlemen are very correct. The obtuse instrument was clearly the stone pavement in the yard, upon which the victim had fallen from the window which looked in upon the bed. This idea, however simple it may now seem, escaped the police for the same reason that the breadth of the shutters escaped them—because, by the affair of the nails, their perceptions had been hermetically sealed against the possibility of the windows having ever been opened at all.

"If now, in addition to all these things, you have properly reflected upon the odd disorder of the chamber, we have gone so far as to combine the ideas of an agility astounding, a strength superhuman, a ferocity brutal, a butchery without motive, a *grotesquerie* in horror absolutely alien from humanity, and a voice foreign in tone to the ears of men of many nations, and devoid of all distinct or intelligible syllabification. What result, then, has ensued? What impression have I made upon your fancy?"

I felt a creeping of the flesh as Dupin asked me the question. "A madman," I said, "has done this deed—some raving maniac, escaped from a neighboring *Maison de Santé.*"

"In some respects," he replied, "your idea is not irrelevant. But the voices of madmen, even in their wildest paroxysms, are never found to tally with that peculiar voice heard upon the stairs. Madmen are of some nation, and their language, however incoherent in its words, has always the coherence of syllabification. Besides, the hair of a madman is not such as I now hold in my hand. I disentangled this little tuft from the rigidly clutched fingers of Madame L'Espanaye. Tell me what you can make of it."

"Dupin!" I said, completely unnerved; "this hair is most unusual—this is no *human* hair."

"I have not asserted that it is," said he; "but, before we decide this point, I wish you to glance at the little sketch I have here traced upon this paper. It is a *fac-simile* drawing of what has been described in one portion of the testimony as 'dark bruises, and deep indentations of finger nails' upon the throat of Mademoiselle L'Espanaye, and in another (by Messrs. Dumas and Etienne) as a 'series of livid spots, evidently the impression of fingers.'

"You will perceive," continued my friend, spreading out the paper upon the table before us, "that this drawing gives the idea of a firm and fixed hold. There is no *slipping* apparent. Each finger has retained—possibly until the death of the victim—the fearful grasp by which it originally imbedded itself. Attempt, now, to place all your fingers, at the same time, in the respective impressions as you see them."

I made the attempt in vain.

"We are possibly not giving this matter a fair trial," he said. "The paper is spread out upon a plane surface; but the human throat is cylindrical. Here is a billet of wood, the circumference of which is about that of the throat. Wrap the drawing around it, and try the experiment again."

I did so; but the difficulty was even more obvious than before. "This," I said, "is the mark of no human hand."

"Read now," replied Dupin, "this passage from Cuvier."

It was a minute anatomical and generally descriptive account of the large fulvous Ourang-Outang of the East Indian Islands. The gigantic stature, the prodigious strength and activity, the wild ferocity, and the imitative propensities of these mammalia are sufficiently well known to all. I understood the full horrors of the murder at once.

"The description of the digits," said I, as I made an end of the reading, "is in exact accordance with this drawing. I see no animal but an Ourang-Outang, of the species here mentioned, could have impressed the indentations as you have traced them. This tuft of tawny hair, too, is identical in character with that of the beast of Cuvier. But I cannot possibly comprehend the particulars of this frightful mystery. Besides, there were *two* voices heard in contention, and one of them was unquestionably the voice of a Frenchman."

"True; and you will remember an expression attributed almost unanimously, by the evidence, to this voice,—the expression, '*mon Dieu!*' This, under the circumstances, has been justly characterized by one of the witnesses (Montani, the confectioner) as an expression of remonstrance or expostulation. Upon these two words, therefore, I have mainly built my hopes of a full solution of the riddle. A Frenchman was cognizant of the murder. It is possible—indeed it is far more than probable—that he was innocent of all participation in the bloody transactions which took place. The Ourang-Outang may have escaped from him. He may have traced it to the chamber; but, under the agitating circumstances which ensued, he could never have recaptured it. It is still at large. I will not pursue these guesses—for I have no right to call them more—since the shades of reflection upon which they are based are scarcely of sufficient depth to be appreciated by my own intellect, and since I could not pretend to make them intelligible to the understanding of another. We will call them guesses, then, and speak of them as such. If the Frenchman in question is indeed, as I suppose, innocent of this atrocity, this advertisement, which I left last might, upon our return home, at the office of 'Le Monde' (a paper devoted to the shipping interest, and much sought by sailors), will bring him to our residence."

He handed me a paper, and I read thus:

> "CAUGHT—*In the Bois de Boulogne, early in the morning of the —— inst. (the morning of the murder), a very large, tawny Ourang-Outang of the Bornese species. The owner (who is ascertained to be a sailor, belonging to a Maltese vessel) may have the animal again, upon identifying it satisfactorily, and paying a few charges arising from its capture and keeping. Call at No. —— Rue ——, Faubourg St. Germain—au troisième.*"

"How was it possible," I asked, "that you should know the man to be a sailor, and belonging to a Maltese vessel?"

"I do *not* know it," said Dupin. "I am not *sure* of it. Here, however, is a small piece of ribbon, which from its form, and from its greasy appearance, has evidently been used in tying the hair in one of those long *queues* of which sailors are so fond. Moreover, this knot is one which few besides sailors can tie, and is peculiar to the Maltese. I picked the ribbon up at the foot of the lighting-rod. It could not have belonged to either of the deceased. Now if, after all, I am wrong in my induction from this ribbon, that the Frenchman was a sailor belonging to a Maltese vessel, still I can have done no harm in saying what I did in the advertisement. If I am in error, he will merely suppose that I had been misled by some circumstance into which he will not take the trouble to inquire. But if I am right, a great point is gained. Cognizant although innocent of the murder, the Frenchman will naturally hesitate about replying to the advertisement—about demanding the Ourang-Outang. He will reason thus: —'I am innocent; I am poor; my Ourang-Outang is of great value—to one in my circumstances a fortune of itself—why should I lose it through idle apprehensions of danger? Here it is, within my grasp. It was found in the Bois de Boulogne—at a vast distance from the scene of that butchery. How can it ever be suspected that a brute beast should have done the deed? The police are at fault—they have failed to procure the slightest clew. Should they even trace the animal, it would be impossible to prove me cognizant of the murder, or to implicate me in guilt on account of that cognizance. Above all, *I am known*. The advertiser designates me as the possessor of the beast. I am not sure to what limit his knowledge may extend. Should I avoid claiming a property of so great value, which it is known that I possess, I will render the animal at least, liable to suspicion. It is not my policy to attract attention either to myself or to the beast. I will answer the advertisement, get the Ourang-Outang, and keep it close until this matter has blown over.'"

At this moment we heard a step upon the stairs.

"Be ready," said Dupin, "with your pistols, but neither use them nor show them until at a signal from myself."

The front door of the house had been left open, and the visitor had entered, without ringing, and advanced several steps upon the staircase. Now, however, he seemed to hesitate. Presently we heard him descending. Dupin was moving quickly to the door, when we again heard him coming up. He did not turn back a second time, but stepped up with decision, and rapped at the door of our chamber.

"Come in," said Dupin, in a cheerful and hearty tone.

A man entered. He was a sailor, evidently—a tall, stout, and muscular-looking person, with a certain dare-devil expression of countenance, not altogether unprepossessing. His face, greatly sunburnt, was more than half hidden by whisker and *mustachio*. He had with him a huge oaken cudgel, but appeared to be otherwise unarmed. He bowed awkwardly, and bade us "good evening," in French accents, which, although somewhat Neufchatelish, were still sufficiently indicative of a Parisian origin.

"Sit down, my friend," said Dupin. "I suppose you have called about the Ourang-Outang. Upon my word, I almost envy you the possession of him; a remarkably fine, and no doubt very valuable animal. How old do you suppose him to be?"

The sailor drew a long breath, with the air of a man relieved of some intolerable burden, and then replied in an assured tone:

"I have no way of telling—but he can't be more than four or five years old. Have you got him here?"

"Oh, no; we had no conveniences for keeping him here. He is at a livery stable in the Rue Dubourg, just by. You can get him in the morning. Of course you are prepared to identify the property?"

"To be sure I am, sir."

"I shall be sorry to part with him," said Dupin.

"I don't mean that you should be at all this trouble for nothing, sir," said the man. "Couldn't expect it. Am very willing to pay a reward for the finding of the animal—that is to say, any thing in reason."

"Well," replied my friend, "that is all very fair, to be sure. Let me think! —what should I have? Oh! I will tell you. My reward shall be this. You shall give me all the information in your power about these murders in the Rue Morgue."

Dupin said the last words in a very low tone, and very quietly. Just as quietly, too, he walked toward the door, locked it, and put the key in his pocket. He then drew a pistol from his bosom and placed it, without the least flurry, upon the table.

The sailor's face flushed up as if he were struggling with suffocation. He started to his feet and grasped his cudgel; but the next moment he fell back into his seat, trembling violently, and with the countenance of death itself. He spoke not a word. I pitied him from the bottom of my heart.

"My friend," said Dupin, in a kind tone, "you are alarming yourself unnecessarily—you are indeed. We mean you no harm whatever. I pledge you the honor of a gentleman, and of a Frenchman, that we intend you no injury. I perfectly well know that you are innocent of the atrocities in the Rue Morgue. It will not do, however, to deny that you are in some measure implicated in them. From what I have already said, you must know that I have had means of information about this matter—means of which you could never have dreamed. Now the thing stands thus. You have done nothing which you could have avoided—nothing, certainly, which renders you culpable. You were not even guilty of robbery, when you might have robbed with impunity. You have nothing to conceal. You have no reason for concealment. On the other hand, you are bound by every principle of honor to confess all you know. An innocent man is now imprisoned, charged with a crime of which you can point out the perpetrator."

The sailor had recovered his presence of mind, in a great measure, while Dupin uttered these words; but his original boldness of bearing was all gone.

"So help me God," said he, after a brief pause, "I will tell you all I know about this affair—but I do not expect you to believe one half

I say—I would be a fool indeed if I did. Still, I *am* innocent, and I will make a clean breast if I die for it."

What he stated was, in substance, this. He had lately made a voyage to the Indian Archipelago. A party, of which he formed one, landed at Borneo, and passed into the interior on an excursion of pleasure. Himself and a companion had captured the Ourang-Outang. This companion dying, the animal fell into his own exclusive possession. After great trouble, occasioned by the intractable ferocity of his captive during the home voyage, he at length succeeded in lodging it safely at his own residence in Paris, where, not to attract toward himself the unpleasant curiosity of his neighbors, he kept it carefully secluded, until such time as it should recover from a wound in the foot, received from a splinter on board ship. His ultimate design was to sell it.

Returning home from some sailors' frolic on the night, or rather in the morning, of the murder, he found the beast occupying his own bedroom, into which it had broken from a closet adjoining, where it had been, as was thought, securely confined. Razor in hand, and fully lathered, it was sitting before a looking-glass, attempting the operation of shaving, in which it had no doubt previously watched its master through the key-hole of the closet. Terrified at the sight of so dangerous a weapon in the possession of an animal so ferocious, and so well able to use it, the man, for some moments, was at a loss what to do. He had been accustomed, however, to quiet the creature, even in its fiercest moods, by the use of a whip, and to this he now resorted. Upon sight of it, the Ourang-Outang sprang at once through the door of the chamber, down the stairs, and thence, through a window, unfortunately open, into the street.

The Frenchman followed in despair; the ape, razor still in hand, occasionally stopping to look back and gesticulate at his pursuer, until the latter had nearly come up with it. It then again made off. In this manner the chase continued for a long time. The streets were profoundly quiet, as it was nearly three o'clock in the morning. In passing down an alley in the rear of the Rue Morgue, the fugitive's attention was arrested by a light gleaming from the open window of Madame L'Espanaye's chamber, in the fourth story of her house. Rushing to the building, it perceived the lightning-rod, clambered up with inconceivable agility, grasped the shutter, which was thrown fully back against the wall, and, by its means, swung itself directly upon the headboard of the bed. The whole feat did not occupy a minute. The shutter was kicked open again by the Ourang-Outang as it entered the room.

The sailor, in the meantime, was both rejoiced and perplexed. He had strong hopes of now recapturing the brute, as it could scarcely escape from the trap into which it had ventured, except by the rod, where it might be intercepted as it came down. On the other hand, there was much cause for anxiety as to what it might do in the house. This latter reflection urged the man still to follow the fugitive. A lightning-rod is ascended without difficulty, especially by a sailor; but, when he had arrived as high as the window, which lay far to his left, his career was stopped; the most that he could accomplish was to reach over so as to obtain a glimpse of the interior of the room. At this glimpse he nearly fell from his hold through excess of horror. Now it was that those hideous shrieks arose upon the night, which had startled from slumber the inmates of the Rue Morgue. Madame L'Espanaye and her daughter, habited in their night clothes, had apparently been occupied in arranging some papers in the iron chest already mentioned, which had been wheeled into the middle of the room. It was open, and its contents lay beside it on the floor. The victims must have been sitting with their backs toward the window; and, from the time elapsing between the ingress of the beast and the screams, it seems probable that it was not immediately perceived. The flapping-to of the shutter would naturally have been attributed to the wind.

As the sailor looked in, the gigantic animal had seized Madame L'Espanaye by the hair (which was loose, as she had been combing it), and was flourishing the razor about her face, in imitation of the motions of a barber. The daughter lay prostrate and motionless; she had swooned. The screams and struggles of the old lady (during which the hair was torn from her head) had the effect of changing the probably pacific purposes of the Ourang-Outang into those of wrath. With one determined sweep of its muscular arm it nearly severed her head from her body. The sight of blood inflamed its anger into phrensy. Gnashing its teeth, and flashing fire from its eyes, it flew upon the body of the girl, and imbedded its fearful talons in her throat, retaining its grasp until she expired. Its wandering and wild glances fell at this moment upon the head of the bed, over which the face of its master, rigid with horror, was just discernible. The fury of the beast, who no doubt bore still in mind the dreaded whip, was instantly converted into fear. Conscious of having deserved punishment, it seemed desirous of concealing its bloody deeds, and skipped about the chamber in an agony of nervous agitation; throwing down and breaking the furniture as it moved, and dragging the bed from the bedstead. In conclusion, it seized first the corpse of the daughter, and thrust it up the chimney, as it was found; then that of the old lady, which it immediately hurled through the window headlong.

As the ape approached the casement with its mutilated burden, the sailor shrank aghast to the rod, and, rather gliding than clambering down it, hurried at once home—dreading the consequences of the butchery, and gladly abandoning, in his terror, all solicitude about the fate of the Ourang-Outang. The words heard by the party upon the staircase were the Frenchman's exclamations of horror and affright, commingled with the fiendish jabberings of the brute.

I have scarcely anything to add. The Ourang-Outang must have escaped from the chamber, by the rod, just before the breaking of the door. It must have closed the window as it passed through it. It was subsequently caught by the owner himself, who obtained for it a very large sum at the *Jardin des Plantes*. Le Bon was instantly released, upon our narration of the circumstances (with some comments from Dupin) at the bureau of the Prefect of Police. This functionary, however well disposed to my friend, could not altogether conceal his chagrin at the turn which affairs had taken, and was fain to indulge in a sarcasm or two, about the propriety of every person minding his own business.

"Let him talk," said Dupin, who had not thought it necessary to reply. "Let him discourse; it will ease his conscience. I am satisfied with having defeated him in his own castle. Nevertheless, that he failed in the solution of this mystery, is by no means that matter for wonder which he supposes it; for, in truth, our friend the Prefect is somewhat too cunning to be profound. In his wisdom is no *stamen*. It is all head and no body, like the pictures of the Goddess Laverna, —or, at best, all head and shoulders, like a codfish. But he is a good creature after all. I like him especially for one master stroke of cant, by which he has attained his reputation for ingenuity. I mean the way he has '*de nier ce qui est, et d'expliquer ce qui n'est pas.*'"[1]

---

1   "...of denying what is, and explaining what isn't" from a footnote in Letter xi in Part VI of Rousseau's *La Nouvelle Héloïse* (1761). "It is crotchet common to philosophers of all ages to deny what is, and explain what is not."

EVIL ROBOT MONKEY

Mary Robinette Kowal

Possibly the shortest story ever nominated for a Hugo, Kowal's charming piece of flash fiction introduces Sly, a chimp implanted with a chip that makes him smarter than his brethren.

Sliding his hands over the clay, Sly relished the moisture oozing around his fingers. The clay matted down the hair on the back of his hands making them look almost human. He turned the potter's wheel with his prehensile feet as he shaped the vase. Pinching the clay between his fingers he lifted the wall of the vase, spinning it higher.

Someone banged on the window of his pen. Sly jumped and then screamed as the vase collapsed under its own weight. He spun and hurled it at the picture window like feces. The clay spattered against the Plexiglas, sliding down the window.

In the courtyard beyond the glass, a group of school kids leapt back, laughing. One of them swung his arms aping Sly crudely. Sly bared his teeth, knowing these people would take it as a grin, but he meant it as a threat. Swinging down from his stool, he crossed his room in three long strides and pressed his dirty hand against the window. Still grinning, he wrote SSA. Outside, the letters would be reversed.

The students' teacher flushed as red as a female in heat and called the children away from the window. She looked back once as she led them out of the courtyard, so Sly grabbed himself and showed her what he would do if she came into his pen.

Her naked face turned brighter red and she hurried away. When they were gone, Sly rested his head against the glass. The metal in his skull thunked against the window. It wouldn't be long now, before a handler came to talk to him.

Damn.

He just wanted to make pottery. He loped back to the wheel and sat down again with his back to the window. Kicking the wheel into movement, Sly dropped a new ball of clay in the center and tried to lose himself.

In the corner of his vision, the door to his room snicked open. Sly let the wheel spin to a halt, crumpling the latest vase.

Vern poked his head through. He signed, "You okay?"

Sly shook his head emphatically and pointed at the window.

"Sorry." Vern's hands danced. "We should have warned you that they were coming."

"You should have told them that I was not an animal."

Vern looked down in submission. "I did. They're kids."

"And I'm a chimp. I know." Sly buried his fingers in the clay to silence his thoughts.

"It was Delilah. She thought you wouldn't mind because the other chimps didn't."

Sly scowled and yanked his hands free. "I'm not *like* the other chimps." He pointed to the implant in his head. "Maybe Delilah should have one of these. Seems like she needs help thinking."

"I'm sorry." Vern knelt in front of Sly, closer than anyone else would come when he wasn't sedated. It would be so easy to reach out and snap his neck. "It was a lousy thing to do."

Sly pushed the clay around on the wheel. Vern was better than the others. He seemed to understand the hellish limbo where Sly lived—too smart to be with other chimps, but too much of an animal to be with humans. Vern was the one who had brought Sly the potter's wheel which, by the Earth and Trees, Sly loved. Sly looked up and raised his eyebrows. "So what did they think of my show?"

Vern covered his mouth, masking his smile. The man had manners. "The teacher was upset about the 'evil robot monkey.'"

Sly threw his head back and hooted. Served her right.

"But Delilah thinks you should be disciplined." Vern, still so close that Sly could reach out and break him, stayed very still. "She wants me to take the clay away since you used it for an anger display."

Sly's lips drew back in a grimace built of anger and fear. Rage threatened to blind him, but he held on, clutching the wheel. If he lost it with Vern—rational thought danced out of his reach. Panting, he spun the wheel trying to push his anger into the clay.

The wheel spun. Clay slid between his fingers. Soft. Firm and smooth. The smell of earth lived in his nostrils. He held the world in his hands. Turning, turning, the walls rose around a kernel of anger, subsuming it.

His heart slowed with the wheel and Sly blinked, becoming aware again as if he were slipping out of sleep. The vase on the wheel still seemed to dance with life. Its walls held the shape of the world within them. He passed a finger across the rim.

Vern's eyes were moist. "Do you want me to put that in the kiln for you?"

Sly nodded.

"I have to take the clay. You understand that, don't you."

Sly nodded again, staring at his vase. It was beautiful.

Vern scowled. "The woman makes *me* want to hurl feces."

Sly snorted at the image, then sobered. "How long before I get it back?"

Vern picked up the bucket of clay next to the wheel. "I don't know." He stopped at the door and looked past Sly to the window. "I'm not cleaning your mess. Do you understand me?"

For a moment, rage crawled on his spine, but Vern did not meet his eyes and kept staring at the window. Sly turned.

The vase he had thrown lay on the floor in a pile of clay.

Clay.

"I understand." He waited until the door closed, then loped over and scooped the clay up. It was not much, but it was enough for now.

Sly sat down at his wheel and began to turn.

APES IN LITERATURE

Jess Nevins

Apes have appeared in literature as a metaphor for various sins and as a proxy for humanity for centuries. From ancient Egyptian religious writings to a 2011 Oscar-nominated film, apes are a constant part of human culture. However, their meanings, usages, and portrayal have changed over time.

Apes were known to the ancient Greeks and Romans first-hand from their experiences in Africa. To both groups apes were seen as ugly, malicious, and dangerous, and "ape" was commonly used as an insult. Heraclitus wrote that "the handsomest ape is ugly compared with humanity; the wisest man appears as an ape compared with a god" (in Plato, *Hippias Major*, c. 390 BCE) and Horace wrote that "that ape of yours who knows nothing but how to imitate Calvus and Catullus" (*Satirae*, c. 35 BCE). Early Christian writers and artists used apes as a symbol for the vices of vanity, greed, and lechery, and as a symbol of unrestrained, uninhibited humanity. In Dante's *Inferno* (1308–1321 CE) an alchemist describes himself as "a fine ape of nature," and in Shakespeare's *The Winter's Tale* (1623 CE) a painter is praised as being so skilled that he "would beguile Nature of her custom, so perfectly he is her ape."

Not all early portrayals of apes were negative. In the French story of "Milles et Amys," which has been dated back to Alberic de Troisfontaines' *Chronicle* (circa 1240), the two friends Milles and Amys are killed by Ogier the Dane during his rebellion against Charlemagne. The children of Milles are guarded by a talking ape nursemaid, who protects them from Amys' evil widow until two angels of paradise spirit the children away. And Wu Cheng'en's *Journey to the West* (circa 1550) has a heroic trickster monkey, Sun Wu Kong, as its main character. But most portrayals of apes, especially in the West, followed Christian teachings and portrayed them as vain and lecherous, if not worse: in the English *Wagner Book* (1593), an elaboration on the Faust legend, Faust's assistant Wagner is accompanied by an ape assistant, making explicit the traditionally implicit ties between apes and supernatural evil.

Apes took on a still darker edge at the turn of the seventeenth century. John Donne's *Progresse of the Soule* (1601) played up the apes' supposedly lust-filled nature by showing an ape fall in love with Siphatecia, Adam's fifth daughter, and have sex with her. This was the beginning of the "rape ape" theme, the motif of the crazed ape dragging a woman away in order to violate her. The "rape ape" motif, embodied in an anecdote of a male ape carrying off a female "Hottentot," became a common part of seventeenth-century travel narratives and eighteenth-century prose narratives such as Swift's *Gulliver's Travels* (1726).

At about this time scientists in the West began to experience apes first-hand. In 1698 a live chimpanzee was captured in Angola and brought to England, and his death and that of other primates in the seventeenth century were opportunities for scientists, including Carl Linnaeus, to dissect them and eventually create a taxonomy of primates. In 1766 the French naturalist Georges-Louis Leclerc, Count de Buffon, used the term "Jocko" to describe the smaller species of African apes, and the term entered common usage, though it was eventually limited to being synonymous with chimpanzees, as were the terms "orang" and "orangutan."

A competing view of apes had arisen in the mid-eighteenth century. Jean-Jacques Rousseau's *Discourse on the Origin of Inequality* (1755) countered Hobbes' view, that man's life was "poor, nasty, brutish and short," with the idea that original man was free, happy, and good. Rousseau's "Discourse" popularized the concept of the Noble Savage. When Rousseau wrote "Discourse" he was working under the influence of the Count de Buffon. In Note Ten of "Discourse" Rousseau quotes Buffon regarding "orang-outangs" and compares them to men, going so far as to theorize that some kinds of apes, like the orangutan, are actually primitive men.

It was in the Rousseauvian mode that the French writer Charles de Pougens wrote *Jocko* (1824), the story of an orangutan who falls in love with the novel's narrator. Unfortunately for Jocko, the narrator is greedy and forces Jocko to bring him precious stones. Jocko dies and the narrator returns to Europe a rich man. De Pougens wrote under the influence of Rousseau, and de Pougens' audience viewed Jocko as a Noble Savage. *Jocko* was immensely popular and widely imitated. However, the novel's lack of condemnation of the narrator's greed and heartlessness toward Jocko prompted the Russian author Alekseii Perovskii to write a satire of *Jocko*: "Journey in a Stagecoach" (1828). "Journey" tells the story of Fritz, a man raised by Tutu, a female gorilla, but who chooses a wife over Tutu. Tutu breaks a locket with the wife's picture in it, and Fritz shoots her. But he is haunted by her voice forever after. Perovskii includes in "Journey" all the irony de Pougens left out of *Jocko* as well as the balancing of the moral scales.

The proposed innocent simian of de Pougens and Perovskii were, with the evil/depraved ape of tradition, one-half of the most common mode of portrayal of the apes in the nineteenth century. The other half consisted of parodies, satires, and fables.

•

As early as 1727 apes were being used in parodies of popular works. Peter Longueville's *The Hermit*, a parody of *Robinson Crusoe*, has the titular character be adopted by Beaufidelle, a Friday-like ape sidekick. *The Hermit* was nearly as popular as *Robinson Crusoe* and was reprinted for over a century. Less well known, but popular in France, was Albert Robida's *Saturnin Faroundal* (1879), a parody of Jules Verne's *romans d'aventures*, in which the titular character is raised by monkeys, becomes their king, and with their help conquers Australia.

Far more authors found primates useful as vehicles of satire. John Gay's "The Monkey Who Has Seen the World" (1728) satirizes humanity by having a monkey who has lived among humans escape to the wild, only to bring human vices with him. Apes were common vehicles for a satire of human civilization or of other cultures: Thomas Bond's "A Merry Tale" (1823) and Arthur Brookfield's *Simiocracy* (1884) of England, William Hauff's "The Young Englishman" (1826) of Germany, James Fenimore Cooper's *Monikins* (1835) of both Great Britain and the United States.

Apes also appeared in a more fabular role. Zaccaria Seriman's *Viaggi di Enrico Wanton alle terre Incognite Australi* (1772) portrays a race of dog-headed monkeys living in Australia who are visited by a pair of shipwrecked men, while Pilpai's "The Monkey and the Tortoise" (1854) tells the story of a monkey who sacrifices himself to help take his people's land back from a group of bear invaders.

During the first half of the nineteenth century apes lost their symbolic weight and largely became just another plot element. In T. L. Peacock's *Melincourt* (1817) the ape, Sir Oran Haut-Ton, becomes a Member of Parliament (for a rotten borough), but *Melincourt* is a satire of the British government rather than of humanity as a whole. And when Edgar Allan Poe used an orangutan as the murderer in "The Murders in the Rue Morgue" (1841), it was not to convey a symbolic message or to make a political or religious point. The orangutan was used solely as a plot element.

This changed in the 1860s, following the 1859 publication of Darwin's *On the Origin of Species* and the resulting furor over evolution. Darwin's controversial linking of apes and humanity led dozens of writers to comment fictionally on the similarity or lack of same, and on the truth or falsity of Darwin's claims. One of the earliest of these fictional comments was the Reverend Charles Kingsley's *The Water-Babies* (1862–1863), which equates apes with degenerated, stupid humans. A year later, the poet Robert Browning wrote "Caliban Upon Setibos," a soliloquy by Shakespeare's Caliban, in which Caliban ponders his place in existence and his god, and in so doing comments on the ideas of evolution and natural selection.

Not every fictional primate following Darwin was used to comment on Darwin: L. D. Nichols' "Sam's Monkey" (1867) is a straightforward tale of a pet monkey destroying a household, Élie Berthet's *The Wild Man of the Woods* (1868) is an adventure tale with a number of similarities to Burroughs' *Tarzan of the Apes*, and the monkey in J. S. Le Fanu's "Green Tea" (1869) is either hallucinatory or demonic. But through the 1860s and 1870s primates were used often enough as a comment on evolution that William Allingham spoke for many with his poem "How Man is like to Ape we have now heard enough and to spare" (1884).

During this time period three separate developments appeared which would permanently affect how apes were portrayed in literature.

The first was Modernism. As a literary and cultural movement reacting to a widely perceived cultural malaise, Modernism was full of ambivalence about culture in general. One element Modernism was ambivalent about and even hostile to was science and its efforts to understand the universe. Modernism was equally concerned with what it saw as the evils of progress and the destructiveness of science.

Modernism most often manifested itself in high art and the avant-garde, but during the first half of the twentieth century there was a discernible stream of influence, deliberate and otherwise, on creators of low art. And with the widespread use of primates in popular culture (see below) it was inevitable that modernist ape stories would be told.

As early as 1886, in Émile Dodillon's *Hemo*, the scientific attempt to improve the "blood-line" of humanity through the use of "strong ancestral stock"—a response to Sir Francis Galton's theories on eugenics—is treated with Modernist contempt, and the attempt ends in bestiality, homicide, and suicide. In Frank Constable's *The Curse of Intellect* (1895), teaching a monkey how to speak English and interact with humans socially causes the ape, and its teacher, nothing but misery and bitterness. In Leopoldo Lugones' "Yzur" (1906), the attempt to teach an ape sign language exposes the narrator's cruelty. And in Ilya Selvinksy's play *Pao-Pao* (1933) giving the titular orangutan the power of speech through a brain transplant only convinces Pao-Pao of the truth of nihilism.

The second was anthropology. Although the study of the origins, development, and customs of human societies began in the eighteenth century with Immanuel Kant's *Anthropology from a Pragmatic Point of View*, anthropology began to develop as a separate academic discipline in the second half of the nineteenth century, and what might be thought of as an anthropological approach to primates began to appear in fiction. Henry Curwen's *Zit and Xoe* (1886) examines how two advanced apes, Zit and Xoe, are ostracized by ape society and how they make their own. Willy Speyer's "Bobbi the Chimp" (1909) shows how an ape brought into society clashes with human society's rules and is ultimately ostracized. And Yevgeni Zamyatin's play *Afrikanskii Gost'* (1929–1930) mixed anthropology and Soviet science in its story of the proper conversion of an African ape to Soviet Communism.

But the third and largest major development was the creation of modern popular fiction and especially genre fiction. As modern popular fiction and genre fiction evolved from preceding forms in the nineteenth century, its writers seized on previously existing motifs and images for use. One of these was primates, who proved to be a reliable standby until the middle of the twentieth century.

An exhaustive list of primates in modern fiction is far beyond the limits of this essay, so instead I will cover a few of the highlights in some of the major genres.

Examples in adventure fiction are numerous and obvious. In Westerns, two typical examples appeared in the German pulp *Reo Ratt - Im Kampf Gegen List und Gewalt* in 1924 and in the English story paper *Wizard* in 1939. In *Reo Ratt* the titular German cowboy hero pursues Kaku, an ape trained by a gang of thieves to hold up stagecoaches. In *Wizard* a serial, "Six Gun Gorilla," ran over several months; the serial was about O'Neil, a gun-slinging gorilla whose owner is killed and who pursues the killers across the Old West.

In mysteries, when primates appeared, they were in the mode of the orangutan of "Murders in the Rue Morgue," but occasionally more unusual variations appeared. Primate detectives occasionally appear in modern comic books, but the first was Jacko the Detective, who appeared in an English story paper from 1911 to 1917. Jacko was the assistant and chauffeur to a Willoughby Homes, a Sherlock Holmesian Great Detective, and occasionally Jacko would solve cases on his own.

Primates were often used in science fiction, primarily as monsters or henchmen, but occasionally in more interesting ways. In the pseudonymously published "The Upper Hand" (1894), set in 1993, apes have taken over the world and developed advanced technology, including a device for communicating with Mars. And in Marcel Roland's "Gulluliou, ou, Le Presqu'homme" (1905), set in the twenty-fourth century, an attempt to integrate the titular superintelligent ape leads to love between the ape and a socialite.

Primates were most commonly used in horror stories: as a jealous pet who murders his owner's wife in Rudyard Kipling's "Bertran and Bimi" (1891), as the crazed result of a Moreau-like mad scientist's experiments in Epes Winthrop Sargent's "Beyond the Banyans" (1909), and as inhabitants of a lost African city and the ancestor of the title character in H. P. Lovecraft's "Facts Concerning the Late Arthur Jermyn and His Family" (1921).

Some political writers found primates to be useful symbols. The Polish writer Tadeusz Miciński, in his *Nietota* (1910) and *Żywia Słoneczna* (1912), the forces of good and evil clash, good being represented by the holy warrior Ariaman and evil being represented by the demonic ape de Mangro and his ally, the "sultan of souls," Pope Pius X. And in response to the Japanese invasion during World War Two the Kids' Theatre of Shanghai put on the play *The Gorilla King* (1941?), a retelling of *Journey to the West* but one in which China is invaded by a group of conspicuously unnamed invaders, leading Sun Wukong, who is actually King Kong, to swim to China from Skull Island and liberate China.

Internationally, primates were as common in popular fiction as they were in the West: in Japan, in Kaita Murayama's "Maenden" (1915), a retelling of "Murders in the Rue Morgue" set in contemporary Tokyo and featuring a superpowered gorilla; in Spain, in Jesús de Aragón's *Los Piratas del Aire* (1929), as the pilot of the Yellow Peril's war-zeppelin; and in Portugal, in Reinaldo Ferreira's *Aventuras Extraordinarias do Mosqueteiro do Ar* (1933), as the assassins of the international crime syndicate Trust Z.

Primates were common in twentieth-century popular literature, but only a handful of works with primates achieved iconic status, such as Edgar Rice Burroughs' Tarzan, whose hundreds of appearances began with the twenty-four novels and story collections written by Burroughs beginning in 1912. Although there were numerous influences on Burroughs, most notably Rudyard Kipling's *The Jungle Book* (1894), Burroughs succeeded in creating the most famous and enduring character from the American pulps and one of the archetypal characters of twentieth-century popular literature, as well as one of the two most imitated characters in global popular fiction. (Sherlock Holmes is the first.) An inextricable part of Tarzan's adventures are the *mangani*, the intelligent apes who helped raise him and so imprinted themselves on him that he is known, not as "Tarzan," but as "Tarzan the Ape Man."

Although the film *King Kong* was preceded by a magazine

story version in late 1932, it was the 1933 film that became the primate-centric work of popular culture, and had the most impact on popular culture. *King Kong* has become the archetypal giant monster movie, and its primate protagonist has become a movie icon. Though clearly not based on any real species of primate, King Kong nonetheless remains the most famous ape in the world, and in the 2005 remake Kong became a sympathetic protagonist rather than simply a giant monster.

In 1941 German Jews H. A. and Margret Rey, who had fled Europe because of the Nazis, published *Curious George*, the first of seven children's books the Reys wrote about a well-meaning, childlike chimpanzee. Like King Kong, Curious George become iconic, but in a much different fashion: through international translations, television shows, movies, and generations of children readers, George became the iconic friendly primate and ideal fantasy pal for children.

The shift to visual culture in the 1950s led to the next two iconic primate characters appearing in visual media rather than in prose. The 1959 debut of John Broome's Gorilla Grodd, in the comic book *The Flash*, gave the world the archetypal hostile, intelligent primate. Grodd has been a recurring character in superhero comics since his debut, and arguably every hostile talking primate since then has been, to some degree, an imitation of Grodd.

Like *King Kong*, the Planet of the Apes franchise began in print, in a 1963 novel, *La Planète des Singes*, by French author Pierre Boulle. But like *King Kong* far more people were exposed to the film version of the novel than to the novel itself. In all, seven films and two television series were made based (however lightly) on Boulle's novel, in the process creating the most iconic post-apocalyptic world and the best-known world, in which apes, not humanity, are the rulers.

Finally, Will Self's novel *Great Apes* (1997), a satire about a world in which chimpanzees and humans have switched places, was critically acclaimed and remains popular. But *Great Apes*' real importance was in establishing the idea that a novel about intelligent primates could be treated seriously by critics and even achieve canonical status. The 2011 *Rise of the Planet of the Apes*, though superficially belonging to the *Planet of the Apes* franchise, is far more serious than the previous films, and the result is far closer to *Great Apes* than to the earlier films in its portrayal of simian psychology.

After 1500 years apes are finally being treated seriously in high culture. As apes achieve more legal rights in Western civilization, this trend will only continue and accelerate.

TARZAN'S FIRST LOVE

Edgar Rice Burroughs

Burroughs tackles the thorny topic of Tarzan's adolescence when the future Jungle Lord attempts to woo Teeka, a female ape. The outcome forces the young man to confront his genetic distance from his animal brethren.

Teeka, stretched at luxurious ease in the shade of the tropical forest, presented, unquestionably, a most alluring picture of young, feminine loveliness. Or at least so thought Tarzan of the Apes, who squatted upon a low-swinging branch in a near-by tree and looked down upon her.

Just to have seen him there, lolling upon the swaying bough of the jungle-forest giant, his brown skin mottled by the brilliant equatorial sunlight which percolated through the leafy canopy of green above him, his clean-limbed body relaxed in graceful ease, his shapely head partly turned in contemplative absorption and his intelligent, gray eyes dreamily devouring the object of their devotion, you would have thought him the reincarnation of some demigod of old.

You would not have guessed that in infancy he had suckled at the breast of a hideous, hairy she-ape, nor that in all his conscious past since his parents had passed away in the little cabin by the landlocked harbor at the jungle's verge, he had known no other associates than the sullen bulls and the snarling cows of the tribe of Kerchak, the great ape.

Nor, could you have read the thoughts which passed through that active, healthy brain, the longings and desires and aspirations which the sight of Teeka inspired, would you have been any more inclined to give credence to the reality of the origin of the ape-man. For, from his thoughts alone, you could never have gleaned the truth—that he had been born to a gentle English lady or that his sire had been an English nobleman of time-honored lineage.

Lost to Tarzan of the Apes was the truth of his origin. That he was John Clayton, Lord Greystoke, with a seat in the House of Lords, he did not know, nor, knowing, would have understood.

Yes, Teeka was indeed beautiful!

Of course Kala had been beautiful—one's mother is always that—but Teeka was beautiful in a way all her own, an indescribable sort of way which Tarzan was just beginning to sense in a rather vague and hazy manner.

For years had Tarzan and Teeka been play-fellows, and Teeka still continued to be playful while the young bulls of her own age were rapidly becoming surly and morose. Tarzan, if he gave the matter much thought at all, probably reasoned that his growing attachment for the young female could be easily accounted for by the fact that of the former playmates she and he alone retained any desire to frolic as of old.

But today, as he sat gazing upon her, he found himself noting the beauties of Teeka's form and features—something he never had done before, since none of them had aught to do with Teeka's ability to race nimbly through the lower terraces of the forest in the primitive games of tag and hide-and-go-seek which Tarzan's fertile brain evolved. Tarzan scratched his head, running his fingers deep into the shock of black hair which framed his shapely, boyish face—he scratched his head and sighed. Teeka's new-found beauty became as suddenly his despair. He envied her the handsome coat of hair which covered her body. His own smooth, brown hide he hated with a hatred born of disgust and contempt. Years back he had harbored a hope that some day he, too, would be clothed in hair as were all his brothers and sisters; but of late he had been forced to abandon the delectable dream.

Then there were Teeka's great teeth, not so large as the males, of course, but still mighty, handsome things by comparison with Tarzan's feeble white ones. And her beetling brows, and broad, flat nose, and her mouth! Tarzan had often practiced making his mouth into a little round circle and then puffing out his cheeks while he winked his eyes rapidly; but he felt that he could never do it in the same cute and irresistible way in which Teeka did it.

And as he watched her that afternoon, and wondered, a young bull ape who had been lazily foraging for food beneath the damp, matted carpet of decaying vegetation at the roots of a near-by tree lumbered awkwardly in Teeka's direction. The other apes of the tribe of Kerchak moved listlessly about or lolled restfully in the midday heat of the equatorial jungle. From time to time one or another of them had passed close to Teeka, and Tarzan had been uninterested. Why was it then that his brows contracted and his muscles tensed as he saw Taug pause beside the young she and then squat down close to her?

Tarzan always had liked Taug. Since childhood they had romped together. Side by side they had squatted near the water, their quick, strong fingers ready to leap forth and seize Pisah, the fish, should that wary denizen of the cool depths dart surfaceward to the lure of the insects Tarzan tossed upon the face of the pool.

Together they had baited Tublat and teased Numa, the lion. Why, then, should Tarzan feel the rise of the short hairs at the nape of his neck merely because Taug sat close to Teeka?

It is true that Taug was no longer the frolicsome ape of yesterday. When his snarling-muscles bared his giant fangs no one could longer imagine that Taug was in as playful a mood as when he and Tarzan had rolled upon the turf in mimic battle. The Taug of today was a huge, sullen bull ape, somber and forbidding. Yet he and Tarzan never had quarreled.

For a few minutes the young ape-man watched Taug press closer to Teeka. He saw the rough caress of the huge paw as it stroked the sleek shoulder of the she, and then Tarzan of the Apes slipped catlike to the ground and approached the two.

As he came his upper lip curled into a snarl, exposing his fighting fangs, and a deep growl rumbled from his cavernous chest. Taug looked up, batting his blood-shot eyes. Teeka half raised herself and looked at Tarzan. Did she guess the cause of his perturbation? Who may say? At any rate, she was feminine, and so she reached up and scratched Taug behind one of his small, flat ears.

Tarzan saw, and in the instant that he saw, Teeka was no longer the little playmate of an hour ago; instead she was a wondrous thing—the most wondrous in the world—and a possession for which Tarzan would fight to the death against Taug or any other who dared question his right of proprietorship.

Stooped, his muscles rigid and one great shoulder turned toward the young bull, Tarzan of the Apes sidled nearer and nearer. His face was partly averted, but his keen gray eyes never left those of Taug, and as he came, his growls increased in depth and volume.

Taug rose upon his short legs, bristling. His fighting fangs were bared. He, too, sidled, stiff-legged, and growled.

"Teeka is Tarzan's," said the ape-man, in the low gutturals of the great anthropoids.

"Teeka is Taug's," replied the bull ape.

Thaka and Numgo and Gunto, disturbed by the growlings of the two young bulls, looked up half apathetic, half interested. They were sleepy, but they sensed a fight. It would break the monotony of the humdrum jungle life they led.

Coiled about his shoulders was Tarzan's long grass rope, in his hand was the hunting knife of the long-dead father he had never known. In Taug's little brain lay a great respect for the shiny bit of sharp metal which the ape-boy knew so well how to use. With it had he slain Tublat, his fierce foster father, and Bolgani, the gorilla. Taug knew these things, and so he came warily, circling about Tarzan in search of an opening. The latter, made cautious because of his lesser bulk and the inferiority of his natural armament, followed similar tactics.

For a time it seemed that the altercation would follow the way of the majority of such differences between members of the tribe and that one of them would finally lose interest and wander off to prosecute some other line of endeavor. Such might have been the end of it had the *casus belli* been other than it was; but Teeka was flattered at the attention that was being drawn to her and by the fact that these two young bulls were contemplating battle on her account. Such a thing never before had occurred in Teeka's brief life. She had seen other bulls battling for other and older shes, and in the depth of her wild little heart she had longed for the day when the jungle grasses would be reddened with the blood of mortal combat for her fair sake.

So now she squatted upon her haunches and insulted both her admirers impartially. She hurled taunts at them for their cowardice, and called them vile names, such as Histah, the snake, and Dango, the hyena. She threatened to call Mumga to chastise them with a stick—Mumga, who was so old that she could no longer climb and so toothless that she was forced to confine her diet almost exclusively to bananas and grub-worms.

The apes who were watching heard and laughed. Taug was infuriated. He made a sudden lunge for Tarzan, but the ape-boy leaped nimbly to one side, eluding him, and with the quickness of a cat wheeled and leaped back again to close quarters. His hunting knife was raised above his head as he came in, and he aimed a vicious blow at Taug's neck. The ape wheeled to dodge the weapon so that the keen blade struck him but a glancing blow upon the shoulder.

The spurt of red blood brought a shrill cry of delight from Teeka. Ah, but this was something worth while! She glanced about to see if others had witnessed this evidence of her popularity. Helen of Troy was never one whit more proud than was Teeka at that moment.

If Teeka had not been so absorbed in her own vaingloriousness she might have noted the rustling of leaves in the tree above her—a rustling which was not caused by any movement of the wind, since there was no wind. And had she looked up she might have seen a sleek body crouching almost directly over her and wicked yellow eyes glaring hungrily down upon her, but Teeka did not look up.

With his wound Taug had backed off growling horribly. Tarzan had followed him, screaming insults at him, and menacing him with his brandishing blade. Teeka moved from beneath the tree in an effort to keep close to the duelists.

The branch above Teeka bent and swayed a trifle with the movement of the body of the watcher stretched along it. Taug had halted now and was preparing to make a new stand. His lips were flecked with foam, and saliva drooled from his jowls. He stood with head lowered and arms outstretched, preparing for a sudden charge to close quarters. Could he but lay his mighty hands upon that soft, brown skin the battle would be his. Taug considered Tarzan's manner of fighting unfair. He would not close. Instead, he leaped nimbly just beyond the reach of Taug's muscular fingers.

The ape-boy had as yet never come to a real trial of strength with a bull ape, other than in play, and so he was not at all sure that it would be safe to put his muscles to the test in a life and death struggle. Not that he was afraid, for Tarzan knew nothing of fear. The instinct of self-preservation gave him caution—that was all. He took risks only when it seemed necessary, and then he would hesitate at nothing.

His own method of fighting seemed best fitted to his build and to his armament. His teeth, while strong and sharp, were, as weapons of offense, pitifully inadequate by comparison with the mighty fighting fangs of the anthropoids. By dancing about, just out of reach of an antagonist, Tarzan could do infinite injury with his long, sharp hunting knife, and at the same time escape many of the painful and dangerous wounds which would be sure to follow his falling into the clutches of a bull ape.

And so Taug charged and bellowed like a bull, and Tarzan of the Apes danced lightly to this side and that, hurling jungle billingsgate at his foe, the while he nicked him now and again with his knife.

There were lulls in the fighting when the two would stand panting for breath, facing each other, mustering their wits and their forces for a new onslaught. It was during a pause such as this that Taug chanced to let his eyes rove beyond his foeman. Instantly the entire aspect of the ape altered. Rage left his countenance to be supplanted by an expression of fear.

With a cry that every ape there recognized, Taug turned and fled. No need to question him—his warning proclaimed the near presence of their ancient enemy.

Tarzan started to seek safety, as did the other members of the tribe, and as he did so he heard a panther's scream mingled with the frightened cry of a she-ape. Taug heard, too; but he did not pause in his flight.

With the ape-boy, however, it was different. He looked back to see if any member of the tribe was close pressed by the beast of prey, and the sight that met his eyes filled them with an expression of horror.

Teeka it was who cried out in terror as she fled across a little clearing toward the trees upon the opposite side, for after her leaped Sheeta, the panther, in easy, graceful bounds. Sheeta appeared to be in no hurry. His meat was assured, since even though the ape reached the trees ahead of him she could not climb beyond his clutches before he could be upon her.

Tarzan saw that Teeka must die. He cried to Taug and the other bulls to hasten to Teeka's assistance, and at the same time he ran toward the pursuing beast, taking down his rope as he came. Tarzan knew that once the great bulls were aroused none of the jungle, not even Numa, the lion, was anxious to measure fangs with them, and that if all those of the tribe who chanced to be present today would charge, Sheeta, the great cat, would doubtless turn tail and run for his life.

Taug heard, as did the others, but no one came to Tarzan's assistance or Teeka's rescue, and Sheeta was rapidly closing up the distance between himself and his prey.

The ape-boy, leaping after the panther, cried aloud to the beast in an effort to turn it from Teeka or otherwise distract its attention until the she-ape could gain the safety of the higher branches where Sheeta dared not go. He called the panther every opprobrious name that fell to his tongue. He dared him to stop and do battle with him; but Sheeta only loped on after the luscious titbit now almost within his reach.

Tarzan was not far behind and he was gaining, but the distance was so short that he scarce hoped to overhaul the carnivore before it had felled Teeka. In his right hand the boy swung his grass rope above his head as he ran. He hated to chance a miss, for the distance was much greater than he ever had cast before except in practice. It was the full length of his grass rope which separated him from Sheeta, and yet there was no other thing to do. He could not reach the brute's side before it overhauled Teeka. He must chance a throw.

And just as Teeka sprang for the lower limb of a great tree, and Sheeta rose behind her in a long, sinuous leap, the coils of the ape-boy's grass rope shot swiftly through the air, straightening into a long thin line as the open noose hovered for an instant above the savage head and the snarling jaws. Then it settled—clean and true about the tawny neck it settled, and Tarzan, with a quick twist of his rope-hand, drew the noose taut, bracing himself for the shock when Sheeta should have taken up the slack.

Just short of Teeka's glossy rump the cruel talons raked the air as the rope tightened and Sheeta was brought to a sudden stop—a stop that snapped the big beast over upon his back. Instantly Sheeta was up—with glaring eyes, and lashing tail, and gaping jaws, from which issued hideous cries of rage and disappointment.

He saw the ape-boy, the cause of his discomfiture, scarce forty feet before him, and Sheeta charged.

Teeka was safe now; Tarzan saw to that by a quick glance into the tree whose safety she had gained not an instant too soon, and Sheeta was charging. It was useless to risk his life in idle and unequal combat from which no good could come; but could he escape a battle with the enraged cat? And if he was forced to fight, what chance had he to survive? Tarzan was constrained to admit that his position was aught but a desirable one. The trees were too far to hope to reach in time to elude the cat. Tarzan could but stand facing that hideous charge. In his right hand he grasped his hunting knife—a puny, futile thing indeed by comparison with the great rows of mighty teeth which lined Sheeta's powerful jaws, and the sharp talons encased within his padded paws; yet the young Lord Greystoke faced it with the same courageous resignation with which some fearless ancestor went down to defeat and death on Senlac Hill by Hastings.

From safety points in the trees the great apes watched, screaming hatred at Sheeta and advice at Tarzan, for the progenitors of man have, naturally, many human traits. Teeka was frightened. She screamed at the bulls to hasten to Tarzan's assistance; but the bulls were otherwise engaged—principally in giving advice and making faces. Anyway, Tarzan was not a real Mangani, so why should they risk their lives in an effort to protect him?

And now Sheeta was almost upon the lithe, naked body, and—the body was not there. Quick as was the great cat, the ape-boy was quicker. He leaped to one side almost as the panther's talons were closing upon him, and as Sheeta went hurtling to the ground beyond, Tarzan was racing for the safety of the nearest tree.

The panther recovered himself almost immediately and, wheeling, tore after his prey, the ape-boy's rope dragging along the ground behind him. In doubling back after Tarzan, Sheeta had passed around a low bush. It was a mere nothing in the path of any jungle creature of the size and weight of Sheeta—provided it had no trailing rope dangling behind. But Sheeta was handicapped by such a rope, and as he leaped once again after Tarzan of the Apes the rope encircled the small bush, became tangled in it and brought the panther to a sudden stop. An instant later Tarzan was safe among the higher branches of a small tree into which Sheeta could not follow him.

Here he perched, hurling twigs and epithets at the raging feline beneath him. The other members of the tribe now took up the bombardment, using such hard-shelled fruits and dead branches as came within their reach, until Sheeta, goaded to frenzy and snapping at the grass rope, finally succeeded in severing its strands. For a moment the panther stood glaring first at one of his tormentors and then at another, until, with a final scream of rage, he turned and slunk off into the tangled mazes of the jungle.

A half hour later the tribe was again upon the ground, feeding as though naught had occurred to interrupt the somber dullness of their lives. Tarzan had recovered the greater part of his rope and was busy fashioning a new noose, while Teeka squatted close behind him, in evident token that her choice was made.

Taug eyed them sullenly. Once when he came close, Teeka bared her fangs and growled at him, and Tarzan showed his canines in an ugly snarl; but Taug did not provoke a quarrel. He seemed to accept after the manner of his kind the decision of the she as an indication that he had been vanquished in his battle for her favors.

Later in the day, his rope repaired, Tarzan took to the trees in search of game. More than his fellows he required meat, and so, while they were satisfied with fruits and herbs and beetles, which could be discovered without much effort upon their part, Tarzan spent considerable time hunting the game animals whose flesh alone satisfied the cravings of his stomach and furnished sustenance and strength to the mighty thews which, day by day, were building beneath the soft, smooth texture of his brown hide.

Taug saw him depart, and then, quite casually, the big beast hunted closer and closer to Teeka in his search for food. At last he was within a few feet of her, and when he shot a covert glance at her he saw that she was appraising him and that there was no evidence of anger upon her face.

Taug expanded his great chest and rolled about on his short legs, making strange growlings in his throat. He raised his lips, baring his fangs. My, but what great, beautiful fangs he had! Teeka could not but notice them. She also let her eyes rest in admiration upon Taug's beetling brows and his short, powerful neck. What a beautiful creature he was indeed!

Taug, flattered by the unconcealed admiration in her eyes, strutted about, as proud and as vain as a peacock. Presently he began to inventory his assets, mentally, and shortly he found himself comparing them with those of his rival.

Taug grunted, for there was no comparison. How could one compare his beautiful coat with the smooth and naked hideousness of Tarzan's bare hide? Who could see beauty in the stingy nose of the Tarmangani after looking at Taug's broad nostrils? And Tarzan's eyes! Hideous things, showing white about them, and entirely unrimmed with red. Taug knew that his own blood-shot eyes were beautiful, for he had seen them reflected in the glassy surface of many a drinking pool.

The bull drew nearer to Teeka, finally squatting close against her. When Tarzan returned from his hunting a short time later it was to see Teeka contentedly scratching the back of his rival.

Tarzan was disgusted. Neither Taug nor Teeka saw him as he swung through the trees into the glade. He paused a moment, looking at them; then, with a sorrowful grimace, he turned and faded away into the labyrinth of leafy boughs and festooned moss out of which he had come.

Tarzan wished to be as far away from the cause of his heartache as he could. He was suffering the first pangs of blighted love, and he didn't quite know what was the matter with him. He thought that he was angry with Taug, and so he couldn't understand why it was that he had run away instead of rushing into mortal combat with the destroyer of his happiness.

He also thought that he was angry with Teeka, yet a vision of her many beauties persisted in haunting him, so that he could only see her in the light of love as the most desirable thing in the world.

The ape-boy craved affection. From babyhood until the time of her death, when the poisoned arrow of Kulonga had pierced her savage heart, Kala had represented to the English boy the sole object of love which he had known.

In her wild, fierce way Kala had loved her adopted son, and Tarzan had returned that love, though the outward demonstrations of it were no greater than might have been expected from any other beast of the jungle. It was not until he was bereft of her that the boy realized how deep had been his attachment for his mother, for as such he looked upon her.

In Teeka he had seen within the past few hours a substitute for Kala—someone to fight for and to hunt for—someone to caress; but now his dream was shattered. Something hurt within his breast. He placed his hand over his heart and wondered what had happened to him. Vaguely he attributed his pain to Teeka. The more he thought of Teeka as he had last seen her, caressing Taug, the more the thing within his breast hurt him.

Tarzan shook his head and growled; then on and on through the jungle he swung, and the farther he traveled and the more he thought upon his wrongs, the nearer he approached becoming an irreclaimable misogynist.

Two days later he was still hunting alone—very morose and very unhappy; but he was determined never to return to the tribe. He could not bear the thought of seeing Taug and Teeka always together. As he swung upon a great limb Numa, the lion, and Sabor, the lioness, passed beneath him, side by side, and Sabor leaned against the lion and bit playfully at his cheek. It was a half-caress. Tarzan sighed and hurled a nut at them.

Later he came upon several of Mbonga's black warriors. He

was upon the point of dropping his noose about the neck of one of them, who was a little distance from his companions, when he became interested in the thing which occupied the savages. They were building a cage in the trail and covering it with leafy branches. When they had completed their work the structure was scarcely visible.

Tarzan wondered what the purpose of the thing might be, and why, when they had built it, they turned away and started back along the trail in the direction of their village.

It had been some time since Tarzan had visited the blacks and looked down from the shelter of the great trees which overhung their palisade upon the activities of his enemies, from among whom had come the slayer of Kala.

Although he hated them, Tarzan derived considerable entertainment in watching them at their daily life within the village, and especially at their dances, when the fires glared against their naked bodies as they leaped and turned and twisted in mimic warfare. It was rather in the hope of witnessing something of the kind that he now followed the warriors back toward their village, but in this he was disappointed, for there was no dance that night.

Instead, from the safe concealment of his tree, Tarzan saw little groups seated about tiny fires discussing the events of the day, and in the darker corners of the village he descried isolated couples talking and laughing together, and always one of each couple was a young man and the other a young woman.

Tarzan cocked his head upon one side and thought, and before he went to sleep that night, curled in the crotch of the great tree above the village, Teeka filled his mind, and afterward she filled his dreams—she and the young black men laughing and talking with the young black women.

Taug, hunting alone, had wandered some distance from the balance of the tribe. He was making his way slowly along an elephant path when he discovered that it was blocked with undergrowth. Now Taug, come into maturity, was an evil-natured brute of an exceeding short temper. When something thwarted him, his sole idea was to overcome it by brute strength and ferocity, and so now when he found his way blocked, he tore angrily into the leafy screen and an instant later found himself within a strange lair, his progress effectually blocked, notwithstanding his most violent efforts to forge ahead.

Biting and striking at the barrier, Taug finally worked himself into a frightful rage, but all to no avail; and at last he became convinced that he must turn back. But when he would have done so, what was his chagrin to discover that another barrier had dropped behind him while he fought to break down the one before him! Taug was trapped. Until exhaustion overcame him he fought frantically for his freedom; but all for naught.

In the morning a party of blacks set out from the village of Mbonga in the direction of the trap they had constructed the previous day, while among the branches of the trees above them hovered a naked young giant filled with the curiosity of the wild things. Manu, the monkey, chattered and scolded as Tarzan passed, and though he was not afraid of the familiar figure of the ape-boy, he hugged closer to him the little brown body of his life's companion. Tarzan laughed as he saw it; but the laugh was followed by a sudden clouding of his face and a deep sigh.

A little farther on, a gaily feathered bird strutted about before the admiring eyes of his somber-hued mate. It seemed to Tarzan that everything in the jungle was combining to remind him that he had lost Teeka; yet every day of his life he had seen these same things and thought nothing of them.

When the blacks reached the trap, Taug set up a great commotion. Seizing the bars of his prison, he shook them frantically, and all the while he roared and growled terrifically. The blacks were elated, for while they had not built their trap for this hairy tree man, they were delighted with their catch.

Tarzan pricked up his ears when he heard the voice of a great ape and, circling quickly until he was down wind from the trap, he sniffed at the air in search of the scent spoor of the prisoner. Nor was it long before there came to those delicate nostrils the familiar odor that told Tarzan the identity of the captive as unerringly as though he had looked upon Taug with his eyes. Yes, it was Taug, and he was alone.

Tarzan grinned as he approached to discover what the blacks would do to their prisoner. Doubtless they would slay him at once. Again Tarzan grinned. Now he could have Teeka for his own, with none to dispute his right to her. As he watched, he saw the black warriors strip the screen from about the cage, fasten ropes to it and drag it away along the trail in the direction of their village.

Tarzan watched until his rival passed out of sight, still beating upon the bars of his prison and growling out his anger and his threats. Then the ape-boy turned and swung rapidly off in search of the tribe, and Teeka.

Once, upon the journey, he surprised Sheeta and his family in a little overgrown clearing. The great cat lay stretched upon the ground, while his mate, one paw across her lord's savage face, licked at the soft white fur at his throat.

Tarzan increased his speed then until he fairly flew through the forest, nor was it long before he came upon the tribe. He saw them before they saw him, for of all the jungle creatures, none passed more quietly than Tarzan of the Apes. He saw Kamma and her mate feeding side by side, their hairy bodies rubbing against each other. And he saw Teeka feeding by herself. Not for long would she feed thus in loneliness, thought Tarzan, as with a bound he landed amongst them.

There was a startled rush and a chorus of angry and frightened snarls, for Tarzan had surprised them; but there was more, too, than mere nervous shock to account for the bristling neck hair which remained standing long after the apes had discovered the identity of the newcomer.

Tarzan noticed this as he had noticed it many times in the past— that always his sudden coming among them left them nervous and unstrung for a considerable time, and that they one and all found it necessary to satisfy themselves that he was indeed Tarzan by smelling about him a half dozen or more times before they calmed down.

Pushing through them, he made his way toward Teeka; but as he approached her the ape drew away.

"Teeka," he said, "it is Tarzan. You belong to Tarzan. I have come for you."

The ape drew closer, looking him over carefully. Finally she sniffed at him, as though to make assurance doubly sure.

"Where is Taug?" she asked.

"The Gomangani have him," replied Tarzan. "They will kill him."

In the eyes of the she, Tarzan saw a wistful expression and a troubled look of sorrow as he told her of Taug's fate; but she came quite close and snuggled against him, and Tarzan, Lord Greystoke, put his arm about her.

As he did so he noticed, with a start, the strange incongruity of that smooth, brown arm against the black and hairy coat of his lady-love. He recalled the paw of Sheeta's mate across Sheeta's face—no incongruity there. He thought of little Manu hugging his she, and how the one seemed to belong to the other. Even the proud male bird, with his gay plumage, bore a close resemblance to his quieter spouse, while Numa, but for his shaggy mane, was almost a counterpart of Sabor, the lioness. The males and the females differed, it was true; but not with such differences as existed between Tarzan and Teeka.

Tarzan was puzzled. There was something wrong. His arm dropped from the shoulder of Teeka. Very slowly he drew away from her. She looked at him with her head cocked upon one side. Tarzan rose to his full height and beat upon his breast with his fists. He raised his head toward the heavens and opened his mouth. From the depths of his lungs rose the fierce, weird challenge of the victorious bull ape. The tribe turned curiously to eye him. He had killed nothing, nor was there any antagonist to be goaded to madness by the savage scream. No, there was no excuse for it, and they turned back to their feeding, but with an eye upon the ape-man lest he be preparing to suddenly run amuck.

As they watched him they saw him swing into a near-by tree and disappear from sight. Then they forgot him, even Teeka.

Mbonga's black warriors, sweating beneath their strenuous task, and resting often, made slow progress toward their village. Always the savage beast in the primitive cage growled and roared when they moved him. He beat upon the bars and slavered at the mouth. His noise was hideous.

They had almost completed their journey and were making their final rest before forging ahead to gain the clearing in which lay their village. A few more minutes would have taken them out of the forest, and then, doubtless, the thing would not have happened which did happen.

A silent figure moved through the trees above them. Keen eyes inspected the cage and counted the number of warriors. An alert and daring brain figured upon the chances of success when a certain plan should be put to the test.

Tarzan watched the blacks lolling in the shade. They were exhausted. Already several of them slept. He crept closer, pausing just above them. Not a leaf rustled before his stealthy advance. He waited in the infinite patience of the beast of prey. Presently but two of the warriors remained awake, and one of these was dozing.

Tarzan of the Apes gathered himself, and as he did so the black who did not sleep arose and passed around to the rear of the cage. The ape-boy followed just above his head. Taug was eyeing the warrior and emitting low growls. Tarzan feared that the anthropoid would awaken the sleepers.

In a whisper which was inaudible to the ears of the Negro, Tarzan whispered Taug's name, cautioning the ape to silence, and Taug's growling ceased.

The black approached the rear of the cage and examined the fastenings of the door, and as he stood there the beast above him launched itself from the tree full upon his back. Steel fingers circled his throat, choking the cry which sprang to the lips of the terrified man. Strong teeth fastened themselves in his shoulder, and powerful legs wound themselves about his torso.

The black in a frenzy of terror tried to dislodge the silent thing which clung to him. He threw himself to the ground and rolled about; but still those mighty fingers closed more and more tightly their deadly grip.

The man's mouth gaped wide, his swollen tongue protruded, his eyes started from their sockets; but the relentless fingers only increased their pressure.

Taug was a silent witness of the struggle. In his fierce little brain he doubtless wondered what purpose prompted Tarzan to attack the black. Taug had not forgotten his recent battle with the ape-boy, nor the cause of it. Now he saw the form of the Gomangani suddenly go limp. There was a convulsive shiver and the man lay still.

Tarzan sprang from his prey and ran to the door of the cage. With nimble fingers he worked rapidly at the thongs which held the door in place. Taug could only watch—he could not help. Presently Tarzan pushed the thing up a couple of feet and Taug crawled out. The ape would have turned upon the sleeping blacks that he might wreak his pent vengeance; but Tarzan would not permit it.

Instead, the ape-boy dragged the body of the black within the cage and propped it against the side bars. Then he lowered the door and made fast the thongs as they had been before.

A happy smile lighted his features as he worked, for one of his principal diversions was the baiting of the blacks of Mbonga's village. He could imagine their terror when they awoke and found the dead body of their comrade fast in the cage where they had left the great ape safely secured but a few minutes before.

Tarzan and Taug took to the trees together, the shaggy coat of the fierce ape brushing the sleek skin of the English lordling as they passed through the primeval jungle side by side.

"Go back to Teeka," said Tarzan. "She is yours. Tarzan does not want her."

"Tarzan has found another she?" asked Taug.

The ape-boy shrugged.

"For the Gomangani there is another Gomangani," he said; "for Numa, the lion, there is Sabor, the lioness; for Sheeta there is a she of his own kind; for Bara, the deer; for Manu, the monkey; for all the beasts and the birds of the jungle is there a mate. Only for Tarzan of the Apes is there none. Taug is an ape. Teeka is an ape. Go back to Teeka. Tarzan is a man. He will go alone."

RACHEL IN LOVE

Pat Murphy

A superintelligent chimpanzee's life quickly descends into chaos following the death of her beloved caretaker. Placed in a primate research center, the terrified Rachel discovers the true meanings of despair, love, and life. This powerful tale won the 1987 Nebula Award for best novelette and the 1987 Theodore Sturgeon Memorial Award for Short Fiction.

It is a Sunday morning in summer and a small brown chimpanzee named Rachel sits on the living room floor of a remote ranch house on the edge of the Painted Desert. She is watching a Tarzan movie on television. Her hairy arms are wrapped around her knees and she rocks back and forth with suppressed excitement. She knows that her father would say that she's too old for such childish amusements—but since Aaron is still sleeping, he can't chastise her.

On the television, Tarzan has been trapped in a bamboo cage by a band of wicked Pygmies. Rachel is afraid that he won't escape in time to save Jane from the ivory smugglers who hold her captive. The movie cuts to Jane, who is tied up in the back of a jeep, and Rachel whimpers softly to herself. She knows better than to howl: she peeked into her father's bedroom earlier, and he was still in bed. Aaron doesn't like her to howl when he is sleeping.

When the movie breaks for a commercial, Rachel goes to her father's room. She is ready for breakfast and she wants him to get up. She tiptoes to the bed to see if he is awake.

His eyes are open and he is staring at nothing. His face is pale and his lips are a purplish color. Dr. Aaron Jacobs, the man Rachel calls father, is not asleep. He is dead, having died in the night of a heart attack.

When Rachel shakes him, his head rocks back and forth in time with her shaking, but his eyes do not blink and he does not breathe. She places his hand on her head, nudging him so that he will waken and stroke her. He does not move. When she leans toward him, his hand falls limply to dangle over the edge of the bed.

In the breeze from the open bedroom window, the fine wisps of gray hair that he had carefully combed over his bald spot each morning shift and flutter, exposing the naked scalp. In the other room, elephants trumpet as they stampede across the jungle to rescue Tarzan. Rachel whimpers softly, but her father does not move.

Rachel backs away from her father's body. In the living room, Tarzan is swinging across the jungle on vines, going to save Jane. Rachel ignores the television. She prowls through the house as if searching for comfort—stepping into her own small bedroom, wandering through her father's laboratory. From the cages that line the walls, white rats stare at her with hot red eyes. A rabbit hops across its cage, making a series of slow dull thumps, like a feather pillow tumbling down a flight of stairs.

She thinks that perhaps she made a mistake. Perhaps her father is just sleeping. She returns to the bedroom, but nothing has changed. Her father lies open-eyed on the bed. For a long time, she huddles beside his body, clinging to his hand.

He is the only person she has ever known. He is her father, her teacher, her friend. She cannot leave him alone.

The afternoon sun blazes through the window, and still Aaron does not move. The room grows dark, but Rachel does not turn on the lights. She is waiting for Aaron to wake up. When the moon rises, its silver light shines through the window to cast a bright rectangle on the far wall.

Outside, somewhere in the barren rocky land surrounding the ranch house, a coyote lifts its head to the rising moon and wails, a thin sound that is as lonely as a train whistling through an abandoned station. Rachel joins in with a desolate howl of loneliness and grief. Aaron lies still and Rachel knows that he is dead.

When Rachel was younger, she had a favorite bedtime story. —Where did I come from? she would ask Aaron, using the abbreviated gestures of ASL, American Sign Language. —Tell me again.

"You're too old for bedtime stories," Aaron would say.

—Please, she signed. —Tell me the story.

In the end, he always relented and told her. "Once upon a time, there was a little girl named Rachel," he said. "She was a pretty girl, with long golden hair like a princess in a fairy tale. She lived with her father and her mother and they were all very happy."

Rachel would snuggle contentedly beneath her blankets. The story, like any good fairy tale, had elements of tragedy. In the story, Rachel's father worked at a university, studying the workings of the brain and charting the electric fields that the nervous impulses of an active brain produced. But the other researchers at the university didn't understand Rachel's father; they distrusted his research and cut off his funding. (During this portion of the story, Aaron's voice took on a bitter edge.) So he left the university and took his wife and daughter to the desert, where he could work in peace.

He continued his research and determined that each individual brain produced its own unique pattern of fields, as characteristic as a fingerprint. (Rachel found this part of the story quite dull, but Aaron insisted on including it.) The shape of this "Electric Mind," as he called it, was determined by habitual patterns of thoughts and emotions. Record the Electric Mind, he postulated, and you could capture an individual's personality.

Then one sunny day, the doctor's wife and beautiful daughter went for a drive. A truck barreling down a winding cliffside road lost its brakes and met the car head-on, killing both the girl and her mother. (Rachel clung to Aaron's hand during this part of the story, frightened by the sudden evil twist of fortune.)

But though Rachel's body had died, all was not lost. In his desert lab, the doctor had recorded the electrical patterns produced by his daughter's brain. The doctor had been experimenting with the use of external magnetic fields to impose the patterns from one animal onto the brain of another. From an animal supply house, he obtained a young chimpanzee. He used a mixture of norepinephrine-based transmitter substances to boost the speed of neural processing in the chimp's brain, and then he imposed the pattern of his daughter's mind upon the brain of this young chimp, combining the two after his own fashion, saving his daughter in his own way. In the chimp's brain was all that remained of Rachel Jacobs.

The doctor named the chimp Rachel and raised her as his own daughter. Since the limitations of the chimpanzee larynx made speech very difficult, he instructed her in ASL. He taught her to read and to write. They were good friends, the best of companions.

By this point in the story, Rachel was usually asleep. But it didn't matter—she knew the ending. The doctor, whose name was Aaron Jacobs, and the chimp named Rachel lived happily ever after.

Rachel likes fairy tales and she likes happy endings. She has the mind of a teenage girl, but the innocent heart of a young chimp.

Sometimes, when Rachel looks at her gnarled brown fingers, they seem alien, wrong, out of place. She remembers having small, pale, delicate hands. Memories lie upon memories, layers upon layers, like the sedimentary rocks of the desert buttes.

Rachel remembers a blonde-haired, fair-skinned woman who smelled sweetly of perfume. On a Halloween long ago, this woman (who was, in these memories, Rachel's mother) painted Rachel's fingernails bright red because Rachel was dressed as a gypsy and gypsies liked red. Rachel remembers the woman's hands: white hands with faintly blue veins hidden just beneath the skin, neatly clipped nails painted rose pink.

But Rachel also remembers another mother and another time. Her mother was dark and hairy and smelled sweetly of overripe fruit. She and Rachel lived in a wire cage in a room filled with chimps and she hugged Rachel to her hairy breast whenever any people came into the room. Rachel's mother groomed Rachel constantly, picking delicately through her fur in search of lice that she never found.

Memories upon memories: jumbled and confused, like random pictures clipped from magazines, a bright collage that makes no sense. Rachel remembers cages: cold wire mesh beneath her feet, the smell of fear around her. A man in a white lab coat took her from the arms of her hairy mother and pricked her with needles. She could hear her mother howling, but she could not escape from the man.

Rachel remembers a junior high school dance where she wore a new dress: she stood in a dark corner of the gym for hours, pretending to admire the crepe paper decorations because she felt too shy to search among the crowd for her friends.

She remembers when she was a young chimp: she huddled with five other adolescent chimps in the stuffy freight compartment of a train, frightened by the alien smells and sounds.

She remembers gym class: gray lockers and ugly gym suits that revealed her skinny legs. The teacher made everyone play softball, even Rachel who was unathletic and painfully shy. Rachel at bat, standing at the plate, was terrified to be the center of attention. "Easy out," said the catcher, a hard-edged girl who ran with the wrong crowd and always smelled of cigarette smoke. When Rachel swung at the ball and missed, the outfielders filled the air with malicious laughter.

Rachel's memories are as delicate and elusive as the dusty moths and butterflies that dance among the rabbit brush and sage. Memories of her girlhood never linger; they land for an instant, then take flight, leaving Rachel feeling abandoned and alone.

Rachel leaves Aaron's body where it is, but closes his eyes and pulls the sheet up over his head. She does not know what else to do. Each day she waters the garden and picks some greens for the rabbits. Each day, she cares for the rats and the rabbits, bringing them food and refilling their water bottles. The weather is cool, and Aaron's body does not smell too bad, though by the end of the week, a wide line of ants runs from the bed to the open window.

At the end of the first week, on a moonlit evening, Rachel decides to let the animals go free. She releases the rabbits one by one, climbing on a stepladder to reach down into the cage and lift each placid bunny out. She carries each one to the back door, holding it for a moment and stroking the soft warm fur. Then she sets the animal down and nudges it in the direction of the green grass that grows around the perimeter of the fenced garden.

The rats are more difficult to deal with. She manages to wrestle the large rat cage off the shelf, but it is heavier than she thought it would be. Though she slows its fall, it lands on the floor with a crash and the rats scurry to and fro within. She shoves the cage across the linoleum floor, sliding it down the hall, over the doorsill, and onto the back patio. When she opens the cage door, rats burst out like popcorn from a popper, white in the moonlight and dashing in all directions.

Once, while Aaron was taking a nap, Rachel walked along the dirt track that led to the main highway. She hadn't planned on going far. She just wanted to see what the highway looked like, maybe hide near the mailbox and watch a car drive past. She was curious about the outside world and her fleeting fragmentary memories did not satisfy that curiosity.

She was halfway to the mailbox when Aaron came roaring up in his old jeep. "Get in the car," he shouted at her. "Right now!" Rachel had never seen him so angry. She cowered in the jeep's passenger seat, covered with dust from the road, unhappy that Aaron was so upset. He didn't speak until they got back to the ranch house, and then he spoke in a low voice, filled with bitterness and suppressed rage.

"You don't want to go out there," he said. "You wouldn't like it out there. The world is filled with petty, narrow-minded, stupid people. They wouldn't understand you. And anyone they don't understand, they want to hurt. They hate anyone who's different. If they know that you're different, they punish you, hurt you. They'd lock you up and never let you go."

He looked straight ahead, staring through the dirty windshield. "It's not like the shows on TV, Rachel," he said in a softer tone. "It's not like the stories in books."

He looked at her then and she gestured frantically. —I'm sorry. I'm sorry.

"I can't protect you out there," he said. "I can't keep you safe."

Rachel took his hand in both of hers. He relented then, stroking her head. "Never do that again," he said. "Never."

Aaron's fear was contagious. Rachel never again walked along the dirt track and sometimes she had dreams about bad people who wanted to lock her in a cage.

●

Two weeks after Aaron's death, a black-and-white police car drives slowly up to the house. When the policemen knock on the door, Rachel hides behind the couch in the living room. They knock again, try the knob, then open the door, which she had left unlocked.

Suddenly frightened, Rachel bolts from behind the couch, bounding toward the back door. Behind her, she hears one man yell, "My God! It's a gorilla!"

By the time he pulls his gun, Rachel has run out the back door and away into the hills. From the hills she watches as an ambulance drives up and two men in white take Aaron's body away. Even after the ambulance and the police car drive away, Rachel is afraid to go back to the house. Only after sunset does she return.

Just before dawn the next morning, she wakens to the sound of a truck jouncing down the dirt road. She peers out the window to see a pale green pickup. Sloppily stenciled in white on the door are the words: PRIMATE RESEARCH CENTER. Rachel hesitates as the truck pulls up in front of the house. By the time she has decided to flee, two men are getting out of the truck. One of them carries a rifle.

She runs out the back door and heads for the hills, but she is only halfway to hiding when she hears a sound like a sharp intake of breath and feels a painful jolt in her shoulder. Suddenly, her legs give way and she is tumbling backward down the sandy slope, dust coating her red-brown fur, her howl becoming a whimper, then fading to nothing at all. She falls into the blackness of sleep.

The sun is up. Rachel lies in a cage in the back of the pickup truck. She is partially conscious and she feels a tingling in her hands and feet. Nausea grips her stomach and bowels. Her body aches.

Rachel can blink, but otherwise she can't move. From where she lies, she can see only the wire mesh of the cage and the side of the truck. When she tries to turn her head, the burning in her skin intensifies. She lies still, wanting to cry out, but unable to make a sound. She can only blink slowly, trying to close out the pain. But the burning and nausea stay.

The truck jounces down a dirt road, then stops. It rocks as the men get out. The doors slam. Rachel hears the tailgate open.

A woman's voice: "Is that the animal the county sheriff wanted us to pick up?" A woman peers into the cage. She wears a white lab coat and her brown hair is tied back in a single braid. Around her eyes, Rachel can see small wrinkles, etched by years of living in the desert. The woman doesn't look evil. Rachel hopes that the woman will save her from the men in the truck.

"Yeah. It should be knocked out for at least another half hour. Where do you want it?"

"Bring it into the lab where we had the rhesus monkeys. I'll keep it there until I have an empty cage in the breeding area."

Rachel's cage scrapes across the bed of the pickup. She feels each bump and jar as a new pain. The man swings the cage onto a cart and the woman pushes the cart down a concrete corridor. Rachel watches the walls pass just a few inches from her nose.

The lab contains rows of cages in which small animals sleepily move. In the sudden stark light of the overhead fluorescent bulbs, the eyes of white rats gleam red.

With the help of one of the men from the truck, the woman manhandles Rachel onto a lab table. The metal surface is cold and hard, painful against Rachel's skin. Rachel's body is not under her control; her limbs will not respond. She is still frozen by the tranquilizer, able to watch, but that is all. She cannot protest or plead for mercy.

Rachel watches with growing terror as the woman pulls on rubber gloves and fills a hypodermic needle with a clear solution. "Mark down that I'm giving her the standard test for tuberculosis; this eyelid should be checked before she's moved in with the others. I'll add thiabendazole to her feed for the next few days to clean out any intestinal worms. And I suppose we might as well de-flea her as well," the woman says. The man grunts in response.

Expertly, the woman closes one of Rachel's eyes. With her open eye, Rachel watches the hypodermic needle approach. She feels a sharp pain in her eyelid. In her mind, she is howling, but the only sound she can manage is a breathy sigh.

The woman sets the hypodermic aside and begins methodically spraying Rachel's fur with a cold, foul-smelling liquid. A drop strikes Rachel's eye and burns. Rachel blinks, but she cannot lift a hand to rub her eye. The woman treats Rachel with casual indifference, chatting with the man as she spreads Rachel's legs and sprays her genitals. "Looks healthy enough. Good breeding stock."

Rachel moans, but neither person notices. At last, they finish their torture, put her in a cage, and leave the room. She closes her eyes, and the darkness returns.

Rachel dreams. She is back at home in the ranch house. It is night and she is alone. Outside, coyotes yip and howl. The coyote is the voice of the desert, wailing as the wind wails when it stretches itself thin to squeeze through a crack between two boulders. The people native to this land tell tales of Coyote, a god who was a trickster, unreliable, changeable, mercurial.

Rachel is restless, anxious, unnerved by the howling of the coyotes. She is looking for Aaron. In the dream, she knows he is not dead, and she searches the house for him, wandering from his cluttered bedroom to her small room to the linoleum-tiled lab.

She is in the lab when she hears something tapping: a small dry scratching, like a wind-blown branch against the window, though no tree grows near the house and the night is still. Cautiously, she lifts the curtain to look out.

She looks into her own reflection: a pale oval face, long blonde hair. The hand that holds the curtain aside is smooth and white with carefully clipped fingernails. But something is wrong. Superimposed on the reflection is another face peering through the glass: a pair of dark brown eyes, a chimp face with red-brown hair and jug-handle ears. She sees her own reflection and she sees the outsider; the two images merge and blur. She is afraid, but she can't drop the curtain and shut the ape face out.

She is a chimp looking in through the cold, bright windowpane; she is a girl looking out; she is a girl looking in; she is an ape looking out. She is afraid and the coyotes are howling all around.

Rachel opens her eyes and blinks until the world comes into focus. The pain and tingling has retreated, but she still feels a little sick. Her left eye aches. When she rubs it, she feels a raised lump on the eyelid where the woman pricked her. She lies on the floor of a wire mesh cage. The room is hot and the air is thick with the smell of animals.

In the cage beside her is another chimp, an older animal with scruffy dark brown fur. He sits with his arms wrapped around his knees, rocking back and forth, back and forth. His head is down. As he rocks, he murmurs to himself, a meaningless cooing that goes on and on. On his scalp, Rachel can see a gleam of metal: a permanently implanted electrode protrudes from a shaven patch. Rachel makes a soft questioning sound, but the other chimp will not look up.

Rachel's own cage is just a few feet square. In one corner is a bowl of monkey pellets. A water bottle hangs on the side of the cage. Rachel ignores the food, but drinks thirstily.

Sunlight streams through the windows, sliced into small sections by the wire mesh that covers the glass. She tests her cage door, rattling it gently at first, then harder. It is securely latched. The gaps in the mesh are too small to admit her hand. She can't reach out to work the latch.

The other chimp continues to rock back and forth. When Rachel rattles the mesh of her cage and howls, he lifts his head wearily and looks at her. His red-rimmed eyes are unfocused; she can't be sure he sees her.

—Hello, she gestures tentatively. —What's wrong?

He blinks at her in the dim light. —Hurt, he signs in ASL. He reaches up to touch the electrode, fingering skin that is already raw from repeated rubbing.

—Who hurt you? she asks. He stares at her blankly and she repeats the question. —Who?

—Men, he signs.

As if on cue, there is the click of a latch and the door to the lab opens. A bearded man in a white coat steps in, followed by a clean-shaven man in a suit. The bearded man seems to be showing the other man around the lab. "...only preliminary testing, so far," the bearded man is saying. "We've been hampered by a shortage of chimps trained in ASL." The two men stop in front of the old chimp's cage. "This old fellow is from the Oregon center. Funding for the language program was cut back and some of the animals were dispersed to other programs." The old chimp huddles at the back of the cage, eying the bearded man with suspicion.

—Hungry? the bearded man signs to the old chimp. He holds up an orange where the old chimp can see it.

—Give orange, the old chimp gestures. He holds out his hand, but comes no nearer to the wire mesh than he must to reach the orange. With the fruit in hand, he retreats to the back of his cage.

The bearded man continues, "This project will provide us with the first solid data on neural activity during use of sign language. But we really need greater access to chimps with advanced language skills. People are so damn protective of their animals."

"Is this one of yours?" the clean-shaven man asks, pointing to Rachel. She cowers in the back of the cage, as far from the wire mesh as she can get.

"No, not mine. She was someone's household pet, apparently. The county sheriff had us pick her up." The bearded man peers into her cage. Rachel does not move; she is terrified that he will somehow guess that she knows ASL. She stares at his hands and thinks about those hands putting an electrode through her skull. "I think she'll be put in breeding stock," the man says as he turns away.

Rachel watches them go, wondering at what terrible people these are. Aaron was right: they want to punish her, put an electrode in her head.

After the men are gone, she tries to draw the old chimp into conversation, but he will not reply. He ignores her as he eats his orange. Then he returns to his former posture, hiding his head and rocking himself back and forth.

Rachel, hungry despite herself, samples one of the food pellets. It has a strange medicinal taste, and she puts it back in the bowl. She needs to pee, but there is no toilet and she cannot escape the cage. At last, unable to hold it, she pees in one corner of the cage. The urine flows through the wire mesh to soak the litter below, and the smell of warm piss fills her cage. Humiliated, frightened, her head aching, her skin itchy from the flea spray, Rachel watches as the sunlight creeps across the room.

The day wears on. Rachel samples her food again, but rejects it, preferring hunger to the strange taste. A black man comes and cleans the cages of the rabbits and rats. Rachel cowers in her cage and watches him warily, afraid that he will hurt her too.

When night comes, she is not tired. Outside, coyotes howl. Moonlight filters in through the high windows. She draws her legs up toward her body, then rests with her arms wrapped around her knees. Her father is dead, and she is a captive in a strange place. For a time, she whimpers softly, hoping to awaken from this nightmare and find herself at home in bed. When she hears the click of a key in the door to the room, she hugs herself more tightly.

A man in green coveralls pushes a cart filled with cleaning supplies into the room. He takes a broom from the cart, and begins sweeping the concrete floor. Over the rows of cages, she can see the top of his head bobbing in time with his sweeping. He works slowly and methodically, bending down to sweep carefully under each row of cages, making a neat pile of dust, dung, and food scraps in the center of the aisle.

The janitor's name is Jake. He is a middle-aged deaf man who has been employed by the Primate Research Center for the past seven years. He works night shift. The personnel director at the Primate Research Center likes Jake because he fills the federal quota for handicapped employees, and because he has not asked for a raise in five years. There have been some complaints about Jake—his work is often sloppy—but never enough to merit firing the man.

Jake is an unambitious, somewhat slow-witted man. He likes the Primate Research Center because he works alone, which allows him to drink on the job. He is an easy-going man, and he likes the animals. Sometimes, he brings treats for them. Once, a lab assistant caught him feeding an apple to a pregnant rhesus monkey. The monkey was part of an experiment on the effect of dietary restrictions on fetal brain development, and the lab assistant warned Jake that he would be fired if he was ever caught interfering with the animals again. Jake still feeds the animals, but he is more careful about when he does it, and he has never been caught again.

As Rachel watches, the old chimp gestures to Jake. —Give banana, the chimp signs. —Please banana. Jake stops sweeping for a minute and reaches down to the bottom shelf of his cleaning cart. He returns with a banana and offers it to the old chimp. The chimp accepts the banana and leans against the mesh while Jake scratches his fur.

When Jake turns back to his sweeping, he catches sight of Rachel and sees that she is watching him. Emboldened by his kindness to the old chimp, Rachel timidly gestures to him. —Help me.

Jake hesitates, then peers at her more closely. Both his eyes are shot with a fine lacework of red. His nose displays the broken blood vessels of someone who has been friends with the bottle for too many years. He needs a shave. But when he leans close, Rachel catches the scent of whiskey and tobacco. The smells remind her of Aaron and give her courage.

—Please help me, Rachel signs. —I don't belong here.

For the last hour, Jake has been drinking steadily. His view of the world is somewhat fuzzy. He stares at her blearily.

Rachel's fear that he will hurt her is replaced by the fear that he will leave her locked up and alone. Desperately she signs again. —Please please please. Help me. I don't belong here. Please help me go home.

He watches her, considering the situation. Rachel does not move. She is afraid that any movement will make him leave. With a majestic speed dictated by his inebriation, Jake leans his broom on the row of cages behind him and steps toward Rachel's cage again. —You talk? he signs.

—I talk, she signs.

—Where did you come from?

—From my father's house, she signs. —Two men came and shot me and put me here. I don't know why. I don't know why they locked me in jail.

Jake looks around, willing to be sympathetic, but puzzled by her talk of jail. —This isn't jail, he signs. —This is a place where scientists raise monkeys.

Rachel is indignant. —I am not a monkey, she signs. —I am a girl.

Jake studies her hairy body and her jug-handle ears. —You look like a monkey.

Rachel shakes her head. —No. I am a girl.

Rachel runs her hands back over her head, a very human gesture of annoyance and unhappiness. She signs sadly, —I don't belong here. Please let me out.

Jake shifts his weight from foot to foot, wondering what to do. —I can't let you out. I'll get in big trouble.

—Just for a little while? Please?

Jake glances at his cart of supplies. He has to finish off this room and two corridors of offices before he can relax for the night.

—Don't go, Rachel signs, guessing his thoughts.

—I have work to do.

She looks at the cart, then suggests eagerly, —Let me out and I'll help you work.

Jake frowns. —If I let you out, you will run away.

—No, I won't run. I will help. Please let me out.

—You promise to go back?

Rachel nods.

Warily he unlatches the cage. Rachel bounds out, grabs a whisk broom from the cart, and begins industriously sweeping bits of food and droppings from beneath the row of cages. —Come on, she signs to Jake from the end of the aisle. —I will help.

When Jake pushes the cart from the room filled with cages, Rachel follows him closely. The rubber wheels of the cleaning cart rumble softly on the linoleum floor. They pass through a metal door into a corridor where the floor is carpeted and the air smells of chalk dust and paper.

Offices let off the corridor, each one a small room furnished with a desk, bookshelves, and a blackboard. Jake shows Rachel how to empty the wastebaskets into a garbage bag. While he cleans the blackboards, she wanders from office to office, trailing the trash-filled garbage bag.

At first, Jake keeps a close eye on Rachel. But after cleaning each blackboard, he pauses to sip whiskey from a paper cup. At the end of the corridor, he stops to refill the cup from the whiskey bottle that he keeps wedged between the Sani-flush and the window cleaner. By the time he is halfway through the second cup, he is treating her like an old friend, telling her to hurry up so that they can eat dinner.

Rachel works quickly, but she stops sometimes to gaze out the office windows. Outside, moonlight shines on a sandy plain, dotted here and there with scrubby clumps of rabbit brush.

At the end of the corridor is a larger room in which there are several desks and typewriters. In one of the wastebaskets, buried beneath memos and candybar wrappers, she finds a magazine. The title is *Love Confessions* and the cover has a picture of a man and woman kissing. Rachel studies the cover, then takes the magazine, tucking it on the bottom shelf of the cart.

Jake pours himself another cup of whiskey and pushes the cart to another hallway. Jake is working slower now, and as he works he makes humming noises, tuneless sounds that he feels only as pleasant vibrations. The last few blackboards are sloppily done, and Rachel, finished with the wastebaskets, cleans the places that Jake missed.

They eat dinner in the janitor's storeroom, a stuffy windowless room furnished with an ancient grease-stained couch, a battered black-and-white television, and shelves of cleaning supplies. From a shelf, Jake takes the paper bag that holds his lunch: a baloney sandwich, a bag of barbequed potato chips, and a box of vanilla wafers. From behind the gallon jugs of liquid cleanser, he takes a magazine. He lights a cigarette, pours himself another cup of whiskey, and settles down on the couch. After a moment's hesitation, he offers Rachel a drink, pouring a shot of whiskey into a chipped ceramic cup.

Aaron never let Rachel drink whiskey, and she samples it carefully. At first the smell makes her sneeze, but she is fascinated by the way that the drink warms her throat, and she sips some more.

As they drink, Rachel tells Jake about the men who shot her and the woman who pricked her with a needle, and he nods. —The people here are crazy, he signs.

—I know, she says, thinking of the old chimp with the electrode in his head. —You won't tell them I can talk, will you?

Jake nods. —I won't tell them anything.

—They treat me like I'm not real, Rachel signs sadly. Then she hugs her knees, frightened at the thought of being held captive by crazy people. She considers planning her escape: she is out of the cage and she is sure she could outrun Jake. As she wonders about it, she finishes her cup of whiskey. The alcohol takes the edge off her fear. She sits close beside Jake on the couch, and the smell of his cigarette smoke reminds her of Aaron. For the first time since Aaron's death she feels warm and happy.

She shares Jake's cookies and potato chips and looks at the *Love Confessions* magazine that she took from the trash. The first story that she reads is about a woman named Alice. The headline reads: "I became a go-go dancer to pay off my husband's gambling debts, and now he wants me to sell my body."

Rachel sympathizes with Alice's loneliness and suffering. Alice, like Rachel, is alone and misunderstood. As Rachel slowly reads, she sips her second cup of whiskey. The story reminds her of a fairy tale: the nice man who rescues Alice from her terrible husband replaces the handsome prince who rescued the princess. Rachel glances at Jake and wonders if he will rescue her from the wicked people who locked her in the cage.

She has finished the second cup of whiskey and eaten half of Jake's cookies when Jake says that she must go back to her cage. She goes reluctantly, taking the magazine with her. He promises that he will come for her again the next night, and with that she must be content. She puts the magazine in one corner of the cage and curls up to sleep.

She wakes early in the afternoon. A man in a white coat is wheeling a low cart into the lab.

Rachel's head aches with hangover and she feels sick. As she crouches in one corner of her cage, he stops the cart beside her cage and then locks the wheels. "Hold on there," he mutters to her, then slides her cage onto the cart.

The man wheels her through long corridors, where the walls are cement blocks, painted institutional green. Rachel huddles unhappily in the cage, wondering where she is going and whether Jake will ever be able to find her.

At the end of a long corridor, the man opens a thick metal door and a wave of warm air strikes Rachel. It stinks of chimpanzees, excrement, and rotting food. On either side of the corridor are metal bars and wire mesh. Behind the mesh, Rachel can see dark hairy shadows. In one cage, five adolescent chimps swing and play. In another, two females huddle together, grooming each other. The man slows as he passes a cage in which a big male is banging on the wire with his fist, making the mesh rattle and ring.

"Now, Johnson," says the man. "Cool it. Be nice. I'm bringing you a new little girlfriend."

With a series of hooks, the man links Rachel's cage with the cage next to Johnson's and opens the doors. "Go on, girl," he says. "See the nice fruit." In the new cage is a bowl of sliced apples with an attendant swarm of fruit flies.

At first, Rachel will not move into the new cage. She crouches in the cage on the cart, hoping that the man will decide to take her back to the lab. She watches him get a hose and attach it to a water facet. But she does not understand his intention until he turns the stream of water on her. A cold blast strikes her on the back and she howls, fleeing into the new cage to avoid the cold water. Then the man closes the doors, unhooks the cage, and hurries away.

The floor is bare cement. Her cage is at one end of the corridor and two walls are cement block. A door in one of the cement block walls leads to an outside run. The other two walls are wire mesh: one facing the corridor; the other, Johnson's cage.

Johnson, quiet now that the man has left, is sniffing around the door in the wire mesh wall that joins their cages. Rachel watches him anxiously. Her memories of other chimps are distant, softened by time. She remembers her mother; she vaguely remembers playing with other chimps her age. But she does not know how to react to Johnson when he stares at her with great intensity and makes a loud huffing sound. She gestures to him in ASL, but he only stares harder and huffs again. Beyond Johnson, she can see other cages and other chimps, so many that the wire mesh blurs her vision and she cannot see the other end of the corridor.

To escape Johnson's scrutiny, she ducks through the door into the outside run, a wire mesh cage on a white concrete foundation. Outside there is barren ground and rabbit brush. The afternoon sun is hot and all the other runs are deserted until Johnson appears in the run beside hers. His attention disturbs her and she goes back inside.

She retreats to the side of the cage farthest from Johnson. A crudely built wooden platform provides her with a place to sit. Wrapping her arms around her knees, she tries to relax and ignore Johnson. She dozes off for a while, but wakes to a commotion across the corridor.

In the cage across the way is a female chimp in heat. Rachel recognizes the smell from her own times in heat. Two keepers are opening the door that separates the female's cage from the adjoining cage, where a male stands, watching with great interest. Johnson is shaking the wire mesh and howling as he watches.

"Mike here is a virgin, but Susie knows what she's doing," one keeper was saying to the other. "So it should go smoothly. But keep the hose ready."

"Yeah?"

"Sometimes they fight. We only use the hose to break it up if it gets real bad. Generally, they do okay."

Mike stalks into Susie's cage. The keepers lower the cage door, trapping both chimps in the same cage. Susie seems unalarmed. She continues eating a slice of orange while Mike sniffs at her genitals with every indication of great interest. She bends over to let Mike finger her pink bottom, the sign of estrus.

Rachel finds herself standing at the wire mesh, making low moaning noises. She can see Mike's erection, hear his grunting cries. He squats on the floor of Susie's cage, gesturing to the female.

Rachel's feelings are mixed: she is fascinated, fearful, confused. She keeps thinking of the description of sex in the *Love Confessions* story: When Alice feels Danny's lips on hers, she is swept away by the passion of the moment. He takes her in his arms and her skin tingles as if she were consumed by an inner fire.

Susie bends down and Mike penetrates her with a loud grunt, thrusting violently with his hips. Susie cries out shrilly and suddenly leaps up, knocking Mike away. Rachel watches, overcome with fascination. Mike, his penis now limp, follows Susie slowly to the corner of the cage, where he begins grooming her carefully. Rachel finds that the wire mesh has cut her hands where she gripped it too tightly.

It is night, and the door at the end of the corridor creaks open. Rachel is immediately alert, peering through the wire mesh and trying to see down to the end of the corridor. She bangs on the wire mesh. As Jake comes closer, she waves a greeting.

When Jake reaches for the lever that will raise the door to Rachel's cage, Johnson charges toward him, howling and waving his arms above his head. He hammers on the wire mesh with his fists, howling and grimacing at Jake. Rachel ignores Johnson and hurries after Jake.

Again Rachel helps Jake clean. In the laboratory, she greets the old chimp, but the animal is more interested in the banana that Jake has brought than in conversation. The chimp will not reply to her questions, and after several tries, she gives up.

While Jake vacuums the carpeted corridors, Rachel empties the trash, finding a magazine called *Modern Romance* in the same wastebasket that had provided *Love Confessions*.

Later, in the janitor's lounge, Jake smokes a cigarette, sips whiskey, and flips through one of his own magazines. Rachel reads love stories in *Modern Romance*.

Every once in a while, she looks over Jake's shoulder at grainy pictures of naked women with their legs spread wide apart. Jake looks for a long time at a picture of a blonde woman with big breasts, red fingernails, and purple-painted eyelids. The woman lies on her back and smiles as she strokes the pinkness between her legs. The picture on the next page shows her caressing her own breasts, pinching the dark nipples. The final picture shows her looking back over her shoulder. She is in the position that Susie took when she was ready to be mounted.

Rachel looks over Jake's shoulder at the magazine, but she does not ask questions. Jake's smell began to change as soon as he opened the magazine; the scent of nervous sweat mingles with the aromas of tobacco and whiskey. Rachel suspects that questions would not be welcome just now.

At Jake's insistence, she goes back to her cage before dawn.

Over the next week, she listens to the conversations of the men who come and go, bringing food and hosing out the cages. From the men's conversation, she learns that the Primate Research Center is primarily a breeding facility that supplies researchers with domestically bred apes and monkeys of several species. It also maintains its own research staff. In indifferent tones, the men talk of horrible things. The adolescent chimps at the end of the corridor are being fed a diet high in cholesterol to determine cholesterol's effects on the circulatory system. A group of pregnant females are being injected with male hormones to determine how that will affect the female offspring. A group of infants is being fed a low protein diet to determine adverse effects on their brain development.

The men look through her as if she were not real, as if she were a part of the wall, as if she were no one at all. She cannot speak to them; she cannot trust them.

Each night, Jake lets her out of her cage and she helps him clean.

He brings treats: barbequed potato chips, fresh fruit, chocolate bars, and cookies. He treats her fondly, as one would treat a precocious child. And he talks to her.

At night, when she is with Jake, Rachel can almost forget the terror of the cage, the anxiety of watching Johnson pace to and fro, the sense of unreality that accompanies the simplest act. She would be content to stay with Jake forever, eating snack food and reading confessions magazines. He seems to like her company. But each morning, Jake insists that she must go back to the cage and the terror. By the end of the first week, she has begun plotting her escape.

Whenever Jake falls asleep over his whiskey, something that happens three nights out of five, Rachel prowls the center alone, surreptitiously gathering things that she will need to survive in the desert: a plastic jug filled with water, a plastic bag of food pellets, a large beach towel that will serve as a blanket on the cool desert nights, a discarded plastic shopping bag in which she can carry the other things. Her best find is a road map on which the Primate Center is marked in red. She knows the address of Aaron's ranch and finds it on the map. She studies the roads and plots a route home. Cross country, assuming that she does not get lost, she will have to travel about fifty miles to reach the ranch. She hides these things behind one of the shelves in the janitor's storeroom.

Her plans to run away and go home are disrupted by the idea that she is in love with Jake, a notion that comes to her slowly, fed by the stories in the confessions magazines. When Jake absent-mindedly strokes her, she is filled with a strange excitement. She longs for his company and misses him on the weekends when he is away. She is happy only when she is with him, following him through the halls of the center, sniffing the aroma of tobacco and whiskey that is his own perfume. She steals a cigarette from his pack and hides it in her cage, where she can savor the smell of it at her leisure.

She loves him, but she does not know how to make him love her back. Rachel knows little about love: she remembers a high school crush where she mooned after a boy with a locker near hers, but that came to nothing. She reads the confessions magazines and Ann Landers' column in the newspaper that Jake brings with him each night, and from these sources, she learns about romance. One night, after Jake falls asleep, she types a badly punctuated, ungrammatical letter to Ann. In the letter, she explains her situation and asks for advice on how to make Jake love her. She slips the letter into a sack labeled "Outgoing Mail," and for the next week she reads Ann's column with increased interest. But her letter never appears.

Rachel searches for answers in the magazine pictures that seem to fascinate Jake. She studies the naked women, especially the big-breasted woman with the purple smudges around her eyes.

One night, in a secretary's desk, she finds a plastic case of eye shadow. She steals it and takes it back to her cage. The next evening, as soon as the Center is quiet, she upturns her metal food dish and regards her reflection in the shiny bottom. Squatting, she balances the eye shadow case on one knee and examines its contents: a tiny makeup brush and three shades of eye shadow—INDIAN BLUE, FOREST GREEN, and WILDLY VIOLET. Rachel chooses the shade labeled WILDLY VIOLET.

Using one finger to hold her right eye closed, she dabs her eyelid carefully with the makeup brush, leaving a gaudy orchid-colored smudge on her brown skin. She studies the smudge critically, then adds to it, smearing the color beyond the corner of her eyelid until it disappears in her brown fur. The color gives her eye a carnival brightness, a lunatic gaiety. Working with great care, she matches the effect on the other side, then smiles at herself in the glass, blinking coquettishly.

In the other cage, Johnson bares his teeth and shakes the mesh. She ignores him.

When Jake comes to let her out, he frowns at her eyes. —Did you hurt yourself? he asks.

—No, she says. Then, after a pause, —Don't you like it?

Jake squats beside her and stares at her eyes. Rachel puts a hand on his knee and her heart pounds at her own boldness. —You are a very strange monkey, he signs.

Rachel is afraid to move. Her hand on his knee closes into a fist; her face folds in on itself, puckering around the eyes.

Then, straightening up, he signs, —I liked your eyes better before.

He likes her eyes. She nods without taking her eyes from his face. Later, she washes her face in the women's restroom, leaving dark smudges the color of bruises on a series of paper towels.

Rachel is dreaming. She is walking through the Painted Desert with her hairy brown mother, following a red rock canyon that Rachel somehow knows will lead her to the Primate Research Center. Her mother is lagging behind: she does not want to go to the Center; she is afraid. In the shadow of a rock outcropping, Rachel stops to explain to her mother that they must go to the Center because Jake is at the Center.

Rachel's mother does not understand sign language. She watches Rachel with mournful eyes, then scrambles up the canyon wall, leaving Rachel behind. Rachel climbs after her mother, pulling herself over the edge in time to see the other chimp loping away across the wind-blown red cinder-rock and sand.

Rachel bounds after her mother, and as she runs she howls like an abandoned infant chimp, wailing her distress. The figure of her mother wavers in the distance, shimmering in the heat that rises from the sand. The figure changes. Running away across the red sands is a pale blonde woman wearing a purple sweatsuit and jogging shoes, the sweet-smelling mother that Rachel remembers. The woman looks back and smiles at Rachel. "Don't howl like an ape, daughter," she calls. "Say Mama."

Rachel runs silently, dream running that takes her nowhere. The sand burns her feet and the sun beats down on her head. The blonde woman vanishes in the distance, and Rachel is alone. She collapses on the sand, whimpering because she is alone and afraid.

She feels the gentle touch of fingers grooming her fur, and for a moment, still half asleep, she believes that her hairy mother has returned to her. In the dream, she opens her eyes and looks into a pair of dark brown eyes, separated from her by wire mesh. Johnson. He has reached through a gap in the fence to groom her. As he sorts through her fur, he makes soft cooing sounds, gentle comforting noises.

Still half asleep, she gazes at him and wonders why she was so fearful. He does not seem so bad. He grooms her for a time, and then sits nearby, watching her through the mesh. She brings a slice of apple from her dish of food and offers it to him. With her free hand, she makes the sign for apple. When he takes it, she signs again: apple. He is not a particularly quick student, but she has time and many slices of apple.

All Rachel's preparations are done, but she cannot bring herself to leave the Center. Leaving the Center means leaving Jake, leaving potato chips and whiskey, leaving security. To Rachel, the thought of love is always accompanied by the warm taste of whiskey and potato chips.

Some nights, after Jake is asleep, she goes to the big glass doors that lead to the outside. She opens the doors and stands on the steps, looking down into the desert. Sometimes a jackrabbit sits on its haunches in the rectangles of light that shine through the glass doors. Sometimes she sees kangaroo rats, hopping through the moonlight like rubber balls bouncing on hard pavement. Once, a coyote trots by, casting a contemptuous glance in her direction.

The desert is a lonely place. Empty. Cold. She thinks of Jake snoring softly in the janitor's lounge. And always she closes the door and returns to him.

Rachel leads a double life: janitor's assistant by night, prisoner and teacher by day. She spends her afternoons drowsing in the sun and teaching Johnson new signs.

On a warm afternoon, Rachel sits in the outside run, basking in the sunlight. Johnson is inside, and the other chimps are quiet. She can almost imagine she is back at her father's ranch, sitting in her own yard. She naps and dreams of Jake.

She dreams that she is sitting in his lap on the battered old couch. Her hand is on his chest: a smooth pale hand with red-painted fingernails. When she looks at the dark screen of the television set, she can see her reflection. She is a thin teenager with blonde hair and blue eyes. She is naked.

Jake is looking at her and smiling. He runs a hand down her back and she closes her eyes in ecstasy.

But something changes when she closes her eyes. Jake is grooming her as her mother used to groom her, sorting through her hair in search of fleas. She opens her eyes and sees Johnson, his diligent fingers searching through her fur, his intent brown eyes watching her. The reflection on the television screen shows two chimps, tangled in each other's arms.

Rachel wakes to find that she is in heat for the first time since she came to the Center. The skin surrounding her genitals is swollen and pink.

For the rest of the day, she is restless, pacing to and fro in her cage. On his side of the wire mesh wall, Johnson is equally restless, following her when she goes outside, sniffing long and hard at the edge of the barrier that separates him from her.

That night, Rachel goes eagerly to help Jake clean. She follows him closely, never letting him get far from her. When he is sweeping, she trots after him with the dustpan and he almost trips over her twice. She keeps waiting for him to notice her condition, but he seems oblivious.

As she works, she sips from a cup of whiskey. Excited, she drinks more than usual, finishing two full cups. The liquor leaves her a little disoriented, and she sways as she follows Jake to the janitor's lounge. She curls up close beside him on the couch. He relaxes with his arms resting on the back of the couch, his legs stretching out before him. She moves so that she presses against him.

He stretches, yawns, and rubs the back of his neck as if trying to rub away stiffness. Rachel reaches around behind him and begins to gently rub his neck, reveling in the feel of his skin, his hair against the backs of her hands. The thoughts that hop and skip though her mind are confusing. Sometimes it seems that the hair that tickles her hands is Johnson's; sometimes, she knows it is Jake's. And sometimes it doesn't seem to matter. Are they really so different? They are not so different.

She rubs his neck, not knowing what to do next. In the confessions magazines, this is where the man crushes the woman in his arms. Rachel climbs into Jake's lap and hugs him, waiting for him to crush her in his arms. He blinks at her sleepily. Half asleep, he strokes her, and his moving hand brushes near her genitals. She presses herself against him, making a soft sound in her throat. She rubs her hip against his crotch, aware now of a slight change in his smell, in the tempo of his breathing. He blinks at her again, a little more awake now. She bares her teeth in a smile and tilts her head back to lick his neck. She can feel his hands on her shoulders, pushing her away, and she knows what he wants. She slides from his lap and turns, presenting him with her pink genitals, ready to be mounted, ready to have him penetrate her. She moans in anticipation, a low inviting sound.

He does not come to her. She looks over her shoulder and he is still sitting on the couch, watching her through half-closed eyes. He reaches over and picks up a magazine filled with pictures of naked women. His other hand drops to his crotch and he is lost in his own world.

Rachel howls like an infant who has lost its mother, but he does not look up. He is staring at the picture of the blonde woman.

Rachel runs down dark corridors to her cage, the only home she has. When she reaches the corridor, she is breathing hard and making small lonely whimpering noises. In the dimly lit corridor, she hesitates for a moment, staring into Johnson's cage. The male chimp is asleep. She remembers the touch of his hands when he groomed her.

From the corridor, she lifts the gate that leads into Johnson's cage and enters. He wakes at the sound of the door and sniffs the air. When he sees Rachel, he stalks toward her, sniffing eagerly. She lets him finger her genitals, sniff deeply of her scent. His penis is erect and he grunts in excitement. She turns and presents herself to him and he mounts her, thrusting deep inside. As he penetrates, she thinks, for a moment, of Jake and of the thin blonde teenage girl named Rachel, but then the moment passes. Almost against her will she cries out, a shrill exclamation of welcoming and loss.

After he withdraws his penis, Johnson grooms her gently, sniffing her genitals and softly stroking her fur. She is sleepy and content, but she knows that they cannot delay.

Johnson is reluctant to leave his cage, but Rachel takes him by the hand and leads him to the janitor's lounge. His presence gives her courage. She listens at the door and hears Jake's soft breathing. Leaving Johnson in the hall, she slips into the room. Jake is lying on the couch, the magazine draped over his legs. Rachel takes the equipment that she has gathered and stands for a moment, staring at the sleeping man. His baseball cap hangs on the arm of a broken chair, and she takes that to remember him by.

Rachel leads Johnson through the empty halls. A kangaroo rat, collecting seeds in the dried grass near the glass doors, looks up curiously as Rachel leads Johnson down the steps. Rachel carries the plastic shopping bag slung over her shoulder. Somewhere in the distance, a coyote howls, a long yapping wail. His cry is joined by others, a chorus in the moonlight.

Rachel takes Johnson by the hand and leads him into the desert.

A cocktail waitress, driving from her job in Flagstaff to her home in Winslow, sees two apes dart across the road, hurrying away from the bright beams of her headlights. After wrestling with her conscience (she does not want to be accused of drinking on the job), she notifies the county sheriff.

A local newspaper reporter, an eager young man fresh out of journalism school, picks up the story from the police report and interviews the waitress. Flattered by his enthusiasm for her story and delighted to find a receptive ear, she tells him details that she failed to mention to the police: one of the apes was wearing a baseball cap and carrying what looked like a shopping bag.

The reporter writes up a quick humorous story for the morning edition, and begins researching a feature article to be run later in the week. He knows that the newspaper, eager for news in a slow season, will play a human-interest story up big—kind of *Lassie, Come Home* with chimps.

Just before dawn, a light rain begins to fall, the first rain of spring. Rachel searches for shelter and finds a small cave formed by three tumbled boulders. It will keep off the rain and hide them from casual observers. She shares her food and water with Johnson. He has followed her closely all night, seemingly intimidated by the darkness and the howling of distant coyotes. She feels protective toward him. At the same time, having him with her gives her courage. He knows only a few gestures in ASL, but he does not need to speak. His presence is comfort enough.

Johnson curls up in the back of the cave and falls asleep quickly. Rachel sits in the opening and watches dawnlight wash the stars from the sky. The rain rattles against the sand, a comforting sound.

She thinks about Jake. The baseball cap on her head still smells of his cigarettes, but she does not miss him. Not really. She fingers the cap and wonders why she thought she loved Jake.

The rain lets up. The clouds rise like fairy castles in the distance and the rising sun tints them pink and gold and gives them flaming red banners. Rachel remembers when she was younger and Aaron read her the story of Pinocchio, the little puppet who wanted to be a real boy. At the end of his adventures, Pinocchio, who has been brave and kind, gets his wish. He becomes a real boy.

Rachel had cried at the end of the story and when Aaron asked why, she had rubbed her eyes on the backs of her hairy hands. —I want to be a real girl, she signed to him. —A real girl.

"You are a real girl," Aaron had told her, but somehow she had never believed him.

The sun rises higher and illuminates the broken rock turrets of the desert. There is a magic in this barren land of unassuming grandeur. Some cultures send their young people to the desert to seek visions and guidance, searching for true thinking spawned by the openness of the place, the loneliness, the beauty of emptiness.

Rachel drowses in the warm sun and dreams a vision that has the clarity of truth. In the dream, her father comes to her. "Rachel," he says to her, "it doesn't matter what anyone thinks of you. You're my daughter."

—I want to be a real girl, she signs.

"You *are* real," her father says. "And you don't need some two-bit drunken janitor to prove it to you." She knows she is dreaming, but she also knows that her father speaks the truth. She is warm and happy and she doesn't need Jake at all. The sunlight warms her and a lizard watches her from a rock, scurrying for cover when she moves. She picks up a bit of loose rock that lies on the floor of the cave. Idly, she scratches on the dark red sandstone wall of the cave. A lopsided heart shape. Within it, awkwardly printed: Rachel and Johnson. Between them, a plus sign. She goes over the letters again and again, leaving scores of fine lines on the smooth rock surface.

Then, late in the morning, soothed by the warmth of the day, she sleeps.

Shortly after dark, an elderly rancher in a pickup truck spots two apes in a remote corner of his ranch. They run away and lose him in the rocks, but not until he has a good look at them. He calls the police, the newspaper, and the Primate Center.

The reporter arrives first thing the next morning, interviews the rancher, and follows the men from the Primate Research Center as they search for evidence of the chimps. They find monkey shit near the cave, confirming that the runaways were indeed nearby. The news reporter, an eager and curious young man, squirms on his belly into the cave and finds the names scratched on the cave wall. He peers at it. He might have dismissed them as the idle scratchings of kids, except that the names match the names of the missing chimps. "Hey," he called to his photographer, "take a look at this."

The next morning's newspaper displays Rachel's crudely scratched letters. In a brief interview, the rancher mentioned that the chimps were carrying bags. "Looked like supplies," he said. "They looked like they were in for the long haul."

On the third day, Rachel's water runs out. She heads toward a small town, marked on the map. They reach it in the early morning—thirst forces them to travel by day. Beside an isolated ranch house, she finds a faucet. She is filling her bottle when Johnson grunts in alarm.

A dark-haired woman watches from the porch of the house. She does not move toward the apes, and Rachel continues filling the bottle. "It's all right, Rachel," the woman, who has been following the story in the papers, calls out. "Drink all you want."

Startled, but still suspicious, Rachel caps the bottle and, keeping her eyes on the woman, drinks from the faucet. The woman steps back into the house. Rachel motions Johnson to do the same, signaling for him to hurry and drink. She turns off the faucet when he is done.

They are turning to go when the woman emerges from the house carrying a plate of tortillas and a bowl of apples. She sets them on the edge of the porch and says, "These are for you."

The woman watches through the window as Rachel packs the food into her bag. Rachel puts away the last apple and gestures her thanks to the woman. When the woman fails to respond to the sign language, Rachel picks up a stick and writes in the sand of the yard. "THANK YOU," Rachel scratches, then waves good-bye and sets out across the desert. She is puzzled, but happy.

The next morning's newspaper includes an interview with the dark-haired woman. She describes how Rachel turned on the faucet and turned it off when she was through, how the chimp packed the apples neatly in her bag and wrote in the dirt with a stick.

The reporter also interviews the director of the Primate Research Center. "These are animals," the director explains angrily. "But people want to treat them like they're small hairy people." He describes the Center as "primarily a breeding center with some facilities for medical research." The reporter asks some pointed questions about their acquisition of Rachel.

But the biggest story is an investigative piece. The reporter reveals that he has tracked down Aaron Jacobs' lawyer and learned that Jacobs left a will. In this will, he bequeathed all his possessions—including his house and surrounding land—to "Rachel, the chimp I acknowledge as my daughter."

The reporter makes friends with one of the young women in the typing pool at the research center, and she tells him the office scuttlebutt: people suspect that the chimps may have been released by a deaf and drunken janitor, who was subsequently fired for negligence. The reporter, accompanied by a friend who can communicate in sign language, finds Jake in his apartment in downtown Flagstaff.

Jake, who has been drinking steadily since he was fired, feels betrayed by Rachel, by the Primate Center, by the world. He complains at length about Rachel: they had been friends, and then she took his baseball cap and ran away. He just didn't understand why she had run away like that.

"You mean she could talk?" the reporter asks through his interpreter.

—Of course she can talk, Jake signs impatiently. —She is a smart monkey.

The headlines read: "Intelligent chimp inherits fortune!" Of course, Aaron's bequest isn't really a fortune and she isn't just a chimp, but close enough. Animal rights activists rise up in Rachel's defense. The case is discussed on the national news. Ann Landers reports receiving a letter from a chimp named Rachel; she had thought it was a hoax perpetrated by the boys at Yale. The American Civil Liberties Union assigns a lawyer to the case.

By day, Rachel and Johnson sleep in whatever hiding places they can find: a cave; a shelter built for range cattle; the shell of an abandoned car, rusted from long years in a desert gully. Sometimes Rachel dreams of jungle darkness, and the coyotes in the distance become a part of her dreams, their howling becomes the cries of fellow apes.

The desert and the journey have changed her. She is wiser, having passed through the white-hot love of adolescence and emerged on the other side. She dreams, one day, of the ranch house. In the dream, she has long blonde hair and pale white skin. Her eyes are red from crying and she wanders the house restlessly, searching for something that she has lost. When she hears coyotes howling, she looks through a window at the darkness outside. The face that looks in at her has jug-handle ears and shaggy hair. When she sees the face, she cries out in recognition and opens the window to let herself in.

By night, they travel. The rocks and sands are cool beneath Rachel's feet as she walks toward her ranch. On television, scientists and politicians discuss the ramifications of her case, describe the technology uncovered by investigation of Aaron Jacobs' files. Their debates do not affect her steady progress toward her ranch or the stars that sprinkle the sky above her.

It is night when Rachel and Johnson approach the ranch house. Rachel sniffs the wind and smells automobile exhaust and strange humans. From the hills, she can see a small camp beside a white van marked with the name of a local television station. She hesitates, considering returning to the safety of the desert. Then she takes Johnson by the hand and starts down the hill. Rachel is going home.

HER FURRY FACE

Leigh Kennedy

This Nebula-nominated story explores an unusually intense and unnaturally close relationship between the orangutan Annie, who learns sign language and can read, and her trainer Douglas.

Douglas was embarrassed when he saw Annie and Vernon mating.

He'd seen hours of sex between orangutans, but this time was different. He'd never seen *Annie* doing it. He stood in the shade of the pecan tree for a moment, iced tea glasses sweating in his hand, shocked, then he backed around the corner of the brick building. He was confused. The cicadas seemed louder than usual, the sun hotter, and the squeals of pleasure from the apes strange.

He walked back to the front porch and sat down. His mind still saw the two giant mounds of red-orange fur moving together like one being.

When the two orangs came back around, Douglas thought he saw smugness in Vernon's face. Why not, he thought? I guess I would be smug, too.

Annie flopped down on the grassy front yard and crossed one leg over the other, her abdomen bulging high; she gazed upward into the heavy white sky.

Vernon bounded toward Douglas. He was young and red-chocolate-colored. His face was still slim, without the older orangutan jowls yet.

"Be polite," Douglas warned him.

"Drink tea, please?" Vernon signed rapidly, the fringe on his elbows waving. "Dry as bone."

Douglas handed Vernon one of the glasses of tea, though he'd brought it out for Annie. The handsome nine-year-old downed it in a gulp. "Thank you," he signed. He touched the edge of the porch and withdrew his long fingers. "Could fry egg," he signed, and instead of sitting, swung out hand-over-hand on the ropes between the roof of the schoolhouse and the trees. It was a sparse and dry substitute for the orang's native rain forest.

He's too young and crude for Annie, Douglas thought.

"Annie," Douglas called. "Your tea."

Annie rolled onto one side and lay propped on an elbow, staring at him. She was lovely. Fifteen years old, her fur was glossy and coppery, her small yellow eyes in the fleshy face expressive and intelligent. She started to rise up toward him, but turned toward the road.

The mail jeep was coming down the highway.

In a blurred movement, she set off at a four-point gallop down the half-mile drive toward the mailbox. Vernon swung down from his tree and followed, giving a small groan.

Reluctant to go out in the sun, Douglas put down the tea anyway and followed the apes along the drive. By the time he got near them, Annie was sitting with mail sorted between her toes, holding an opened letter in her hands. She looked up with an expression on her face that he'd never seen—it could have been fear, but it wasn't.

She handed the letter to Vernon, who pestered her for it. "Douglas," she signed, "they want to buy my story."

Therese lay in the bathwater, her knees sticking up high, her hair floating beside her face. Douglas sat on the edge of the tub; as he talked to her he was conscious that he spoke a double language—the one with his lips and the other with his hands.

"As soon as I called Ms Young, the magazine editor, and told her who Annie was, she got really excited. She asked me why we hadn't sent a letter explaining it with the story, so I told her that Annie didn't want anyone to know first."

"Did Annie decide that?" Therese sounded skeptical, as she always seemed to when Douglas talked about Annie.

"We talked about it and she wanted it that way." Douglas felt the resistance from Therese. Why she never understood, he didn't know, unless she did it to provoke him. She acted as though she thought an ape was still just an ape, no matter what he or she could do. "Anyway," he said, "she talked about doing a whole publicity thing to the hilt—talk shows, autograph parties. You know. But Dr Morris thinks it would be better to keep things quiet."

"Why?" Therese sat up; her legs went underwater and she soaped her arms.

"Because she'd be too nervous. Annie, I mean. It might disrupt her education to become a celebrity. Too bad. Even Dr Morris knows that it would be great for fund-raising. But I guess we'll let the press in some."

Therese began to shampoo her hair. "I brought home that essay that Sandy wrote yesterday. The one I told you about. Now if she were an orangutan instead of just a deaf kid, she could probably get it published in *Fortune*." Therese smiled.

Douglas stood. He didn't like the way Therese headed for the old argument—no matter what one of Therese's deaf students did, if Annie could do it one one-hundredth as well, it was more spectacular. Douglas knew it was true, but why Therese was so bitter about it, he didn't understand.

"That's great," he said, trying to sound enthusiastic.

"Will you wash my back?" she asked.

He crouched and absent-mindedly washed her. "I'll never forget Annie's face when she read that letter."

"Thank you," Therese said. She rinsed. "Do you have any plans for this evening?"

"I've got work to do," he said, leaving the bathroom. "Would you like me to work in the bedroom so you can watch television?"

After a long pause, she said, "No, I'll read."

He hesitated in the doorway. "Why don't you go to sleep early? You look tired."

She shrugged. "Maybe I am."

In the playroom at the school, Douglas watched Annie closely. It was still morning, though late. In the recliner across the room from him, she seemed a little sleepy. Staring out the window, blinking, she marked her place in Pinkwater's *Fat Men from Space* with a long brown finger.

He had been thinking about Therese, who'd been silent and morose that morning. Annie was never morose, though often quiet. He wondered if Annie was quiet today because she sensed that Douglas was not happy. When he'd come to work, she'd given him an extra hug.

He wondered if Annie could have a crush on him, like many schoolgirls have on their teachers. Remembering her mating with Vernon days before, he idly wandered into a fantasy of touching those petals of her genitals and gently, gently moving inside her.

The physical reaction to his fantasy embarrassed him. *God, what am I thinking?* He shook himself out of the reverie, averting his gaze for a few moments, until he'd gotten control of himself again.

"Douglas," Annie signed. She walked erect, towering, to him and sat down on the floor at his feet. Her flesh folded into her lap like dough.

"What?" he asked, wondering suddenly if orangutans were tele-pathic.

"Why you say my story children's?"

He looked blankly at her.

"Why not send *Harper's?*" she asked, having to spell out the name of the magazine.

He repressed a laugh, knowing it would upset her. "It's...it's the kind of story children would like."

"Why?"

He sighed. "The level of writing is...*young.* Like you, sweetie." He stroked her head, looking into the small, intense eyes. "You'll get more sophisticated as you grow."

"I smart as you," she signed. "You understand me always because I talk smart. You not always talk smart."

Douglas was dumbfounded by her logic.

She tilted her head and waited. When Douglas shrugged, she seemed to assume victory and returned to her recliner.

Dr Morris came in. "Here we go," she said, handing him the paper and leaving again.

Douglas skimmed the page until he came to an article about the "ape author." He scanned it. It contained one of her flashpoints; this and the fact that she was irritable from being in estrus made him consider hiding it. But that wouldn't be right.

"Annie," he said softly.

She looked up.

"There's an article about you."

"Me read," she signed, putting her book on the floor. She came and crawled up on the sofa next to him. He watched her eyes as they jerked across every word. He grew edgy. She read on.

Suddenly she took off as if from a diving board. He ran after her as she bolted out the door. The stuffed dog which had always been a favorite toy was being shredded in those powerful hands even before he knew she had it. Annie screamed as she pulled the toy apart, running into the yard.

Terrified by her own aggression, she ran up the tree with stuffing falling like snow behind her.

Douglas watched as the shade filled with foam rubber and fake fur. The tree branches trembled. After a long while, she stopped pummeling the tree and sat quietly.

She spoke to herself with her long ape hand. "Not animal," she said, "not animal."

Douglas suddenly realized that Therese was afraid of the apes.

She watched warily as the four of them strolled along the edge of the school acreage. Douglas knew that Therese didn't appreciate the grace of Annie's muscular gait as he did; the sign language that passed between them was as similar to the Ameslan that Therese used for her deaf children as British to Jamaican. Therese couldn't appreciate Annie in creative conversation.

It wasn't good to be afraid of the apes, no matter how educated they were.

He had invited her out, hoping it would please her to be included in his world here. She had only visited briefly twice before.

Vernon lagged behind them, snapping pictures now and then with his expensive but hardy camera modified for his hands. Vernon took several pictures of Annie and one of Douglas, but only when Therese had separated from him to peer in between the rushes at the edge of the creek.

"Annie," Douglas called, pointing ahead. "A cardinal. The red bird."

Annie lumbered forward. She glanced back to see where Douglas pointed, then stood still, squatting. Douglas walked beside her and they watched the bird.

It flew.

"Gone," Annie signed.

"Wasn't it pretty, though?" Douglas asked.

They ambled on. Annie stopped often to investigate shiny bits of trash or large bugs. They rarely came this far from the school. Vernon whizzed past them, a dark auburn streak of youthful energy.

Remembering Therese, Douglas turned. She sat on a stump far behind. He was annoyed. He'd told her to wear her jeans and a straw hat because there would be grass burrs and hot sun. But there she sat, bare-headed, wearing shorts, miserably rubbing at her ankles.

He grunted impatiently. Annie looked up at him. "Not you," he said, stroking her fur. She patted his butt.

"Go on," Douglas said, turning his back. When he came to Therese, he said, "What's the problem?"

"No problem." She started forward without looking at him. "I was just resting."

Annie had paused to poke at something on the ground with a stick. Douglas quickened his step. Even though his students were smart, they had orangutan appetites. He always worried that they would eat something that would sicken them. "What is it?" he called.

"Dead cat," Vernon signed back. He took a picture as Annie flipped the carcass with her stick.

Therese hurried forward. "Oh, poor kitty," she said, kneeling.

Annie had seemed too absorbed in poking the cat to notice Therese approach. Only a quick eye could follow her leap. Douglas was stunned.

Both screamed. It was over.

Annie clung to Douglas's legs, whimpering.

"Shit!" Therese said. She lay on the ground, rolling from side to side, holding her left arm. Blood dripped from between her fingers.

Douglas pushed Annie back. "That was bad, *very bad*," he said. "Do you hear me?"

Annie sank down on her rump and covered her head. She hadn't gotten a child-scolding for a long time. Vernon stood beside her, shaking his head, signing, "Not wise, baboon-face."

"Stand up," Douglas said to Therese. "I can't help you right now."

Therese was pale, but dry-eyed. Clumsily, she stood and grew even paler. A hunk of flesh hung loosely from above her elbow, meaty and bleeding. "Look."

"Go on. Walk back to the house. We'll come right behind you." He tried to keep his voice calm, holding a warning hand on Annie's shoulder.

Therese moaned, catching her breath. "It hurts," she said, but stumbled on.

"We're coming," Douglas said sternly. "Just walk and—Annie, don't you dare step out of line."

They walked silently, Therese ahead, leaving drops of blood in the dirt. The drops got larger and closer together. Once, Annie dipped her finger into a bloody spot and sniffed her fingertip.

Why can't things just be easy and peaceful, he wondered? Something always happens. *Always.* He should have known better than to bring Therese around Annie. Apes didn't understand that vulnerable quality that Therese was made of. He himself didn't understand it, though at one time he'd probably been attracted to it. No—maybe he had never really seen it until it was too late. He'd only thought of Therese as "sweet" until their lives were too tangled up to keep clear of it.

Why couldn't she be as tough as Annie? Why did she always take everything so seriously?

They reached the building. Douglas sent Annie and Vernon to their rooms and guided Therese to the infirmary. He watched as Jim, their all-purpose nurse and veterinary assistant, examined her arm. "I think you should probably have stitches."

He left the room to make arrangements.

Therese looked at Douglas, holding the gauze over her still-bleeding arm. "Why did she bite me?" she asked.

Douglas didn't answer. He couldn't think of how to express it.

"Do you have any idea?" she asked.

"You asked for it, all your wimping around."

"I..."

Douglas saw the anger rising in her. He didn't want to argue now. He wished he'd never brought her. He'd done it all for her, and she had ruined it.

"Don't start," he said simply, giving her a warning look.

"But, Douglas, I didn't do anything."

"Don't start," he repeated.

"I see now," she said coldly. "Somehow it's my fault again."

Jim returned with his supplies.

"Do you want me to stay?" Douglas asked. He suddenly felt a pang of guilt, realizing that she was actually hurt enough for all this attention.

"No," she said softly.

And her eyes looked far, far from him as he left her.

On the same day that the largest donation ever came to the school, a television news team came out to tape.

Douglas could tell that everyone was excited. Even the chimps that lived on the north half of the school hung on the fence and watched the TV van being unloaded. The reporter decided upon the playroom as the best location for the taping, though she didn't seem to relish sitting on the floor with the giant apes. People went over scripts, strung cords and microphones, set up hot lights, and discussed angles and sound while pointing at the high ceiling's jungle-gym design. All this to talk to a few people and an orangutan.

They brought Annie's desk into the playroom, contrary to Annie's wishes. Douglas explained that it was temporary, that these people would go away after they talked a little. Douglas and Annie stayed outside as long as possible and played Tarzan around the big tree. He tickled her. She grabbed him as he swung from a limb. "Kagoda?" she signed, squeezing him with one arm.

"Kagoda!" he shouted, laughing.

They relaxed on the grass. Douglas was hot. He felt flushed all over. "Douglas," Annie signed, "they read story?"

"Not yet. It isn't published yet."

"Why talk me?"

"Because you wrote it and sold it and people like to interview famous authors." He groomed her shoulder. "Time to go in," he said, seeing a wave from inside.

Annie picked him up in a big hug and carried him in.

"Here it is!" Douglas called to Therese, and turned on the video-recorder.

First, a long shot of the school from the dusty drive, looking only functional and square, without personality. The reporter's voice said, "Here, just southeast of town, is a special school with unusual young students. The students here have little prospect for employment when they graduate, but millions of dollars each year fund this institution."

A shot of Annie at her typewriter, picking at the keyboard with her long fingers; a sheet of paper is slowly covered with large block letters.

"This is Annie, a fifteen-year-old orangutan, who has been a student with the school for five years. She graduated with honors from another 'ape school' in Georgia before coming here. And now Annie has become a writer. Recently, she sold a story to a children's magazine. The editor who bought the story didn't know that Annie was an orangutan until after she had selected the story for publication."

Annie looked at the camera uncertainly.

"Annie can read and write and understand spoken English, but she cannot speak. She uses a sign language similar to the one hearing-impaired use." Change in tone from narrative to interrogative. "Annie, how did you start writing?"

Douglas watched himself on the small screen watching Annie sign, "Teacher told me write." He saw himself grin, eyes shift slightly toward the camera, but generally watching Annie. His name and "Orangutan Teacher" appeared on the screen. The scene made him uneasy.

"What made you send in Annie's story for publication?" the reporter asked.

Douglas signed to Annie, she came to him for a hug, and turned a winsome face to the camera. "Our administrator, Dr Morris, and I both thought it was as good as any kids' story, so Dr Morris said, 'Send it in.' The editor liked it." Annie nervously made "pee" sign to Douglas.

Then, a shot of Dr Morris in her office, a chimp on her lap, clapping her brown hands.

"Dr Morris, your school was established five years ago by grants and government funding. What is your purpose here?"

"Well, in the last few decades, apes—mostly chimpanzees like Rose here—have been taught sign language experimentally. Mainly to prove that apes could indeed use language." Rosie put the tip of her finger through the gold hoop in Dr Morris's ear. Dr Morris took her hand away gently. "We were established with the idea of *educating* apes, a comparable education to the primary grades." She looked at the chimp. "Or however far they will advance."

"Your school has two orangutans and six chimpanzees. Are there differences in their learning?" the reporter asked.

Dr Morris nodded emphatically. "Chimpanzees are very clever, but the orang has a different brain structure which allows for more abstract reasoning. Chimps learn many things quickly, orangs are slower. But the orangutan has the ability to learn in greater depth."

Shot of Vernon swinging on the ropes in front of the school.

Assuming that Vernon is Annie, the reporter said, "Her teacher felt from the start that Annie was an especially promising student. The basic sentences that she types out on her typewriter are simple but original entertainment."

Another shot of Annie at the typewriter.

"If you think this is just monkey business, you'd better think again. Tolstoy, watch out!"

Depressed by the lightness, brevity, and the stupid "monkey business" remark, Douglas turned off the television.

He sat for a long time. Whenever Therese had gone to bed, she had left him silently. After half an hour of staring at the blank screen, he rewound his video-recorder and ran it soundlessly until Annie's face appeared.

And then froze it. He could almost feel again the softness of her halo of red hair against his chin.

He couldn't sleep.

Therese had rumpled her way out of the sheet and lay on her side, her back to him. He looked at the shape of her shoulder and back, downward to the dip of the waist, up the curve of her hip. Her buttocks were round ovals, one atop the other. Her skin was sleek and shiny in the filtered street light coming through the window. She smelled slightly of shampoo and even more slightly of female.

What he felt for her, when he thought of her generally, anyone could call love. And yet, he found himself helplessly angry with her most of the time. When he thought he could amuse her, it would end with her feelings being hurt for some obscure reason. He heard cruel words come barging out of an otherwise gentle mouth. She took everything seriously; mishaps and misunderstandings occurred beyond his control, beyond his repair.

Under this satiny skin, she was troubled and tense. A lot of sensitivity and fear. He had stopped trying to gain access to what had been the happier parts of her person, not understanding where they had gone. He had stopped wanting to love her, but he didn't *not* want to love her, either. It just did not seem to matter.

Sometimes, he thought, it would be easier to have someone like Annie for a wife.

Annie.

He loved her furry face. He loved the unconditional joy in her face when she saw him. She was bright and warm and unafraid. She didn't read things into what he said, but listened and talked with him. They were so natural together. Annie was so filled with vitality.

Douglas withdrew his hand from Therese, whose skin seemed a bare blister of dissatisfaction.

He lay on the floor of the apes' playroom with the fan blowing across his chest. He held Annie's report on Lawrence's *Sons and Lovers* by diagonal corners to keep it from flapping.

Annie lazily swung from bars crisscrossing the ceiling.

"Paul wasn't happy at work because the boss looked over his shoulder at his handwriting," she had written. "But he was happy again later. His brother died and his mother was sad. Paul got sick. He was better and visited his friends again. His mother died and his friends didn't tickle him any more."

Douglas looked over the top of the paper at Annie. True, it was the first time she'd read an "adult" novel, but he had expected something better than this. He considered asking her if Vernon had written the report for her, but thought better of it.

"Annie," he said, sitting up. "What do you think this book is really about?"

She swung down and landed on the sofa. "About man," she said.

Douglas waited. There was no more. "But what about it? Why this man instead of another? What was special about him?"

Annie rubbed her hands together, answerless.

"What about his mother?"

"She help him," Annie answered in a flurry of dark fingers. "Especially when he paint."

Douglas frowned. He looked at the page again, disappointed.

"What I do?" Annie asked, worried.

He tried to brighten up. "You did just fine. It was a hard book."

"Annie smart," the orang signed. "Annie smart."

Douglas nodded. "I know."

Annie rose, then stood on her legs, looking like a two-story fuzzy building, teetering from side to side. "Annie smart. Writer. Smart," she signed. "Write book. Bestseller."

Douglas made a mistake. He laughed. Not as simple as a human laughing at another, this was an act of aggression. His bared teeth and uncontrolled guff-guff struck out at Annie. He tried to stop.

She made a gulping sound and galloped out of the room.

"Wait, Annie!" He chased after her.

By the time he got outside she was far ahead. He stopped running when his chest hurt and trotted slowly through the weeds toward her. She sat forlornly far away and watched him come.

When he was near, she signed "hug" three times.

Douglas collapsed, panting, his throat raw. "Annie, I'm sorry," he said. "I didn't mean it." He put his arms around her.

She held onto him.

"I love you, Annie. I love you so much I don't want ever to hurt you. Ever, ever, ever. I want to be with you all the time. Yes, you're smart and talented and good." He kissed her tough face.

Whether forgotten or forgiven, the hurt of his laughter was gone from her eyes. She held him tighter, making a soft sound in her throat, a sound for him.

They lay together in the crackling yellow weeds, clinging. Douglas felt his love physically growing for her. More passionately than ever before in his life, he wanted to make love to her. He touched her. He felt that she understood what he wanted, that her breath on his neck was anticipation. A consummation as he'd never imagined, the joining of their species in language and body. Not dumb animal-banging but mutual love... He climbed over her and hugged her back.

Annie went rigid when he entered her.

Slowly, she rolled away from him, but he held onto her. "No." A horrible grimace came across her face that raised the hairs on the back of Douglas's neck. "Not you," she said.

She's going to kill me, he thought.

His passion declined; Annie disentangled herself and walked away.

He sat for a moment, stunned at what he'd done, at what had happened, wondering what he would do for the rest of his life with the memory of it. Then he zipped up his pants.

Staring at his dinner plate, he thought, it's just the same as if I had been rejected by a woman.

His hands could still remember the matted feel of her fur; tucked in his groin was the memory of being in an alien place. It had made him throw up out in the field that afternoon, and afterwards he'd come straight home. He hadn't even said good night to the orangs.

"What's the matter?" Therese asked.

He shrugged.

She half-rose out of her chair to kiss him on the temple. "You don't have a fever, do you?"

"No."

"Can I do something to make you feel better?" Her hand slid along his thigh.

He stood up. "Stop it."

She sat still. "Are you in love with another woman?"

Why can't she just leave me alone. "No. I have a lot on my mind."

"It never was like this, even when you were working on your thesis."

"Therese," he said, with what he felt was undeserved patience, "just leave me alone. It doesn't help with you at me all the time."

"But I'm scared. I don't know what to do. You act like you don't want me around."

"All you do is criticize me." He stood and took his dishes to the sink.

Slowly, she trailed after him, carrying her plate. "I'm just trying to understand. It's my life, too."

He said nothing and she walked away as if someone had told her not to leave footsteps.

In the bathroom, he stripped and stood under the shower for a long time. He imagined that Annie's smell clung to him. He felt that Therese could smell it on him.

What have I done, what have I done...?

And when he came out of the shower, Therese was gone.

He had considered calling in sick, but he knew that it would be just as miserable to stay around the house and think about Annie, think about Therese, and worse, to think about himself.

He dressed for work, but couldn't eat breakfast. Realizing that his pain showed, he straightened his shoulders, but found them drooping again as he got out of the car at work.

With some fear, he came through the office. The secretary greeted him with rolling eyes. "Someone's given out our number again," she said as the phone buzzed. Another line was on hold. "This morning there was a man standing at the window watching me until Gramps kicked him off the property."

Douglas shook his head in sympathy with her and approached the orang's door. He felt nauseated again.

Vernon sat at his typewriter, composing captions for his photo album. He didn't get up to greet Douglas, but gave him an evaluative stare.

Douglas patted his shoulder. "Working?" he asked.

"Like dog," Vernon said and returned to typing.

Annie sat outside on the back porch. Douglas opened the door and stood beside her. She looked up at him, but—like Vernon—made no move toward the customary hug. The morning was still cool, the shadow of the building still long in front of them. Douglas sat down.

"Annie," he said softly. "I'm sorry. I'll never do it again. You see, I felt..." He stopped. It wasn't any easier than it had been to talk to Oona, or Wendy, or Shelley, or Therese... He realized then that he didn't understand her any more than he'd understood them. Why had she rejected him? What was she thinking? What would happen from now on? Would they be friends again?

"Oh, hell," he said. He stood. "It won't happen again."

Annie gazed away into the trees.

He felt strained all over, especially in his throat. He stood by her a long time.

"I don't want write stories," she signed.

Douglas stared at her. "Why?"

"Don't want." She seemed to shrug.

Douglas wondered what had happened to the confident ape who'd planned to write a bestseller the day before. "Is that because of me?"

She didn't answer.

"I don't understand," he said. "Do you want to write it down for me? Could you explain it that way?"

"No," she signed, "can't explain. Don't want."

He continued. "What *do* you want?"

"Sit tree. Eat bananas, chocolate. Drink brandy." She looked at him seriously. "Sit tree. Day, day, day, week, month, year."

Christ almighty, he thought, she's having a goddamned existential crisis. All the years of education. All the accomplishments. The hopes of an entire field of primatology. All shot to hell because of a moody ape. It can't just be me. This would have happened sooner or later, maybe... He thought of all the effort he would have to make to repair their relationship. It made him tired.

"Annie, why don't we just ease up a little on your work. You can rest today. You can go sit in the trees all of today and I'll bring you a glass of wine."

She shrugged again.

Oh, I've botched it, he thought. What an idiot. He felt a pain coming back, a pain like poison, with a focal point but shooting through his heart and hands, making him dizzy and short of breath.

At least she doesn't hate me, he thought, squatting to touch her hand.

She bared her teeth.

Douglas froze. She slid away from him and headed for the trees.

He sat alone at home and watched the newscast. In a small Midwestern town they burned the issues of the magazine with Annie's story in it.

A heavy woman in a windbreaker was interviewed with the bonfire in the background. "I don't want my children reading things that weren't even written by humans. I have human children and this godless ape is not going to tell its stories to them."

A quick interview with Dr Morris, who looked even more tired and introverted than usual. "The story is a very innocent tale, told by an innocent personality. I really don't think she has any ability or intention to corrupt..."

He turned the television off. He picked up the phone and dialed one of Therese's friends. "Jan, have you heard from Therese yet?"

"No, sure haven't."

"Well, let me know, okay?"

"Sure."

He thought vaguely about trying to catch her at work, but he left earlier in the morning and came home later in the evening than she did.

Looking at her pictures on the wall, he thought of when they had first met, first lived together. There had been a time when he had loved her so much, he'd been bursting with it. Now he felt empty. He didn't want her to hate him, but he still didn't know if he could talk to her about what had happened. The idea that she would sit and listen to him didn't seem realistic.

Even Annie wouldn't listen to him any more.

He was alone. He'd done a big, dumb, terrible thing. It would have been different if Annie had reciprocated, if somehow they could have become lovers. Then it would have been them against the world, a new kind of relationship.

But Annie didn't seem any different than Therese when it really came down to it. She didn't have any more interest in him than Dr Morris would have in Vernon. He'd imagined it.

He was alone. And without Annie's consent, he was just a jerk who'd fucked an ape.

"I made a mistake," he said aloud to Therese's picture. "So let's forget it."

But he couldn't forget.

"Dr Morris wants to see you," the secretary said as he came in.

"Okay." He changed course for the administrative office. He whistled. In the past few days, Annie had been cool, but he felt that everything would settle down eventually. He felt better. Wondering what horrors or marvels Dr Morris had to share with him, he knocked at her door and peered through the glass window. Probably another magazine burning, he thought.

She signaled him to come in. "Hello, Douglas."

Annie, he thought, *something's happened.*

He stood until she motioned him to sit down. She looked at his face for several seconds. "This is difficult for me," she said.

She's found out, he thought. But he put that aside, figuring it was paranoia that made him worry. There's no way. No way. I have to calm down or I'll show it.

She held up a photograph.

There it was—a dispassionate and cold document of that one

moment in his life. She held it up to him like an accusation. It shocked him as if it hadn't been himself.

Defiance forced him to stare at the picture instead of looking for compassion in Dr Morris's eyes. He knew exactly where the picture had come from.

Vernon and his new telephoto lens.

He visualized the image of his act rising up in a tray of chemicals. Slowly, he looked away from it. Dr Morris could not know how he had changed since that moment. He could make no protest or denial.

"I have no choice," Dr Morris said flatly. "I'd always thought that even if you weren't good with people, at least you worked well with the apes. Thank God Henry, who does Vernon's darkroom work, has promised not to say anything."

Douglas was rising from his chair. He wanted to tear the picture out of her hands. He didn't want her to see it. He wanted her to ask him if he had changed, let him reassure her that it would never happen again, that he understood he'd been wrong.

But her eyes were flat and shuttered against him. "We'll send your things," she said.

He paused at his car and saw two big red shapes—one coppery orange, one chocolate-red—sitting in the trees. Vernon bellowed out a groan that ended with an alien burbling. It was a wild sound full of the jungle and steaming rain.

Douglas watched Annie scratch herself and look toward some chimps walking the land beyond their boundary fence. As she started to turn her gaze in his direction, he ducked into his car.

I guess an ape wouldn't understand me any more than a human, he thought, angrily trying to drive his shame away.

THE FOUR-COLOR APE

Scott A. Cupp

It was not a remarkable beginning. A simple cover on an inauspicious science fiction comic title with the name *Strange Adventures* in issue number 8 from 1951. The cover features a gorilla holding up a blackboard with the message: "Ruth...Please believe me! I am the victim of a terrible scientific experiment! Ralph." A woman, obviously Ruth, seems taken aback by the message. The cover additionally proclaims: "Featuring 'Evolution Plus!' The incredible story of an ape with a human mind!"

The story was one of several in the issue which featured stories with a trick ending, standard on the anthology comics of the period. It is nothing remarkable. What was remarkable was the result of the issue on the sales stand. The issue sold much better than any previous issue. This did not go unnoticed. The next issue featured the origin of Captain Comet, a midlevel science fiction superhero, that did not sell particularly well. Later, another comic had an ape on the cover and sales took another spike upward.

The editors at DC Comics, which had published the *Strange Adventures* comic, began to take notice. Suddenly covers featuring apes in a variety of situations began to appear. Those individual issues began to sell as much as 20 percent more than a regular issue. The rush was on. Apes appeared on no less than sixteen issues of *Strange Adventures* during its run (though several were for reprint stories late in the series). The ape phenomenon got so out of hand at DC Comics that, according to the editor of DC's science fiction titles, Julius Schwartz, in his autobiography *Man of Two Worlds*, "Irwin Donenfeld (Editorial Director at DC Comics) called me in and said we should try it again. Finally all the editors wanted to use gorilla covers, and he said no more than one a month."

But what brought this about? Comics had featured apes prior to this time without the noted increases. As early as 1908 with the illustrated book *The Mischievous Monks of Crocodile Island* and later with *Action Comics* #6 (1938) with a beautiful cover by Leo O'Mealia, gorillas and other apes were the frequent menace of the heroes. And the superheroes of the day (including Superman) did not have their powers clearly defined and had some trouble battling a full grown gorilla. Not so the Superman of later years.

Before the discovery of the lowland gorilla in 1847, there were rumors of the wild creatures. With their discovery and subsequent exhibition, man began to recognize a distant cousin. Charles Darwin made his evolutionary researches known and suddenly apes of various sizes and skills began to appear everywhere.

Apes represented Man in his baser instincts. With the same basic DNA, opposable thumbs, and Darwin all right there it was easy to substitute an ape for a man to make a basic moral point.

Throughout the Golden Age (generally defined as the period from the beginning of the superhero age with *Action Comics* #1 in 1938 until the reintroduction of The Flash in *Showcase Comics* #4 in 1956), apes in various forms appeared to no great acclaim. Mostly they were sidekicks as in the various jungle-related comics such as *Jumbo, Jungle, Sheena, Nyoka The Jungle Girl*, and more.

Chief among the jungle-related comics would have to be *Tarzan*. Created in 1912 by Edgar Rice Burroughs, Tarzan first appeared in the Sunday comics as *Tarzan of the Apes* in 1929 with art from

Harold (Hal) Foster, whose gloriously detailed pen work would later grace *Prince Valiant*. Foster started the strip in 1928, left it to Rex Maxon, and then took it back from 1931 through 1937. Other artists who drew the Sunday strip included Burne Hogarth, Ruben Moreira, Russ Manning, and Mike Grell.

In the Tarzan strip, Tarzan had a unique relationship with the apes, having been raised by a great she-ape and thinking of himself as a pale-skinned member of the tribe. He could talk their talk and walk their walk and he considered them family and equals.

Over the years Tarzan appeared in numerous comic incarnations, starting with newspaper reprints in such titles as *Sparkler*, *Tip Top Comics*, and *Single Series*. Later Western Publishing started printing original stories in their Dell *Four Color* series followed by the *Tarzan* series. In 1962 the title switched to Gold Key publishing (still a part of Western) and continued until 1972. The *Tarzan* series ran for 206 issues under Dell and Gold Key before being picked up by DC comics in 1972. Dell and Gold Key artists included such greats as Jesse Marsh, Russ Manning, and Doug Wildey, and included adaptations of most of the Burroughs' Tarzan novels.

It should also be noted that Burroughs created the giant white apes that terrorize Martians in his Mars novels, many of which were adapted to comics by DC Comics writers and artists in the *Weird Worlds* comics of the 1970s.

Between 1972 and 1977 DC Comics took over the *Tarzan* comic book and continued the numbering, publishing issues 207 through 258. In 1977 Marvel Comics took it over but started a new numbering sequence, running 29 issues and three annuals before ceasing in 1979. Later other comics houses including Dark Horse and Charlton published *Tarzan* comics. At the Grand Comics Database there are more than 180 entries for comics with Tarzan in the title from at least fifteen different countries and totaling over 6,600 individual issues!

So, what made the *Strange Adventures* title with its ape cover take off? It appears to have been a matter of timing: 1951 was when the first of the postwar baby boomers began to go to school. As they learned to read, they sought something other than *Fun with Dick and Jane*. Comics were available and they were cheap. Television was still in its infancy and it had not encroached on most of their lives. The superheroes of The Golden Age were gone for the most part. Sure, *Superman*, *Batman*, *Wonder Woman*, and *Blackhawk* continued but their stories were frequently bland. There was no continuity from one story to the next. Superman found himself facing Titano, the Super-Ape with kryptonite vision. While Titano maintained his beastly personality, he brought Superman to his knees in their few encounters.

Horror, western, science fiction, and crime comics were on the rise and fearsome apes filled in where previously Nazis and Japanese criminals flooded the market. The simians could be seen as a substitute for all of Man's evil practices. And, since they were not human, there could be some respite from the evils of the war years. There were ape witches, ape policemen, apes copying superheroes. Jimmy Olsen even married an ape in one issue.

Among the more interesting titles during this period was *Congo Bill*. Previously Congo Bill was a hunter working in Africa, much like Clyde Beatty or Jungle Jim. The stories were, again, nothing special. But in 1952 Bill found a magic ring which allowed him to exchange bodies with a wild golden ape. Bill's mind inhabited the ape's body while the ape's mind went into Bill's body. The Congorilla stories were an occasional feature of *Action Comics* beginning with issue #248 (1959) but they never really caught on. Congorilla/Congo Bill appeared sporadically throughout the years, with a disappointing miniseries in 1999 and a teamup with Starman in 2011, even eventually joining the Justice League in 2009.

In 1952, the comic *Rex the Wonder Dog* introduced Detective Chimp, which had thirteen appearances in the title. The character was later revived for the DC *Infinite Crisis* series and was a member of *Shadowpact* (created by *Fables* scribe Bill Willingham).

Inquiring minds may have enjoyed the proliferation of apes in the various anthology titles of the period, but it was not until the superhero reinvention of the mid to late 1950s, when the Flash was reintroduced in *Showcase #4* in 1956, that readers got to see a new type of ape. In issue 106 of *The Flash* readers were introduced to Gorilla Grodd. Oddly enough, this issue of *The Flash* did NOT feature an ape on the cover, preferring to show the Pied Piper in his first appearance. Grodd did not appear on the cover of *The Flash* until issue 127.

Grodd was an outcast from Gorilla City located in central Africa. He was strong, superintelligent, possessed of remarkable psychic power, and purely evil. It took all that the Flash had to stop him in the initial encounter and, in subsequent encounters; it sometimes took all of the Justice League to stop him.

The dam began to break. Gorillas as something other than beasts became the new norm. *Konga* (Charlton Comics, 1960) was based on the Hammer film of the same year and featured art by Steve Ditko. The success of the movie tie-in led to a regular series featuring the giant ape which ran more than twenty issues. *The Brave and the Bold #49* (1963) featured "Strange Sports Stories" and had a winning team with gorillas and baseball in "Gorilla Wonders of the Diamond!"

Other super villains of a simian nature were soon on the market. There were ape villains menacing most of the DC universe at this time. Among the notables here was *The Doom Patrol #86* with the first appearance of The Brain and Monsieur Mallah. That first cover with Mallah is classic. The Doom Patrol, one of the many superteams of the period, was facing a giant television screen. On the screen a disembodied brain in a vat of chemicals was giving instructions to Mallah, standing beside the equipment with his Thompson submachine gun at the ready, and a bandolier of ammunition crossing his chest. As the Brain gives him his instructions, the gorilla speaks. The combination of gorilla and disembodied brain took a very strange twist when in *The Doom Patrol #34* (1990) Mallah and the Brain declare their undying love for each other. The two are destroyed in that issue when Robotman's body with the Brain inside explodes as Mallah and the Brain kiss. But, as comic characters do, reappeared later, and in the *Salvation Run* series (2007–2008) are both killed by Grodd.

And the ape phenomenon was not confined to the DC universe. Gorilla-Man first appeared in *Men's Adventures* #26 (1954). In this story hunter Kenneth Hale is seeking to live forever, which can be done by killing the Gorilla-Man. He does this and finds that his immortality comes at the price of becoming the new Gorilla-Man. Gorilla-Man later worked with the X-Men, S.H.I.E.L.D., and the Agents of Atlas. During the fifties, Marvel tried two other incarnations of a Gorilla-Man in *Mystery Tales* #21 (1954) and *Tales to Astonish* #28 but neither of these incarnations led to other stories.

In *Fantastic Four* #13 (1963) creators Stan Lee (writer), Jack Kirby (penciler), and Steve Ditko (inker) featured a villain, Ivan Kragoff, known as the Red Ghost, who takes three apes with him into space to duplicate the cosmic ray bombardment that gave the Fantastic Four their powers. And it works, as Mikhlo, a lowland gorilla, acquires super strength, Peotor the orangutan acquires magnetic powers, and Igor, a baboon, becomes a shapeshifter. Kragoff acquires the ability to become intangible. They fight the Fantastic Four on the moon in a fun battle. Marvel was never much into the ape culture so this marked a significant issue in their continuity. Spider-Man fought a few monkeys when he faced the Circus of Crime, but, for the most part, apes did not fall into the Marvel milieu for a while. They appeared as beasts again in the sword and sorcery titles such as *Conan*, *Solomon Kane*, and *Savage Sword of Conan*, as well as the jungle strips *Ka-zar* and *Shanna the She-Devil*.

So with gorilla supervillains, there must be gorilla superheroes somewhere on the horizon. There were several notable near heroes, including *Angel and the Ape*. Created by writer E. Nelson Bridwell and artist Bob Oksner (often with inks by Wally Wood!), the titular ape is one Sam Simeon, a comic book artist who also partners with Angel O'Day at the O'Day and Simeon Detective Agency. The stories here are humorous rather than a normal superhero title. The pair was featured in *Showcase #77* and then had their own title for seven issues. They have been revived for a couple of miniseries, including one by *Girl Genius* mastermind Phil Foglio in 1991.

Taking the *Angel and the Ape* model a different direction, Arthur Adams' *Monkeyman and O'Brien* (1993) featured huge ten-foot-tall superintelligent gorilla Axewell Tiberius (Monkeyman) from another dimension who teamed up with a beautiful seven-foot-tall superstrong Amazonian woman, Ann O'Brien. The pair had interesting adventures against the Froglodytes and the Shrewmanoid without lapsing into slapstick.

King Kong may be greatest fantastic gorilla of them all. According to Wikipedia, he was also the subject of a Mexican comic book that ran 185 issues. It was later followed by another title *King Kong in the Microcosmos*, which ran thirty-five issues. In 1991 Monster Comics produced a six-issue adaptation of *King Kong* written and illustrated by Don Simpson with covers from Dave Stevens, Mark Schultz, Al Williamson, William Stout, Tom Luth, and Ken Steacy. The adaptation was based on the film novelization by Delos Lovelace rather than the filmed screenplay. The novelization differs significantly from the film as it was produced from an earlier version of the script in order to be published in advance of the film for promotional purposes. Consequently it features the famous spider sequence, a fight with three Triceratops, and a fight with a Styracosaurus which do not appear in the film.

In 1999 DC comics used the Justice League of Apes (JLApe) across their various titles' annuals as a connecting theme. In this series, the Justice League is turned into simian form by a Gorillabomb initiated by the Simian Scarlet, a gorilla terrorist group led by Grodd who have already assassinated the Gorilla City leader Solovar. Later Marvel would produce an entire ape version of their superhero pantheon in Karl Kesel and Ramon Bach's *Marvel Apes* (2008). The Gibbon, an apelike mutant named Martin Blank, finds himself transported to another universe where ape characters, the Ape-vengers led by a gorilla Captain America, take on Doctor Ooktavius. There are many simian versions of Marvel heroes including Spider-Monkey, Ms. Marvape, Gro-Rilla, Invisible Simian, Simian Torch, Marvel Chimp, and the Silver Simian.

But the 800-pound gorilla hanging around in the room has to be the *Planet of the Apes* series. The story has been handled through a variety of companies and titles, beginning with a single-issue adaptation of the second film, *Beneath the Planet of the Apes*, in 1970 by Gold Key comics. The Grand Comics Database lists twenty-eight combinations of titles and publishers totaling 246 individual issues including ten combinations for the title *Planet of the Apes* (200 individual issues including one annual). The biggest run is for the Marvel UK *Planet of the Apes* which ran 123 issues. This included reprints of Marvel's twenty-nine-issue magazine-size *Planet of the Apes* title (with breathtaking art from Mike Ploog and Tom Sutton), which had done adaptations of the five films and, according to one source, reprints of the Killraven series retitled as "Apeslayer" with alien apes as the enemy. Marvel also had an eleven-issue run of *Adventures on the Planet of the Apes* beginning in 1975, which did color versions of the adaptations of the first two feature films.

There followed some foreign comic adaptations featuring TV or film characters. In 1990 Adventure Comics did twenty-four original issues as well as five miniseries—*Urchak's Folly*, *Forbidden Zone*, *Ape City*, *Blood of the Apes*, and *Ape Nation* (a crossover with *Alien Nation*). Beginning in spring 2011 BOOM! Studios began a new *Planet of the Apes* comic written by Daryl Gregory and illustrated by Carlos Magno. This comic covers a timeline similar to that of the first two movies. Also *Betrayal of the Planet of the Apes* from BOOM! began in late 2011 following a totally different storyline set prior to the first film.

BOOM! Studios introduced a ten-page prequel to the *Rise of the Planet of the Apes* movie, on the web, with a script from writer Daryl Gregory and art from Damian Couceiro and Tony Parker, which ran prior to the film's opening and finished two days before the premiere.

Other non Marvel or DC comics include such titles as *The Adventures of Barry Ween, Boy Genius: Monkey Tales* (2001–2002) written and illustrated by Judd Winick. In this six-issue story arc, the ten-year-old foul-mouthed genius befriends bigfoot and sends his girlfriend Sara back to prehistoric age. *Sky Ape,* by writers Phil Amara, Mike Russo, Tim McCarney, and artist Richard Jenkins, features Kirk Madge as Sky Ape (an ape with a jet pack), who fights crime in a style similar to how the Monty Python guys might have done it, with non sequiturs and insanity.

Image Comics has Cy-Gor, a half-gorilla, half-man, cyborg, created by Todd McFarlane (writer) and Tony Daniel (artist), who first appeared in *Spawn # 38* and later had his own mini-series and maybe an incarnation of Kali, the goddess of death.

Grease Monkey, created in 1996 by Tim Eldred, features an Earth where 60 percent of the population has been destroyed by alien invasion. Good aliens come in and offer to enhance the intelligence of dolphins (who refuse) and gorillas (who accept) to help turn around the recovery process. Mac is an accelerated gorilla who serves as chief mechanic to the Barbarian Squadron of female fighter pilots aboard the battlecruiser *Fist of Earth.*

Banana Sunday by Paul Tobin, under the name Root Nibot (writer), and Colleen Coover (illustrator), saw its four-issue mini-series appear from Oni Press in 2005. The comic deals with high school student Kirby Steinberg, who has three intelligent apes who go to school with her. The three are an orangutan (Chuck), a chimp (Knobby), and a gorilla (Go-Go). Tobin and Coover are husband and wife. The comic explores themes of alienation and friendship.

The internet and the introduction of webcomics allowed the passion for apes to appear unhindered by the commercial restrictions that face print media. Apes proliferated around the web with such titles as *Joe and Monkey*; *Ape, Not Monkey* (which has some discussions of science and religion), and *The Thinking Ape Blues*. While not always successful, they were frequently entertaining. A fairly recent entry is *Apes 'n' Capes*, a webcomic begun in 2011. It has not progressed far enough yet to establish a firm feel, but it looks promising.

Many great artists have tackled the apes over the years. In 1966 Frank Frazetta did the amazing cover to *Creepy* #11 (not illustrating anything in particular) as well as (and this is small stretch) the 1955 Flash Gordon versus the caveman cover for *Weird Science Fantasy* #29, considered by many to be the greatest comic cover of all time. The cavemen appear more simian than human. Frazetta had also done some Tarzan paperback book covers as well as other Burroughs characters. Hal Foster and Burne Hogarth did wonderful apes for their *Tarzan* Sunday pages, as did Alex Raymond for his *Jungle Jim* Sunday pages. Joe Kubert's apes in the DC *Tarzan* series were also superbly drawn. Noted science fiction artist Richard Powers even produced a King Kong coloring book.

Over the last twenty years, though, one artist has to be singled out for his ape work: Frank Cho frequently included apes in his *Liberty Meadows* newspaper Sunday pages. He frequently depicted himself as a Monkeyboy when speaking to his readership. He still does this on his apesandbabes.com website. While no apes were regular characters, Cho liked to draw them and, with little provocation, they would show up in movie advertisements that the characters watched, as daydreams, or, just because Cho had new pens and wanted to try them out. And, since he also like dinosaurs, there were many wondrous and epic battles portrayed.

For the last 100 years apes have been a part of the illustrated entertainment for adults and children everywhere. While never wildly successful, they have endured bringing visions of heroes and derring-do to their readers. Whether hero or villain, pawn or instigator, they remain fascinating now and will continue on through this century.

Suggested Additional Reading

Joy, Bob. *DC Goes Ape!*
DC Comics, 2008.

Eury, Michael. *Comics Gone Ape!*
TwoMorrows Publishing, 2007.

Schwartz, Julius and Thomsen, Brian M.. *Man of Two Worlds*.
Harper Paperbacks, 2000.

Websites

Grand Comics Database
http://www.comics.org/

Comic Book Gorillarama
http://members.shaw.ca/comicbookgorillarama/cbgindex.htm

Frank Cho
http://www.libertymeadows.com

The Gorilla Gallery
http://cravenlovelace.com/cravenblog/the-gorilla-gallery/

Gorilla Age of Comics
http://www.lethargiclad.com/gorilla/

List of Fictional Apes
http://en.wikipedia.org/wiki/List_of_fictional_apes

Joe and Monkey
http://www.joeandmonkey.com/

The Thinking Ape Blues
http://thinkingapeblues.com/

Ape, Not Monkey
http://www.apenotmonkey.com/

Apes 'n' Capes
http://apesncapes.com/

RED SHADOWS
Robert E. Howard

The first published Solomon Kane adventure follows the legendary Puritan as he chases the murderous Le Loup across the wilds of Africa. Complete with sword fights, mysticism, and apes, this *Weird Tales* contribution ranks among Howard's best works.

I: The Coming of Solomon

The moonlight shimmered hazily, making silvery mists of illusion among the shadowy trees. A faint breeze whispered down the valley, bearing a shadow that was not of the moon-mist. A faint scent of smoke was apparent.

The man whose long, swinging strides, unhurried yet unswerving, had carried him for many a mile since sunrise, stopped suddenly. A movement in the trees had caught his attention, and he moved silently toward the shadows, a hand resting lightly on the hilt of his long, slim rapier.

Warily he advanced, his eyes striving to pierce the darkness that brooded under the trees. This was a wild and menacing country; death might be lurking under those trees. Then his hand fell away from the hilt and he leaned forward. Death indeed was there, but not in such shape as might cause him fear.

"The fires of Hades!" he murmured. "A girl! What has harmed you, child? Be not afraid of me."

The girl looked up at him, her face like a dim white rose in the dark.

"You—who are—you?" her words came in gasps.

"Naught but a wanderer, a landless man, but a friend to all in need." The gentle voice sounded somehow incongruous, coming from the man.

The girl sought to prop herself up on her elbow, and instantly he knelt and raised her to a sitting position, her head resting against his shoulder. His hand touched her breast and came away red and wet.

"Tell me." His voice was soft, soothing, as one speaks to a babe.

"Le Loup," she gasped, her voice swiftly growing weaker. "He and his men—descended upon our village—a mile up the valley. They robbed—slew—burned—"

"That, then, was the smoke I scented," muttered the man. "Go on, child."

"I ran. He, the Wolf, pursued me—and—caught me—" The words died away in a shuddering silence.

"I understand, child. Then—?"

"Then—he—he—stabbed me—with his dagger—oh, blessed saints!—mercy—"

Suddenly the slim form went limp. The man eased her to the earth, and touched her brow lightly.

"Dead!" he muttered.

Slowly he rose, mechanically wiping his hands upon his cloak. A dark scowl had settled on his somber brow. Yet he made no wild, reckless vow, swore no oath by saints or devils.

"Men shall die for this," he said coldly.

II: The Lair of the Wolf

"You are a fool!" The words came in a cold snarl that curdled the hearer's blood.

He who had just been named a fool lowered his eyes sullenly without answer.

"You and all the others I lead!" The speaker leaned forward, his fist pounding emphasis on the rude table between them. He was a tall, rangy-built man, supple as a leopard and with a lean, cruel, predatory face. His eyes danced and glittered with a kind of reckless mockery.

The fellow spoken to replied sullenly, "This Solomon Kane is a demon from hell, I tell you."

"Faugh! Dolt! He is a man—who will die from a pistol ball or a sword thrust."

"So thought Jean, Juan and La Costa," answered the other grimly. "Where are they? Ask the mountain wolves that tore the flesh from their dead bones. Where does this Kane hide? We have searched the mountains and the valleys for leagues, and we have found no trace. I tell you, Le Loup, he comes up from hell. I knew no good would come from hanging that friar a moon ago."

The Wolf strummed impatiently upon the table. His keen face, despite lines of wild living and dissipation, was the face of a thinker. The superstitions of his followers affected him not at all.

"Faugh! I say again. The fellow has found some cavern or secret vale of which we do not know where he hides in the day."

"And at night he sallies forth and slays us," gloomily commented the other. "He hunts us down as a wolf hunts deer—by God, Le Loup, you name yourself Wolf but I think you have met at last a fiercer and more crafty wolf than yourself! The first we know of this man is when we find Jean, the most desperate bandit unhung, nailed to a tree with his own dagger through his breast, and the letters S.L.K. carved upon his dead cheeks. Then the Spaniard Juan is struck down, and after we find him he lives long enough to tell us that the slayer is an Englishman, Solomon Kane, who has sworn to destroy our entire band! What then? La Costa, a swordsman second only to yourself, goes forth swearing to meet this Kane. By the demons of perdition, it seems he met him! For we found his sword-pierced corpse upon a cliff. What now? Are we all to fall before this English fiend?"

"True, our best men have been done to death by him," mused the bandit chief. "Soon the rest return from that little trip to the hermit's; then we shall see. Kane can not hide forever. Then—ha, what was that?"

The two turned swiftly as a shadow fell across the table. Into the entrance of the cave that formed the bandit lair, a man staggered. His eyes were wide and staring; he reeled on buckling legs, and a dark red stain dyed his tunic. He came a few tottering steps forward, then pitched across the table, sliding off onto the floor.

"Hell's devils!" cursed the Wolf, hauling him upright and propping him in a chair. "Where are the rest, curse you?"

"Dead! All dead!"

"How? Satan's curses on you, speak!" The Wolf shook the man savagely, the other bandit gazing on in wide-eyed horror.

"We reached the hermit's hut just as the moon rose," the man muttered. "I stayed outside—to watch—the others went in—to torture the hermit—to make him reveal—the hiding-place—of his gold."

"Yes, yes! Then what?" The Wolf was raging with impatience.

"Then the world turned red—the hut went up in a roar and a red rain flooded the valley—through it I saw—the hermit and a tall man clad all in black—coming from the trees—"

"Solomon Kane!" gasped the bandit. "I knew it! I—"

"Silence, fool!" snarled the chief. "Go on!"

"I fled—Kane pursued—wounded me—but I outran—him—got—here—first—"

The man slumped forward on the table.

"Saints and devils!" raged the Wolf. "What does he look like, this Kane?"

"Like—Satan—"

The voice trailed off in silence. The dead man slid from the table to lie in a red heap upon the floor.

"Like Satan!" babbled the other bandit. "I told you! 'Tis the Horned One himself! I tell you—"

He ceased as a frightened face peered in at the cave entrance.

"Kane?"

"Aye." The Wolf was too much at sea to lie. "Keep close watch, La Mon; in a moment the Rat and I will join you."

The face withdrew and Le Loup turned to the other.

"This ends the band," said he. "You, I, and that thief La Mon are all that are left. What would you suggest?"

The Rat's pallid lips barely formed the word: "Flight!"

"You are right. Let us take the gems and gold from the chests and flee, using the secret passageway."

"And La Mon?"

"He can watch until we are ready to flee. Then—why divide the treasure three ways?"

A faint smile touched the Rat's malevolent features. Then a sudden thought smote him.

"He," indicating the corpse on the floor, "said, 'I got here first.' Does that mean Kane was pursuing him here?" And as the Wolf nodded impatiently the other turned to the chests with chattering haste.

The flickering candle on the rough table lighted up a strange and wild scene. The light, uncertain and dancing, gleamed redly in the slowly widening lake of blood in which the dead man lay; it danced upon the heaps of gems and coins emptied hastily upon the floor from the brass-bound chests that ranged the walls; and it glittered in the eyes of the Wolf with the same gleam which sparkled from his sheathed dagger.

The chests were empty, their treasure lying in a shimmering mass upon the blood-stained floor. The Wolf stopped and listened. Outside was silence. There was no moon, and Le Loup's keen imagination pictured the dark slayer, Solomon Kane, gliding through the blackness, a shadow among shadows. He grinned crookedly; this time the Englishman would be foiled.

"There is a chest yet unopened," said he, pointing.

The Rat, with a muttered exclamation of surprise, bent over the chest indicated. With a single, catlike motion, the Wolf sprang upon him, sheathing his dagger to the hilt in the Rat's back, between the shoulders. The Rat sagged to the floor without a sound.

"Why divide the treasure two ways?" murmured Le Loup, wiping his blade upon the dead man's doublet. "Now for La Mon."

He stepped toward the door; then stopped and shrank back.

At first he thought that it was the shadow of a man who stood in the entrance; then he saw that it was a man himself, though so dark and still he stood that a fantastic semblance of shadow was lent him by the guttering candle.

A tall man, as tall as Le Loup he was, clad in black from head to foot, in plain, close-fitting garments that somehow suited the somber face. Long arms and broad shoulders betokened the swordsman, as plainly as the long rapier in his hand. The features of the man were saturnine and gloomy. A kind of dark pallor lent him a ghostly appearance in the uncertain light, an effect heightened by the satanic darkness of his lowering brows. Eyes, large, deep-set and unblinking, fixed their gaze upon the bandit, and looking into them, Le Loup was unable to decide what color they were. Strangely, the Mephistophelean trend of the lower features was offset by a high, broad forehead, though this was partly hidden by a featherless hat.

That forehead marked the dreamer, the idealist, the introvert, just as the eyes and the thin, straight nose betrayed the fanatic. An observer would have been struck by the eyes of the two men who stood there, facing each other. Eyes of both betokened untold deeps of power, but there the resemblance ceased.

The eyes of the bandit were hard, almost opaque, with a curious scintillant shallowness that reflected a thousand changing lights and gleams, like some strange gem; there was mockery in those eyes, cruelty and recklessness.

The eyes of the man in black, on the other hand, deep-set and staring from under prominent brows, were cold but deep; gazing into them, one had the impression of looking into countless fathoms of ice.

Now the eyes clashed, and the Wolf, who was used to being feared, felt a strange coolness on his spine. The sensation was new to him—a new thrill to one who lived for thrills, and he laughed suddenly.

"You are Solomon Kane, I suppose?" he asked, managing to make his question sound politely incurious.

"I am Solomon Kane." The voice was resonant and powerful. "Are you prepared to meet your God?"

"Why, Monsieur," Le Loup answered, bowing, "I assure you I am as ready as I ever will be. I might ask Monsieur the same question."

"No doubt I stated my inquiry wrongly," Kane said grimly. "I will change it: Are you prepared to meet your master, the Devil?"

"As to that, Monsieur"—Le Loup examined his fingernails with elaborate unconcern—"I must say that I can at present render a most satisfactory account to his Horned Excellency, though really I have no intention of so doing—for a while at least."

Le Loup did not wonder as to the fate of La Mon; Kane's presence in the cave was sufficient answer that did not need the trace of blood on his rapier to verify it.

"What I wish to know, Monsieur," said the bandit, "is why in the Devil's name have you harassed my band as you have, and how did you destroy that last set of fools?"

"Your last question is easily answered, sir," Kane replied. "I myself had the tale spread that the hermit possessed a store of gold, knowing that would draw your scum as carrion draws vultures. For days and nights I have watched the hut, and tonight, when I saw your villains coming, I warned the hermit, and together we went among the trees back of the hut. Then, when the rogues were inside, I struck flint and steel to the train I had laid, and flame ran through the trees like a red snake until it reached the powder I had placed beneath the hut floor. Then the hut and thirteen sinners went to hell in a great roar of flame and smoke. True, one escaped, but him I had slain in the forest had not I stumbled and fallen upon a broken root, which gave him time to elude me."

"Monsieur," said Le Loup with another low bow, "I grant you the admiration I must needs bestow on a brave and shrewd foeman. Yet tell me this: Why have you followed me as a wolf follows deer?"

"Some moons ago," said Kane, his frown becoming more menacing, "you and your fiends raided a small village down the valley. You know the details better than I. There was a girl there, a mere child, who, hoping to escape your lust, fled up the valley; but you, you jackal of hell, you caught her and left her, violated and dying. I found her there, and above her dead form I made up my mind to hunt you down and kill you."

"H'm," mused the Wolf. "Yes, I remember the wench. Mon Dieu, so the softer sentiments enter into the affair! Monsieur, I had not thought you an amorous man; be not jealous, good fellow, there are many more wenches."

"Le Loup, take care!" Kane exclaimed, a terrible menace in his voice. "I have never yet done a man to death by torture, but by God, sir, you tempt me!"

The tone, and more especially the unexpected oath, coming as it did from Kane, slightly sobered Le Loup; his eyes narrowed and his hand moved toward his rapier. The air was tense for an instant; then the Wolf relaxed elaborately.

"Who was the girl?" he asked idly. "Your wife?"

"I never saw her before," answered Kane.

"Nom d'un nom!" swore the bandit. "What sort of a man are you, Monsieur, who takes up a feud of this sort merely to avenge a wench unknown to you?"

"That, sir, is my own affair; it is sufficient that I do so."

Kane could not have explained, even to himself, nor did he ever seek an explanation within himself. A true fanatic, his promptings were reasons enough for his actions.

"You are right, Monsieur." Le Loup was sparring now for time; casually he edged backward inch by inch, with such consummate acting skill that he aroused no suspicion even in the hawk who watched him. "Monsieur," said he, "possibly you will say that you are merely a noble cavalier, wandering about like a true Galahad, protecting the weaker; but you and I know different. There on the floor is the equivalent to an emperor's ransom. Let us divide it peaceably; then if you like not my company, why—nom d'un nom!—we can go our separate ways."

Kane leaned forward, a terrible brooding threat growing in his cold eyes. He seemed like a great condor about to launch himself upon his victim.

"Sir, do you assume me to be as great a villain as yourself?"

Suddenly Le Loup threw back his head, his eyes dancing and leaping with a wild mockery and a kind of insane recklessness. His shout of laughter sent the echoes flying.

"Gods of hell! No, you fool, I do not class you with myself! Mon Dieu, Monsieur Kane, you have a task indeed if you intend to avenge all the wenches who have known my favors!"

"Shades of death! Shall I waste time in parleying with this base scoundrel!" Kane snarled in a voice suddenly blood-thirsting, and his lean frame flashed forward like a bent bow suddenly released.

At the same instant Le Loup with a wild laugh bounded backward with a movement as swift as Kane's. His timing was perfect; his back-flung hands struck the table and hurled it aside, plunging the cave into darkness as the candle toppled and went out.

Kane's rapier sang like an arrow in the dark as he thrust blindly and ferociously.

"Adieu, Monsieur Galahad!" The taunt came from somewhere in front of him, but Kane, plunging toward the sound with the savage fury of baffled wrath, caromed against a blank wall that did not yield to his blow. From somewhere seemed to come an echo of a mocking laugh.

Kane whirled, eyes fixed on the dimly outlined entrance, thinking his foe would try to slip past him and out of the cave; but no form bulked there, and when his groping hands found the candle and lighted it, the cave was empty, save for himself and the dead men on the floor.

III: The Chant of the Drums

Across the dusky waters the whisper came: boom, boom, boom!—a sullen reiteration. Far away and more faintly sounded a whisper of different timbre: thrum, throom, thrum! Back and forth went the vibrations as the throbbing drums spoke to each other. What tales did they carry? What monstrous secrets whispered across the sullen, shadowy reaches of the unmapped jungle?

"This, you are sure, is the bay where the Spanish ship put in?"

"Yes, Senhor; the negro swears this is the bay where the white man left the ship alone and went into the jungle."

Kane nodded grimly.

"Then put me ashore here, alone. Wait seven days; then if I have not returned and if you have no word of me, set sail wherever you will."

"Yes, Senhor."

The waves slapped lazily against the sides of the boat that carried Kane ashore. The village that he sought was on the river bank but set back from the bay shore, the jungle hiding it from sight of the ship.

Kane had adopted what seemed the most hazardous course, that of going ashore by night, for the reason that he knew, if the man he sought were in the village, he would never reach it by day. As it was, he was taking a most desperate chance in daring the nighttime jungle, but all his life he had been used to taking desperate chances. Now he gambled his life upon the slim chance of gaining the negro village under cover of darkness and unknown to the villagers.

At the beach he left the boat with a few muttered commands, and as the rowers put back to the ship which lay anchored some distance out in the bay, he turned and engulfed himself in the blackness of the jungle. Sword in one hand, dagger in the other, he stole forward, seeking to keep pointed in the direction from which the drums still muttered and grumbled.

He went with the stealth and easy movement of a leopard, feeling his way cautiously, every nerve alert and straining, but the way was not easy. Vines tripped him and slapped him in the face, impeding his progress; he was forced to grope his way between the huge boles of towering trees, and all through the underbrush about him sounded vague and menacing rustlings and shadows of movement. Thrice his foot touched something that moved beneath it and writhed away, and once he glimpsed the baleful glimmer of feline eyes among the trees. They vanished, however, as he advanced.

Thrum, thrum, thrum, came the ceaseless monotone of the drums: war and death (they said); blood and lust; human sacrifice and human feast! The soul of Africa (said the drums); the spirit of the jungle; the chant of the gods of outer darkness, the gods that roar and gibber, the gods men knew when dawns were young, beast-eyed, gaping-mouthed, huge-bellied, bloody-handed, the Black Gods (sang the drums).

All this and more the drums roared and bellowed to Kane as he worked his way through the forest. Somewhere in his soul a responsive chord was smitten and answered. You too are of the night (sang the drums); there is the strength of darkness, the strength of the primitive in you; come back down the ages; let us teach you, let us teach you (chanted the drums).

Kane stepped out of the thick jungle and came upon a plainly defined trail. Beyond, through the trees came the gleam of the village fires, flames glowing through the palisades. Kane walked down the trail swiftly.

He went silently and warily, sword extended in front of him, eyes straining to catch any hint of movement in the darkness ahead, for the trees loomed like sullen giants on each hand; sometimes their great branches intertwined above the trail and he could see only a slight way ahead of him.

Like a dark ghost he moved along the shadowed trail; alertly he stared and harkened; yet no warning came first to him, as a great, vague bulk rose up out of the shadows and struck him down, silently.

IV: The Black God

Thrum, thrum, thrum! Somewhere, with deadening monotony, a cadence was repeated, over and over, bearing out the same theme: "Fool—fool—fool!" Now it was far away, now he could stretch out his hand and almost reach it. Now it merged with the throbbing in his head until the two vibrations were as one: "Fool—fool—fool—fool—"

The fogs faded and vanished. Kane sought to raise his hand to his head, but found that he was bound hand and foot. He lay on the floor of a hut—alone? He twisted about to view the place. No, two eyes glimmered at him from the darkness. Now a form took shape, and Kane, still mazed, believed that he looked on the man who had struck him unconscious. Yet no; this man could never strike such a blow. He was lean, withered and wrinkled. The only thing that seemed alive about him were his eyes, and they seemed like the eyes of a snake.

The man squatted on the floor of the hut, near the doorway, naked save for a loin-cloth and the usual paraphernalia of bracelets, anklets and armlets. Weird fetishes of ivory, bone and hide, animal and human, adorned his arms and legs. Suddenly and unexpectedly he spoke in English.

"Ha, you wake, white man? Why you come here, eh?"

Kane asked the inevitable question, following the habit of the Caucasian.

"You speak my language—how is that?"

The black man grinned.

"I slave—long time, me boy. Me, N'Longa, ju-ju man, me, great fetish. No black man like me! You white man, you hunt brother?"

Kane snarled. "I! Brother! I seek a man, yes."

The negro nodded. "Maybe so you find um, eh?"

"He dies!"

Again the negro grinned. "Me pow'rful ju-ju man," he announced apropos of nothing. He bent closer. "White man you hunt, eyes like a leopard, eh? Yes? Ha! ha! ha! ha! Listen, white man: man-with-eyes-of-a-leopard, he and Chief Songa make pow'rful palaver; they blood brothers now. Say nothing, I help you; you help me, eh?"

"Why should you help me?" asked Kane suspiciously.

The ju-ju man bent closer and whispered, "White man Songa's right-hand man; Songa more pow'rful than N'Longa. White man mighty ju-ju! N'Longa's white brother kill man-with-eyes-of-a-leopard, be blood brother to N'Longa, N'Longa be more pow'rful than Songa; palaver set."

And like a dusky ghost he floated out of the hut so swiftly that Kane was not sure but that the whole affair was a dream.

Without, Kane could see the flare of fires. The drums were still booming, but close at hand the tones merged and mingled, and the impulse-producing vibrations were lost. All seemed a barbaric clamor without rime or reason, yet there was an undertone of mockery there, savage and gloating. "Lies," thought Kane, his mind still swimming, "jungle lies like jungle women that lure a man to his doom."

Two warriors entered the hut—black giants, hideous with paint and armed with crude spears. They lifted the white man and carried him out of the hut. They bore him across an open space, leaned him upright against a post and bound him there. About him, behind him and to the side, a great semicircle of black faces leered and faded in the firelight as the flames leaped and sank. There in front of him loomed a shape hideous and obscene—a black, formless thing, a grotesque parody of the human. Still, brooding, blood-stained, like the formless soul of Africa, the horror, the Black God.

And in front and to each side, upon roughly carven thrones of teakwood, sat two men. He who sat upon the right was a black man, huge, ungainly, a gigantic and unlovely mass of dusky flesh and muscles. Small, hoglike eyes blinked out over sin-marked cheeks; huge, flabby red lips pursed in fleshly haughtiness.

The other—

"Ah, Monsieur, we meet again." The speaker was far from being the debonair villain who had taunted Kane in the cavern among the mountains. His clothes were rags; there were more lines in his face; he had sunk lower in the years that had passed. Yet his eyes still gleamed and danced with their old recklessness and his voice held the same mocking timbre.

"The last time I heard that accursed voice," said Kane calmly, "was in a cave, in darkness, whence you fled like a hunted rat."

"Aye, under different conditions," answered Le Loup imperturbably. "What did you do after blundering about like an elephant in the dark?"

Kane hesitated, then: "I left the mountain—"

"By the front entrance? Yes? I might have known you were too stupid to find the secret door. Hoofs of the Devil, had you thrust against the chest with the golden lock, which stood against the wall, the door had opened to you and revealed the secret passageway through which I went."

"I traced you to the nearest port and there took ship and followed you to Italy, where I found you had gone."

"Aye, by the saints, you nearly cornered me in Florence. Ho! ho! ho! I was climbing through a back window while Monsieur Galahad was battering down the front door of the tavern. And had your horse not gone lame, you would have caught up with me on the road to Rome. Again, the ship on which I left Spain had barely put out to sea when Monsieur Galahad rides up to the wharfs. Why have you followed me like this? I do not understand."

"Because you are a rogue whom it is my destiny to kill," answered Kane coldly. He did not understand. All his life he had roamed about the world aiding the weak and fighting oppression, he neither knew nor questioned why. That was his obsession, his driving force of life. Cruelty and tyranny to the weak sent a red blaze of fury, fierce and lasting, through his soul. When the full flame of his hatred was wakened and loosed, there was no rest for him until his vengeance had been fulfilled to the uttermost. If he thought of it at all, he considered himself a fulfiller of God's judgment, a vessel of wrath to be emptied upon the souls of the unrighteous. Yet in the full sense of the word Solomon Kane was not wholly a Puritan, though he thought of himself as such.

Le Loup shrugged his shoulders. "I could understand had I wronged you personally. Mon Dieu! I, too, would follow an enemy across the world, but, though I would have joyfully slain and robbed you, I never heard of you until you declared war on me."

Kane was silent, his still fury overcoming him. Though he did not realize it, the Wolf was more than merely an enemy to him; the bandit symbolized, to Kane, all the things against which the Puritan had fought all his life: cruelty, outrage, oppression and tyranny.

Le Loup broke in on his vengeful meditations. "What did you do with the treasure, which—gods of Hades!—took me years to accumulate? Devil take it, I had time only to snatch a handful of coins and trinkets as I ran."

"I took such as I needed to hunt you down. The rest I gave to the villages which you had looted."

"Saints and the devil!" swore Le Loup. "Monsieur, you are the greatest fool I have yet met. To throw that vast treasure—by Satan, I rage to think of it in the hands of base peasants, vile villagers! Yet, ho! ho! ho! ho! they will steal, and kill each other for it! That is human nature."

"Yes, damn you!" flamed Kane suddenly, showing that his conscience had not been at rest. "Doubtless they will, being fools. Yet what could I do? Had I left it there, people might have starved and gone naked for lack of it. More, it would have been found, and theft and slaughter would have followed anyway. You are to blame, for had this treasure been left with its rightful owners, no such trouble would have ensued."

The Wolf grinned without reply. Kane not being a profane man, his rare curses had double effect and always startled his hearers, no matter how vicious or hardened they might be.

It was Kane who spoke next. "Why have you fled from me across the world? You do not really fear me."

"No, you are right. Really I do not know; perhaps flight is a habit which is difficult to break. I made my mistake when I did not kill you that night in the mountains. I am sure I could kill you in a fair fight, yet I have never even, ere now, sought to ambush you. Somehow I have not had a liking to meet you, Monsieur—a whim of mine, a mere whim. Then—mon Dieu!—mayhap I have enjoyed a new sensation—and I had thought that I had exhausted the thrills of life. And then, a man must either be the hunter or the hunted. Until now, Monsieur, I was the hunted, but I grew weary of the role—I thought I had thrown you off the trail."

"A negro slave, brought from this vicinity, told a Portugal ship captain of a white man who landed from a Spanish ship and went into the jungle. I heard of it and hired the ship, paying the captain to bring me here."

"Monsieur, I admire you for your attempt, but you must admire me, too! Alone I came into this village, and alone among savages and cannibals I—with some slight knowledge of the language learned from a slave aboard ship—I gained the confidence of King Songa and supplanted that mummer, N'Longa. I am a braver man than you, Monsieur, for I had no ship to retreat to, and a ship is waiting for you."

"I admire your courage," said Kane, "but you are content to rule amongst cannibals—you the blackest soul of them all. I intend to return to my own people when I have slain you."

"Your confidence would be admirable were it not amusing. Ho, Gulka!"

A giant negro stalked into the space between them. He was the hugest man that Kane had ever seen, though he moved with catlike ease and suppleness. His arms and legs were like trees, and the great, sinuous muscles rippled with each motion. His apelike head was set squarely between gigantic shoulders. His great, dusky hands were like the talons of an ape, and his brow slanted back from above bestial eyes. Flat nose and great, thick red lips completed this picture of primitive, lustful savagery.

"That is Gulka, the gorilla-slayer," said Le Loup. "He it was who lay in wait beside the trail and smote you down. You are like a wolf, yourself, Monsieur Kane, but since your ship hove in sight you have been watched by many eyes, and had you had all the powers of a leopard, you had not seen Gulka nor heard him. He hunts the most terrible and crafty of all beasts, in their native forests, far to the north, the beasts-who-walk-like-men—as that one, whom he slew some days since."

Kane, following Le Loup's fingers, made out a curious, manlike thing, dangling from a roof-pole of a hut. A jagged end thrust through the thing's body held it there. Kane could scarcely distinguish its characteristics by the firelight, but there was a weird, humanlike semblance about the hideous, hairy thing.

"A female gorilla that Gulka slew and brought to the village," said Le Loup.

The giant black slouched close to Kane and stared into the white man's eyes. Kane returned his gaze somberly, and presently the negro's eyes dropped sullenly and he slouched back a few paces. The look in the Puritan's grim eyes had pierced the primitive hazes of the gorilla-slayer's soul, and for the first time in his life he felt fear. To throw this off, he tossed a challenging look about; then, with unexpected animalness, he struck his huge chest resoundingly, grinned cavernously and flexed his mighty arms. No one spoke. Primordial bestiality had the stage, and the more highly developed types looked on with various feelings of amusement, tolerance or contempt.

Gulka glanced furtively at Kane to see if the white man was watching him, then with a sudden beastly roar, plunged forward and dragged a man from the semicircle. While the trembling victim screeched for mercy, the giant hurled him upon the crude altar before the shadowy idol. A spear rose and flashed, and the screeching ceased. The Black God looked on, his monstrous features seeming to leer in the flickering firelight. He had drunk; was the Black God pleased with the draft—with the sacrifice?

Gulka stalked back, and stopping before Kane, flourished the bloody spear before the white man's face.

Le Loup laughed. Then suddenly N'Longa appeared. He came from nowhere in particular; suddenly he was standing there, beside the post to which Kane was bound. A lifetime of study of the art of illusion had given the ju-ju man a highly technical knowledge of appearing and disappearing—which after all, consisted only in timing the audience's attention.

He waved Gulka aside with a grand gesture, and the gorilla-man slunk back, apparently to get out of N'Longa's gaze—then with incredible swiftness he turned and struck the ju-ju man a terrific blow upon the side of the head with his open hand. N'Longa went down like a felled ox, and in an instant he had been seized and bound to a post close to Kane. An uncertain murmuring rose from the negroes, which died out as King Songa stared angrily toward them.

Le Loup leaned back upon his throne and laughed uproariously.

"The trail ends here, Monsieur Galahad. That ancient fool thought I did not know of his plotting! I was hiding outside the hut and heard the interesting conversation you two had. Ha! ha! ha! ha! The Black God must drink, Monsieur, but I have persuaded Songa to have you two burnt; that will be much more enjoyable, though we shall have to forego the usual feast, I fear. For after the fires are lit about your feet the devil himself could not keep your carcasses from becoming charred frames of bone."

Songa shouted something imperiously, and blacks came bearing wood, which they piled about the feet of N'Longa and Kane. The ju-ju man had recovered consciousness, and he now shouted something in his native language. Again the murmuring arose among the shadowy throng. Songa snarled something in reply.

Kane gazed at the scene almost impersonally. Again, somewhere in his soul, dim primal deeps were stirring, age-old thought memories, veiled in the fogs of lost eons. He had been here before, thought Kane; he knew all this of old—the lurid flames beating back the sullen night, the bestial faces leering expectantly, and the god, the Black God, there in the shadows! Always the Black God, brooding back in the shadows. He had known the shouts, the frenzied chant of the worshipers, back there in the gray dawn of the world, the speech of the bellowing drums, the singing priests, the repellent, inflaming, all-pervading scent of freshly spilt blood. All this have I known, somewhere, sometime, thought Kane; now I am the main actor—

He became aware that someone was speaking to him through the roar of the drums; he had not realized that the drums had begun to boom again. The speaker was N'Longa: "Me pow'rful ju-ju man! Watch now: I work mighty magic. Songa!" His voice rose in a screech that drowned out the wildly clamoring drums.

Songa grinned at the words N'Longa screamed at him. The chant of the drums now had dropped to a low, sinister monotone and Kane plainly heard Le Loup when he spoke:

"N'Longa says that he will now work that magic which it is death to speak, even. Never before has it been worked in the sight of living men; it is the nameless ju-ju magic. Watch closely, Monsieur; possibly we shall be further amused." The Wolf laughed lightly and sardonically.

A black man stooped, applying a torch to the wood about Kane's feet. Tiny jets of flame began to leap up and catch. Another bent to do the same with N'Longa, then hesitated. The ju-ju man sagged in his bonds; his head drooped upon his chest. He seemed dying.

Le Loup leaned forward, cursing, "Feet of the Devil! Is the scoundrel about to cheat us of our pleasure of seeing him writhe in the flames?"

The warrior gingerly touched the wizard and said something in his own language.

Le Loup laughed: "He died of fright. A great wizard, by the—"

His voice trailed off suddenly. The drums stopped as if the drummers had fallen dead simultaneously. Silence dropped like a fog upon the village and in the stillness Kane heard only the sharp crackle of the flames whose heat he was beginning to feel.

All eyes were turned upon the dead man upon the altar, for the corpse had begun to move!

First a twitching of a hand, then an aimless motion of an arm, a motion which gradually spread over the body and limbs. Slowly, with blind, uncertain gestures, the dead man turned upon his side, the trailing limbs found the earth. Then, horribly like something being born, like some frightful reptilian thing bursting the shell of non-existence, the corpse tottered and reared upright, standing on legs wide apart and stiffly braced, arms still making useless, infantile motions. Utter silence, save somewhere a man's quick breath sounded loud in the stillness.

Kane stared, for the first time in his life smitten speechless and thoughtless. To his Puritan mind this was Satan's hand manifested.

Le Loup sat on his throne, eyes wide and staring, hand still half raised in the careless gesture he was making when frozen into silence by the unbelievable sight. Songa sat beside him, mouth and eyes wide open, fingers making curious jerky motions upon the carved arms of the throne.

Now the corpse was upright, swaying on stiltlike legs, body tilting far back until the sightless eyes seemed to stare straight into the red moon that was just rising over the black jungle. The thing tottered uncertainly in a wide, erratic half-circle, arms flung out grotesquely as if in balance, then swayed about to face the two thrones—and the Black God. A burning twig at Kane's feet cracked like the crash of a cannon in the tense silence. The horror thrust forth a black foot—it took a wavering step—another. Then with stiff, jerky and automatonlike steps, legs straddled far apart, the dead man came toward the two who sat in speechless horror to each side of the Black God.

"Ah-h-h!" from somewhere came the explosive sigh, from that

shadowy semicircle where crouched the terror-fascinated worshipers. Straight on stalked the grim specter. Now it was within three strides of the thrones, and Le Loup, faced by fear for the first time in his bloody life, cringed back in his chair; while Songa, with a superhuman effort breaking the chains of horror that held him helpless, shattered the night with a wild scream and, springing to his feet, lifted a spear, shrieking and gibbering in wild menace. Then as the ghastly thing halted not its frightful advance, he hurled the spear with all the power of his great, black muscles, and the spear tore through the dead man's breast with a rending of flesh and bone. Not an instant halted the thing—for the dead die not—and Songa the king stood frozen, arms outstretched as if to fend off the terror.

An instant they stood so, leaping firelight and eery moonlight etching the scene forever in the minds of the beholders. The changeless staring eyes of the corpse looked full into the bulging eyes of Songa, where were reflected all the hells of horror. Then with a jerky motion the arms of the thing went out and up. The dead hands fell on Songa's shoulders. At the first touch, the king seemed to shrink and shrivel, and with a scream that was to haunt the dreams of every watcher through all the rest of time, Songa crumpled and fell, and the dead man reeled stiffly and fell with him. Motionless lay the two at the feet of the Black God, and to Kane's dazed mind it seemed that the idol's great, inhuman eyes were fixed upon them with terrible, still laughter.

At the instant of the king's fall, a great shout went up from the blacks, and Kane, with a clarity lent his subconscious mind by the depths of his hate, looked for Le Loup and saw him spring from his throne and vanish in the darkness. Then vision was blurred by a rush of black figures who swept into the space before the god. Feet knocked aside the blazing brands whose heat Kane had forgotten, and dusky hands freed him; others loosed the wizard's body and laid it upon the earth. Kane dimly understood that the blacks believed this thing to be the work of N'Longa, and that they connected the vengeance of the wizard with himself. He bent, laid a hand on the ju-ju man's shoulder. No doubt of it: he was dead, the flesh was already cold. He glanced at the other corpses. Songa was dead, too, and the thing that had slain him lay now without movement.

Kane started to rise, then halted. Was he dreaming, or did he really feel a sudden warmth in the dead flesh he touched? Mind reeling, he again bent over the wizard's body, and slowly he felt warmness steal over the limbs and the blood begin to flow sluggishly through the veins again.

Then N'Longa opened his eyes and stared up into Kane's, with the blank expression of a new-born babe. Kane watched, flesh crawling, and saw the knowing, reptilian glitter come back, saw the wizard's thick lips part in a wide grin. N'Longa sat up, and a strange chant arose from the negroes.

Kane looked about. The blacks were all kneeling, swaying their bodies to and fro, and in their shouts Kane caught the word, "N'Longa!" repeated over and over in a kind of fearsomely ecstatic refrain of terror and worship. As the wizard rose, they all fell prostrate.

N'Longa nodded, as if in satisfaction.

"Great ju-ju—great fetish, me!" he announced to Kane. "You see? My ghost go out—kill Songa—come back to me! Great magic! Great fetish, me!"

Kane glanced at the Black God looming back in the shadows, at N'Longa, who now flung out his arms toward the idol as if in invocation.

I am everlasting (Kane thought the Black God said); I drink, no matter who rules; chiefs, slayers, wizards, they pass like the ghosts of dead men through the gray jungle; I stand, I rule; I am the soul of the jungle (said the Black God).

Suddenly Kane came back from the illusory mists in which he had been wandering. "The white man! Which way did he flee?"

N'Longa shouted something. A score of dusky hands pointed; from somewhere Kane's rapier was thrust out to him. The fogs faded and vanished; again he was the avenger, the scourge of the unrighteous; with the sudden volcanic speed of a tiger he snatched the sword and was gone.

V: The End of the Red Trail

Limbs and vines slapped against Kane's face. The oppressive steam of the tropic night rose like mist about him. The moon, now floating high above the jungle, limned the black shadows in its white glow and patterned the jungle floor in grotesque designs. Kane knew not if the man he sought was ahead of him, but broken limbs and trampled underbrush showed that some man had gone that way, some man who fled in haste, nor halted to pick his way. Kane followed these signs unswervingly. Believing in the justice of his vengeance, he did not doubt that the dim beings who rule men's destinies would finally bring him face to face with Le Loup.

Behind him the drums boomed and muttered. What a tale they had to tell this night! of the triumph of N'Longa, the death of the black king, the overthrow of the white-man-with-eyes-like-a-leopard, and a more darksome tale, a tale to be whispered in low, muttering vibrations: the nameless ju-ju.

Was he dreaming? Kane wondered as he hurried on. Was all this part of some foul magic? He had seen a dead man rise and slay and die again; he had seen a man die and come to life again. Did N'Longa in truth send his ghost, his soul, his life essence forth into the void, dominating a corpse to do his will? Aye, N'Longa died a real death there, bound to the torture stake, and he who lay dead on the altar rose and did as N'Longa would have done had he been free. Then, the unseen force animating the dead man fading, N'Longa had lived again.

Yes, Kane thought, he must admit it as a fact. Somewhere in the darksome reaches of jungle and river, N'Longa had stumbled upon the Secret—the Secret of controlling life and death, of overcoming the shackles and limitations of the flesh. How had this dark wisdom, born in the black and blood-stained shadows of this grim land, been given to the wizard? What sacrifice had been so pleasing to the Black Gods, what ritual so monstrous, as to make them give up the knowledge of this magic? And what thoughtless, timeless journeys had N'Longa taken, when he chose to send his ego, his ghost, through the far, misty countries, reached only by death?

There is wisdom in the shadows (brooded the drums), wisdom and magic; go into the darkness for wisdom; ancient magic shuns the light; we remember the lost ages (whispered the drums), ere man became wise and foolish; we remember the beast gods—the serpent gods and the ape gods and the nameless, the Black Gods, they who drank blood and whose voices roared through the shadowy hills, who feasted and lusted. The secrets of life and of death are theirs; we remember, we remember (sang the drums).

Kane heard them as he hastened on. The tale they told to the feathered black warriors farther up the river, he could not translate; but they spoke to him in their own way, and that language was deeper, more basic.

The moon, high in the dark blue skies, lighted his way and gave him a clear vision as he came out at last into a glade and saw Le Loup standing there. The Wolf's naked blade was a long gleam of silver in the moon, and he stood with shoulders thrown back, the old, defiant smile still on his face.

"A long trail, Monsieur," said he. "It began in the mountains of France; it ends in an African jungle. I have wearied of the game at last, Monsieur—and you die. I had not fled from the village, even, save that—I admit it freely—that damnable witchcraft of N'Longa's shook my nerves. More, I saw that the whole tribe would turn against me."

Kane advanced warily, wondering what dim, forgotten tinge of chivalry in the bandit's soul had caused him thus to take his chance in the open. He half suspected treachery, but his keen eyes could detect no shadow of movement in the jungle on either side of the glade.

"Monsieur, on guard!" Le Loup's voice was crisp. "Time that we ended this fool's dance about the world. Here we are alone."

The men were now within reach of each other, and Le Loup, in the midst of his sentence, suddenly plunged forward with the speed of light, thrusting viciously. A slower man had died there, but Kane parried and sent his own blade in a silver streak that slit Le Loup's tunic as the Wolf bounded backward. Le Loup admitted the failure of his trick with a wild laugh and came in with the breath-taking speed and fury of a tiger, his blade making a white fan of steel about him.

Rapier clashed on rapier as the two swordsmen fought. They were fire and ice opposed. Le Loup fought wildly but craftily, leaving no openings, taking advantage of every opportunity. He was a living flame, bounding back, leaping in, feinting, thrusting, warding, striking—laughing like a wild man, taunting and cursing.

Kane's skill was cold, calculating, scintillant. He made no waste movement, no motion not absolutely necessary. He seemed to devote more time and effort toward defense than did Le Loup, yet there was no hesitancy in his attack, and when he thrust, his blade shot out with the speed of a striking snake.

There was little to choose between the men as to height, strength and reach. Le Loup was the swifter by a scant, flashing margin, but Kane's skill reached a finer point of perfection. The Wolf's fencing was fiery, dynamic, like the blast from a furnace. Kane was more steady—less the instinctive, more the thinking fighter, though he, too, was a born slayer, with the co-ordination that only a natural fighter possessed.

Thrust, parry, a feint, a sudden whirl of blades—

"Ha!" the Wolf sent up a shout of ferocious laughter as the blood started from a cut on Kane's cheek. As if the sight drove him to further fury, he attacked like the beast men named him. Kane was forced back before that blood-lusting onslaught, but the Puritan's expression did not alter.

Minutes flew by; the clang and clash of steel did not diminish. Now they stood squarely in the center of the glade, Le Loup untouched, Kane's garments red with the blood that oozed from wounds on cheek, breast, arm and thigh. The Wolf grinned savagely and mockingly in the moonlight, but he had begun to doubt.

His breath came hissing fast and his arm began to weary; who was this man of steel and ice who never seemed to weaken? Le Loup knew that the wounds he had inflicted on Kane were not deep, but even so, the steady flow of blood should have sapped some of the man's strength and speed by this time. But if Kane felt the ebb of his powers, it did not show. His brooding countenance did not change in expression, and he pressed the fight with as much cold fury as at the beginning.

Le Loup felt his might fading, and with one last desperate effort he rallied all his fury and strength into a single plunge. A sudden, unexpected attack too wild and swift for the eye to follow, a dynamic burst of speed and fury no man could have withstood, and Solomon Kane reeled for the first time as he felt cold steel tear through his body. He reeled back, and Le Loup, with a wild shout, plunged after him, his reddened sword free, a gasping taunt on his lips.

Kane's sword, backed by the force of desperation, met Le Loup's in midair; met, held and wrenched. The Wolf's yell of triumph died on his lips as his sword flew singing from his hand.

For a fleeting instant he stopped short, arms flung wide as a crucifix, and Kane heard his wild, mocking laughter peal forth for the last time, as the Englishman's rapier made a silver line in the moonlight.

Far away came the mutter of the drums. Kane mechanically cleansed his sword on his tattered garments. The trail ended here, and Kane was conscious of a strange feeling of futility. He always felt that, after he had killed a foe. Somehow it always seemed that no real good had been wrought; as if the foe had, after all, escaped his just vengeance.

With a shrug of his shoulders Kane turned his attention to his bodily needs. Now that the heat of battle had passed, he began to feel weak and faint from the loss of blood. That last thrust had been close; had he not managed to avoid its full point by a twist of his body, the blade had transfixed him. As it was, the sword had struck glancingly, plowed along his ribs and sunk deep in the muscles beneath the shoulder-blade, inflicting a long, shallow wound.

Kane looked about him and saw that a small stream trickled through the glade at the far side. Here he made the only mistake of that kind that he ever made in his entire life. Mayhap he was dizzy from loss of blood and still mazed from the weird happenings of the night; be that as it may, he laid down his rapier and crossed, weaponless, to the stream. There he laved his wounds and bandaged them as best he could, with strips torn from his clothing.

Then he rose and was about to retrace his steps when a motion among the trees on the side of the glade where he first entered, caught his eye. A huge figure stepped out of the jungle, and Kane saw, and recognized, his doom. The man was Gulka, the gorilla-slayer. Kane remembered that he had not seen the black among those doing homage to N'Longa. How could he know the craft and hatred in that dusky, slanting skull that had led the negro, escaping the vengeance of his tribesmen, to trail down the only man he had ever feared? The Black God had been kind to his neophyte; had led him upon his victim helpless and unarmed. Now Gulka could kill his man openly—and slowly, as a leopard kills, not smiting him down from ambush as he had planned, silently and suddenly.

A wide grin split the negro's face, and he moistened his lips. Kane, watching him, was coldly and deliberately weighing his chances. Gulka had already spied the rapiers. He was closer to them than was Kane. The Englishman knew that there was no chance of his winning in a sudden race for the swords.

A slow, deadly rage surged in him—the fury of helplessness. The blood churned in his temples and his eyes smoldered with a terrible light as he eyed the negro. His fingers spread and closed like claws. They were strong, those hands; men had died in their clutch. Even Gulka's huge black column of a neck might break like a rotten branch between them—a wave of weakness made the futility of these thoughts apparent to an extent that needed not the verification of the moonlight glimmering from the spear in Gulka's black hand. Kane could not even have fled had he wished—and he had never fled from a single foe.

The gorilla-slayer moved out into the glade. Massive, terrible, he was the personification of the primitive, the Stone Age. His mouth yawned in a red cavern of a grin; he bore himself with the haughty arrogance of savage might.

Kane tensed himself for the struggle that could end but one way. He strove to rally his waning forces. Useless; he had lost too much blood. At least he would meet his death on his feet, and somehow he stiffened his buckling knees and held himself erect, though the glade shimmered before him in uncertain waves and the moonlight seemed to have become a red fog through which he dimly glimpsed the approaching black man.

Kane stooped, though the effort nearly pitched him on his face; he dipped water in his cupped hands and dashed it into his face. This revived him, and he straightened, hoping that Gulka would charge and get it over with before his weakness crumpled him to the earth.

Gulka was now about the center of the glade, moving with the slow, easy stride of a great cat stalking a victim. He was not at all in a hurry to consummate his purpose. He wanted to toy with his victim, to see fear come into those grim eyes which had looked him down, even when the possessor of those eyes had been bound to the death stake. He wanted to slay, at last, slowly, glutting his tigerish blood-lust and torture-lust to the fullest extent.

Then suddenly he halted, turned swiftly, facing another side of the glade. Kane, wondering, followed his glance.

At first it seemed like a blacker shadow among the jungle shadows. At first there was no motion, no sound, but Kane instinctively knew that some terrible menace lurked there in the darkness that masked and merged the silent trees. A sullen horror brooded there, and Kane felt as if, from that monstrous shadow, inhuman eyes seared his very soul. Yet simultaneously there came the fantastic sensation that these eyes were not directed on him. He looked at the gorilla-slayer.

The black man had apparently forgotten him; he stood, half crouching, spear lifted, eyes fixed upon that clump of blackness. Kane looked again. Now there was motion in the shadows; they merged fantastically and moved out into the glade, much as Gulka had done. Kane blinked: was this the illusion that precedes death? The shape he looked upon was such as he had visioned dimly in wild nightmares, when the wings of sleep bore him back through lost ages.

He thought at first it was some blasphemous mockery of a man, for it went erect and was tall as a tall man. But it was inhumanly broad and thick, and its gigantic arms hung nearly to its misshapen feet. Then the moonlight smote full upon its bestial face, and Kane's mazed mind thought that the thing was the Black God coming out of the shadows, animated and blood-lusting. Then he saw that it was covered with hair, and he remembered the manlike thing dangling from the roof-pole in the native village. He looked at Gulka.

The negro was facing the gorilla, spear at the charge. He was not afraid, but his sluggish mind was wondering over the miracle that brought this beast so far from his native jungles.

The mighty ape came out into the moonlight and there was a terrible majesty about his movements. He was nearer Kane than Gulka but he did not seem to be aware of the white man. His small, blazing eyes were fixed on the black man with terrible intensity. He advanced with a curious swaying stride.

Far away the drums whispered through the night, like an accompaniment to this grim Stone Age drama. The savage crouched in the middle of the glade, but the primordial came out of the jungle with eyes bloodshot and blood-lusting. The negro was face to face with a thing more primitive than he. Again ghosts of memories whispered to Kane: you have seen such sights before (they murmured), back in the dim days, the dawn days, when beast and beast-man battled for supremacy.

Gulka moved away from the ape in a half-circle, crouching, spear ready. With all his craft he was seeking to trick the gorilla, to make a swift kill, for he had never before met such a monster as this, and though he did not fear, he had begun to doubt. The ape made no attempt to stalk or circle; he strode straight forward toward Gulka.

The black man who faced him and the white man who watched could not know the brutish love, the brutish hate that had driven the monster down from the low, forest-covered hills of the north to follow for leagues the trail of him who was the scourge of his kind— the slayer of his mate, whose body now hung from the roof-pole of the negro village.

The end came swiftly, almost like a sudden gesture. They were close, now, beast and beast-man; and suddenly, with an earth-shaking roar, the gorilla charged. A great hairy arm smote aside the thrusting spear, and the ape closed with the negro. There was a shattering sound as of many branches breaking simultaneously, and Gulka slumped silently to the earth, to lie with arms, legs and body flung in strange, unnatural positions. The ape towered an instant above him, like a statue of the primordial triumphant.

Far away Kane heard the drums murmur. The soul of the jungle, the soul of the jungle: this phrase surged through his mind with monotonous reiteration.

The three who had stood in power before the Black God that night, where were they? Back in the village where the drums rustled lay Songa—King Songa, once lord of life and death, now a shriveled corpse with a face set in a mask of horror. Stretched on his back in the middle of the glade lay he whom Kane had followed many a league by land and sea. And Gulka the gorilla-slayer lay at the feet of his killer, broken at last by the savagery which had made him a true son of this grim land which had at last overwhelmed him.

Yet the Black God still reigned, thought Kane dizzily, brooding back in the shadows of this dark country, bestial, blood-lusting, caring naught who lived or died, so that he drank.

Kane watched the mighty ape, wondering how long it would be before the huge simian spied and charged him. But the gorilla gave no evidence of having even seen him. Some dim impulse of vengeance yet unglutted prompting him, he bent and raised the negro. Then he slouched toward the jungle, Gulka's limbs trailing limply and grotesquely. As he reached the trees, the ape halted, whirling the giant form high in the air with seemingly no effort, and dashed the dead man up among the branches. There was a rending sound as a broken projecting limb tore through the body hurled so powerfully against it, and the dead gorilla-slayer dangled there hideously.

A moment the clear moon limned the great ape in its glimmer, as he stood silently gazing up at his victim; then like a dark shadow he melted noiselessly into the jungle.

Kane walked slowly to the middle of the glade and took up his rapier. The blood had ceased to flow from his wounds, and some of his strength was returning, enough, at least, for him to reach the coast where his ship awaited him. He halted at the edge of the glade for a backward glance at Le Loup's upturned face and still form, white in the moonlight, and at the dark shadow among the trees that was Gulka, left by some bestial whim, hanging as the she-gorilla hung in the village.

Afar the drums muttered: "The wisdom of our land is ancient; the wisdom of our land is dark; whom we serve, we destroy. Flee if you would live, but you will never forget our chant. Never, never," sang the drums.

Kane turned to the trail which led to the beach and the ship waiting there.

THE CULT OF THE WHITE APE

Hugh B. Cave

In another selection from *Weird Tales*, Cave delivers a riveting tale set in the hills of Congo. Full of supernatural, romance, brutality, and terror, this story lingers long after the last page.

The hour is midnight. The oil lamp on the table before me, casting its weird glow over my face, is a feeble, inadequate thing that flickers constantly as the corrugated iron roof of the shack trembles with the throbbing beat of incessant rain. It has rained here in the village of Kodagi for the last four months—a horrible maddening dirge that drives its way into a man's brain and undermines his reason. The M'Boto Hills of the Congo, sunk in the stinking sweat of the rain belt, are cursed with such torment.

It was raining when Matthew Betts came here. I was outside at the time, working on the veranda inside my cage of mosquito-netting. A man must have some relief from the monotony or else go mad; and I had found, after being sent here by the Belgian government to fill the position of *chef de poste*, that my hobby of entomology was a heaven-sent blessing.

When Betts came, I was busily sorting specimens and mounting them on the little oki-wood table in my veranda laboratory. Beside me, on the stoop, squatted old Kodagi. A cunning man, Kodagi. A wizened monkey of a man with parchment face and filed teeth and a broad grin that bespeaks much hidden knowledge. He belongs, I believe, to the Zapo Zaps—a queerly deformed race which inhabits these mysterious jungles. For years he has been the village Ngana, the witch-doctor and magician of the tribe.

Kodagi, I like to believe, is my friend. It is a peculiar half-dead friendship at most, and yet I am thankful for the little that is allotted me. There are rumours—more than rumours—that Kodagi disliked intensely the white man who held the position of *chef de poste* before me, and that this white man died a slow, unpleasant, and altogether inexplicable death. More than once I have suspected that Kodagi is one of the all-powerful members of the Bakanzenzi—the terrible, cannibalistic secret cult which even the natives of my village speak of in fearful undertones.

Kodagi was watching me astutely as I went about my work. His beady eyes followed me everywhere, saw every movement. Occasionally he muttered something to me under his breath; but the monotonous beat of the rain smothered his voice.

All at once he turned, to stare at the opposite wall of the clearing.

"Look, *Bwana!*" he pointed.

I jerked about obediently, to see the nose of a safari winding its sluggish way into our silent domain. Sloshing through the soft mud they came, with heads down and backs bowed under the weight of their burdens. At their head strode a white man—a hulking buffalo of a man with coarse red face and loose-fitting white drill which hung from him like a drenched winding-sheet. In one hand he carried a *kiboko*. The other hand he flung up to salute me, and shouted boisterously, at the same time turning in his tracks to snarl at the cringing natives behind him. They were afraid of him evidently, for they cowered back in silence and huddled together in whispering groups while he strode forward to the veranda.

I watched him quietly. I thought I knew his identity, since I had been informed that certain land close to the village had been leased by the officials of a powerful rubber company. This company, the report stated, would send a chap named Betts—Matthew Betts—

to the village of Kodagi, where he would experiment with various types of latex-producing trees and vines.

If this was the man they were sending, I decided instantly that I disliked him. He was drunk; and it is not good for white men to drink native rum in the sweating, fever-ridden murk of the Congo, less than five degrees from the equator. I was infinitely glad when my Jopaluo house-boy, Njo, relieved me of the task of opening the veranda door for him.

I saw then that he was very drunk. He stumbled on the step and lurched forward. Perhaps he did not see Kodagi crouching there; perhaps he saw but did not care. At any rate, his outstretched foot entwined between Kodagi's black legs. He stumbled and caught himself on the mosquito-netting. Then, before I could prevent it, he swung upon Kodagi with a rasping snarl. His heavy boot drove into the Ngana's naked ribs. Kodagi, screaming in pain and writhing hideously, tumbled off the stoop into the mud.

The result was instantaneous. Straightening up, Betts stepped toward me with, a livid grin. Two steps he took, and opened his mouth to speak. Then the grin faded with uncanny abruptness, leaving an expression of unholy fear on his bloated face. I saw his eyes dilate. His features lost colour. He flung himself sideways and jerked up a Luger in his fist. A sudden belch of flame seared through the muzzle; and the bullets, whining dangerously close to me, roared blindly into a patch of thick scrub beside the veranda rail.

After that there was complete silence for a moment. Betts stood rigid, trembling. Behind him, at the rim of the clearing, the porters of his safari were running madly to safety, screeching in terror. Njo, my house-boy, was down on his knees in the middle of the doorway, muttering in his native tongue. Kodagi, who had been lying prone in the mud at the foot of the stoop, had vanished!

I turned slowly, mechanically, to stare at the clump of brush which had excited Betts' drunken attention. I saw nothing—nothing at all. Frowning, I strode to Betts' side and gripped his arm.

"What the devil," I snapped, "are you doing? Are you mad?"

"Mad? *Mad!*" the words came from his dry mouth in a thick whisper. "You—you didn't see it, Varicks?"

"See what?" I said curtly.

"The—the thing—there in the reeds!" His eyes shifted furtively. Reddish brown eyes, they were, sunk in fatty pits that made them incredibly small and pointed.

"You're drunk," I shrugged. "Come inside."

"I—I saw it, Varicks," he muttered again. "An ape-thing—a *white* ape—big as a man—standing there snarling at me—"

"Come inside," I ordered, taking hold of him. Evidently he had swilled enough native rum to put a less powerful man under the ground. White apes—in the Congo! That was about the limit—the nearest thing to D.T.'s I had seen in many months.

But he refused to be led away. He wrenched his arm from my grip and continued to stand there, staring, muttering something about not daring to turn his back. I saw that I should have to use extreme measures, or else have a raving fever-drunk lunatic on my hands.

"You're seeing things," I said quietly. "Come on—we'll have a look. If anything was hiding in the reeds, there will be footprints in the mud. You'll see."

He went with me unwillingly, holding back so much that I was practically forced to drag him along. Together we stumped down the veranda steps and wallowed through the mud to the suspicious patch of brush. He stood beside me, uneasy and twitching, as I pushed forward and parted the high reeds with my hands.

Then, very suddenly, I froze in my tracks. My arms remained outflung, like the wings of a great bat. My groping foot stiffened in the very act of kicking the reeds aside; and there, directly beneath it, lay the soggy imprint of another foot!

Betts' eyes went horribly wide and filled with fear. His fingers dug into my forearm. He whispered something, but I did not hear, for I was already on my knees, examining the thing in front of me.

It was the mark of a man's foot—a naked, human foot. In the

heel of it, where a little pool of water should have accumulated, lay a well of something else—something red and sticky that was blood.

Without a word I stood up again. Carefully, painstakingly, I examined every inch of that clump of reeds. I found nothing else— nothing but that damning, significant imprint of a human foot and the spilled human blood in the heel of it. When I finally pushed Betts toward the shack, my fists were clenched and my mouth was screwed into a thin, troubled line. I was afraid.

On the veranda, inside the screen of mosquito-netting, I lowered myself heavily into a chair. Betts sat close to me, facing me, peering fearfully into my face. For an instant neither of us offered to break the silence which had crept over us. Then, leaning forward, Betts extended an unsteady hand to clutch my knee. His lips sucked open.

"What—what was it?" he whispered thickly.

I did not answer him immediately. I was thinking of Kodagi, whom he had kicked into the mud, and who had disappeared with such incredible swiftness. One moment the village sorcerer had been lying lifeless in the filth. Next moment Betts had seen that hideous apparition in the reeds, and Kodagi, all at once, had vanished.

"I don't know what it was," I said evenly, replying to Betts' query. "I only know that you've made a horrible blunder."

"A—blunder? Me?"

"In this village," I said meaningly, "one doesn't kick and beat the natives. This is deep-jungle territory. The natives are not the half-civilised, peaceful breed you're accustomed to handling. They are atavistic. Many of them are members of the Bakanzenzi."

"You—you mean—"

"Up here," I said quietly, "you are in the heart of strange jungles and strange people, where queer things take place. That's the best explanation I can offer you."

"But the ape—" he mumbled. "I saw—"

"This is not gorilla country, Betts. The big apes never come here. They never leave their stamping-grounds in the Ogowwi and Kivu districts."

He blinked at me uncomprehendingly. His fat hand came up shakily to wipe the sweat from his jowls. Evidently my words had made a deep impression upon him, for his eyes were quite colourless and his mouth twitched.

"Get me—a drink, Varicks," he said gutturally. "I need it."

I hesitated. He had had enough to drink already. But one more might serve to steady his nerves and prevent a collapse. I got out of my chair to get it.

He rose with me and turned clumsily to the veranda door. Jerking it open, he looked toward the opposite end of the clearing, where his safari had first appeared.

"Lucilia!" he bellowed. "Lucilia!"

I was bewildered—even more bewildered when I followed the direction of his stare and saw what I had not noticed before. A *masheela* chair—a kind of covered hammock carried by four bearers—had been set down at the edge of the jungle. The bearers, having fled like frightened rodents at the sight of Betts' demonstration, had now returned. At the sound of the big man's voice, they lifted the *masheela* and carried it forward.

"My God!" I said thickly. "You haven't brought a woman here?"

"Why not?" Betts grumbled.

"This is no country for a white woman, Betts. You know damned well—"

"That's my business," he snapped. "She's my wife."

I choked the retort that came to my lips. Then I turned to stare at the woman who was approaching us. She was young—much younger than her bull-necked husband—hardly more than a slim, very lovely girl. When Betts spoke her name and she placed her hand in mine, I felt that I should be more than glad to endure her husband's drunken presence during his stay in Kodagi's village. A white woman, here in this horrible place, was an angel from Heaven.

During the following day I saw little of Betts and his wife. They drove their safari to the far end of the village and took possession, with their entire equipment, of a huddled group of broken-down abandoned huts. Njo, my house-boy, brought news to me late in the afternoon that Betts had gone alone into the jungle on a preliminary tour of inspection.

"Alone?" I frowned, peering into Njo's yellow-toothed mouth.

"Yes, *Bwana*. He is an ignorant fool!"

"Drunk?" I said curtly.

"So drunk, *Bwana*, that he can not walk straight!"

"Hmm. You think he was drunk before, when he claimed to see a white ape in the brush, Njo?" I asked meaningly.

The little Jopaluo's eyes widened in fear. He fell away from me, grimacing. I had to repeat the question before he would answer.

"Others have seen the white ape, *Bwana*," he whispered uneasily. "I myself have looked upon it one night in the jungle near the moon-tower of the Bakanzenzi; and many of the Manyimas and Zapo Zaps have seen it. It is *mafui*—the were-ape. It is not of this world, *Bwana!*"

"You are afraid, eh?"

"Afraid! Aiiiii! The *mafui* means death!"

I glanced at him quickly. There was no doubt about the terror in his face; it was genuine and abject. With a shrug of indifference, altogether assumed to mask my own forebodings, I turned away— and then turned back again.

"Where is Kodagi?" I demanded.

"He is in his hut, *Bwana*, across the village."

"Go to him then," I ordered, "and tell him that I am sorry for what the big man did to him. Tell him to come here and I will take the pain from his bruises."

"Yes, *Bwana!*"

Njo scurried out, leaving me alone. For some time I paced back and forth in the central room of the shack, listening to the throb of rain on the roof above me. Presently I went out on the veranda. I made sure that my revolver—a Webley forty-four—hung in its holster at my belt.

An hour later Betts came to visit me. He came alone, wallowing and sloughing through the black mud, completely drunk and in ill temper. He fell shakily into a veranda chair beside me.

"Stinkin' weather!" he cursed. "Rain, rain—"

"You're drinking too much," I said curtly. "A man can't bloat himself with liquor up here and remain alive as well, Betts. He can't—"

"*Can't!*" he bellowed. "You and the rest of the fools in this country make a bloody creed out of that word. Can't do this; can't do that. They told me I can't grow rubber in the Ituri district. Well, by God, I've got the concession and I'm going to!"

I shrugged. If he wished to kill himself with native poison, that was his affair. But I thought of his girl-wife—slim, flower-faced, and so very lovely. I pitied her from the bottom of my heart.

It would be the inevitable conclusion. He would drink himself semi-insane. The rain would beat into his mind and drive out reason. He would turn on Lucilia, make life a living hell for her. From the momentary glance I had already had of her troubled face, it was evident that the process had already begun.

"Look here," I began curtly. "You've got to send your wife out of this. You've no right to keep her here and—"

The door opened behind me. I turned quickly, to see Njo, the house-boy, scuffling toward me. He had returned from the village. He had a message for me. Bending over, he delivered it in a whisper.

"Kodagi says, *Bwana*," he muttered, "that he will come and he thanks you. He says that you are his friend, but the red-eyed white man had better beware. That is all, *Bwana*."

Njo stepped back and vanished. With tight-pressed lips I turned back to Betts.

"There is danger here," I said grimly. "You have no right to expose your wife to it."

"No? You're gettin' pretty damned interested in her, ain't you?"

"I am doing what you are too drunk to do!" I snapped, choking back my temper. It was an effort, just then, to keep from taking his thick throat between my fingers and twisting some sense into him.

"If it's so almighty dangerous," he leered, "what are *you* stayin' here for then?"

"Because the danger does not concern me. I don't kick witch-doctors, Betts. I don't shoot at white apes. I make a point of minding my own business."

"Well?"

"My predecessor was a man of your type, Betts. He did about as he pleased. He died very slowly and unpleasantly—and mysteriously."

My words had no effect. Betts lumbered to his feet, swaying unsteadily, and grinned down at me.

"You're worse than the niggers with your damned superstitions," he scoffed. "Me—I'm hard-headed and sensible. I'm goin' to finish what I started."

"You refuse to send Lucilia—"

"She stays right here with me. I got to have some one to pour drinks for me, Varicks. She ain't much good for anythin' else, but she'll learn."

"Have you—" I began, then caught myself. My question was too delicate.

"Wot?"

"Have you been married long?"

"About a month," he grumbled, turning away. "That's all—about a month. I'm thinkin' it was a mistake. But I reckon she'll learn. I'll teach her."

Then he groped down the steps and staggered away into the darkness.

I saw him many times after that. He was continually under the effect of liquor, and he came to me bragging and boasting about the progress he was making. Already he had repaired his huts to withstand the hammering rain.

Already he had made preparations for planting his latex-producing shrubs and vines.

His wife seldom accompanied him when he came to visit me. At first I could not understand this; but then, one night when she did come with him, I knew the reason. She was ashamed.

Her lovely throat bore indelible marks of finger-prints. Her left cheek, pallid and colourless, was scratched with a livid red welt, where he had either struck her or raked her with his fingernails. Yet, even though we met by chance occasionally when he was not about, she refrained from mentioning these things to me.

Then one night Betts said to me quizzically:

"I been lookin' at a big clearin' about a quarter of a mile back in the jungle, Varicks. What in hell is the tower affair in the middle of it?"

I knew what he meant. He had stumbled upon a wide amphitheatre far from the village proper, where members of the secret cult of the Bakanzenzi, according to whispered rumours, were supposed to meet. As for the tower, it was a solid pillar of gleaming white stone, somewhat squat and encircled by a platform at the top, which rose, like a thing of another world, from the reeds of the clearing.

During my four months' stay in Kodagi's village, I had examined this tower many times. It was not hollow, but solid and thick; and the stones had evidently been brought from a great distance, since I could find no others like them in the surrounding district. It is my belief—and I am sure that the belief is no idle supposition—that this tower was built many hundreds of years ago by the Phoenicians.

There are many such towers scattered throughout Africa's gloomy interior. They were originally erected to the Phoenician goddess, Astarte—but now, naturally enough, they are sacred to native gods and exponents of black magic and *mafui*.

I explained this, as best I could, to the man who sat before me. He shrugged at the mention of Astarte; he sneered when I spoke of *mafui*.

"What is this Bakanzenzi of yours?" he grinned.

"What is it?" I said quietly. "I am not sure, Betts. For that matter, no white man is ever sure of the secret cults. The Bakanzenzi are cannibals, who are said to be able to transform themselves into animals at certain times. Kodagi has told me that the tower-glade is sacred to the Bakanzenzi. They hold their rites by the old white tower. The walls of the glade are made up of twisted, writhing-limbed oki-trees, said to be magic. According to Kodagi, the penalty for disturbing the sacred amphitheatre is death—horrible and certain."

"Rot," Betts grunted. "You're an old woman, Varicks."

"I have lived in these jungles long enough to be careful," I said simply.

"Yeah? Well, I've been here long enough to know that the glade is good planting-ground. Tomorrow I'm diggin' up the ground around the white tower and plantin' it with rubber vines. Tell *that* to your blasted Bakanzenzi!"

I argued with him. He told me curtly that the ground came within his jurisdiction and he intended to do as he pleased. Moreover, he did it. The following day he put his entire gang of blacks to work, planting the glade of Astarte with indigenous rubber plants and vines. He drove the natives brutally; and while they did his work for him, he sprawled in the shadow of the tower and swilled rotten whisky into his stomach.

●

That night his wife came to my shack alone. We sat inside, out of the chill, moisture-ridden air; and I saw, as she leaned close to me in the glow of the lamp, that fresh marks of brutality were livid on her face and neck.

"I—I am afraid," she whispered tensely. "He is drinking more than ever. He has whipped some of our black boys until they can hardly walk!"

"He has also—beaten you?" I suggested softly.

She turned her face away. A dull line of crimson crept about her throat and rose higher. Reaching out, I took her hand and held it.

"There is bound to be trouble," I said bitterly. "You say he has beaten the natives—and yet no natives have come to me with complaints. That is ominous. They would ordinarily bring their troubles to me, since I am in charge. This silence means that they intend to settle the score on their own account."

"You—you can do nothing?"

"I will do my best. Kodagi is coming here tomorrow, to have his wounds re-dressed. He was kicked brutally, severely. I am afraid there are internal injuries."

Lucilia's hand slipped unconsciously to her own side. She winced and stifled an exclamation of pain as her fingers touched some hidden bruise. I knew then that Betts had used his heavy boots on more than Kodagi; and a sullen rage found its way into my heart. God—if I ever *caught* him kicking her!

"Does he know you are here?" I said suddenly.

"No," she said, shaking her head heavily. "He—he has taken to going into the bush at night—alone. I do not know where he goes. He is always drunk—savage. I dare not question him."

My fists clenched. I saw that she was crying softly, and drew her close to me so that her head rested on my shoulder.

"Why does he hate you, Lucilia?" I pleaded.

"Because—because he is drunk. And because he is jealous of you. You are all that he would like to be. Clean—strong—"

"If I were strong in courage," I said bitterly, "I would take you away from him."

She raised her face slowly, almost entreatingly.

"I—wish you would—Lyle," she whispered.

Then I caught myself. She was his wife; I was a civilised white man, in spite of our surroundings. I could kill him—and would kill him—if I found him mistreating her. But I could not make love to her, in spite of my emotions. There was a difference between protection and theft.

I walked back with her, through the rain. The hut where she lived was empty. Betts had not returned. I whispered farewell to her and returned, with slow steps and heavy heart, to my own dreary shanty on the other side of the village.

Kodagi came the next afternoon, limping painfully and supporting himself on the shoulders of two of the Zapo Zaps. I dressed his wounds with infinite care. Then, thinking to insure his friendship, I led him and his two henchmen into the rear room of the shanty. There I gave them presents of cigarettes and other valueless odds and ends which might catch their fancy. In addition, I allowed them to peer through the high-powered microscope which stood on the table—a thing which had always excited their curiosity in the past.

Kodagi bent over the instrument for many minutes, finally stepping aside to make room for one of his companions. He grinned at me gratefully. I attempted, then, to explain the secret of it to him.

"You see," I said, "the high-powered lenses make things seem larger than they really are and—"

The door slammed open behind me, drowning my words. I swung about, ready for any kind of emergency in view of what had already occurred. I found myself face to face with Betts, who stood swaying in the doorway.

He was savagely drunk—more drunk than I had ever before seen him. He lunged toward me with both hands outflung, snarling like an animal.

"So you're here, are you!" he rasped. "You—"

The curse was not pleasant. It was a livid torrent of abuse and epithet.

"What do you want?" I said crisply. Kodagi and his men had stepped away from the table and were watching me intently.

"You know damned well what I want!" he bellowed. "My wife comes here when I'm away in the jungle, does she? You and her—"

There was but one answer possible. I seized his arms and flung him away from me.

"You're drunk!" I said curtly. "If you say another word—by God, Betts, you're not fit to live with a woman. If you don't stop your infernal drinking and quit beating the natives, I'll have you sent back to the coast. You—you scum!"

He caromed across the floor like a top-heavy bullock. For thirty seconds he stared at me; and the utter hate and jealousy in his face must have been visible even to Kodagi and the Zapo Zaps. Then, with a burning oath, he clawed at the revolver in his belt.

He was drunk enough to have killed me. Luckily his fingers were clumsy, slippery with sweat. Before he could get the thing free and level it, I was upon him. My fist ground into his mouth. He jerked erect under the impetus of the blow; then, groping for support with lifeless fingers, he slumped to the floor unconscious.

Kodagi and the two natives faded silently through the open doorway. They said nothing; they departed like ghosts. I was left alone with the limp thing on the floor.

For a moment I stood stiff by the table, undecided whether to leave him there or to make some attempt to revive him. Then I considered that after all he had been drunk; he had not known what he was doing. I dropped to my knees beside him and wiped the blood from his face.

Someone else entered the shack then. I heard the veranda door open and close, and hesitant steps crossed the outer room. I glanced up to find Lucilia standing above me, on the threshold.

"You—you have killed him?" she whispered tensely.

"No. He would have killed me."

A soft, choking exclamation came from her pale lips. She stared into Betts' face; and as she did so, the renegade's eyes twitched open.

We were silent, all three of us, for a long moment. Presently Betts groped to his feet and stood confronting us. A sneer curled his mouth.

"I suppose you're damned glad," he said gutturally, turning to his wife, "that Varicks did for me."

"Yes," she said simply. "I am."

"Yeah?" he snarled. "Well, by God, I'll change *that* before I'm done!"

He turned heavily, without a word to me, and lurched over the sill. I heard him stagger through the outer room. The veranda door thudded. Lucilia and I were alone.

"Why did you come here?" I shrugged. "You know it brings his madness to the surface."

"I had to come, Lyle. When he left me, he was insane. He—he might have killed you."

She seized my arm passionately. Her face was ghastly white.

"I'm afraid of him, Lyle!" she said fervently. "He—he is becoming an animal. At the slightest sound, he turns with horrible quickness to stare behind him, like a thing of the jungle. He walks on tiptoe and talks in a whisper when we are alone. When he thinks I am not looking, he mutters to himself and claws at the empty air, as if bats were fighting him."

"Vampire bats," I said aloud, without meaning to utter the words.

"What?" she said suddenly.

"Nothing," I mumbled. "You had better go back. It is not safe for you to excite his temper. If anything happens, come to me at once."

"I wish—oh, I wish I could stay here with you!"

"So do I," I said sincerely. "But it's impossible."

She walked out with dragging steps. I could read the anguish in her stooped shoulders and hanging head. But I could do nothing, then. I could only stare, and let her go.

When she had gone, I made an attempt to be rational. For an hour I worked over my case of entomological specimens, labelling them and separating them into their proper groups. But my mind was not on the work. My thoughts persisted in returning to her description of Betts' mysterious behaviour.

I have studied medicine to some extent; and I knew that a medical diagnosis of Betts' malady was simple enough and completely devoid of mystery. The man had delirium tremens. He was on the verge of madness, brought on by an excess of native rum and bad whisky. And yet when I considered old Kodagi's sudden disappearance in that first hour of torment—when I considered the tower of Astarte and the horrible cult of the Bakanzenzi—I knew that the medical explanation was not complete. Other things—unknown, unnamed things of darkness and the jungle—had taken possession.

An hour dragged on. It was nearly midnight when I heard the door of my shanty clatter open. I turned from the specimen table with both of my arms uplifted to defend myself—and then my arms dropped helplessly as Lucilia stumbled into the room.

"He is gone!" she said sibilantly.

"Gone?" I repeated. "Where?"

"He was in the house when I returned. I heard him pacing back and forth in his own room, mumbling and talking to himself. I sat on the stoop and waited—waited for him to come out and—and beat me. I must have fallen asleep—from exhaustion. When I awoke, the shack was abandoned. He has gone into the jungle again, Lyle!"

I stood rigid, undecided what to do. She came closer and stared pitifully into my face.

"Lyle," she whispered, "his—his clothes are thrown on the bunk where he sleeps. He—he must be naked!"

"In the jungle—*naked?*" I said roughly. "Good God, no!"

"It is true, Lyle. He is an animal. He—"

But I thrust her aside. This ghastly affair had reached its climax, and I was determined to settle it once and for all.

"Stay here," I ordered crisply. "I intend to find him."

She slumped into a chair. I threw a coat about my shoulders and strode into the outer room, where Njo was asleep upon his bunk in the corner. I prodded him to consciousness and swore at him because he sat like a monkey on the edge of the bunk, blinking at me in bewilderment. Then, with the little Jopaluo trailing at my heels, I stepped into the night.

The clearing lay in nearly complete darkness. For once, the rain had ceased its monotonous drizzle; and the jungle was buried under a steaming mist. The sky was greyish black, void of stars. The moon, hanging in the middle of it like a blurred lantern, was blood-red.

We went straight to Betts' hut. There, with the aid of the search-lamp in my clenched fist, we found the man's spoor leading from the rear door—and the prints were those of naked feet! It was not difficult to trail that curious line of tracks into the jungle.

For twenty minutes we continued, following a well-beaten path through the jungle. In this manner we came to that significant grove in the midst of the great trees, where the gleaming tower of Astarte stuck up from the reeds like a white tooth.

And there, at the base of the tower, we found a continuation of Betts' naked footprints. Round and round the tower they went—a circular, deep-beaten path of fresh imprints made by naked feet. And there they ended.

Confused, bewildered, not at all sure of my own sanity, I led the way back to my own shanty. For a long time I talked to Lucilia of what I had seen; and finally, mastering the fear of her heart, she returned to her hut. Far into the night I sat on the veranda of my place, smoking and waiting and wondering. It was the night before the full moon.

In the morning, Betts came to me cursing. He made no mention of the previous night. He was blind with rage because many of the euphorbias, which he had brought all the way from Madagascar and planted in the grove, had been uprooted. He demanded that I find the culprit.

I could do nothing, and I told him so. Still cursing, he slunk into the jungle. I heard no more from him during the hours of daylight. Nor did I hear from Lucilia, who, for the sake of her own safety, refrained from coming near me. But when night came, and the moon swung into a sky of pitch, the village chief made a visit to my shanty and stood before me on the veranda.

"I come, *Bwana*," he said bitterly, "for justice. The red-eyed white man has done murder. He has killed two of the men who worked for him."

I did not bother to ask useless questions. My position of *chef de poste* demanded that I do one thing—and one thing only. Strapping a revolver holster about my belt, I went directly to Betts' abode.

His wife opened the door to me and stared at me in consternation. She must have read the anger in my face, for I confess that I made no attempt to conceal it. Betts himself sat slumped in a chair close to the table.

I accused him outright of murdering two of the blacks. He lurched to his feet and snarled into my mouth.

"Why wouldn't I?" he rasped. "They were pullin' up my rubber plants in the grove. I caught 'em at it! By God, I'll murder the whole bloody tribe if they don't leave my plants alone!"

"You're under arrest!" I snapped. "This is my village. I won't stand for—" He moved with such uncanny quickness that I could not prevent it. His fist hammered into my eyes, hurling me into the wall. I heard Lucilia scream as I went down. I saw Betts, running with tremendous speed and agility, swirl across the threshold and race into the jungle. Staggering up, I wiped the blood from my face and plunged after him. The jungle closed over me.

I had no flash-lamp this time. There was nothing to light the trail. The moon above the trees was full and vivid, but here it was blotted out completely by interlaced branches and creepers. I stumbled headlong, plunging into unseen thickets and strangling vines. For half an hour I groped through the bush, stopping at intervals to listen for sounds of the fugitive. Once I heard a scream—a woman's scream. At that moment I did not realise the hellish portent of it, and so I continued to fight my way forward.

Then it came. I had no defense against it, since it fell upon me from behind. As I faltered in the darkness, the underbrush broke apart behind me. I heard a sudden terrifying suck of breath. Then something—God, I cannot force myself to call it human!—something hideously powerful, stark naked, reeking with the stench of liquor, crushed me into the dank floor of the jungle. A white arm lashed about my throat. I was lifted bodily and flung over a sweat-soaked shoulder. At terrific speed I was borne through the jungle. Overhanging vines tore at my face and beat against me, filling my eyes with blood. I believe I lost consciousness.

What happened from then on is a blur of agony. I felt the naked form beneath me heaving and panting as it raced on and on through the pitch. Then the jungle opened wide and a gleaming white glare, from the moon above, blinded me. I was carried another hundred steps, then flung to the ground. When my eyes opened, staring through a mask of blood, I found myself bound hand and foot with reed ropes and lying in a contorted position at the foot of that mysterious, curious tower of Astarte, in the centre of the forbidden amphitheatre of the Bakanzenzi!

Something stirred beside me. I jerked myself about fearfully, expecting anything. My eyes went wide in horror. There, flung brutally against the stone not two yards away from me, and moaning with the pain of the reeds that cut into her wrists and ankles, lay Lucilia. I can see her face a hundred times over, so deeply was it engraved with fear!

I could say nothing. My mouth welled with blood; my lips were thick and swollen. Dumbly I stared out into the clearing. The moon, hanging very low over the great ceiba silk-cotton trees and borassus palms at the rim of the amphitheatre, had not yet swung deep enough to illuminate the tower. The entire centre of the clearing lay in mottled blackness, masking the tower in shadow.

But we were not alone. Out there, half hidden in the gloom, a huge white shape inhabited the shadows with us. I could see it lumbering around the tower, mumbling and wailing to itself in a guttural voice that rose, at sudden intervals, into a screaming chant. In a mad circle it rushed, and as it hurtled past in front of me I saw something more—a jet-black bat-shape flapping and fluttering about its head. I saw the flame of fireflies swirling.

Terror came to me then. I shrank close to the girl beside me, and I was mortally afraid. The thing out there was Betts. I *knew* it was Betts. Yet the thought brought no consolation, for the creature was a stark naked raving madman in the grip of some weird occult power beyond my comprehension.

I stared into Lucilia's eyes.

"How—how did you come here?" I choked. "Did he—"

"He came back as soon as you had gone, Lyle! He was naked, mad! He seized me—carried me here—"

Something in her voice gave me courage, because I knew that she needed me. It was a strange time to think of love; and yet I knew, at that moment, that I loved her, that she loved me in return. This ordeal had thrown us together and made us realise the truth.

I lifted my head then and shouted to the terrible thing that lumbered about us.

"Betts!" I screamed. "Betts! Get hold of yourself, man. You're mad!"

The naked thing stopped in its tracks and laughed hideously. I saw it point to the rising moon. Behind it, at the edge of the jungle, I thought I saw the massive underbrush sway and rustle with a significant, peculiar movement, as if a horde of unseen things lay in wait there. Then, chattering frantically, the horrible mad thing continued its ceaseless circle.

Once again fear gripped me. I stared with unblinking eyes, waiting and wondering what the end would be. Somehow I knew that Betts was not alone. The Bakanzenzi—the dreaded cult which held its rites in this clearing at the height of the full moon—were somewhere about, only waiting until the moon-white should reach the sacred tower.

Then, at my feet, a shaft of moonlight fell upon the base of the column. The great white shape stopped its prowling and stepped full into the glow. I saw every detail of Betts' unclad form—a terrible naked figure covered with self-inflicted cuts and slashes.

He approached with short, jerky steps, flinging his arms wildly.

"Betts!" I shouted. "For God's sake—"

He ignored me. In a shrill, screeching voice he began to speak, turning his bloody head in all directions as if he were addressing some immense gathering. The man was gripped with some tremendous power of hallucination. He saw things which did not exist—or perhaps they *did* exist and were beyond my human perceptions!

"The time has come!" he muttered. "The moon has risen to the sacred tower. The unbelievers must die, as it was ordained by the Goddess of the Tower! The time—is—now!"

He flung himself forward. I saw his arm lunge up. The pallid white light gleamed on the blade of a horribly long knife clenched in his fist. I closed my eyes with a shudder. Lucilia, pressed close against me, moaned softly and tried to take my hand.

But Betts did not reach us. A furious burst of sound stopped him in his tracks. From all sides of the tower it came—the wild, thunderous beat of drums. It rose out of the jungle like the hammering of rain on a tent-top, deafening in its intensity. At the same moment a hairy arm, stark white and gleaming in the moonlight, twisted about my waist from behind and lifted me from the base of the tower. A sudden stench of rancid flesh came over me, strong enough to be nauseating. I felt myself carried, at a curious lumbering, rolling gait, through the high reeds to the jungle rim. There, in the protecting shadow of the borassus palms, I was flung down. Lucilia Betts was tossed beside me; and when I regained my senses long enough to stare about me, the monstrous hairy creature had vanished. Vanished just as Kodagi had vanished from the mud of the village floor!

Then it began in earnest.

The drums took up a wild reverberation. There was no steady beat; merely a continuous roar of noise emanating out of nothing. Betts, adding his voice to the tumult, had dropped his knife and was once more lumbering round and round the white tower, trotting with the shifting gait of a great gorilla. Beyond him, all about him, I saw native forms, glistening black in the glare of the moon. Like ants they were, crouching in the reeds; and their faces were hidden behind triangular black masks of carved wood—the sign of the Bakanzenzi!

They watched Betts with a hungry stare, as if waiting for something. He saw them. His even, rolling stride became a peculiar jumping, hopping gait, altogether erratic. But still he moved in the same mad circle!

There could be no more horror—so I thought. The only thing that kept me from going insane was the touch of Lucilia's hands on my manacled arms. Then her voice screamed beside me.

"The tower! Oh—God! Look!"

She shrank against me, trembling. But my eyes were riveted to the top of the tower, open wide in the culmination of horror. There, peering down at Betts with savage lust, hung a face—a hideous face, white and hairy and huge, with drooling fangs that glistened in the light. An ape's face—a white ape of enormous size, larger than the gorillas of the Kivu country!

The thing dropped down behind Betts. It followed him in his

route about the tower, trotting clumsily behind him and making no attempt to close the intervening distance. Then Lucilia screamed again; and I saw another of those horrible white shapes appear in the top of the tower, to drop down and join in the procession. One after another they came, as if by magic, to leap into the rushing circle of monstrosities headed by Betts. When I finally closed my eyes, overcome by the horror of it, more than a score of them had joined the ring.

I think then that the moon-glow struck the tip of the tower, as a signal. A peculiar vibrating chant rose all about me, rising and falling like a tide of water. A dozen scattered fires leaped into being about the clearing, as if they had been waiting for some hidden sign. The light was blinding, bewildering. It roared and flickered and threw great blotches of sparks into the vivid sky. The Bakanzenzi were dancing—dancing and screaming and hammering on their infernal drums.

And suddenly the natives were no longer there—no longer before me. In their place appeared creatures of the jungle. I saw leopards swirling in the reeds; great rock pythons coiled in the glare of the fires, filling the night with their hissing voices; crocodiles thrashing about with open jaws; bush-pigs racing madly! The terrible lingas and dinwinti drums roared faster and faster.

Lucilia fainted then. I pressed her close to me and stared in horror. The great apes were rumbling, hammering upon their chests as they lumbered about the tower. Their fanged mouths were open, dripping saliva. And Betts was no longer leading them in the ritual—he was racing at top speed, as fast as his sweating legs would carry him, to *escape!* His voice rose in a tortured screech, full of terror. He raised his arms to the moon, blubbering in torment.

I could not close my eyes. Every detail of that mad scene burned into my brain. The fires, already burning and waiting for their cannibalistic offering—the jungle creatures writhing and leaping about the flames—the great apes of the tower closing in on their victim with relentless certainty. God!

Then they caught him. I heard a heart-rending scream that rose in livid crescendo and was smothered at its peak. Then came a mighty crash of sound, a deafening bellow; and the giant *mafui* apes dragged their victim down. I fainted.

When I opened my eyes again, I peered into the frightened face of Njo, my house-boy. I lay on the veranda of my own shanty, in the village of Kodagi, and Lucilia Betts lay ten feet distant from me, sprawled pitifully on the stoop. Njo was struggling faithfully to pour brandy between my clenched teeth.

"Who—who brought me here?" I said thickly, gripping his arm.

The Jopaluo peered into my face and shuddered.

"You were here, *Bwana*," he whispered fearfully. "I found both of you here at daylight, when the screams of leopards and the dinwinti drums awakened me."

I could get no more out of him, in spite of my questioning. That was his story—he had found us there on the veranda at daylight.

When I had recovered strength I left him to care for Lucilia, while I stumbled back through the jungle to the clearing of the Bakanzenzi. I was determined to know the truth.

The amphitheatre was deserted. At the base of the tower I found stains of blood and many, many footprints—*human* footprints. Side by side in the muddy ground I found two other things of mystery. One was a crescent-shaped disk of mother-of-pearl—the ancient symbol of Astarte. The other, half buried in the mud, was a gold seal ring bearing Betts' initials—and inside it, curled maliciously and staring up at me with cloudy gold eyes, lay a tiny green whip-snake—the symbol of the Bakanzenzi.

On my way back to the shanty, I made a visit to the hut of old Kodagi, for the purpose of asking him a single significant question. Quietly I pushed aside the reed mat that hung over the entrance; and Kodagi was sitting there on the floor, blinking at me.

"Do you know," I said simply, squatting beside him, "where Betts is?"

He peered into my face for a long time. A wealth of uncanny wisdom and knowledge was engraved in his parchment features at that particular moment. "Last night, *Bwana*," he shrugged, "I heard the screams of the leopards and the victory cries of the great apes. It is possible that Betts was torn by the big cats—or killed by a wandering tribe of gorillas from the Kivu."

"Apes—" I muttered. "It was an ape who carried Lucilia and me to safety under the borassus palms. An ape—"

"Perhaps, *Bwana*," Kodagi said softly, "the ape was your friend. Perhaps he saved you because you were kind to him, healing his wounds and letting him peer through your magic instruments and—"

My head came up with a jerk.

"What?" I snapped.

"Nothing, *Bwana*. I was talking to myself. I always talk to myself when it is raining, *Bwana*—and you see for yourself it is raining again."

And so I left him. And tonight, now that the ordeal is finished, I find myself unable to sleep. I am sitting here with pencil and paper in the inner room of my shanty, with the flickering lamplight playing over my shrunken face. Lucilia has gone to her own hut, with Njo to keep guard over her until morning. Then she and I, together, will depart from this strange village and leave behind us, for ever, the domain of the Bakanzenzi and the hideous region of *mafui*. We shall be married at the mission of the white fathers in the village of Bugani, twenty miles down-river, and from there we shall go directly to the coast.

There I shall make my report to the government, and in it I shall say that Betts was devoured by leopards. But Lucilia and I—and old Kodagi, who squats for ever on the floor of his hut and is wiser by far than any of us—we know better.

THE MAZE OF MAÂL DWEB

Clark Ashton Smith

In his suspenseful tale of terror from the pages of *Weird Tales*, this master of super-natural horror recounts the Tiglari's assault upon the lair of the despot Maâl Dweb. There is a reason why no one has ever survived an attack on the tyrant king.

By the light of the four small waning moons of Xiccarph, Tiglari had crossed that bottomless swamp wherein no reptile dwelt and no dragon descended; but where the pitch-black ooze was alive with incessant heavings. He had not cared to use the high causey of corundum that spanned the fen, and had threaded his way with much peril from isle to sedgy isle that shuddered gelatinously beneath him. When he reached the solid shore and the shelter of the palm-tall rushes, he did not approach the porphyry stairs that wound skyward through giddy chasms and along glassy scarps to the house of Maâl Dweb. The causey and the stairs were guarded by the silent, colossal automatons of Maâl Dweb, whose arms ended in long crescent blades of tempered steel which were raised in implacable scything against any who came thither without their master's permission.

Tiglari's naked body was smeared with the juice of a plant repugnant to all the fauna of Xiccarph. By virtue of this he hoped to pass unharmed the ferocious ape-like creatures that roamed at will through the tyrant's cliff-hung gardens. He carried a coil of woven root-fibre, strong and light, and weighted with a brazen ball, for use in climbing the mesa. At his side, in a sheath of chimera-skin, he wore a needle-sharp knife that had been dipped in the poison of winged vipers.

Many, before Tiglari, with the same noble dream of tyrannicide, had attempted to cross the fen and scale the scarps. But none had returned; and the fate of such as had won to the palace of Maâl Dweb was a much-disputed problem. But Tiglari, the skilled jungle hunter, was undeterred by the hideous dubieties before him.

That escalade would have been an improbable feat by the full light of the three suns of Xiccarph. With eyes keen as those of some night-flying pterodactyl, Tiglari hurled his weighted coil about narrow coigns and salients. He climbed with simian ease from foothold to foothold; and at length he gained a little buttress beneath the last cliff. From this vantage it was easy to fling his rope around a crooked tree that leaned gulfward with scimitar-like foliage from the gardens.

Evading the sharp, semi-metallic leaves that slashed downward as the tree bent limberly with his weight, he stood, stooping warily, on the fearsome and fabled mesa. Here, it was said, with no human aid, the half-demoniac sorcerer had carved a mountain's pinnacles into walls, domes and turrets, and had leveled the rest of the mountain to a flat space about them. This space he had covered with loamy soil, produced by magic; and therein he had planted curious baneful trees from outlying worlds, together with flowers that might have been those of some exuberant hell.

Little enough was known of these gardens; but the flora that grew upon the northern, southern and western sides of the palace was believed to be less deadly than that which faced the dawning of the three suns. Much of this latter vegetation, according to myth, had been trained and topiarized in the form of a labyrinth, balefully ingenious, that concealed atrocious traps and unknown dooms.

Mindful of this labyrinth, Tiglari had approached the palace on the side toward the sunset.

Breathless from his climb, he crouched in the garden shadows. About him heavy-hooded blossoms leaned in venomous languor, or fawned with open mouths that exhaled a narcotic perfume or diffused a pollen of madness. Anomalous, multiform, with silhouettes that curdled the blood or touched the mind with nightmare, the trees of Maâl Dweb appeared to gather and conspire against him. Some arose with the sinuous towering of plumed pythons, of aigretted dragons. Others crouched with radiating limbs like the hairy members of giant spiders. They seemed to close in upon Tiglari. They waved their frightful darts of thorn, their scythe-like leaves. They blotted the four moons with webs of arabesque menace.

With endless caution the hunter made his way forward, seeking a rift in the monstrous hedge. His faculties, ever alert, were quickened still more by fear and hatred. The fear was not for himself but for the girl Athlé, his beloved and the fairest of his tribe, who had gone up alone that evening by the causey of corundum and the porphyry stairs, at the summons of Maâl Dweb. His hatred was that of an outraged lover for the all-powerful, all-dreaded tyrant whom no man had ever seen, and from whose abode no woman ever came back; who spoke with an iron voice audible in far cities or outmost jungles; who punished the disobedient with a doom of falling fire swifter than the thunderstone.

Maâl Dweb had taken ever the fairest from among the maidens of the planet Xiccarph; and no mansion of the walled towns, or outland cave, was exempt from his scrutiny. He had chosen no less than fifty girls during the period of his tyranny; and these, forsaking their lovers and kinsfolk voluntarily, lest the wrath of Maâl Dweb should descend upon them, had gone one by one to the mountain citadel and were lost behind its cryptic walls. There, as the odalisques of the ageing sorcerer, they were supposed to dwell in halls that multiplied their beauty with a thousand mirrors; and were said to have for servants women of brass and men of iron.

Tiglari had poured before Athlé his uncouth adoration and the spoils of the chase, but having many rivals, was unsure of her favor. Cool as a river-lily, she had accepted inpartially his worship and that of the others, among whom the warrior Mocair was perhaps the most formidable. Returning from the hunt, Tiglari had found the tribe in lamentation; and learning that Athlé had departed to the harem of Maâl Dweh, was swift to follow. He had not told his intention to anyone, since the ears of Maâl Dweb were everywhere; and he did not know whether Mocair or any of the others had preceded him in his desperate errantry. But it was not unlikely that Mocair had already dared the obscure and hideous perils of the mountain.

The thought of this was enough to drive Tiglari forward with a rash disregard of the clutching foliations and reptile flowers. He came to a gap in the horrible grove, and saw the saffron lights from the sorcerer's windows. The lights were vigilant as dragons' eyes, and appeared to regard him with an evil awareness. But Tiglari leapt toward them, across the gap, and heard the clash of sabered leaves meeting behind him.

Before him was an open lawn, covered with a queer grass that squirmed like innumerable worms under his feet. He did not care to linger upon that lawn. There were no footmarks in the grass; but, nearing the palace portico, he saw a coil of thin rope that someone had flung aside, and surmised that Mocair had preceded him.

There were paths of mottled marble about the palace, and fountains that played from the throats of carven monsters. The open portals were unguarded, and the whole building was still as a mausoleum lit by windless lamps. Tiglari, however, mistrusted this appearance of quietude and slumber, and followed the bordering paths for some distance before daring to approach nearer to the palace.

Certain large and shadowy animals, which he took for the apish monsters of Maâl Dweb, went by him in the gloom. Some of them ran in four-footed fashion, while others maintained the half-erect posture of anthropoids; but all were hairy and uncouth. They did not offer to molest Tiglari; but, whining dismally, they slunk away as if to avoid him. By this token he knew that they were actual beasts, and could not abide the odor with which he had smeared his limbs and torso.

At length he came to a lampless, column-crowded portico; and, gliding silently as a jungle snake, he entered the mysterious house of Maâl Dweb. A door stood open behind the dark pillars; and beyond the door he discerned the dim reaches of an empty hall.

Tiglari went in with redoubled caution, and began to follow the arrased wall. The place was full of unknown perfumes, languorous and somnolent: a subtle reek as of censers in hidden alcoves of love. He did not like the perfumes; and the silence troubled him more and more. It seemed to him that the darkness was thick with unheard breathings, was alive with invisible movements.

Slowly, like the opening of great yellow eyes, yellow flames arose in lamps of copper along the hall. Tiglari hid himself behind an arras; and peering forth presently, he saw that the hall was still deserted. Finally he dared to resume his progress. All around him the rich hangings, broidered with purple men and blue women on a field of blood, appeared to stir with uneasy life in a wind he could not feel. But there was no sign of the presence of Maâl Dweb or his metal servitors and human odalisques.

The doors on either side of the hall, with cunningly mated valves of ebony and ivory, were all closed. At the far end Tiglari saw a thin rift of light in a somber double arras. Parting the arras very slowly, he peered through into a huge, brilliantly lit chamber that seemed to be the harem of Maâl Dweb, peopled with all the girls that the enchanter had summoned to his dwelling. It seemed, in fact, that there were hundreds, leaning or lying on ornate couches, or standing in attitudes of languor or terror. Tiglari discerned in the throng the women of Ommu-Zain, whose flesh is whiter than desert salt; the slim girls of Uthmai, who are moulded from breathing, palpitating jet; the queenly topaz girls of equatorial Xala; and the small women of Ilap, who have the tones of newly greening bronze. But among them all he could not find the lotus-like beauty of Athlé.

Much he marvelled at the number of the women and the perfect stillness with which they maintained their various postures. They were like goddesses that slept in some enchanted hall of eternity. Tiglari, the intrepid hunter, was awed and frightened. These women—if indeed they were women and not mere statues—were surely the thralls of a death-like spell. Here, indeed, was proof of the sorcery of Maâl Dweb.

However, if Tiglari were to continue his search, he must traverse that enchanted chamber. Feeling that a marble sleep might descend upon him at the crossing of the sill, he went in with held breath and furtive leopard-like paces. About him the women preserved their eternal stillness. Each, it seemed, had been overcome by the spell at the instant of same particular emotion, whether of fear, wonder, curiosity, vanity, weariness, anger or voluptuousness. Their number was fewer than he had supposed; and the room itself was smaller: but metal mirrors, panelling the walls, had created an illusion of multitude and immensity.

At the further end he parted a second double arras, and peered into a twilight chamber illumined dimly by two censers that gave forth a parti-colored glow. The censers stood on tripods, facing each other. Between them, beneath a canopy of some dark and smouldering stuff with hinges braided like women's hair, was a couch of night-deep purples bordered with silver birds that fought against golden snakes.

On the couch, in sober garments, a man reclined as if weary or asleep. The man's face was dim with ever-wavering shadows; but it did not occur to Tiglari that this was any other than the redoubtable tyrant whom he had come to slay. He knew that this was Maâl Dweb, whom no man had seen in the flesh but whose power was manifest to all: the occult, omniscient ruler of Xiccarph; the suzerain of the three suns and of all their planets and moons.

Like ghostly sentinels, the symbols of the grandeur of Maâl Dweb, the images of his frightful empire, rose up to confront Tiglari. But the thought of Athlé was a red mist that blotted all. He forgot his eerie terrors, his awe of that wizard palace. The rage of the bereaved lover, the blood-thirst of the cunning hunter, awoke within him. He neared the unconscious sorcerer; and his hand tightened on the hilt of the needle-sharp knife that had been dipped in viper-venom.

The man before him lay with closed eyes and a cryptic weariness on his mouth and eyelids. He seemed to meditate rather than sleep, like one who wanders in a maze of distant memories or profound reveries. About him the walls were draped with funereal hangings, darkly figured. Above him the twin censers wrought a cloudly glow, and diffused throughout the room their drowsy myrrh, which made Tiglari's senses swim with a strange dimness.

Crouching tiger-wise, he made ready for the stroke. Then, mastering the subtle vertigo of the perfume, he rose up; and his arm, with the darting movement of some heavy but supple adder, struck fiercely at the tyrant's heart.

It was as if he had tried to pierce a wall of stone. In midair, before and above the recumbent enchanter, the knife clashed on some unseen, impenetrable substance; and the point broke off and tinkled on the floor at Tiglari's feet. Uncomprehending, baffled, he peered at the being whom he had sought to slay. Maâl Dweb had not stirred nor opened his eyes; but his look of enigmatic weariness was somehow touched with a faint and cruel amusement.

Tiglari put out his hand to verify a curious notion that had occurred to him. Even as he had suspected, there was no couch or canopy between the censers—only a vertical, unbroken, highly polished surface in which the couch and its occupant were apparently reflected. But, to his further mystification, he himself was not visible in the mirror.

He whirled about, thinking that Maâl Dweb must be somewhere in the room. Even as he turned, the funereal draperies rushed back with a silken, evil whispering from the walls, as if drawn by unseen hands. The chamber leapt into sudden glaring light; the walls appeared to recede illimitably; and naked giants whose umber-brown limbs and torsos glistened as if smeared with ointment, stood in menacing postures on every side. Their eyes glowered like those of jungle creatures; and each of them held an enormous knife, from which the point had been broken.

This, thought Tiglari, was a fearsome thaumaturgy; and he crouched down, wary as a trapped animal, to await the assault of the giants. But these beings, crouching simultaneously, mimicked his every movement. It came to him that what he saw was his own reflection, multiplied in the mirrors.

He turned again. The tasselled canopy, the couch of night-dark purples, the reclining dreamer, had vanished. Only the censers remained, rearing before a glassy wall that gave back like the others the reflection of Tiglari himself.

Baffled and terrified, he felt that Maâl Dweb, the all-seeing, all-potent magician, was playing a game and was deluding him with elaborate mockeries. Rashly indeed had Tiglari pitted his simple brawn and forest craft against a being capable of such demoniac artifice. He dared not stir, he scarcely ventured to breathe. The monstrous reflections appeared to watch him like giants guarding a captive pigmy. The light, which streamed as if from hidden lamps in the mirrors, took on a more pitiless and alarming luster. The reaches of the room seemed to deepen; and far away in their shadows he saw the gathering of vapors with human faces that melted and re-formed incessantly and were never twice the same.

Ever the weird radiance brightened; ever the mist of faces, like a hell-born smoke, dissolved and relimned itself behind the immobile giants, in the lengthening vistas. How long Tiglari waited, he could not tell: the bright frozen horror of that room was a thing apart from time.

Now, in the lit air, a voice began to speak; a voice that was toneless, deliberate, and disembodied. It was faintly contemptuous; a little weary, slightly cruel. It was near as the beating of Tiglari's heart—and yet infinitely far.

"What do you seek, Tiglari?" said the voice. "Do you think to enter with impunity the palace of Maâl Dweb? Others—many others, with the same intentions—have come before you. But all have paid a price for their temerity."

"I seek the maiden Athlé," said Tiglari. "What have you done with her?"

"Athlé is very beautiful," returned the voice. "It is the will of Maâl Dweb to make a certain use of her loveliness. The use is not one that should concern a hunter of wild beasts....You are unwise, Tiglari."

"Where is Athlé?" persisted the hunter,

"She has gone to find her fate in the labyrinth of Maâl Dweb. Not long ago, the warrior Mocair, who had followed her to my palace, went out at my suggestion to pursue his search amid the threadless windings of that never-to-be-exhausted maze. Go now, Tiglari, and seek her also. There are many mysteries in my labyrinth; and among them, perhaps, is one which you are destined to solve."

A door had opened in the mirror-panelled wall. Emerging as if from the mirrors, two of the metal slaves of Maâl Dweb had appeared. Taller than living men, and gleaming from head to foot with implacable lusters as of burnished swords, they came forward upon Tiglari. The right arm of each was handed with a great sickle. Hastily, the hunter went out through the opened door, and heard behind him the surly clash of its meeting valves.

The short night of the planet Xiccarph was not yet over; and the moons had all gone down. But Tiglari saw before him the beginning of the fabled maze, illumined by glowing globular fruits that hung lantern-wise from arches of foliage. Guided only by their light, he entered the labyrinth.

At first, it was a place of elfin fantasies. There were quaint paths, pillared with antic trees, latticed with drolly peering faces of extravagant orchids, that led the seeker to hidden, surprising bowers of goblinry. It was as if those outer mazes had been planned wholly to entice and beguile.

Then, by vague degrees, it seemed that the designer's mood had darkened, had become more ominous and baleful. The trees that lined the way with their twisted, intertwining boles were Laocoöns of struggle and torture, lit by enormous fungi that seemed to lift unholy tapers. The path ran downward to eerie pools alight with wreathing witch-fires, or climbed with evilly tilted steps through caverns of close-set leafage that shone like brazen dragon-scales. It divided at every turn; the branching multiplied; and skilled though he was in jungle-craft, it would have been impossible for Tiglari to retrace his wanderings. He kept on, hoping that chance would somehow lead him to Athlé; and many times he called her name aloud but was answered only by remote, derisive echoes or by the dolorous howling of some unseen beast.

Now he was mounting through arbors of malignant hydra growths that coiled and uncoiled tumultuously about him. The way lightened more and more; the night-shining fruits and blossoms were pale and sickly as the dying tapers of a witches' revel. The earliest of the three suns had risen; and its gamboge-yellow beams were filtering in through the frilled and venomous vines.

Far off, and seeming to fall from some hidden height in the maze before him, he heard a chorus of brazen voices that were like articulate bells. He could not distinguish the words; but the accents were those of a solemn announcement, fraught with portentous finality. They ceased; and there was no sound other than the hiss and rustle of swaying plants.

It seemed now, as Tiglari went on, that his every step was predestined. He was no longer free to choose his way; for many of the paths were overgrown by things that he did not care to face; and others were blocked by horrid portcullises of cacti, or ended in pools that teemed with leeches larger than tunnies. The second and third suns arose, heightening with their emerald and carmine rays the horror of the strange web closing ineluctably about him.

He climbed on by stairs that reptilian vines had taken, and gradients lined with tossing, clashing aloes. Rarely could he see the reaches below, or the levels toward which he was tending. Somewhere on the blind path he met one of the ape-like animals of Maâl Dweb: a dark, savage creature, sleek and glistening like a wet otter, as if it bathed in one of the pools. It passed him with a hoarse growl, recoiling as the others had done from his repulsively smeared body.... But nowhere could he find the maiden Athlé, or the warrior Mocair, who had preceded him into the maze.

Now he came to a curious little pavement of onyx, oblong, and surrounded by enormous flowers with bronze-like stems and great leaning bells that might have been the mouths of chimeras, yawning to disclose their crimson throats. He stepped forward upon the pavement through a narrow gap in this singular hedge, and stood staring irresolutely at the serried blooms: for here the way seemed to end.

The onyx beneath his feet was wet with some unknown, sticky fluid. A quick sense of peril stirred within him, and he turned to retrace his steps. At his first movement toward the opening through which he had entered, a long tendril like a wire of bronze uncoiled with lightning rapidity from the base of each of the flower sterns, and closed about his ankles. He stood trapped and helpless at the center of a taut net. Then, while he struggled impotently, the stems began to lean and tilt toward him, till the red mouths of their blossoms were close about his knees like a circle of fawning monsters.

Nearer they came, almost touching him. From their lips a clear, hueless liquid, dripping slowly at first, and then running in little rills, descended on his feet and ankles and shanks. Indescribably, his flesh crawled beneath it; then there was a passing numbness; then a furious stinging like the bites of innumerable insects. Between the crowding heads of the flowers, he saw that his legs had undergone a mysterious and horrifying change. Their natural hairiness had thickened, had assumed a shaggy pile like the fur of apes; the shanks themselves had somehow shortened and the feet had grown longer, with uncouth finger-like toes such as were possessed by the animals of Maâl Dweb.

In a frenzy of nameless alarm, he drew his broken-tipped knife and began to slash at the flowers. It was as if he had assailed the armored heads of dragons, or had struck at ringing bells of iron. The blade snapped at the hilt. Then the blossoms, lifting hideously, were leaning about his waist, were laving his hips and thighs in their thin, evil slaver.

With the senses of one who drowns in nightmare, he heard the startled cry of a woman. Above the tilted flowers he beheld a strange scene which the hitherto impenetrable maze, parting as if by magic, had revealed. Fifty feet away, on the same level as the onyx pavement, there stood an elliptic dais of moon-white stone at whose center the maiden Athlé, emerging from the labyrinth on a raised porphyry walk, had paused in an attitude of wonder. Before her, in the claws of an immense marble lizard that reared above the dais, a round mirror of steely metal was held upright. Athlé, as if fascinated by some strange vision, was peering into the disk. Midway between the pavement and the dais, a row of slender brazen columns rose at broad intervals, topped with graven heads like demoniac Termini.

Tiglari would have called out to Athlé. But at that moment she took a single step toward the mirror, as if drawn by something that she saw in its depths; and the dull disk seemed to brighten with some internal, incandescent flame. The hunter's eyes were blinded by the spiky rays that leapt forth from it for an instant, enveloping and transfixing the maiden. When the dimness cleared away in whirling blots of color, he saw that Athlé, in a pose of statuesque rigidity, was still regarding the mirror with startled eyes. She had not moved; the wonder was frozen on her face; and it came to Tiglari that she was like the women who slept an enchanted slumber in the harem of Maâl Dweb. Even as this thought occurred to him, he heard a ringing chorus of metallic voices that seemed to emanate from the graven demon heads of the columns.

"The maiden Athlé," announced the voices in solemn and portentous tones, "has beheld herself in the mirror of Eternity, and has passed beyond the changes and corruptions of Time."

Tiglari felt as if he were sinking into some obscure and terrible fen. He could comprehend nothing of what had befallen Athlé; and his own fate was an equally dark and dreadful enigma, beyond the solution of a simple hunter.

Now the blossoms had lifted about his shoulders, were laving his arms, his body. Beneath their abhorrent alchemy the transformation continued. A long fur sprang up on the thickening torso; the arms lengthened; they became simian; the hands took on a likeness to the feet. From the neck downward, Tiglari differed in no wise from the apish creatures of the garden.

In helpless abject horror, he waited for the completion of the metamorphosis. Then he became aware that a man in sober garments, with eyes and mouth filled with the weariness of strange things, was standing before him. Behind the man were two of the sickle-handed iron automatons.

In a somewhat languid voice, the man uttered an unknown word that vibrated in the air with prolonged, mysterious aftertones. The circle of craning flowers drew back from Tiglari, resuming their former upright positions in a close hedge; and the wiry tendrils were withdrawn from his ankles. Hardly able to comprehend his release, he heard a sound of brazen voices, and knew dimly that the demon heads of the columns had spoken, saying:

"The hunter Tiglari has been laved in the nectar of the blossoms of primordial life, and has become in all ways, *from the neck downward*, even as the beasts that he hunted."

When the chorus ceased, the weary man in sober raiment came nearer and addressed him:

"I, Maâl Dweb, had planned to deal with you precisely as I dealt with Mocair and many others. Mocair was the beast that you met in the labyrinth, with new-made fur still sleek and wet from the liquor of the flowers; and you saw some of his predcecssors about the palace. However, I find that my whims are not always the same. You, Tiglari, unlike the others, shall at least remain a man from the neck upward; you are free to resume your wanderings in the labyrinth, and escape from it if you can. I do not wish to see you again, and my clemency springs from another reason than esteem for your kind. Go now: the maze has many windings which you are yet to traverse."

A great awe was upon Tiglari; his native fierceness, his savage volition, were tamed by the enchanter's languid will. With one backward look of concern and wonder at Athlé, he withdrew obediently, slouching like a huge ape. His fur glistening wetly to the three suns, he vanished amid the labyrinth.

Maâl Dweb, attended by his metal slaves, went over to the figure of Athlé, which still regarded the mirror with astonished eyes.

"Mong Lut," he said, addressing by name the nearer of the two automatons at his heels, "it has been, as you know, my caprice to eternalize the frail beauty of women. Athlé, like the others before her, has explored my ingenious maze, and has looked into that mirror whose sudden radiance turns the flesh to a stone fairer than marble and no less enduring.... Also, as you know, it has been my whim to turn men into beasts with the copious fluid of certain artificial flowers, so that their outer semblance should conform more strictly to their inner nature. Is it not well, Mong Lut, that I have done these things? Am I not Maâl Dweb, in whom all knowledge and all power reside?"

"Yea, master," echoed the automaton. "You are Maâl Dweb, the all-wise, the all-powerful, and it is well that you have done these things."

"However," continued Maâl Dweb, "the repetition of even the most remarkable thaumaturgies can grow tiresome after a certain number of times. I do not think that I shall deal again in this fashion with any woman, or deal thus with any man. Is it not well, Mong Lut, that I should vary my sorceries in future? Am I not Maâl Dweb, the all-resourceful?"

"Indeed, you are Maâl Dweb," agreed the automaton, "and it would no doubt be well for you to diversify your enchantments."

Maâl Dweb was not ill pleased with the answers that the automaton had given. He cared little for converse, other than the iron echoing of his metal servitors, who assented always to all that he said, and spared him the tedium of arguments. And it may have been that there were times when he wearied a little even of this, and preferred the silence of the petrified women, or the muteness of the beasts that could no longer call themselves men.

QUIDQUID VOLUERIS

Gustave Flaubert
Translated by Gio Clairval

Immersed within the insensitive racial-stereotyping that dominated the early Victorian era, the sixteen-year-old Flaubert successfully presaged the future of horror when he penned this grotesque tale in 1837. The forced mating of an orangutan with a Brazilian female slave as part of a cruel interspecies experiment leads to the tragic story of the resulting hybrid's life.

I

Memories of sleepless nights, come to me! Come to me, my wretched, foolish dreams. Come one, come all, my good friends the imps. You who jump on my feet at night, who run across my window panes and up over my ceiling; you, purple, green, yellow, black, white, with great wings and long beards; you who rattle my walls and the irons on my door. Under your breath the lamp shivers and pales as your greenish lips blow it out.

I see you, more often than not, creeping quietly through pale winter nights, vested in greatcoats that stand out, brown against the snowy rooftops, with your little heads as bony as skulls. You come through my keyhole, and each one of you warms up its long nails at my fireplace, which still diffuses mild warmth.

Come all, spawn of my brain, lend me some of your craziness, let me use your strange dreams. Your presence will spare me a preface in the fashion of the Moderns or an invocation to the muse in the Ancients' tradition.

II

"Tell us the tale of your trip to Brazil, my dear friend," Mrs. de Lansac asked her cousin Paul. "It will entertain Adele." In fact Adele was a nonchalant pretty blond who hung on her cousin's arm while walking the paths across the park. Mr. Paul answered: "But why, my aunt, my trip was delightful, I assure you."

"You already said so."

"Ah!" he said.

And then he said nothing.

The walkers' silence lasted a long time, each walking without being aware of the other. One plucked the petals of a rose, the other churned the sand of the path with his shoes, and the third watched the moon, which appeared bright and calm through the intertwined branches of the great elms.

The moon, again! But surely the moon must play some major role in this story! It is the sine qua non of every lugubrious piece, like teeth clattering and hair standing on end. At any rate, on this day, there was a moon.

Why take it away from me? O my moon, I love you! You shine gracefully over the castle's steep rooftops. You turn the lake into a stretch of silver, and under your pale light every drop of rain that falls, every drop, I say, that hangs from a rose petal is like a pearl on a beautiful woman's breast. Those are old memories! But let's end this digression and go back to our story.

Still, in her affected nonchalance, in her dreamy relaxed attitude, this tall girl whose figure bent gracefully over her cousin's arm held something languorous and flirty about her, as in those pretty white teeth that appeared briefly through her smile, in this blond hair framing with ample curls her pale and lovely face, in all of this there was a fragrance of love that raised a delightful sensation in the soul.

She was not a vibrant Mediterranean beauty, not one of those girls from the South with eyes alit like a volcano, full of burning passion. Her eyes were not black, her skin did not have the velvety touch of an Andalusian complexion, but it had a vaporous and mystical quality, like the Scandinavian faeries with alabaster necks who stand bare-footed in the mountain snow, and who appear on lovely starry nights on the shores of torrents, light and ephemeral, to the bards who sing their love songs.

Her gaze was blue and moist, her complexion pale. She was one of those girls born with gastritis, who drink water, who tap on a noisy piano some music from Liszt, who love poetry, wistful daydreaming, melancholic love, and who have fragile stomachs. She loved... whom? Her swans sliding on the pond, her monkeys cracking the nuts slipped through the bars of their cage by her pretty white hand, and also her birds, squirrels, the flowers in the park, her beautiful books with golden spines, and...her cousin, her childhood friend, Mr. Paul, who had long black whiskers, who was tall and strong, and whom she was supposed to marry in a fortnight.

You could be sure that she would be happy with such a husband. He was a most sensible man, and I include in that category all those who do not love poetry, who have a strong stomach and a dry heart, essential qualities to live a hundred years and be wealthy. A sensible man is a man who knows how to live without ever paying his debts, how to taste a fine glass of wine, who enjoys the love of a woman like a shirt to wear for a while and then throw away, along with the worn old feelings that have gone out of fashion.

"Indeed," would he reply, "what is love? A silly thing of which I take advantage. And tenderness? Stupidity, the geometricians said, and I have none for anyone. And poetry? Does poetry prove anything? And so I stay away from it. And religion? Homeland?

Art? Nonsense and twaddle. As for the soul, long ago Cabanis and Bichat demonstrated that the veins reach the heart, and voilà." Paul was a sensible man, one that was respected and honored, for he was a member of the Home Guard; he dressed like everyone else, talked morality and philanthropy, voted for the railways and the abolition of brothels. He would have a castle, a wife, a son who would become a notary and a daughter who would marry a chemist. If you had met him at the Opera, you would have seen that he wore spectacles and a black coat, carried a cane and took mints to cover the smell of cigars, and never tackled a pipe because it was so horrid, so unfashionable!

Paul had no wife yet, but he would take one, without love, and for the reason that this marriage would double his fortune and he only needed to make a simple calculation to view that he would be fifty thousand a year richer. In college he was good at mathematics. As for literature, he had always thought it stupid.

The walk lasted for a long time, in silent contemplation of the beautiful blue night that enveloped the trees, the grove, the pond under azure mist pierced by the moonlight as if gauze had been draped on the landscape. The three walkers didn't return to the parlor until after eleven. Candles twinkled and a few roses had fallen from the mahogany planter to lie on the polished floor, pell-mell, petals scattered and trampled underfoot.

Who cared! There were so many of them!

Adele felt her satin shoes moistened with dew. She had a headache and fell asleep on the sofa, one arm hanging loosely, the hand resting on the floor.

Madame de Lansac had left to instruct the servants for the following day and lock all the doors. Only Paul and Djalioh remained. The first looked at the gilded candelabra as the bronze clock struck twelve with silvery tones, and he gazed at Pape's piano, the tables, the chairs, a table with a white marble top, the upholstered sofa. And then he went to the window and peered at the thickest corner of the park.

"Tomorrow at four there will be rabbits."

As for Djalioh, he watched the sleeping girl. He wanted to say something, but the single word he uttered came out so soft, so timorous that Paul took it for a sigh.

One word or a sigh, it did not matter. But he had put his entire soul in it.

III

The next day, in fact, by a beautiful sunrise, the hunter went out with his favorite greyhound bitch, his two basset hounds and the gamekeeper, who carried an ample game bag containing powder, bullets, lead, other stuff needed for hunting, and a huge block of Pâté of Duck Foie Gras that our bridegroom had ordered for himself two days before. The huntsman blew the horn, and they advanced rapidly across the plain.

On the second-floor window, a green sliding shutter opened and a head of long blond hair appeared through the jasmine that climbed the wall and lined the castle's red and white bricks with its foliage. She was wearing a negligee, or at least you would have suspected so by the hair flowing freely, her relaxed pose and her unfastened shirt hemmed with muslin, cut low at the shoulders and with sleeves that reached only the elbows. Her arms—round, white, fleshy— she grazed against the walls as she hastily opened the window to glimpse Paul. She waved and blew him a kiss. Paul turned around, after letting his gaze linger on the young girl's head, so young and pure among the flowers, after thinking that all this would soon be his: the flowers, the girl, and the love these things offered. "She is nice!" he said.

Then a white hand closed the canopy, the clock struck four, the rooster began to crow, and a sunbeam punching through the bower darted over the slate rooftop. All was silent and calm.

At ten o'clock, Mr. Paul had not yet returned. The lunch bell rang, and everyone but he took place at table. The room was high and spacious, furnished in the Louis XV style. Over the fireplace could be seen, half-obliterated by dust, a pastoral scene: a much-powdered shepherdess covered in black-velvet beauty spots, with baskets on her arms, sitting among her white sheep. Cupid fluttered above her, and a pretty pug lay at her feet, curled on an embroidered cloth sporting a bouquet of roses tied with a thread of gold. From the cornices hung pigeon eggs strung together and painted white with green spots.

The wall panels were painted a tired white and decorated with a few family portraits, colored pictures of landscapes representing views of Norway and Russia, snowy mountains, harvest and grape picking. Farther on the wall hung prints framed in black: the full-length portrait of a president of the parliament in ermine furs and classical powdered wig with three looped curls sewn on each side; a German rider on the back of a prancing horse whose tail, thick and braided, rippled in the air like snake coils; some pictures of the Flemish school with its music-hall scenes, bawdy figures bloated with beer painted among clouds of tobacco smoke, joyful atmosphere, big naked boobs, huge laughter on thick lips and the frank materialism that prevails from the child whose curly head is plunged in a mug of wine. Finally, the fleshy shape of the Blessed Virgin sits in her niche blackened by the smoke, while beside her, the tall and wide windows let a bright light into the apartment, despite the old-fashioned furniture, lending the place a certain freshness, thanks also to two marble fountains at either end of the room and the black and white tiles on the floor. But the main piece of furniture, the one that attracted the eye most, was a huge sofa, very old, very smooth, very soft, all bedecked in bright colors: green, yellow, with birds of paradise and bouquets of flowers sprinkled lavishly on white satin. Surely, after the servants had removed the remains of supper, the chatelaine of old time used to sit on those satin cushions. The poor woman waited for *Monsieur le*

Chevalier, who arrived discretely for a drink, because by chance he was thirsty. Yes, certainly more than a pretty Marquise used to sit on that sofa, a great Countess wearing ankle-short skirts, a pink-skinned woman with tiny pretty hands and tightly fastened bodice, sitting and listening to the sweet words that many a philosopher and atheistic friendly abbot put in amid a conversation about the feelings and needs of the soul. Yes, many little sighs, tears and stolen kisses happened on that sofa.

And all this had gone! Marquises, abbots, knights, the gentlemen's words, all had vanished, everything had sunk and fled, the kissing, the love, the tender emotions, the seduction of red heels. The sofa remained in place on its four mahogany feet, but the wood was rotten and the gold trimming had tarnished.

Djalioh sat next to Adele. She pouted and pushed back her chair, blushed and hurriedly poured herself some wine. Her neighbor had nothing agreeable about him. He had been with Paul in the castle for an entire month and had not yet spoken; therefore some thought him strange and unpredictable. Melancholic, said others. Stupid, mad, dumb, the wisest said. In Madame de Lansac's home, everyone believed him Paul's friend, a funny friend, according to everyone. He was short, thin and frail. Only his hands announced some strength in his person. He had squat, flat fingers with strong, half-hooked nails. As for the rest of his body, it looked so weak and feeble, it had such a sad and languid coloring, one would have moaned at the sight of this man still young that seemed born on the brink of the grave, like a young tree that grows twisted and leafless. His clothing, all black, made his coppery-yellow complexion even more livid. His lips were large and only half covered two rows of long white teeth, like those of apes and Negroes. As for his head, it was narrow and compressed at the front, but behind it reached a prodigious size: this deformity was visible because his thinning hair did not hide his wrinkled pate.

There was a weird air about him that spoke of savagery and bestiality, which made him resemble some fantastic animal rather than a human being. His eyes were round, large, of a dull yellow, but when this man's leaden gaze weighed upon you, you couldn't help but feel a strange fascination. Still, he had no harsh or fierce features; he smiled at every attention, although his smiles were stupid and cold.

Had he opened the shirt that covered his thick, black skin, you would have beheld a large, hairy chest which seemed that of an athlete, as it contained huge lungs that breathed comfortably within.

Oh! His heart was too vast and immense, but vast like the sea, as vast and empty as his solitude. Often, in the presence of forests, high mountains, the ocean, his brow smoothed out, his nostrils flared violently, and his whole soul expanded in front of Nature like a rose that blooms in the sun, and he trembled in every limb under the weight of an inner delight as he took his head between his hands and fell into a lethargic melancholy. At that very moment, I say, his soul shone through his body, like the beautiful eyes of a woman behind a black veil. Because his figure was so ugly, so hideous, sallow and sickly, his skull shrunken, his limbs stunted, when he took on such an air of happiness and enthusiasm, such fire and passion lighting up those ugly apish eyes, he seemed shaken by some violent galvanism of the soul. Passion in him had to be fury, and love could only be frenzy. The fibers of his heart were softer and louder than those of other people; in him, pain was converted into convulsive spasms of secret pleasure and joy.

His youth was fresh and pure: he was seventeen years old, or rather he was sixty, one hundred years, centuries. He was old and broken, worn and battered by the winds of the heart through all the storms of the soul. Ask the ocean how many wrinkles it wears on its forehead; count the waves in a tempest!

He had lived for a long time, long ago, not by the thought—the meditations of the learned or their dreams had not taken one moment in his life—but he had lived and aged in his soul, and he was already old by the heart.

Still, his affections had turned on no one because there was in him turmoil of the strangest sentiments, confusion of the strangest sensations. Poetry had dethroned logic, and passion had taken the place of science. Sometimes he thought he heard voices speaking to him behind a rose bush and melodies that fell from the heavens; nature possessed him in all its aspects: delight of the soul, burning passion, gluttonous appetite.

It was the sum of a great moral and physical weakness, with a vehemence of the heart but a fragile core that broke before each obstacle, like the senseless lightning bolt that destroys a palace, burns tiaras, cuts down the humble cottages and dies in a puddle.

This was the freak of nature that lived with Paul, who was a monster, too, or rather was a marvel of civilization, a marvel that possessed all the symbols pertaining to greatness of the mind and dryness of the heart. When Paul found little interest in the outpourings of the soul and the sweet talks of the heart, Djalioh loved the dreams of the night and the slumber of reason. His soul attached itself to all things beautiful and sublime: like ivy clings to ruins, flowers to spring, bodies to tombs, woes to men, his soul clung to beautiful things and died with them. Where intelligence found its boundaries, the heart reigned. He was immense and infinite because he understood the world through his love. Therefore he loved Adele. But above everything else, he loved her as he loved Nature, with a gentle and universal sympathy, and then his love for her gradually increased as his tenderness for every other being decreased.

Indeed we are all born with a certain amount of tenderness and love that we throw away merrily on the first things we encounter: horses, places, honors, thrones, women, sensual pleasures, and what else? We throw our love to the winds, to any current. But let us gather all this love, and we will have an immense treasure. Sprinkle tons of gold nuggets on the surface of the desert: the sand will soon swallow them up, but put the chunks of gold all together, in a heap, and you will shape a pyramid. Likewise, Djalioh concentrated all his soul on a single thought, and that thought nourished his life.

IV

The fatal fortnight had passed as a long wait for the girl, and one of cold indifference for her future husband.

The girl saw in the marriage a husband, cashmeres to buy, an opera box, horse racing in the *Bois de Boulogne*, balls all winter long, oh! as many as she liked! And then again everything a girl of eighteen dreams of in her golden dreams in her closed alcove.

The husband instead saw in the marriage a woman, and cashmeres for which he would have to pay, a little doll to dress, and then again everything a poor husband dreams of as he leads his wife to the ball. That man, however, was conceited enough to believe all women were in love with him.

In fact, he addressed the question to himself whenever he looked at his reflection in the mirror and when he had well combed his black whiskers. He would take a wife because he was bored of being alone and he did not want to keep a mistress, since he had discovered that his butler had one. Also, marriage would force him to stay at home and his health would be better for it: he would have an excuse not to go hunting, since hunting bored him, and finally, he needed a wife for the best of all reasons: he would have love, devotion, domestic happiness, tranquility, children...bah! much better than these, he would have fifty thousand a year in good farms, pretty bank notes that he could place in Spain. He had been to Paris, had bought an opera box for ten thousand francs, sent one hundred and twenty invitations to the ball, and returned to his stepmother's castle, all in eight days. He was a wonderful man.

It was a Sunday in September when the wedding took place. The day was damp and cold. A thick fog hung over the valley. The sand of the garden clung to the ladies' new shoes. Mass being said at ten o'clock, few people were attending. Djalioh allowed himself to be pushed inside by the flow of villagers. Incense burned upon the altar. The air was warm and scented. The church was low, old, small, smeared with white; a smart heritage curator had spared the stained-glass windows. Around the choir stood the guests: the mayor, his council, friends, the lawyer, a doctor, and the singers in white surplices. All wore white gloves and a serene air. Each fished out of his purse a five-franc piece. The silvery sound falling on the platter interrupted the monotony of the church songs. The bell rang.

Djalioh remembered having heard the bell sing over a coffin one day. He'd also seen people dressed in black pray over a dead body. And then, with his eyes on the bride in white as she bowed over the altar, with flowers on her dress and a triple string of pearls around her bare, arching neck, a horrible thought froze him. He staggered and leant against a niche that once harbored a saint (only the face remained, and it was grotesque and horrible to look upon).

Next to Adele, there he was, he, her beloved, and she looked so indulgently at him, at his big blue eyes underneath black eyebrows. His eyes shone like two diamonds set in ebony. Through tortoise-shell glasses inlaid with gold he peered at all the women as he waddled on his crimson velvet chair.

Djalioh stood motionless and silent. No one noticed the pallor of his face and the bitterness of his smile because they believed him cold and removed as the stone monster grimacing behind him, but in reality a storm reigned in his soul and anger simmered in his heart, like the volcanoes of Iceland under their heads whitened by snow. It was not a sudden violent frenzy: it was an inner turmoil without cries, without tears, without profanities, without effort. He remained silent and his eyes spoke no more than his lips. His eyes were lead, his face stupid.

Young and pretty women have a fresh, smooth, satin-white skin for many years, and then they languish, their eyes lose their bright-ness, become dull, close forever in the end, and then the lithe and graceful woman who used to run across the salons with flowers in her hair, whose hands were so fair, who smelled like musk and rose, well! One day, a friend, maybe a doctor, tells you that, two inches lower than her cleavage, she had cancer in her lung and she died, that her skin is now as fresh as the skin of a corpse. This is the story of all the intimate passions, of all frozen smiles.

The curse that mars love laughs horribly. Stifling the pain is a greater torture. Do not believe in smiles, joy and mirth. What must we believe?... Believe in tombs: their sanctuary is inviolable and they offer a dreamless slumber.

What an abyss opens under our feet when we hear the word "forever"! Think for a moment about the meaning of these words: life, death, despair, joy, happiness. Ask yourself, the day when you cry over some loved one and moan at night on a pallet strewn with insomnia, ask yourself why we live, why we die, and for what purpose. A wind of misfortune and despair. We are grains of sand that ride the hurricane. What is this hydra that feeds on our tears and delights in our unhappiness? What is this all about?... And then your head spins, and you feel dragged into the boundless abyss, at the bottom of which resounds an enormous, pulsating, mad laughter.

There are things in life and ideas in the soul that draw you inevitably to the satanic worlds, as though your head were made of iron and a magnet for misfortune dragged you there. Oh! a skull! Its hollow and fixed orbits, the yellow color of its surface, its chipped jaw, would death then be reality, and would truth lie in nothingness only?

It is in this bottomless pit of doubt and pain that Djalioh had lost himself. Seeing the festive ambience, these smiling faces, seeing Adele, his love, his life, the charm of her countenance, the sweetness of her gaze, he wondered why he was denied all this: like a person sentenced to death and left to starve while iron bars separated him from the food that could save his life.

He did not know why that feeling was different from any other, because if someone in sunny America had come to ask him to share a palm tree's shade, or a fruit of his garden, he would gladly have offered everything. Why, he asked himself, is the love I have for her so exclusive and intractable? It must be that love is a world, and unity is indivisible. And then he bowed his head on his chest and wept silently, like a child.

Only once a hoarse cry escaped him, piercing as that of an owl, but it mingled with the soft, melodious voice of the organ playing the Te Deum. The sounds, pure and rich, rose and reverberated across the nave along with the incense...

He realized then that the guests were whispering and moving the chairs, and as they rose, a sunbeam fingered through the windows, gleaming on the golden bow in the bride's hair, and for a few moments the sun shone on the gilded bars of the cemetery, the only land between the town hall and the church. The grass is very green in cemeteries, high, thick and well fertilized. The guests' feet were soaked through, their white stockings and shining shoes soiled so that they hurled oaths at the dead.

The mayor had taken position, standing on top of a square table covered with green cloth. When the moment came to pronounce the fatal "I will," Paul smiled, Adele turned pale, and Mrs. de Lansac pulled out her smelling salts. Adele then thought about what had just happened—the poor girl could not believe it. She who, only a few moments before, had been so excited, so pensive, running across the meadows, reading novels, poetry, tales, riding her gray mare down the paths of the forest, she who loved to hear the rustling of leaves, the murmur of streams, she had suddenly become a lady, that is to say something that has a large shawl, and goes alone in the streets! All these vague presentiments, these intimate emotions of the heart, this need for poetry, for sensations that made her dream about the future, about herself. Everything would be explained, she thought, as if she had just woken from a dream! Alas! She didn't know that all the poor children of the heart and of the imagination are fated to be smothered in the cradle between domestic chores and caresses to be provided to a surly creature that has rheumatism and corns, and is called a husband.

When the crowd parted to let the procession pass, Adele felt a sudden pain, as if an iron claw had slit her hand. It was Djalioh who had scratched her with his nails as she passed. Her torn glove soaked red with blood, she wrapped a handkerchief around her hand. As she turned to enter her carriage, she saw Djalioh leaning against the step. A shudder seized her and she rushed into the car.

He was pale as the bride's dress. His thick lips, chapped and covered with cold sores, had moved as if he'd been speaking quickly. His eyelids twitched and his eyes rolled slowly in their sockets, like an idiot's eyes.

V

In the evening there was a ball at the castle and lanterns lit behind every window. A procession of carriages, horses and servants turned up at the gate.

From time to time one could see a light appear through the elms, drawing near, following miles of winding lanes until it stopped before the door: it was a carriage drawn by horses dripping sweat. The carriage door opened and a woman stepped down, and she was young or old, ugly or beautiful, dressed in pink or white, whatever you want, and then, after restoring the architecture of her hair by a few hastily applied strokes, she rushed into the hall. In the light of the lamps, and among the green trees and flowers and grass painted on the walls, she left her coat and boa in the lackeys' hands, and entered. They opened the double doors for her. She was announced, which produced a great noise of chairs and feet, guests rising, greeting her, and then ensued the thousand and one conversations, those little things, these charming trifles that buzz in salons and flutter from side to side as fog-light in a greenhouse.

The dancing began at ten o'clock, and inside one could hear shoes slide on the floor, the swishing of skirts, the sound of music, the rhythms of dance and, outside, the rustling of leaves, carriage wheels rolling over wet earth, swans flapping their wings on the pond; in the village there barked a dog at noises from the castle, and then arose a few naive and mocking remarks among peasants whose heads poked out through lounge windows.

In one corner of the salon was a group of young men, friends of Paul's, his former companions in debauchery, in yellow or azure gloves, with spectacles, tailcoats with swallow-tail, medieval heads and such beards as neither Rembrandt nor any painter of the Flemish school had ever dreamed of.

"Tell me, pray," said one of them, a member of the Jockey Club, "whose is that scowling face, wrinkled as an old saddle, which is behind the sofa where your wife is?"

"That one? That's Djalioh."

"Djalioh who?"

"Oh, it's quite a story."

"Do tell!" said one of the young men, whose hair was flattened and plastered on both ears, and who also had bad eyesight. "Since we have nothing to amuse us."

"Some punch at least?" replied a tall, thin, pale man with high cheekbones. "As for me, I won't have any, and for good reason... It's too much."

"Cigars?" said the Jockey Club member.

"Pooh! Cigars! What are you thinking, Ernest? In front of the women?"

"On the contrary, they are crazy about it. I have ten mistresses who smoke like dragons, including two who have seasoned all my pipes."

"I have one that drinks kirsch delightfully."

"Drink!" said a guest who liked neither cigars nor punch or dance or music. "No! Paul should tell his story."

"My dear friends, it's not a long story. Here it is. I bet with Mr. Petterwell, a friend of mine who is a planter in Brazil. I bet a bundle of Virginia against Mirsa, one of his slaves, that apes...yes, we can raise an ape, that is to say...he challenged me to pass an ape for a man."

"What? Djalioh is an ape?"

"Fool! No, he's not!"

"So what?"

"What I need to explain is that, during my trip to Brazil, I very much amused myself. Petterwell had recently acquired a black slave that had just disembarked from the old Bahamas Channel. I'm damned if I remember her name. Finally, this woman had no husband. The ridicule would befall no one. She was very pretty. I bought her from Petterwell; the fool never wanted to sleep with me. She probably thought I was uglier than a savage!"

All laughed. Paul blushed.

"Finally one day, as I was bored, I bought from a Negro the most beautiful orangutan I'd ever seen. The Academy of Sciences had been trying to solve a mystery for a long time: whether there might be a mongrel of monkey and man. I had to avenge myself on that little fool of a Negress, and so one day, upon my return from hunting, I found my ape, Bell, which I'd locked up in my room with the slave, escaped and gone, the slave in tears and all bloody from Bell's claws. A few weeks after she felt pains in the abdomen and nausea. Well! Finally, five months later, she vomited for several days. I was almost sure of my case. Once she had an attack of nerves so violent that she had to be bled at the four limbs, because I would have been distressed if she'd died. In short, after seven months, one day she gave birth on the manure. She died within hours, but the baby was doing beautifully. I was, well, glad that the scientific issue was resolved.

"I sent my report to the Institute, and the Minister, at their request, sent me the cross of honor."

"Never mind, my dear Paul. Everyone has it now."

"I wear it for a futile reason! Women like it: they look at it with a smile while you talk to them. Finally, I raised the child. I loved him like my own."

"Ah! ah!" said a gentleman who had white teeth and laughed all the time, "Why didn't you bring him to France in one of your other trips?"

"I preferred him to stay in his homeland until my final departure, especially since the age set by the bet was sixteen, because it was concluded the first year of my arrival in Janeiro. In short, I won Mirsa, I had the cross of honor when I was twenty and I had a child by unusual means."

"Infernal! Dantesque!" said a pale friend.

"Laughable! Funny!" said another who had fat cheeks and a ruddy complexion.

"Bravo!" said the horseman.

"I could die laughing!" said a small man, writhing with pleasure on an elastic sofa, leaping and wriggling like a fish. This one had a steep forehead, small eyes, flat nose, thin lips. He was round as an apple and fruiting like a mushroom: the trick Paul had just recounted was quite remarkable and only a master, never an ordinary man, would have pulled it off!

"Well, what does Djalioh do? Does he like cigars?" said the smoker, showing both hands full of cigars and dropping them on purpose on a lady's lap.

"Not at all, my dear, he abhors them."

"Does he hunt, then?"

"Even less. Gunshots scare him."

"Surely he works, he reads, he writes all day?"

"He would, if only he could read and write."

"Does he like horses?" asked the cripple.

"He does not."

"He's a quite inert and dull animal, then. Does he like sex?"

"One day I took him to see the girls, and he fled, after stealing a rose and a mirror."

"Decidedly, he's an idiot," everyone said. And the group went to smile and bow to the simpering ladies who, in the absence of dancers, had been yawning. It was getting late, the hours advancing at the rhythm of the music that bounced on the carpet, and time passed with the dance and the women. The clock struck midnight as everyone galloped. Since the beginning of the ball, Djalioh had been sitting on a chair, near the musicians. Now and then he left his place to change sides. If someone from the party, gay and carefree, happy with the noise, content with the wine—intoxicated by these women with half-bare breasts, smiling lips and soft eyes—glanced at him, he immediately became pale and sad. That's why his presence embarrassed everyone, as he stood out in the middle of the cheery ball like a ghost or a demon. Finally the dancers, tired, sat down. Everything then became quieter. The waiters served barley water, and the only noise was now the tinkling of glasses on the trays that interrupted the buzz of all the voices talking at the same time. The piano was open, a violin resting on it, and a bow beside. Djalioh grabbed the instrument, turned it in his hands several times like a child holding a toy and then he touched the bow and bent it so hard it nearly broke. Then he put the violin to his chin, and everybody laughed, as the music was wrong, weird, incoherent. Djalioh looked at all these men, these women, sitting, doubled over, spread out on benches, chairs, armchairs—he looked at them with big wondering eyes. He did not understand this sudden laughter and merriment. He continued playing.

The notes were initially slow, soft; the bow touched the strings and walked from the bridge to the tuning pegs hardly making any sound. Then gradually Djalioh's head came to life: he lowered it onto the neck of the violin; his forehead furrowed; his eyes closed as the bow leaped around across the strings like a rubber ball, with quick jumps. The music was choppy, full of high notes and heartrending cries. Upon hearing that music everyone fell into the grip of a terrible oppression, as if all these notes were made of lead and weighed on the chest. And then rained a string of bold arpeggios, notes that rumbled together and then flew off, octaves rising like Gothic spires, tumbling jumps, altered chords. And all these sounds, of strings and whistling notes without measure, without voices, no rhythm and no melody, stirred vague thoughts of runners who followed one upon the other like fleeting dreams of demons that fled pushed by others, in a restless whirlwind, constantly in a race. Djalioh gripped the neck of the instrument, and every time one of his fingers rose from the fingerboard, his nail made the string throb and the note whistle as it died. Sometimes he paused, startled by the noise, smiled stupidly and resumed the course of his reverie with more concentration, and finally, tired, he stopped and listened for a long time, to see if it would all come back. But nothing! The last vibration of the last note had died from exhaustion.

Everyone looked surprised to have endured that strange noise for so long. The dance resumed. As it was nearly three in the morning, one danced a cotillion. Only the young single women remained; the old ladies had left, along with the married, consumptive men. To make the waltzing easier, the waiters opened the parlor door, along with those leading to the billiard and the dining rooms, into a long suite. Each man grabbed his waltzing partner; they heard the cracked sound of the bow striking the desk and whirled about energetically.

Djalioh stood, leaning on a door panel as the waltz passed him by, whirling, noisy with laughter and joy. Whenever he saw Adele before him, twirl and then disappear, return, only to disappear again; every time he saw her lean on the arm that encircled her waist—she was tired with all the dancing and the excitement—he felt within him a demon shudder and a savage instinct roar in his soul, as a lion in its cage. Each time, at the same repeated measure, the same bow stroke, the same note, he saw the hem of a white dress with pink flowers, and two satin shoes that yawned a little as they whirled past him, and the dance lasted a long time, about twenty minutes. Then the music stopped. Oppressed, Adele wiped her brow, and then she resumed her dancing, lighter, bouncier, crazier and drunker than ever.

It was a hellish torment. It was the pain of the damned. What!

To feel in his chest all the strength it takes to love, to feel the soul burning like fire, and then not be able to turn off the volcano that consumes, to break the rope that binds. To be there, attached to a barren rock, throat parched, like Prometheus, to see a vulture upon your belly, ripping out your entrails, and still be unable to shake off the anger with both hands and crush it!

"Oh! why," wondered Djalioh in his bitter pain, head down, while the crazed waltz ran swirling, the women danced and the music vibrated and sang. "Why don't I like the happy dancing? Why am I ugly and these women are not? Why do they flee when I smile? Why should I suffer and be bored and hate myself? Oh! If I could take her, and then rip off all the clothes that cover her, and tear apart the veils which hide her, and then take her in my arms, carry her far away, across the woods, the meadows, the grasslands, across the seas, and finally arrive in the shade of a palm tree, and once there, look at her and make her look at me, too, make her seize me with her bare arms, and then...ah..." And he wept with rage.

The lights went out...the clock struck five. They heard a few carriages stop, and then the dancers donned their coats and left. The servants closed the shutters and went away. Djalioh had remained in his place, and when he looked up, everything was gone, women, dance and sounds. All had vanished, and the last light sparkled again in the few drops of oil that remained. At that moment dawn appeared on the horizon behind the lime trees.

VI

He took a candle and went upstairs. After removing his coat and his shoes, he jumped on his bed, lowered his head on his pillow and tried to sleep.

But he could not!

He heard an insistent buzzing in his head, a strange din, a weird music. Fever throbbed in his arteries, and the veins in his forehead were swollen and green. His blood boiled in his veins, rushed into his brain and choked him. He rose and opened the window. The fresh morning air calmed his senses. The day approached, the clouds and the moon fleeing with the first rays of light. As the night paled, he gazed at the thousand fantastic shapes the clouds drew in the sky, and then studied the disk of candlelight that illuminated his green-silk curtains.

After an hour or so he went out. The night was not completely over yet, and dew still hung on every leaf of the trees; quite much rain had fallen during the night, and the paths, driven by wheels, had swollen with mud; Djalioh plunged into the most tortuous and obscure of the paths. He took a long walk in the park, trampling the early autumn leaves, yellowed and carried away by the winds, walking on the wet grass, through the bower, to the rhythm of the rustling breeze that stirred the trees. He heard in the distance the first sounds of nature's awakening.

How sweet it is to dream this way, to listen with delight to your footsteps on fallen leaves and dead wood that cracks under your boots, to let yourself go freely down open paths like the current of reverie that carries your soul! And then a poignant and downhearted thought seizes you as you gaze at the falling leaves, as you listen to the trees groaning in the wind and nature singing sadly upon awakening, as if it were crawling out of its tomb. A dear face appears then in the shadows, your mother, or a friend, and the ghosts that brush against the black wall file on, severe in their white surplices. And then the past returns as well, another ghost, in the company of old sorrows, pains, tears and laughter, and finally the future, more vacillating and undefined, wrapped in a thin gauze like those long-dreamed sylphs that rise from a bush and fly away with the birds. We love to hear the wind passing through the trees, bending their tops, singing like a procession of specters, the wind whose breath tousles your hair and cools your burning forehead.

Djalioh wallowed in the most terrible thoughts. The dreamy

sort of melancholy, full of fancy and whim, oozes from the soul's lukewarm, chronic suffering, while pure despair is physical and acutely palpable. His pain came from reality that crushed his heart. Oh, reality! You are a ghost as heavy as a nightmare, yet you last for as long as the spirit perdures!

He didn't care for the past, as it was already lost, and what the future held for him was summed up in one meaningless word: death? But he had the present, this very minute, the moment that obsessed him. This was what he wanted to destroy, to crush under his foot or slaughter with his bare hands. When he thought of himself, poor and despairing, with empty hands, while the ball twirled with flowers and women, Adele and her half-bare breasts, her shoulders, her white hands—when he thought of all this, wild laughter burst from his mouth and bounced off his teeth like a hungry, dying tiger. In his mind's eye he saw Paul's smile, Paul kissing his wife. He saw the two of them lying on a silky bed, arms intertwined, sighs, cries of delight; he saw everything: the sheets twisted by their passionate embrace; flowers on the tables. He saw the rugs and the furniture and finally all that was there, and when he gazed back at himself, his own shape surrounded by the trees, walking alone on the grass and broken twigs, he trembled, and now he saw the immense distance that separated him from the couple, and when he came to wonder why it was so, an impassable barrier rose before him, and a black veil clouded his thoughts.

And he wondered why Adele was not his. Oh! If he had her, he would be so happy to hold her in his arms, rest his head on her chest, lay burning kisses on her breasts! And he cried and sobbed.

Oh! Had he known, as we men do, how to end a life that haunts you, a life fast gone with the trigger of a pistol. Had he known that six sous made a man happy, and that the river swallowed up the dead!...But no. Unhappiness was in the order of things. Nature gave us the consciousness of existence to keep our unhappiness alive for the longest time.

He soon reached the banks of the pond. Swans were playing

with their young, gliding on crystal water, wings spread and necks arched backwards, heads resting on their backs. The largest among them, male and female, swam together in the swift current of the small river that crossed the pond. From time to time they turned their white necks towards each other and exchanged glances while swimming, and then they plunged most of their bodies underwater and flapped their wings on the rippling surface, and made waves when they advanced with their chests cutting the water like the prows of boats.

Djalioh studied the grace of their movements and the beauty of their bodies. And he wondered why he was not a swan, as beautiful as these animals. When he approached other people, everybody fled; he was despised among men. Why was he not as beautiful as the swimming birds? Why had Heaven not made him swan, bird, something light, something that sang and was loved? Or, rather, why was he not null, unmade and non-existent? "Why," he said, kicking a stone, "why am I not like that? I lash out at her and she runs away unscathed!" Then he jumped into the boat, unfastened the chain, took the oars and went across the pond to the prairie where cattle were beginning to roam.

After a few moments he returned to the castle. The servants had already opened the windows and cleaned the dining room. The table was set, because it was nearly nine o'clock, and Djalioh's moments had been long and slow.

Time flies when one is joyful, and also when one sheds tears, and Old Man Time will never lose his breath.

Run fast, walk tirelessly, cut them down with no mercy, white-haired old thing! Walk on and never stop running. Carry your misery along, you who are condemned to live, and lead us quickly into the common grave where you throw everything that stands in your way!

•

VII

After lunch, it was time for a walk, because the sun had pierced the clouds and was beginning to shine.

The ladies insisted on a boat trip, the freshness of the water promising a rest after last night's exertions.

The company split into three groups. Paul, Djalioh and Adele found themselves together. She looked tired and pale, dressed in blue georgette silk with white flowers, and she was more beautiful than ever.

Adele accompanied her husband out of a sense of propriety.

Djalioh did not understand. Despite his soul's ability to embrace all that pertained to sympathy and love, his mind resisted everything that we call delicacy, custom, honor, decency and propriety. He sat at the prow and pulled on the oars. In the middle of the pond was a small island, created to serve as a refuge for the swans. On the island, rose bushes bent their branches to gaze at their reflections on the water, letting dead flowers drop to trail in the current. The young woman crumbled some bread and threw it on the water, and swans rushed, stretching their necks to grab the crumbs that were running away with the river. Every time she doubled over and the white hand stretched out, Djalioh felt her breath caressing his hair and cheeks, brushing against his head, which was burning. The water was clear and still, but a storm raged in his heart. Several times he thought he was going mad, and he brought his hands to his forehead like a delusional man who believes he is dreaming. He rowed quickly, and yet the boat was advancing less than the others, for his movements were jerky and convulsive. Occasionally his dull gray eyes turned slowly on Adele and then on Paul. Djalioh seemed calm, but it was the quiet of the ash that covers a fire; the only sounds were the oars falling in the water, the water lapping at the sides of the boat and a few words exchanged by the couple, and then they looked at each other and smiled, and the swans ran around the boat, swimming across the pond. The wind had dropped a few leaves on the boat and the sun shone upon the green meadows where the river meandered, and the boat glided in the middle of all this, fast and quiet.

At some point, Djalioh halted, set his hand to his eyes and withdrew it all warm and moist. He resumed pulling on his oars, and the tears that rolled on his hands were lost in the stream. Paul, seeing that the rest of the company was far ahead, took Adele's hand and placed on her sateen glove a long kiss of happiness that resounded in Djalioh's ears.

VIII

Madame de Lansac owned plenty of monkeys—it is an old woman's typical passion, as monkeys are the only creatures that, along with dogs, do not reject their love.

I am saying this without malignant intent, and if there were any, it would rather be the desire to appeal to the young, who hate monkeys wholeheartedly. Lord Byron said he could not watch without disgust a pretty woman eat. But Byron may never have thought of this same woman's company, forty years later, which would amount to her poodle and her monkey. All the women you see so young and fresh, well, if they do not die before their sixties, one day will have a mania for dogs instead of men, and they will live with a monkey instead of a lover.

Alas! It's sad, but true, and then, having thus yellowed for a dozen years and shriveled like old parchment by her fireplace, in the company of a cat, a novel, her dinner and her maid, this angel of beauty dies and becomes a cadaver, that is to say, a stinking corpse, and then a little dust, and nothingness...the foul air trapped in a tomb. There are people I always see as skeletons, people whose yellow complexion seems well steeped in the land that will contain them.

I do not like monkeys, but I am wrong, for they seem to be a perfect imitation of human nature. When I see one of these animals (I do not mean men), I have the impression of seeing myself in a magnifying mirror: same feelings, same brutal appetites, a little less pride and there is nothing more to it.

Djalioh felt drawn to the monkeys by strange sympathy. He often remained for hours, watching them, stock still as he gazed at them, either in deep meditation or in a more attentive observation.

Adele went to their large common cage (because sometimes young women love apes, probably because apes remind them of their husbands) and threw nuts and cakes. The animals immediately rushed over, squabbling, tearing at the pieces like Parliament representatives grabbing the crumbs that fall from the King's chair, and they all yelled like lawyers. One of them seized the biggest morsel, ate it quickly, took the most beautiful hazel, cracked it with its nails, peeled it and threw the shells to its colleagues with an air of generosity. This ape had like a crown of sparse hair on his shrunken head, which made him look quite the king. A second ape was humbly sitting in a corner, looking down with an air of modesty, like a priest, and taking surreptitiously everything he could not steal overtly. Finally, a third—it was a female—had dull long hair and puffy eyes. She went to and fro, flashing lewd gestures that made the ladies blush, biting the males, whistling and pinching their ears. This one looked like many prostitutes I know. Everybody was laughing at the animals' simpering and mincing; it was so funny! Only Djalioh did not laugh. He sat on the floor, knees flush with his head, arms on his legs, and half-dead eyes turned solely to one point.

In the afternoon they left for Paris; Djalioh was still placed in front of Adele, as if fate never stopped mocking his pain. Everyone was tired and fell asleep to the gentle rocking of the suspension and the sound of the wheels that turned slowly in the large ruts left by the rain, and the horses' feet squelching in the mud. A window, open behind Djalioh, let air into the carriage, and the wind blew on his shoulders and down his neck.

All bobbed their slumbering heads with the movement of the carriage. Djalioh alone did not sleep and kept his head bowed upon his chest.

IX

It was the beginning of May; the hour was, I think, seven in the morning. The sun rose and illuminated with his splendor Paris, which awoke to a beautiful spring day.

Mrs. Paul de Monville had risen early and retired to a salon to finish a Balzac novel before bath time, lunch and walk.

The couple dwelled in *Faubourg Saint-Germain*, which was now deserted, vast and covered with the shadow cast by the tall walls of the mansions across the gardens with their acacias and their lime trees, thick foliage overflowing the walls, and grass piercing the cracks between the stones. Seldom was heard any noise in the neighborhood if not that of some carriage wheels rolling on the pavement, pulled by two white horses, or, at night, the din of youth returning from an orgy or a music-hall show with some bare-breasted, red-eyed and debauched creatures wearing torn clothes.

It was in one of those *Faubourg Saint-Germain* mansions that Djalioh lived with Mr. Paul and his wife, and in the past two years many sentiments had unfurled within his soul, where unshed tears had dug a deep pit.

One morning, the very day I want to tell you about, he rose and went into the garden where a child of about a year slept in silk and gauze, embroidered clothes and colored scarves, snug in a cradle gilded by the sunlight.

The nannie had left the child alone. Djalioh looked around, and then drew near, very near the cradle.

He pulled off the blankets in a swift movement and spent some time contemplating the wretched little creature as it slumbered and slept. He watched its plump hands, its rounded shape, white neck and tiny fingernails. Finally he picked the baby up with both hands and whirled it in the air over his head, and then he hurled it with all his strength onto the ground, which resounded with the impact. The child screamed once, and its brain spurted out to fall onto the grass a few steps away, near a carnation.

Djalioh opened his pale lips and gave a forced laugh that was as cold and terrible as that of a specter. He ran back to the house, went upstairs, entered the dining room, turned the key in the keyhole and put it in his pocket. He repeated the same gestures with the corridor door, went to the chamber of curiosities and threw the keys out of a window into the street below. Finally he entered the salon, quietly, on tiptoe, and once inside he closed the lock with a double turn. Only a dim light fingered through the fully drawn shutters.

Djalioh paused. He heard the rustle of the pages Adele turned with her white hand as she reclined limply on a red-velvet sofa, and the chirping of birds in the aviary on the terrace, a sound that seeped through the green blinds along with the flapping of wings on the iron lattice.

In a corner of the room, next to the fireplace, there stood a mahogany planter filled with fragrant flowers: pink, white, blue, tall or thick, green foliage with glossy stems, reflected from behind in a large mirror. He approached the young woman and sat down beside her. She shuddered and her blue eyes briskly fell on him, confused. Her robe was of a vaporous white muslin, open down the front, and the fine fabric limned the shape of her thighs.

All around her floated an intoxicating perfume. Her white gloves, thrown onto the chair alongside her belt, handkerchief and head-cloth, released so delicate and sophisticated a fragrance that Djalioh's large nostrils flared to suck in all the scent.

Oh! Next to the woman whom one loves lingers a scented, inebriating aura.

"What do you want?" she said, frightened.

And there followed a long silence. He said nothing and stared at her with devouring eyes. Then, approaching, he took her waist between his hands and placed a kiss on her neck, a kiss that burned Adele like a snake's bite. He saw her flesh palpitate and blush.

"Oh! I'll call for help," she cried with horror. "Help! Help! Oh! The monster!"

Djalioh did not answer. He only stammered and struck her head angrily. What! Not able to say a word to her! Unable to expound his torments and pain, having nothing to offer but an animal's tears and a monster's sighs! And then to be rejected like a reptile! To be hated for what you love and to be unable to respond! To be cursed and to be unable to curse!

"Leave me, please! Leave me! Don't you see that you fill me with horror and disgust? I'll call Paul. He will kill you."

Djalioh showed her the key he held in his hand and she stopped. The clock struck eight, and the birds twittered in the aviary. A cart passed with a rumble. She drew away from him.

"Well, will you leave? Leave me, for Heaven's sake!"

And she tried to rise, but Djalioh held her by the skirt of her dress, and it tore under his fingernails.

"I need to get out. I must...I must see my child! Let me see my child!"

A terrible thought made her tremble in every limb. She turned pale and said: "Yes, my son! I must see him, and immediately, now!" She turned and saw in front of her the grinning face of a demon. Djalioh laughed so strongly, without stopping, that Adele, petrified with horror, fell at his feet, on her knees.

Djalioh crouched, then he seized her, made her forcibly sit on his knee, and with both hands he tore her clothes; he tore to pieces the veils that covered her, and when he saw her trembling like a leaf, half-undressed and crossing her arms over her breasts, crying, red cheeks and blue lips, he felt the weight of a strange oppression and then he grabbed the flowers, scattered them on the floor. He drew the pink silk curtains and took off his clothes.

Adele, seeing him naked, shuddered in horror and looked away; Djalioh drew near and held her tight against his chest. Therefore she felt on her warm and silky skin the cold flesh of a hairy monster. He jumped on the couch, threw the cushions and balanced a long time on the back of the sofa, with a mechanical regularity and the agility of flexible vertebrae. He uttered from time to time a guttural cry and smiled through his teeth.

What was left to be desired? He had a woman before him, flowers at his feet, the pink daylight on him, the sound of music from the aviary under the pale sunbeams!

He ceased his balancing, pounced on Adele, dug his claws into her flesh and pulled her to him, tearing off her cotton shift.

Glimpsing herself naked in the mirror, in Djalioh's arms, she screamed in horror and prayed to God. She wanted to call for help, but could not utter a single word.

Djalioh in turn, at the sight of her naked and with hair flowing down her shoulders, stood motionless with amazement, like the first man who ever saw a woman. He respected her for some time, simply tearing off her blond hair, putting the strands in his mouth, biting them, kissing them, and then he rolled down on the flowers, among the cushions, over Adele's clothes, happy, mad, drunk with love. Adele cried, a trail of blood running down her alabaster breasts. And then his fierce brutality knew no limits. He sprang on her, spread her hands, spread her on the floor and made her roll, disheveled...He uttered several ferocious cries and extended both arms. Stupid and motionless, he groaned with pleasure, like a man who is dying.

All of a sudden Adele convulsed under him, her muscles stiffening like iron. She screamed and gave sighs that were smothered by kisses. Then he felt her become cold. Her eyelids closed. She rolled over and her mouth slackened.

When he had long felt her still and cold, he rose, turned her body over, kissed her feet, her hands, her mouth, and then he ran about the place, bounding on the walls. For a long time he ran, until he darted headlong into the marble mantelpiece and fell bloodied and still on Adele's body.

X

When one came to find Adele, she had broad and deep furrows clawed all over her body. As for Djalioh, his skull was horribly smashed. Everyone believed that the young woman, defending her honor, had killed him with a knife.

All these details appeared in the newspapers, and you bet there was enough for more than a week's worth of "Ahs!" and "Ohs!"

They buried the dead the next day. The procession was superb: two coffins, the mother and the child, and everything decorated with black plumes, candles, singing priests, the crowd pressing and men in black with white gloves.

XI

A few days later, "It's horrible!" cried a patriarchal family of grocers gathered around a huge haunch with an enticing aroma.

"Poor child!" the wife said to the grocer. "Go and kill a child! What had it done to him?"

"Indeed!" said the grocer, in his indignant righteousness, for he was an eminently moral man, decorated with the cross of honor for good performance in the National Guard and a subscriber to the *Constitutionnel*! "Indeed! Go an' kill 'at poor lil' wife! It's outrageous!"

"I think it was passion," said a fat, chubby boy, the son of the house, who had just completed his eighth grade in seventeen years, because his father felt one should give education to the youth.

"Oh! People have little restraint," said the grocer, asking for his third serving of beans.

One rang in the shop, and he went to sell candles for two sous.

XII

You absolutely want an ending, do you not? And you think I am being slow in delivering it; so be it!

For Adele, she was buried, but after two years she had lost much of her beauty: when they unearthed her to put her remains in the *Père Lachaise* Cemetery, she stank so fiercely that a gravedigger fainted.

And Djalioh?

Oh! He is now splendid, polished, sealed, neat, magnificent. Because you know that a zoology exhibit took hold of his body and made a beautiful skeleton of him.

And Mr. Paul? Well, I forgot to tell you! He remarried. Sometimes I see him in the *Bois de Boulogne,* and tonight you will meet at the *Italiens*[1].

October 8, 1837

---

1 Translator's Note: Several companies of Italian actors, staging *Commedia dell'Arte* plays and later on *operas comiques,* performed in Paris since the first *troupe* was invited to France by Regent Philippe d'Orleans, after Louis XIV's death in 1715.

GORILLA OF YOUR DREAMS:
A BRIEF HISTORY OF SIMIAN CINEMA
Rick Klaw

Similar to their prose cousins, films starring apes abound. Not surprising since simians work well as a proxy for the worst of humanity: a cracked mirror of things we'd rather not confront. In the movies apes usually portray buffoons or the terrifying monster. Through the best films we can safely explore and challenge the darker side of humanity. Racism, violence, greed, sexism, elitism, and cruelty are all present throughout the history of simian cinema. Thanks to their similarities to humans, these creatures fascinate us. While apes have appeared in movies since almost the beginning of film, it wasn't until the 1930s that a movie starring a simian captured the public's attention.

One of the greatest giant-creature movies ever made and the first giant gorilla movie, the original *King Kong* (1933), revolutionized filmmaking, introduced the template for all future monster films, and established the ape as a major player in motion pictures. Developed from an idea by crime writer Edgar Wallace and producer Merian C. Cooper, *King Kong* essentially retold "Beauty & the Beast." The groundbreaking stop-motion effects developed by Willis O'Brien remained the industry standard until the 1980s with the emergence of computer-generated effects. Thanks largely to O'Brien's camera work, an entertaining script, and the stirring Max Steiner soundtrack, *King Kong* quickly entered the cultural zeitgeist. The 1950s re-release inspired another popular monster, Godzilla, and launched that decade's giant monster movie craze.

Due to the enormous success of their picture, O'Brien, Cooper, and Ernest B. Schoedsack (the original's co-director) teamed up once again on the tepid but humorous sequel *Son of Kong* (1933). Produced for half the budget and in half the time, the project proved critically disappointing. Thankfully, the group's third foray into a giant ape film more than made up for it.

Mighty Joe Young (1949) delivered a classic story of friendship and devotion between a young woman and her oversized gorilla companion. A more subtle parallel occurs between this ape and his more famous forefather. Kong, a tragic monster, and Joe Young, a lovable and playful character, both suffer exploitation in service of the dollar. But by the latter film's end, Joe emerges as a hero granted a happy ending. For his efforts, O'Brien won an Oscar for visual effects. Unfortunately, *Mighty Joe Young* was a financial disaster and its failure essentially ended O'Brien's career.

Disney Studios and director Ron Underwood remade *Mighty Joe Young* (1998) with Charlize Theron as the big ape's friend. Underwood and screenwriters Mark Rosenthal and Lawrence Konner successfully modernized the story for contemporary audiences. This version's exceptional Joe Young visuals were created by Oscar-winning special effects artist Rick Baker.

Kong himself experienced a remake in 1976 under the inept guidance of Dino De Laurentiis. The atrocious film, set in the modern era, lacks any of the charm and elegance found in the original. Rather than using the more convincing stop-motion techniques, the movie relied on a man in a gorilla suit for most of the scenes.

Twelve years later, an even more disastrous sequel *King Kong Lives* (1986), starring Linda Hamilton, appeared.

In 2005, Peter Jackson directed an endearing interpretation of the seminal film. While not quite as compelling as the original, this *King Kong* hits most of the right notes. Andy Serkis excels as the sympathetic Kong, heartbroken and hunted. The special effects sizzle, expertly re-creating a 1930s New York City and a far more terrifying Skull Island, littered with cannibals, dinosaurs, and other nasties.

The Japanese seem fascinated with King Kong. In 1933, legendary filmmaker Torajiro Saito directed *Wasei Kingu Kongu* (aka *The Japanese King Kong*), a silent movie based on the Cooper film. Featuring special effects by Fuminori Ôhashi, who later helped develop the first Godzilla suit, the 1934 production *King Kong Appears in Edo* (*Kingu Kongu Edo ni arawareta*) was among the first *kaiju* (giant monster) films. Both films were unlicensed and are presumed lost. Arguments persist about whether a third movie *Kingu Kongu Zenkouhen* (1938), which supposedly included a Kong-versus-samurai fight, was ever actually produced.

In 1962, Kong finally met his spiritual progeny in *King Kong vs. Godzilla* (*Kingu Kongu Tai Gojira*), this time with the permission of the character's license holders. Contrary to the urban legend that two versions of the movie were shot—a different monster wins depending on where the film was shown—only one ending ever existed. Kong wins. The Japanese flirtation with this giant ape ended in 1967 with *King Kong Escapes* (*Kingu Kongu No Gyakushû*).

The classic Kong tale has spawned numerous knockoffs and rip-offs including *Konga* (1961), *Tarzan and King Kong* (1965), *Queen Kong* (1976), *A*P*E** (also released as *Super Kong*, *The New King Kong*, and *Attack of the Giant Horny Gorilla*, 1976), and *The Mighty Kong* (a 1998 animated musical direct-to-video release starring Dudley Moore).

The earliest known simian appearance in film, the largely forgotten short *The Escape of the Ape* (1908), predated *Kong* by a quarter of a century. A gorilla, played by an unknown actor in reportedly convincing makeup and costume, escapes from the zoo, steals a car, interrupts a poker game, and frightens a couple. Only the unusual protagonist differentiated the film from the abundance of "chase" stories that dominated early–twentieth-century cinema. No copies are known to survive.

The oldest extant gorilla movie is Willis O'Brien's animated stop-motion short "The Dinosaur and The Missing Link" (1915). The effects guru created the film to showcase his new techniques, which he later perfected for *The Lost World* (1925) and of course *King Kong*.

Tarzan of the Apes, the first film version of Edgar Rice Burroughs' popular ape man tale and the first feature-length project to feature apes, starred Elmo Lincoln as the adult Tarzan and Enid Markey as Jane. It was the second highest grossing picture of 1918, right beyond *Mickey*, which bore the unfortunate tagline "The Picture You Will Never Forget." Through 1929, Tarzan appeared in eight silent films.

Ushering in the talkies, Olympic swimmer Johnny Weissmuller portrayed the character alongside the lovely Maureen O'Sullivan as Jane in the seminal *Tarzan the Ape Man* (1932). The film introduced two concepts not from the original tales but closely associated with the character: the comedic chimpanzee sidekick Cheeta, who appeared in nearly every Tarzan film and TV show through 1968, and the "Me Tarzan, you Jane" persona. Within the Burroughs books, the very intelligent and articulate Tarzan speaks several languages fluently and even adopts his family title as the Lord Greystoke. Yet today, the dumb savage persona persists.

Despite the fact that many others have played the role, Weissmuller remains the iconic Tarzan. He starred in twelve movies, some of the very best to ever feature Tarzan, including *Ape Man*, *Tarzan and His Mate* (1934), and *Tarzan's New York Adventure* (1942).

Similar to the original in name only, director John Derek's

Tarzan, the Ape Man (1981) featured his wife Bo Derek as Jane and Miles O'Keeffe as the ape man. Purportedly telling the original story from Jane's point of view, the essentially soft-core porn film was just an excuse for the then-popular Bo to bounce around naked in a beautiful locale.

With a screenplay co-written by Oscar-winner Robert Towne and helmed by *Chariots of Fire* director Hugh Hudson, *Greystoke: The Legend of Tarzan, Lord of the Apes* (1984) attempted a more faithful adaptation of the original Burroughs. Despite its noble intentions, the overly long (143 minutes) film stumbled largely due to the casting of the wooden Christopher Lambert in the title role, the need to dub Jane's (Andie MacDowell) voice with Glenn Close, and the movie's glacial pace.

Disney created one of the best interpretations of the character with *Tarzan* (1999). The animated film contains enough original Burroughsian elements (far more than many of the live-action attempts) to overcome the ridiculous Oscar-winning soundtrack by Phil Collins. The near perfect, frenetic, yet controlled action introduced the ape man to a new generation.

The Tarzan films have spawned numerous imitators including *The King of the Kongo* (1929), *Darkest Africa* (1936), the *Bomba* serials (beginning in 1949), and *Sheena, Queen of the Jungle* (two television series [1955, 2000] and a feature film [1984]). Through 2005, at least one movie or TV show featuring Tarzan has been produced in every decade since his big screen introduction, making the Jungle Lord one of the most identifiable characters in the world.

The first known use of an ape suit occurred in the 1918 *Tarzan of the Apes*. This revolutionary concept dominated nearly every simian film that followed with the O'Brien films as notable exceptions. In *Go and Get It* (1920), wrestler Bull Montana was the first person credited for portraying an ape.

George Barrows, Emil Van Horne, Charlie Gemora, Ray "Crash" Corrigan, and Bob Burns were some of the most famous of the small fraternity of "gorilla men." These actors wore suits of their own designs and enjoyed long, successful careers playing apes in films like *Tarzan the Tiger* (1929), *Murders in the Rue Morgue* (1932, starring the famed Bela Lugosi), *Queen of the Jungle* (1935), *The Ape* (1940, with the legendary Boris Karloff), and many others. (For more on the gorilla men see Mark Finn's "The Men in the Monkey Suit" on p.319)

The other big ape movie of the 1930s, the controversial *Ingagi* (1930) promoted itself as a documentary of African life. At the Los Angeles premiere, several actors recognized one of the scantily clad gorilla-kidnapped natives as a frequent movie extra. It turned out the director used African footage from a 1917 documentary interspersed with grainy, poorly lit scenes of beautiful women and Charlie Gemora in a gorilla suit. All of the salacious attention made the film the third largest moneymaker of the year. *Ingagi's* success paved the way for *King Kong* and spawned several imitators including *Son of Ingagi* (1940). Written by Spencer Williams, who would later play Andy on the 1950s television show *The Amos 'N Andy Show*, the project offered no connection with its predecessor, but it was the first horror film with an all African-American cast.

The rare, non-exploitative, reality-based contribution to the sub-genre, *Gorillas in the Mist* (1988) relates the fascinating true story of Dian Fossey, famed animal rights activist and world-renowned expert on the West African gorilla. Sigourney Weaver received a much deserved Oscar nomination for best actress for her portrayal. Excellent special effects by Rick Baker offered some of the finest looking gorillas ever on film.

The use of actors in ape suits achieved critical mass with *Planet of the Apes* (1968). It spawned four sequels, a television series, an animated series, a 2001 remake, a 2011 re-imagining, and a handful of *Simpsons* parodies. A dystopian reflection of American society in the 1960s, the real strength of *Apes* is the brilliant Michael Wilson and Rod Serling script, which was loosely based on Pierre Boulle's Swiftian satire, *La Planete des Singes* (*Monkey Planet*). The most original shock-ending of all time cemented the movie's place in film history.

The 2001 big-budget remake of *Apes*, spearheaded by Tim Burton, certainly looked the part, but lacked the compelling social gravitas of any of the previous endeavors, culminating in a hollow story wrapped in a beautiful container. The perceived need to one-up the surprises of the original further doomed this disappointing film.

Twentieth Century Fox, shepherds of the *Apes* franchise, used a different tact to relaunch the moribund series in 2011. With a modest budget, no marketable star, and an indie director working on his second film, *Rise of the Planet of the Apes* relied on an intelligent script and cutting-edge motion-capture technology to create a prequel worthy of the original. Serkis, much as he did in the 2005 *King Kong*, masterfully portrayed the film's fulcrum as the first superintelligent chimpanzee Caesar, who leads the ape rebellion. Easily the best *Apes* production since the first, *Rise* far exceeded all critical and box office expectations.

Countless other movies featuring apes exist. A few such as *Buddy* (1997), *The Gorilla* (1939), *The Jungle Book* (1967, animated), and the live-action *George of the Jungle* (1997) deserve some praise, but just as many or more should be forgotten. But simian cinema will persevere. As evident by *Rise*, the popularity of the ape film remains unabated.

For more on simian cinema, check out Don Glut's documentary *Hollywood Goes Ape*. The production quality is poor, but overall a very informative film—by far the most complete and interesting reference compiled on the subject.

AFTER KING KONG FELL

Philip José Farmer

Mr. Howller worries that his granddaughter hasn't gotten the full story of what happened after King Kong fell from the Empire State Building. He should know since he was there. Farmer's classic tale shares the untold conclusion.

The first half of the movie was grim and gray and somewhat tedious. Mr. Howller did not mind. That was, after all, realism. Those times had been grim and gray. Moreover, behind the tediousness was the promise of something vast and horrifying. The creeping pace and the measured ritualistic movements of the actors gave intimations of the workings of the gods. Unhurriedly, but with utmost confidence, the gods were directing events toward the climax.

Mr. Howller had felt that at the age of fifteen, and he felt it now while watching the show on TV at the age of fifty-five. Of course, when he first saw it in 1933, he had known what was coming. Hadn't he lived through some of the events only two years before that?

The old freighter, the *Wanderer*, was nosing blindly through the fog toward the surflike roar of the natives' drums. And then: the commercial. Mr. Howller rose and stepped into the hall and called down the steps loudly enough for Jill to hear him on the front porch. He thought, commercials could be a blessing. They give us time to get into the bathroom or the kitchen, or time to light up a cigarette and decide about continuing to watch this show or go on to that show.

And why couldn't real life have its commercials?

Wouldn't it be something to be grateful for if reality stopped in mid-course while the Big Salesman made His pitch? The car about to smash into you, the bullet on its way to your brain, the first cancer cell about to break loose, the boss reaching for the phone to call you in so he can fire you, the spermatozoon about to be launched toward the ovum, the final insult about to be hurled at the once, and perhaps still, beloved, the final drink of alcohol which would rupture the abused blood vessel, the decision which would lead to the light that would surely fail?

If only you could step out while the commercial interrupted these, think about it, talk about it, and then, returning to the set, switch it to another channel.

But that one is having technical difficulties, and the one after that is a talk show whose guest is the archangel Gabriel himself and after some urging by the host he agrees to blow his trumpet, and...

Jill entered, sat down, and began to munch the cookies and drink the lemonade he had prepared for her. Jill was six and a half years old and beautiful, but then what granddaughter wasn't beautiful? Jill was also unhappy because she had just quarreled with her best friend, Amy, who had stalked off with threats never to see Jill again. Mr. Howller reminded her that this had happened before and that Amy always came back the next day, if not sooner. To take her mind off of Amy, Mr. Howller gave her a brief outline of what had happened in the movie. Jill listened without enthusiasm, but she became excited enough once the movie had resumed. And when Kong was feeling over the edge of the abyss for John Driscoll, played by Bruce Cabot, she got into her grandfather's lap. She gave a little scream and put her hands over her eyes when Kong carried Ann Redman into the jungle (Ann played by Fay Wray).

But by the time Kong lay dead on Fifth Avenue, she was rooting for him, as millions had before her. Mr. Howller squeezed her and kissed her and said, "When your mother was about your age, I took her to see this. And when it was over, she was crying, too."

Jill sniffled and let him dry the tears with his handkerchief. When the Roadrunner cartoon came on, she got off his lap and went back to her cookie-munching. After a while she said, "Grandpa, the coyote falls off the cliff so far you can't even see him. When he hits, the whole earth shakes. But he always comes back, good as new. Why can he fall so far and not get hurt? Why couldn't King Kong fall and be just like new?"

Her grandparents and her mother had explained many times the distinction between a "live" and a "taped" show. It did not seem to make any difference how many times they explained. Somehow, in the years of watching TV, she had gotten the fixed idea that people in "live" shows actually suffered pain, sorrow, and death. The only shows she could endure seeing were those that her elders labeled as "taped." This worried Mr. Howller more than he admitted to his wife and daughter. Jill was a very bright child, but what if too many TV shows at too early an age had done her some irreparable harm? What if, a few years from now, she could easily see, and even define, the distinction between reality and unreality on the screen but deep down in her there was a child that still could not distinguish?

"You know that the Roadrunner is a series of pictures that move. People draw pictures, and people can do anything with pictures. So the coyote is drawn again and again, and he's back in the next show with his wounds all healed and he's ready to make a jackass of himself again."

"A jackass? But he's a coyote."

"Now..."

Mr. Howller stopped. Jill was grinning.

"O.K., now you're pulling my leg."

"But is King Kong alive or is he taped?"

"Taped. Like the Disney I took you to see last week. *Bedknobs and Broomsticks*."

"Then *King Kong* didn't happen?"

"Oh, yes, it really happened. But this is a movie they made about King Kong after what really happened was all over. So it's not exactly like it really was, and actors took the parts of Ann Redman and Carl Denham and all the others. Except King Kong himself. He was a toy model."

Jill was silent for a minute and then she said, "You mean, there really *was* a King Kong? How do you know, Grandpa?"

"Because I was there in New York when Kong went on his rampage. I was in the theater when he broke loose, and I was in the crowd that gathered around Kong's body after he fell off the Empire State Building. I was thirteen then, just seven years older than you are now. I was with my parents, and they were visiting my Aunt Thea. She was beautiful, and she had golden hair just like Fay Wray's—I mean, Ann Redman's. She'd married a very rich man, and they had a big apartment high up in the clouds. In the Empire State Building itself."

"High up in the clouds! That must've been fun, Grandpa!"

It would have been, he thought, if there had not been so much tension in that apartment. Uncle Nate and Aunt Thea should have been happy because they were so rich and lived in such a swell place. But they weren't. No one said anything to young Tim Howller, but he felt the suppressed anger, heard the bite of tone, and saw the tightening lips. His aunt and uncle were having trouble of some sort, and his parents were upset by it. But they all tried to pretend everything was as sweet as honey when he was around.

Young Howller had been eager to accept the pretense. He didn't like to think that anybody could be mad at his tall, blonde, and beautiful aunt. He was passionately in love with her; he ached for her in the daytime; at nights he had fantasies about her of which he was ashamed when he awoke. But not for long. She was a thousand times more desirable than Fay Wray or Claudette Colbert or Elissa Landi.

But that night, when they were all going to see the première of *The Eighth Wonder of the World*, King Kong himself, young Howller had managed to ignore whatever it was that was bugging his elders. And even they seemed to be having a good time. Uncle Nate, over his parents' weak protests, had purchased orchestra seats for them. These were twenty dollars apiece, big money in Depression days, enough to feed a family for a month. Everybody got all dressed up, and Aunt Thea looked too beautiful to be real. Young Howller was so excited that he thought his heart was going to climb up and out through his throat. For days the newspapers had been full of stories about King Kong—speculations, rather, since Carl Denham wasn't telling them much. And he, Tim Howller, would be one of the lucky few to see the monster first.

Boy, wait until he got back to the kids in seventh grade in Busiris, Illinois! Would their eyes ever pop when he told them all about it!

But his happiness was too good to last. Aunt Thea suddenly said she had a headache and couldn't possibly go. Then she and Uncle Nate went into their bedroom, and even in the front room, three rooms and a hallway distant, young Tim could hear their voices. After a while Uncle Nate, slamming doors behind him, came out. He was red-faced and scowling, but he wasn't going to call the party off. All four of them, very uncomfortable and silent, rode in a taxi to the theater on Times Square. But when they got inside, even Uncle Nate forgot the quarrel or at least he seemed to. There was the big stage with its towering silvery curtains and through the curtains came a vibration of excitement and of delicious danger. And even through the curtains the hot hairy ape-stink filled the theater.

"Did King Kong get loose just like in the movie?" Jill said.

Mr. Howller started. "What? Oh, yes, he sure did. Just like in the movie."

"Were you scared, Grandpa? Did you run away like everybody else?"

He hesitated. Jill's image of her grandfather had been cast in a heroic mold. To her he was a giant of Herculean strength and perfect courage, her defender and champion. So far he had managed to live up to the image, mainly because the demands she made were not too much for him. In time she would see the cracks and the sawdust oozing out. But she was too young to disillusion now.

"No, I didn't run," he said. "I waited until the theater was cleared of the crowd."

This was true. The big man who'd been sitting in the seat before him had leaped up yelling as Kong began tearing the bars out of his cage, had whirled and jumped over the back of his seat, and his knee had hit young Howller on the jaw. And so young Howller had been stretched out senseless on the floor under the seats while the mob screamed and tore at each other and trampled the fallen.

Later he was glad that he had been knocked out. It gave him a good excuse for not keeping cool, for not acting heroically in the situation. He knew that if he had not been unconscious, he would have been as frenzied as the others, and he would have abandoned his parents, thinking only in his terror of his own salvation. Of course, his parents had deserted him, though they claimed that they had been swept away from him by the mob. This *could* be true; maybe his folks *had* actually tried to get to him. But he had not really thought they had, and for years he had looked down on them because of their flight. When he got older, he realized that he would have done the same thing, and he knew that his contempt for them was really a disguised contempt for himself.

He had awakened with a sore jaw and a headache. The police and the ambulance men were there and starting to take care of the hurt and to haul away the dead. He staggered past them out into the lobby and, not seeing his parents there, went outside. The sidewalks and the streets were plugged with thousands of men, women, and children, on foot and in cars, fleeing northward.

He had not known where Kong was. He should have been able to figure it out, since the frantic mob was leaving the midtown part of Manhattan. But he could think of only two things. Where were his parents? And was Aunt Thea safe? And then he had a third thing to consider. He discovered that he had wet his pants. When he had seen the great ape burst loose, he had wet his pants.

Under the circumstances, he should have paid no attention to this. Certainly no one else did. But he was a very sensitive and shy boy of thirteen, and, for some reason, the need for getting dry underwear and trousers seemed even more important than finding his parents. In retrospect he would tell himself that he would have gone south anyway. But he knew deep down that if his pants had not been wet he might not have dared return to the Empire State Building.

It was impossible to buck the flow of the thousands moving like lava up Broadway. He went east on 43rd Street until he came to Fifth Avenue, where he started southward. There was a crowd to fight against here, too, but it was much smaller than that on Broadway. He was able to thread his way through it, though he often had to go out into the street and dodge the cars. These, fortunately, were not able to move faster than about three miles an hour.

"Many people got impatient because the cars wouldn't go faster," he told Jill, "and they just abandoned them and struck out on foot."

"Wasn't it noisy, Grandpa?"

"Noisy? I've never heard such noise. I think that everyone in Manhattan, except those hiding under their beds, was yelling or talking. And every driver in Manhattan was blowing his car's horn. And then there were the sirens of the fire trucks and police cars and ambulances. Yes, it was noisy."

Several times he tried to stop a fugitive so he could find out what was going on. But even when he did succeed in halting someone for a few seconds, he couldn't make himself heard. By then, as he found out later, the radio had broadcast the news. Kong had chased John Driscoll and Ann Redman out of the theater and across the street to their hotel. They had gone up to Driscoll's room, where they thought they were safe. But Kong had climbed up, using windows as ladder steps, reached into the room, knocked Driscoll out, and grabbed Ann, and had then leaped away with her. He had headed, as Carl Denham figured he would, toward the tallest structure on the island. On King Kong's own island, he lived on the highest point, Skull Mountain, where he was truly monarch of all he surveyed. Here he would climb to the top of the Empire State Building, Manhattan's Skull Mountain.

Tim Howller had not known this, but he was able to infer that Kong had traveled down Fifth Avenue from 38th Street on. He passed a dozen cars with their tops flattened down by the ape's fist or turned over on their sides or tops. He saw three sheet-covered bodies on the sidewalks, and he overheard a policeman telling a reporter that Kong had climbed up several buildings on his way south and reached into windows and pulled people out and thrown them down onto the pavement.

"But you said King Kong was carrying Ann Redman in the crook of his arm, Grandpa," Jill said. "He only had one arm to climb with, Grandpa, so...so wouldn't he fall off the building when he reached in to grab those poor people?"

"A very shrewd observation, my little chickadee," Mr. Howller said, using the W. C. Fields voice that usually sent her into giggles. "But his arms were long enough for him to drape Ann Redman over the arm he used to hang on with while he reached in with the other. And to forestall your next question, even if you had not thought of it, he could turn over an automobile with only one hand."

"But...but why'd he take time out to do that if he wanted to get to the top of the Empire State Building?"

"I don't know why *people* often do the things they do," Mr. Howller said. "So how would I know why an *ape* does the things he does?"

When he was a block away from the Empire State Building, a plane crashed onto the middle of the avenue two blocks behind him and burned furiously. Tim Howller watched it for a few minutes, then he looked upward and saw the red and green lights of the five planes and the silvery bodies slipping in and out of the searchlights.

"Five airplanes, Grandpa? But the movie..."

"Yes, I know. The movie showed about fourteen or fifteen. But the book says that there were six to begin with, and the book is much more accurate. The movie also shows King Kong's last stand taking place in the daylight. But it didn't; it was still nighttime."

The Army Air Force plane must have been going at least 250 mph as it dived down toward the giant ape standing on the top of the observation tower. Kong had put Ann Redman by his feet so he could hang on to the tower with one hand and grab out with the other at the planes. One had come too close, and he had seized the left biplane structure and ripped it off. Given the energy of the plane, his hand should have been torn off, too, or at least he should have been pulled loose from his hold on the tower and gone down with the plane. But he hadn't let loose, and that told something of the enormous strength of that towering body. It also told something of the relative fragility of the biplane.

Young Howller had watched the efforts of the firemen to extinguish the fire and then he had turned back toward the Empire State Building. By then it was all over. All over for King Kong anyway. It was, in after years, one of Mr. Howller's greatest regrets that he had not seen the monstrous dark body falling through the beams of the searchlights—blackness, then the flash of blackness through the whiteness of the highest beam, blackness, the flash through the next beam, blackness, the flash through the third beam, blackness, the flash through the lowest beam. Dot, dash, dot, dash, Mr. Howller was to think afterward. A code transmitted unconsciously by the great ape and received unconsciously by those who witnessed the fall. Or by those who would hear of it and think about it. Or was he going too far in conceiving this? Wasn't he always looking for, codes? And, when he found them, unable to decipher them?

Since he had been thirteen, he had been trying to equate the great falls in man's myths and legends and to find some sort of intelligence in them. The fall of the tower of Babel, of Lucifer, of Vulcan, of Icarus, and, finally, of King Kong. But he wasn't equal to the task; he didn't have the genius to perceive what the falls meant, he couldn't screen out the—to use an electronic term—the "noise."

All he could come up with were folk adages. What goes up must come down. The bigger they are, the harder they fall.

"What'd you say, Grandpa?"

"I was thinking out loud, if you can call that thinking," Mr. Howller said.

Young Howller had been one of the first on the scene, and so he got a place in the front of the crowd. He had not completely forgotten his parents or Aunt Thea, but the danger was over, and he could not make himself leave to search for them. And he had even forgotten about his soaked pants. The body was only about thirty feet from him. It lay on its back on the sidewalk, just as in the movie. But the dead Kong did not look as big or as dignified as in the movie. He was spread out more like an apeskin rug than a body, and blood and bowels and their contents had splashed out around him.

After a while Carl Denham, the man responsible for capturing Kong and bringing him to New York, appeared. As in the movie, Denham spoke his classical lines by the body: "It was Beauty. As always, Beauty killed the Beast."

This was the most appropriately dramatic place for the lines to be spoken, of course, and the proper place to end the movie.

But the book had Denham speaking these lines as he leaned over the parapet of the observation tower to look down at Kong on the sidewalk. His only audience was a police sergeant.

Both the book and the movie were true. Or half true. Denham did speak those lines way up on the 102nd floor of the tower. But, showman that he was, he also spoke them when he got down to the sidewalk, where the newsmen could hear them.

Young Howller didn't hear Denham's remarks. He was too far away. Besides, at that moment he felt a tap on his shoulder and heard a man say, "Hey, kid, there's somebody trying to get your attention!"

Young Howller went into his mother's arms and wept for at least a minute. His father reached past his mother and touched him briefly on the forehead, as if blessing him, and then gave his shoulder a squeeze. When he was able to talk, Tim Howller asked his mother what had happened to them. They, as near as they could remember, had been pushed out by the crowd, though they had fought to get to him, and had run up Broadway after they found themselves in the street because King Kong had appeared. They had managed to get back to the theater, had not been able to locate Tim, and had walked back to the Empire State Building.

"What happened to Uncle Nate?" Tim said.

Uncle Nate, his mother said, had caught up with them on Fifth Avenue and just now was trying to get past the police cordon into the building so he could check on Aunt Thea.

"She must be all right!" young Howller said. "The ape climbed up her side of the building, but she could easily get away from him, her apartment's so big!'

"Well, yes," his father had said. "But if she went to bed with her headache, she would've been right next to the window. But don't worry. If she'd been hurt, we'd know it. And maybe she wasn't even home."

Young Tim had asked him what he meant by that, but his father had only shrugged.

The three of them stood in the front line of the crowd, waiting for Uncle Nate to bring news of Aunt Thea, even though they weren't really worried about her, and waiting to see what happened to Kong. Mayor Jimmy Walker showed up and conferred with the officials. Then the governor himself, Franklin Delano Roosevelt, arrived with much noise of siren and motorcycle. A minute later a big black limousine with flashing red lights and a siren pulled up. Standing on the runningboard was a giant with bronze hair and strange-looking gold-flecked eyes. He jumped off the runningboard and strode up to the mayor, governor, and police commissioner and talked briefly with them. Tim Howller asked the man next to him what the giant's name was, but the man replied that he didn't know because he was from out of town also. The giant finished talking and strode up to the crowd, which opened for him as if it were the Red Sea and he were Moses, and he had no trouble at all getting through the police cordon. Tim then asked the man on the right of his parents if he knew the yellow-eyed giant's name. This man, tall and thin, was with a beautiful woman dressed up in an evening gown and a mink coat. He turned his head when Tim called to him and presented a hawklike face and eyes that burned so brightly that Tim wondered if he took dope. Those eyes also told him that here was a man who asked questions, not one who gave answers. Tim didn't repeat his question, and a moment later the man said, in a whispering voice that still carried a long distance, "Come on, Margo. I've work to do." And the two melted into the crowd.

Mr. Howller told Jill about the two men, and she said, "What about them, Grandpa?"

"I don't really know," he said. "Often I've wondered... Well, never mind. Whoever they were, they're irrelevant to what happened to King Kong. But I'll say one thing about New York—you sure see a lot of strange characters there."

Young Howller had expected that the mess would quickly be cleaned up. And it was true that the sanitation department had sent a big truck with a big crane and a number of men with hoses, scoop shovels, and brooms. But a dozen people at least stopped the cleanup almost before it began. Carl Denham wanted no one to touch the body except the taxidermists he had called in. If he couldn't exhibit a live Kong, he would exhibit a dead one. A colonel from Roosevelt Field claimed the body and, when asked why the Air Force wanted it, could not give an explanation. Rather, he refused to give one, and it was not until an hour later that a phone call from the White House forced him to reveal the real reason. A general wanted the skin for a trophy because Kong was the only ape ever shot down in aerial combat.

A lawyer for the owners of the Empire State Building appeared with a claim for possession of the body. His clients wanted reimbursement for the damage done to the building.

A representative of the transit system wanted Kong's body so it could be sold to help pay for the damage the ape had done to the Sixth Avenue Elevated.

The owner of the theater from which Kong had escaped arrived with his lawyer and announced he intended to sue Denham for an amount which would cover the sums he would have to pay to those who were inevitably going to sue him.

The police ordered the body seized as evidence in the trial for involuntary manslaughter and criminal negligence in which Denham and the theater owner would be defendants in due process.

The manslaughter charges were later dropped, but Denham did serve a year before being paroled. On being released, he was killed by a religious fanatic, a native brought back by the second expedition to Kong's island. He was, in fact, the witch doctor. He had murdered Denham because Denham had abducted and slain his god, Kong.

His Majesty's New York consul showed up with papers which proved that Kong's island was in British waters. Therefore, Denham had no right to anything removed from the island without permission of His Majesty's government.

Denham was in a lot of trouble. But the worst blow of all was to come next day. He would be handed notification that he was being sued by Ann Redman. She wanted compensation to the tune of ten million dollars for various physical indignities and injuries suffered during her two abductions by the ape, plus the mental anguish these had caused her. Unfortunately for her, Denham went to prison without a penny in his pocket, and she dropped the suit. Thus, the public never found out exactly what the "physical indignities and injuries" were, but this did not keep it from making many speculations. Ann Redman also sued John Driscoll, though for a different reason. She claimed breach of promise. Driscoll, interviewed by newsmen, made his famous remark that she should have been suing Kong, not him. This convinced most of the public that what it had suspected had indeed happened. Just how it could have been done was difficult to explain, but the public had never lacked wiseacres who would not only attempt the difficult but would not draw back even at the impossible.

Actually, Mr. Howller thought, the deed was not beyond possibility. Take an adult male gorilla who stood six feet high and weighed 350 pounds. According to Swiss zoo director Ernst Lang, he would have a full erection only two inches long. How did Professor Lang know this? Did he enter the cage during a mating and measure the phallus? Not very likely. Even the timid and amiable gorilla would scarcely submit to this type of handling in that kind of situation. Never mind. Professor Lang said it was so, and so it must be. Perhaps he used a telescope with gradations across the lens like those on a submarine's periscope. In any event, until someone entered the cage and slapped down a ruler during the action, Professor Lang's word would have to be taken as the last word.

By mathematical extrapolation, using the square-cube law, a gorilla twenty feet tall would have an erect penis about twenty-one inches long. What the diameter would be was another guess and perhaps a vital one, for Ann Redman anyway. Whatever anyone else thought about the possibility, Kong must have decided that he would never know unless he tried. Just how well he succeeded, only he and his victim knew, since the attempt would have taken place before Driscoll and Denham got to the observation tower and before the searchlight beams centered on their target.

But Ann Redman must have told her lover, John Driscoll, the truth, and he turned out not to be such a strong man after all.

"What're you thinking about, Grandpa?"

Mr. Howller looked at the screen. The Roadrunner had been succeeded by the Pink Panther, who was enduring as much pain and violence as the poor old coyote.

"Nothing," he said. "I'm just watching the Pink Panther with you."

"But you didn't say what happened to King Kong," she said.

"Oh," he said, "we stood around until dawn, and then the big shots finally came to some sort of agreement. The body just couldn't be left there much longer, if for no other reason than that it was blocking traffic. Blocking traffic meant that business would be held up. And lots of people would lose lots of money. And so Kong's body was taken away by the Police Department, though it used the Sanitation Department's crane, and it was kept in an icehouse until its ownership could be thrashed out."

"Poor Kong."

"No," he said, "not poor Kong. He was dead and out of it."

"He went to heaven?"

"As much as anybody," Mr. Howller said.

"But he killed a lot of people, and he carried off that nice girl. Wasn't he bad?"

"No, he wasn't bad. He was an animal, and he didn't know the difference between good and evil. Anyway, even if he'd been human, he would've been doing what any human would have done."

"What do you mean, Grandpa?"

"Well, if you were captured by people only a foot tall and carried off to a far place and put in a cage, wouldn't you try to escape? And if these people tried to put you back in, or got so scared that they tried to kill you right now, wouldn't you step on them?"

"Sure, I'd step on them, Grandpa."

"You'd be justified, too. And King Kong was justified. He was only acting according to the dictates of his instincts."

"What?"

"He was an animal, and so he can't be blamed, no matter what he did. He wasn't evil. It was what happened around Kong that was evil."

"What do you mean?" Jill said.

"He brought out the bad and the good in the people."

But mostly bad, he thought, and he encouraged Jill to forget about Kong and concentrate on the Pink Panther. And as he looked at the screen, he saw it through tears. Even after forty-two years, he thought, tears. This was what the fall of Kong had meant to him.

The crane had hooked the corpse and lifted it up. And there were two flattened-out bodies under Kong; he must have dropped them onto the sidewalk on his way up and then fallen on them from the tower. But how to explain the nakedness of the corpses of the man and the woman?

The hair of the woman was long and, in a small area not covered by blood, yellow. And part of her face was recognizable.

Young Tim had not known until then that Uncle Nate had returned from looking for Aunt Thea. Uncle Nate gave a long wailing cry that sounded as if he, too, were falling from the top of the Empire State Building.

A second later young Tim Howller was wailing. But where Uncle Nate's was the cry of betrayal, and perhaps of revenge satisfied, Tim's was both of betrayal and of grief for the death of one he had passionately loved with a thirteen-year-old's love, for one whom the thirteen-year-old in him still loved.

"Grandpa, are there any more King Kongs?"

"No," Mr. Howller said. To say yes would force him to try to explain something that she could not understand. When she got older, she would know that every dawn saw the death of the old Kong and the birth of the new.

DEVIATION FROM A THEME

Steven Utley

On an alien world in another dimension, a student relives Ann Darrow's harrowing encounter with the Tyrannosaurus Rex from the classic *King Kong*. Utley's unusual tale of alternative education successfully re-creates the terrifying scene.

Teacher Payeph wagged her wattles in exasperation as she surveyed the shambles I had made of my first continuum.

"How many times must I tell you?" she demanded. "The smaller, the better! Random factors produce effects which spread outward in waves in all directions! Subtlety, Ellease! Subtlety is called for in order to have a smoothly running continuum."

I bent a spine into the apologetic position and said, "I am abjectly sorry, Teacher."

"I'm certain the fact that you're sorry will console all the life-forms suffering in your continuum." She settled at my side and became solicitous, stroking my frill with her whiskers. That egg-gummer Myosa looked up from her continuum and snickered on my private frequency.

Payeph always feels warmth for the retards.

Expel it from your nether vents, I told Myosa, and shut her off.

Payeph punched MEDIUM REDUCTION on my console slate and picked up my continuum. It hung in her pincers like a punctured bagaloon. I colored and clamped the lids shut on my dorsal vents, lest my embarrassment offend.

"What is wrong?" Payeph asked as she returned my limp creation to its mount. "Are you having trouble with your vision? Can't you perceive fine details? Or is it that you simply don't care?"

"Oh, no. It's just...I'm clumsy, Teacher. I *try* to work on a small scale, but every time I attempt to manipulate my life-forms, I accidentally gouge the side off a mountain or punch a hole clean through the planet. Once, I missed altogether and ruptured the sun."

Payeph looked sad. "I think you need more practice, Ellease, before I turn you loose on another continuum of your own. Come over to mine."

I risked a glance at Myosa. She was smoking with envy. It was no secret that Payeph's continuum was the best in existence. Her decision to let me practice there was an undeniable show of favor. I rose and followed my teacher past Myosa, at whom I surreptitiously twitched a nipple.

When we came to her continuum, Payeph punched MEDIUM REDUCTION. Everything became gray shading into black or white.

"Of course," said Payeph, "I can't simply turn you loose on my pride and joy."

"Of course, Teacher." My hearts sank.

"But I am going to allot you control of a quasi-world."

I cocked a spine at her. "A quasi-world, Teacher?"

"A sort of alternate reality which the life-forms in this sector have erected and preserved on light-sensitive film. The absence of color disconcerts you, Ellease? You'll soon become accustomed to it. The process by which images are preserved is rather primitive at this point in my life-forms' development as a technological race. But they learn quickly. They're imaginative, after a fashion. Now I want you to review everything here, and then I'll let you practice handling the random factors."

"Yes, Teacher."

I reviewed the material. Payeph's creations' creations were two-dimensional in addition to being monochromatic, but I nevertheless found them fascinating. My teacher's five-pointed life-forms had grasped the rudiments of continuum-building and, while keeping within the limitations of their technology, had constructed neat, succinct worlds wherein everything contrived to move itself to this point to that. It was rather like a primer in construction.

"I think I have it now," I finally told Payeph.

"You may begin. Just remember to be subtle when selecting your variables."

And I began.

Time was running in circles now, doubling back and catching up with itself, enfolding Ann Darrow in a scramble of images. A skull-shaped mountain rising through the fog. Black hands lashing her between the weathered stone pillars. Monsters crashing through the jungle, blundering into one another in their eagerness to get at her.

It had been a harrowing night for Ann, a night of bad dreams come true, of fearful childhood imaginings spilling over into reality. She had no way of telling how long or how far she had been carried in her monstrous abductor's paw. She could no longer scream. Her throat was raw. She had lost and regained consciousness more times than she could number, and, always, the awakening had been the same.

In the limbo separating nightmare-filled consciousness and total awakening, she tramped the sidewalks of New York City, moving mindlessly, mechanically, like a zombie. She was tired and hungry, but she had no money, no job, no place to go, and it was cold, so very cold.

But the fetid stench in the air was that of decaying vegetation, not automobile-exhaust fumes and ripening garbage. Her clothes were pasted to her skin with perspiration. And a far greater horror than exhaustion or hunger bore her in its hand as though she were a doll.

In the limbo between unconsciousness and awakening, Ann prayed for deliverance.

Make the bad dream go away!

Don't let me—

Please, somebody, save me! Save me!

But the awakening was always the same.

"Ah," said Teacher Payeph. "I'm impressed, Ellease. You reveal a distinct talent for subjectivity."

I retracted my mandibles, a sign of profound thanks, and then, carefully, nervously, started restructuring events in the quasi-world.

Tyrannosaurus sniffed the hot, damp air and began to move through the jungle. The sky was just beginning to lighten, but a thick mist was rising, keeping visibility to a minimum. The dinosaur ploughed through the gloom unconcernedly, letting his acute sense of smell guide him.

Prey-scent was abundant. He crossed the cooling spoor of a nocturnal stegosaurus at one point and, further on, followed the trail of a swamp-dwelling giant until the ground fell off sharply into a bog. Unable to proceed into the swamp, Tyrannosaurus roared out his frustration and swung his twenty-meter length about to seek food elsewhere.

He was aptly named, this Tyrant Lizard; a striding maw of a creature, with teeth like carving knives and jaw muscles like steel cable. He walked on his splayed, talon-tipped toes and held his small forearms close to his scaly chest. He hardly needed the forearms. He did his killing with his jaws and the weight behind those jaws.

He was aptly named, this Tyrannosaurus, and the other denizens of his world feared and respected him accordingly. In their marshes, the thunder lizards headed for deeper water when he approached on the shore. The pterodactyls climbed into the sky. The stegosaurs crouched under their rows of dorsal plates and flicked their spiked tails in alarm.

Tyrannosaurus paused abruptly and listened. He heard a muffled roar in the distance, followed by a series of thin shrieks and a dull crash. There was a sound of large branches snapping. Then the slowly moving air of the jungle brought a faint scent which evoked a fleeting impression, a dim flash of recognition, in the dinosaur's mind: ape.

The Tyrant Lizard began to move again, uprooting saplings and tearing up great clumps of sodden earth as he walked. A lesser scent, intermingled with that of the ape, impinged upon his nostrils. It was a completely unfamiliar odor. Vaguely perplexed, the carnivore slowed his advance. He came to the edge of a clearing and tensed for the attack, for the ape-scent was thick there.

But there was no ape in sight.

A high, plaintive screech brought Tyrannosaurus' head around. His glistening eye fastened upon a strange white thing wedged into the fork of a lightning-blasted tree at the far side of the clearing.

It seemed hardly more than a mouthful, hardly worth the trouble, but its noise was annoying. He hissed and strode forward, and he was almost upon the wailing thing when an enormous ape burst into the clearing like a black mountain on legs.

Tyrannosaurus immediately forgot about the irritating white creature as he wheeled to meet the ape's attack. The simian was as tall as the dinosaur and, though considerably less heavy, very power-fully built. Jaws distended, the reptile lunged. His opponent ducked under his head and clamped its shaggy arms around his neck. He raked his teeth across the beast's broad back, shredding flesh.

Back and forth across the clearing they raged, biting, tearing, kicking, clawing. Locked together, they crashed against the dead tree, felling it. The ape lost its hold on the dinosaur and went down on top of the tree.

Before the mammal could rise, Tyrannosaurus planted an enormous foot upon its stomach, bent down and bit out its throat.

Payeph fluttered her wattles approvingly. "Very good," she said, "but don't forget that the alterations you've made will have a direct bearing on everything which follows."

"Of course. Teacher."

She awoke with a splitting headache. She was pinned beneath the fallen bole, with only a short, thick nub of branch holding it away from her. For several seconds, she could not remember where she was. Through a rift in the jungle canopy, she could see that the stars had faded from the sky, but the effort required to keep her eyes open and focused served only to worsen the agony behind them. She closed her eyes and pressed her cheek into the warm mud.

Then a basso profundo grunt shook her out of her daze. She twisted around as best she could and gave a short, sharp scream.

Her erstwhile captor's inert mass was sprawled across the trunk.

The giant ape was dead. Looming over it was the monster to end all monsters.

Blood dripping from his jaws and dewlap, Tyrannosaurus looked up from his meal when he heard the scream. He peered down at the strange white creature. A growl started to rumble up from his long, deep chest.

It had been a bad night for Ann Darrow. A worse day was dawning.

"Not at all bad, Ellease. See how simple it is?"

"Yes, Teacher."

"All you have to do is exercise the same meticulous care on a cosmic scale. Take your time. Pay attention to details." She clacked her mandibles. "And watch out for your own elbows."

"Yes, Teacher."

"Do you think you've got the hang of it now? Or would you like to practice with another alternate-reality?"

I turned to have another look at the gray quasi-world and quite accidentally ground Tyrannosaurus to mush underfoot just as he was about to nip off Ann Darrow's head and shoulders. Payeph moaned.

I pulled my head down into my carapace. "Er, should I fix it all back the way it was at first?"

"No! I mean, no, Ellease. Let's, uh, leave well enough alone."

"Yes, Teacher." I backed out of the quasi-world as she punched MEDIUM REDUCTION on her console slate. Several of my feet became entangled in something. I gave a tug and pulled free. "Teacher, won't the life-forms who constructed that quasi-world notice the changes I made?"

Payeph made a hooting sound and inflated her wattles in dismay. "I think they have more serious matters to consider now."

I looked into her continuum and groaned. Pulling my feet free, I had broken something else.

"Ellease," Payeph said, "perhaps you should try another line of work."

I stared disconsolately at the mess I had created. Stars were blossoming like variegated flowers. For a brief moment, an entire galaxy flared up into a bouquet.

"Yes, Teacher," I said.

GODZILLA'S TWELVE-STEP PROGRAM

Joe R. Lansdale

It's tough enough for a monster to stop practicing destruction and mayhem. But with miscreants like the asshole Gamera and the Barbie-obsessed Kong around, it's virtually impossible. In his typical Texas Gonzo style, Lansdale doesn't miss a beat in this wild, humorous parody.

ONE: Honest Work

Godzilla, on his way to work at the foundry, sees a large building that seems to be mostly made of shiny copper and dark, reflecting solar glass. He sees his image in the glass and thinks of the old days, wonders what it would be like to stomp on the building, to blow flames at it, kiss the windows black with his burning breath, then dance rapturously in the smoking debris.

One day at a time, he tells himself. One day at a time.

Godzilla makes himself look at the building hard. He passes it by. He goes to the foundry. He puts on his hard hat. He blows his fiery breath into the great vat full of used car parts, turns the car parts to molten metal. The metal runs through pipes and into new molds for new car parts. Doors. Roofs. Etc.

Godzilla feels some of the tension drain out.

TWO: Recreation

After work Godzilla stays away from downtown. He feels tense. To stop blowing flames after work is difficult. He goes over to the BIG MONSTER RECREATION CENTER.

Gorgo is there. Drunk from oily seawater, as usual. Gorgo talks about the old days. She's like that. Always the old days.

They go out back and use their breath on the debris that is deposited there daily for the center's use. Kong is out back. Drunk as a monkey. He's playing with Barbie dolls. He does that all the time. Finally, he puts the Barbies away in his coat pocket, takes hold of his walker and wobbles past Godzilla and Gorgo.

Gorgo says, "Since the fall he ain't been worth shit. And what's with him and the little plastic broads anyway? Don't he know there's real women in the world?"

Godzilla thinks Gorgo looks at Kong's departing walker-supported ass a little too wistfully. He's sure he sees wetness in Gorgo's eyes.

Godzilla blows some scrap to cinders for recreation, but it doesn't do much for him, as he's been blowing fire all day long and has, at best, merely taken the edge off his compulsions. This isn't even as satisfying as the foundry. He goes home.

THREE: Sex and Destruction

That night there's a monster movie on television. The usual one. Big beasts wrecking havoc on city after city. Crushing pedestrians under foot.

Godzilla examines the bottom of his right foot, looks at the scar there from stomping cars flat. He remembers how it was to have people squish between his toes. He thinks about all of that and changes the channel. He watches twenty minutes of *Mr. Ed*, turns off the TV, masturbates to the images of burning cities and squashing flesh.

Later, deep into the night, he awakens in a cold sweat. He goes to the bathroom and quickly carves crude human figures from bars of soap. He mashes the soap between his toes, closes his eyes and imagines. Tries to remember.

FOUR: Beach Trip and the Big Turtle

Saturday, Godzilla goes to the beach. A drunk monster that looks like a big turtle flies by and bumps Godzilla. The turtle calls Godzilla a name, looking for a fight. Godzilla remembers the turtle is called Gamera.

Gamera is always trouble. No one liked Gamera. The turtle was a real asshole.

Godzilla grits his teeth and holds back the flames. He turns his back and walks along the beach. He mutters a secret mantra given him by his sponsor. The giant turtle follows after, calling him names.

Godzilla packs up his beach stuff and goes home. At his back he hears the turtle, still cussing, still pushing. It's all he can do not to respond to the big dumb bastard. All he can do. He knows the turtle will be in the news tomorrow. He will have destroyed something, or will have been destroyed himself.

Godzilla thinks perhaps he should try and talk to the turtle, get him on the twelve-step program. That's what you're supposed to do. Help others. Maybe the turtle could find some peace.

But then again, you can only help those who help themselves. Godzilla realizes he cannot save all the monsters of the world. They have to make these decisions for themselves. But he makes a mental note to go armed with leaflets about the twelve-step program from now on.

Later, he calls in to his sponsor. Tells him he's had a bad day. That he wanted to burn buildings and fight the big turtle. Reptilicus tells him it's okay. He's had days like that. Will have days like that once again.

Once a monster, always a monster. But a recovering monster is where it's at. Take it one day at a time. It's the only way to be happy in the world. You can't burn and kill and chew up humans and their creations without paying the price of guilt and multiple artillery wounds.

Godzilla thanks Reptilicus and hangs up. He feels better for a while, but deep down he wonders just how much guilt he really harbors. He thinks maybe it's the artillery and the rocket-firing jets he really hates, not the guilt.

FIVE: Off the Wagon

It happens suddenly. He falls off the wagon. Coming back from work he sees a small doghouse with a sleeping dog sticking halfway out of a doorway. There's no one around. The dog looks old. It's on a chain. Probably miserable anyway. The water dish is empty. The dog is living a worthless life. Chained. Bored. No water.

Godzilla leaps and comes down on the doghouse and squashes dog in all directions. He burns what's left of the doghouse with a blast of his breath. He leaps and spins on tiptoe through the wreckage. Black cinders and cooked dog slip through his toes and remind him of the old days.

He gets away fast. No one has seen him. He feels giddy. He can hardly walk he's so intoxicated. He calls Reptilicus, gets his answering machine. "I'm not in right now. I'm out doing good. But please leave a message, and I'll get right back to you."

The machine beeps. Godzilla says, "Help."

SIX: His Sponsor

The doghouse rolls around in his head all the next day. While at work he thinks of the dog and the way it burned. He thinks of the little house and the way it crumbled. He thinks of the dance he did in the ruins.

The day drags on forever. He thinks maybe when work is through he might find another doghouse, another dog.

On the way home he keeps an eye peeled, but no doghouses or dogs are seen.

When he gets home his answering machine light is blinking. It's a message from Reptilicus. Reptilicus's voice says, "Call me."

Godzilla does. He says, "Reptilicus. Forgive me, for I have sinned."

SEVEN: Disillusioned. Disappointed.

Reptilicus's talk doesn't help much. Godzilla shreds all the twelve-step program leaflets. He wipes his butt on a couple and throws them out the window. He puts the scraps of the others in the sink and sets them on fire with his breath. He burns a coffee table and a chair, and when he's through, feels bad for it. He knows the landlady will expect him to replace them.

He turns on the radio and lies on the bed listening to an Oldies station. After a while, he falls asleep to Martha and the Vandellas singing "Heat Wave."

●

EIGHT: Unemployed

Godzilla dreams. In it God comes to him, all scaly and blowing fire. He tells Godzilla he's ashamed of him. He says he should do better. Godzilla awakes covered in sweat. No one is in the room.

Godzilla feels guilt. He has faint memories of waking up and going out to destroy part of the city. He really tied one on, but he can't remember everything he did. Maybe he'll read about it in the papers. He notices he smells like charred lumber and melted plastic. There's gooshy stuff between his toes, and something tells him it isn't soap.

He wants to kill himself. He goes to look for his gun, but he's too drunk to find it. He passes out on the floor. He dreams of the devil this time. He looks just like God except he has one eyebrow that goes over both eyes. The devil says he's come for Godzilla

Godzilla moans and fights. He dreams he gets up and takes pokes at the devil, blows ineffective fire on him.

Godzilla rises late the next morning, hung over. He remembers the dream. He calls in to work sick. Sleeps off most of the day. That evening, he reads about himself in the papers. He really did some damage. Smoked a large part of the city. There's a very clear picture of him biting the head off of a woman.

He gets a call from the plant manager that night. The manager's seen the paper. He tells Godzilla he's fired.

NINE: Enticement

Next day some humans show up. They're wearing black suits and white shirts and polished shoes and they've got badges. They've got guns, too. One of them says, "You're a problem. Our government wants to send you back to Japan."

"They hate me there," says Godzilla. "I burned Tokyo down."

"You haven't done so good here either. Lucky that was a colored section of town you burned, or we'd be on your ass. As it is, we've got a job proposition for you."

"What?" Godzilla asks.

"You scratch our back, we'll scratch yours." Then the men tell him what they have in mind.

TEN: Choosing

Godzilla sleeps badly that night. He gets up and plays the "Monster Mash" on his little record player. He dances around the room as if he's enjoying himself, but knows he's not. He goes over to the BIG MONSTER RECREATION CENTER. He sees Kong there, on a stool, undressing one of his Barbies, fingering the smooth spot between her legs. He sees that Kong has drawn a crack there, like a vagina. It appears to have been drawn with a blue ink pen. He's feathered the central line with ink-drawn pubic hair. Godzilla thinks he should have got someone to do the work for him. It doesn't look all that natural.

God, he doesn't want to end up like Kong. Completely spaced. Then again, maybe if he had some dolls he could melt, maybe that would serve to relax him.

No. After the real thing, what was a Barbie? Some kind of form of Near Beer. That's what the debris out back was. Near Beer. The foundry. The Twelve-Step Program. All of it. Near Beer.

ELEVEN: Working for the Government

Godzilla calls the government assholes. "All right," he says. "I'll do it."

"Good," says the government man. "We thought you would. Check your mail box. The map and instructions are there."

Godzilla goes outside and looks in his box. There's a manila envelope there. Inside are instructions. They say: "Burn all the spots you see on the map. You finish those, we'll find others. No penalties. Just make sure no one escapes. Any rioting starts, you finish them. To the last man, woman and child."

Godzilla unfolds the map. On it are red marks. Above the red marks are listings: *Nigger Town. Chink Village. White Trash Enclave. A Clutch of Queers. Mostly Democrats.*

Godzilla thinks about what he can do now. Unbidden. He can burn without guilt. He can stomp without guilt. Not only that, they'll send him a check. He has been hired by his adopted country to clean out the bad spots as they see them.

TWELVE: The Final Step

Godzilla stops near the first place on the list: *Nigger Town.* He sees kids playing in the streets. Dogs. Humans looking up at him, wondering what the hell he's doing here.

Godzilla suddenly feels something move inside him. He knows he's being used. He turns around and walks away. He heads toward the government section of town. He starts with the governor's mansion. He goes wild. Artillery is brought out, but it's no use, he's rampaging. Like the old days.

Reptilicus shows up with a megaphone, tries to talk Godzilla down from the top of the Great Monument Building, but Godzilla doesn't listen. He's burning the top of the building off with his breath, moving down, burning some more, moving down, burning some more, all the way to the ground.

Kong shows up and cheers him on. Kong drops his walker and crawls along the road on his belly and reaches a building and pulls himself up and starts climbing. Bullets spark all around the big ape.

Godzilla watches as Kong reaches the summit of the building and clings by one hand and waves the other, which contains a Barbie doll.

Kong puts the Barbie doll between his teeth. He reaches in his coat and brings out a naked Ken doll. Godzilla can see that Kong has made Ken some kind of penis out of silly putty or something. The penis is as big as Ken's leg.

Kong is yelling, "Yeah, that's right. That's right. I'm AC/DC, you sonsofbitches."

Jets appear and swoop down on Kong. The big ape catches a load of rocket right in the teeth. Barbie, teeth and brains decorate the graying sky. Kong falls.

Gorgo comes out of the crowd and bends over the ape, takes him in her arms and cries. Kong's hand slowly opens, revealing Ken, his penis broken off.

The flying turtle shows up and starts trying to steal Godzilla's thunder, but Godzilla isn't having it. He tears the top off the building Kong had mounted and beats Gamera with it. Even the cops and the army cheer over this.

Godzilla beats and beats the turtle, splattering turtle meat all over the place, like an overheated poodle in a microwave. A few quick pedestrians gather up chunks of the turtle meat to take home and cook, 'cause the rumor is it tastes just like chicken.

Godzilla takes a triple shot of rockets in the chest, staggers, goes down. Tanks gather around him.

Godzilla opens his bloody mouth and laughs. He thinks: If I'd have gotten finished here, then I'd have done the black people too. I'd have gotten the yellow people and the white trash and the homosexuals. I'm an equal opportunity destroyer. To hell with the twelve-step program. To hell with humanity.

Then Godzilla dies and makes a mess on the street. Military men tiptoe around the mess and hold their noses.

Later, Gorgo claims Kong's body and leaves.

Reptilicus, being interviewed by television reporters, says, "Zilla was almost there, man. Almost. If he could have completed the program, he'd have been all right. But the pressures of society were too much for him. You can't blame him for what society made of him."

On the way home, Reptilicus thinks about all the excitement. The burning buildings. The gunfire. Just like the old days when he and Zilla and Kong and that goon-ball turtle were young.

Reptilicus thinks of Kong's defiance, waving the Ken doll, the Barbie in his teeth. He thinks of Godzilla, laughing as he died.

Reptilicus finds a lot of old feelings resurfacing. They're hard to fight. He locates a lonesome spot and a dark house and urinates through an open window, then goes home.

THE MEN IN THE MONKEY SUIT

Mark Finn

Hollywood, the primary twentieth-century architect for the popular misconceptions of great apes, exploited many of the common falsehoods about simian behavior. They quite successfully reduced the chimpanzee to little more than a parodic stand-in for humans; made the orangutan a comic relief figure; and cast the gorilla in the role of the heavy, or the monster.

In the Golden Age of Hollywood, there were no such things as special effects, not in the way we understand them today. Computer-generated imagery was light-years away. If a director wanted a fantastic creature on the screen, they had to build it and film it. Monsters were either animated by hand, on paper, or via articulated puppetry, inch by madding inch at a time. Stop-motion animation may have been preferable for simulating dynamic movements and scale, but it was expensive and time-consuming. Thus, getting an ape on the big screen was best accomplished by the judicious application of a man in a suit. While fashioning a gorilla suit may have been a big undertaking, it was well within the means of a specialized kind of man—the kind of man who didn't mind spending all day in a sixty-five pound, blazing hot suit, who seemed to get a genuine thrill in disappearing under the mountains of latex and yak hair to become something other than himself, who recognized a specific need in his rarefied industry and stepped in to fill it—a job only a handful of men in the history of film ever performed. They are collectively, if not colloquially, known as the Gorilla Men.

There were, all in all, less than a dozen men in the history of Hollywood who made a living wage playing great apes. Some of them were aloof and secretive, while others were extremely giving of their time and talents, even going so far as to encourage and recruit replacements for themselves as age and poor health took their toll on their careers. Despite the seeming constant demand for a gorilla, either as the subject of some mad scientist's demonic whim, or as a companion to the villainous witch doctor in a twelve-chapter serial, only a few men possessed the physical strength and stamina as well as the mental (and possibly even emotional) desire to suit up and spend twelve hours under blistering hot Klieg lights with little assistance from the cast and crew.

It was long, lonely work; there was no fraternity of fellow day-laborers like the legendary stuntmen enjoyed. Most gorilla men weren't a part of the fledgling make-up departments of the new Hollywood studios—they were actually paid the same as day-laborers. They were gunslingers, after a fashion. One day at a time. One day on the Columbia lot, two days on the Republic lot, and then nothing for a week. Most gorilla men had second jobs, or used their ape suits to bolster their income when work on the lots was scarce.

Gorilla suits had been in play as early as 1918, when anonymous actors in suits populated the background in *Tarzan of the Apes*, starring Elmo Lincoln. The suits were crude, and so were the actors' performances. Aside from jumping up and down or sitting hunched over on tree limbs, no effort was made to portray a real ape.

The first and, many say, the greatest, recognized gorilla man was

Charles Gemora. Like so many of the Golden Age of Hollywood's luminaries, Gemora was an immigrant from the Philippines who literally smuggled himself to Los Angeles in 1920, where his skills as an artist were noticed by someone at Universal. At the age of seventeen, he went to work in their art department as a sculptor, working on a number of famous sets (including the Opera House for Lon Chaney's version of *The Phantom of the Opera*). He sculpted his first gorilla suit in 1927 for a film adaptation of the play, *The Gorilla*, while working in the make-up department. By 1928, he'd made a suit for himself, the first of many, and landed the gorilla chores in *The Leopard Lady*. It was destined to be.

Gemora set the gold standard for what the job entailed. He traveled to the San Diego Zoo, one of the only places back then with a gorilla in captivity, and studied the gorilla's movements. A natural mimic, Gemora picked up on the great ape's walk, the way his arms swung out beside him, and more.

His original suit was made by hand, and to fill out his slim, short frame, it was stuffed with kapok, a fibrous plant material used for mattress ticking. Including the underpads Gemora wore to bulk up his 5'4" frame, the suit weighed sixty-five pounds, and thanks to the kapok, trapped his body heat and turned the suit into a pressure cooker. Later, he created more sophisticated apparatus that included water-filled bladders in the stomach of the suit to give a more realistic sway and jiggle, along with improved sculpting on the face and hands. Gemora also used arm extensions for shots when he would be walking in the suit, to better sell the illusion of true apelike proportions.

All of this attention to detail, coupled with Gemora's stirring performances in the suit, earned him the title "The King of the Gorilla Men." He continued his job at Universal, moving into the make-up department, and in his later years became head of make-up for Paramount. He made close to two dozen screen appearances as a gorilla, including the early exploitation flick, *Ingagi*, one of the great-grandfathers of today's "shocking true stories shot on videotape."

The film was allegedly a documentary about a tribe in the jungle that offered up their women as mates for the gorillas, whom they worshiped. Gemora played the titular gorilla, but because of the nature of the production, denied any involvement in the film until the Hayes office got involved and shut the picture down. Despite that little setback, *Ingagi* grossed two million dollars in 1931.

Gemora's oft-cited best role, according to most experts, is 1941's *The Monster and the Girl*, wherein he plays a gorilla with a man's brain. Ignoring the terrible science, Gemora managed to capture the pathos and the power of the great apes, often by using only his eyes, the only visible part of his own face.

Gemora managed to keep Universal stocked with gorillas at a moment's notice, but what about the other studios? Republic and Monogram were two of the largest perpetrators of the "cliffhanger" serials, full of derring-do, endless fights, raucous stunts, and unbelievable villains of every stripe. And where there were villains, especially in the jungle epics, there were bound to be gorillas, mostly played by one man.

What Ray "Crash" Corrigan lacked in finesse, he made up for in enthusiasm. A tall, handsome man, he entered the movies as a stuntman and a gorilla man in the early 1930s, and even had the privilege of doubling Johnny Weissmuller on *Tarzan and his Mate*, in 1934. He also played the part of the gorilla (uncredited at the time) for the production. Crash had a suit made to his specifications, including some creative modifications to the interior armature for the head and jaw that allowed the gorilla face to "snarl" when the jaw was opened past a certain point, triggering the second set of springs and levers. Crash also made a second gorilla suit, for use in the old chestnut of someone dressing up as a gorilla as part of a harebrained scheme, and then his partner encounters a real gorilla and thinks it's the guy in the suit. Hilarity ensures, naturally. Crash even had a white gorilla suit built for one of his more memorable roles, *White Pongo*.

Around the same time that Crash was appearing in such interesting films as 1936's *Darkest Africa*, he was hired as a contract player at Republic Pictures to star as one of the affable cowboys in *The Three Mesquiteers* series. This long-running series of "B" westerns was a Saturday matinee staple and ran for three years, making Crash Corrigan a hit with junior cowboys everywhere. There was just one nagging problem: the studio forbade Corrigan to play gorillas under his own name. They were trying to create a brand with Crash and didn't want this strange sideline to sully their efforts. Crash had no intention of giving up this lucrative sideline that he genuinely enjoyed doing, so he cut a deal with them: he could keep playing gorillas as long as he was never credited. As a result, it's not really clear how many appearances Crash made in the suit, but any time you see "...And...Pongo!" alongside the still of the gorilla, it's a good bet Crash is wearing the suit.

Corrigan did well for himself. He made a lot of money doing westerns and invested in a large swath of land in the Southern California scrub, upon which he built a replica western town and dubbed the place "Corriganville." One of the area's first theme parks, he staffed the place with old actors and stuntmen and put on wild west shows for the kids, and later in the fledgling era of television, rented the entire space out for productions. Crash continued playing gorilla until failing health and a life lived hard took their toll on him. In 1948 he sold the suits to a bartender he knew who wanted to break into movies, Steve Calvert, and taught him some of the signature moves, and passed his legacy forward.

Calvert was another big strapping guy and he led a short but distinguished career behind the mask, appearing in some of the most infamous gorilla movies of all time. These magnum opuses included, but were not limited to: *Bride of the Gorilla* (1951), *Bela Lugosi Meets a Brooklyn Gorilla* (1952), *Panther Girl of the Kongo* (1955), and *The Bride and the Beast* (1958), directed by none other than Ed Wood, Jr.

Another prominent gorilla man who trod the same soundstages as Calvert was George Barrows. The son of silent-era actor Henry Barrows, George was a world-class fencer, and in demand as a stuntman and extra. Again, there are no records of what caused him to take such a bizarre career turn, but he took a leaf out of Gemora's playbook and built his suit from scratch. He was widely used in film and television, appearing on a number of classic television episodes in the fifties and sixties. Barrows' apex (some would say his nadir) was the god-awful *Robot Monster* (1953) wherein he plays the eponymous robot by attaching a modified diving helmet atop his regular gorilla suit. There is no explanation, and if there were, I doubt it would satisfy. Fortunately, Barrows' television work on *The Addams Family*, *F Troop*, *Adventures of Superman*, *The Beverly Hillbillies*, and many others create a far more watchable, if not reasonable, accounting of his time in the suit.

There were many others, of course. Bob Burns made a number of fast and loose, low-budget film appearances as Kogar the Gorilla at the same time that he was collecting discarded props and models from the various studios. Burns made live appearances as "the gorilla" in spook shows and special events held by the Los Angeles movie theaters. Considered the foremost authority on the subject of gorilla men, he tracked down Gemora, chronicling the elderly man's accomplishments in the field. Burns dubbed him the "King of the Gorilla Men." In his own gorilla suit, he is best remembered as the super-intelligent primate Tracy from the 1975 Saturday morning live-action show *The Ghost Busters*.

Another gorilla man who performed both on and off stage was Emil Van Horn. This handsome, compact performer was extremely secretive about his gorilla suit; he never discussed where he got it, who made it, or its operation. And what a strange suit it was! Van Horn's suit was known for his long arm extensions and a more chimp-like performance. His head featured a secondary trigger in the mouth to draw the lips up in a snarl. Van Horn started out in Vaudeville, appearing on stage as a "live" gorilla. Aside from a few bit parts, he only played apes during his film career. When jobs in Hollywood were scarce, Van Horn would play an ape in burlesque houses in what was known as a "beauty and the beast" act. The scrub work paid well, and Van Horn continued to appear more and more as the foil for the beautiful stripper and less on the silver screen as a gorilla man. His threadbare suit was eventually stolen by persons unknown, and he moved to Florida, where he died, alone and broke. His most famous role onscreen was in the 1942 cliffhanger serial *Perils of Nyoka* as the villainous Satan.

As technology became more elaborate, it was possible to make better gorilla suits. One of the most technically proficient gorilla men ever is Rick Baker. Even if he hadn't played the great ape in the not-so-great 1976 Dino De Laurentiis *King Kong* remake, he would still make the list for his impressive make-up contributions. His Kong suit featured a host of cable-controlled armatures for a wide range of expressions, a first in the field. These were improved upon in 1984's *Greystoke: The Legend of Tarzan, Lord of the Apes*, and again in 1988 when he created full body, realistic gorilla suits for *Gorillas in the Mist*. Baker, like so many filmmakers of his generation, credited *King Kong* as a seminal influence adding to his lifelong fascination with apes. In 1998, he created the gorilla for the remake of *Mighty Joe Young*, and completely and convincingly redesigned the iconic ape make-ups for Tim Burton's 2001 "re-interpretation" of *Planet of the Apes*.

There were, of course, even more gorilla men who performed a role once or twice. These men came to the profession through unknown means, and left for a variety of reasons. Janos Prohashka is best remembered for his television work in shows like *The Outer Limits* and *Star Trek*, where he battled William Shatner as the Mugato. He and his son's lives were sadly cut short in a plane crash in 1974. Don McLeod was a noted mime who donned a gorilla suit for several films in the late seventies and early eighties, most notably in the movie *Trading Places*. Peter Elliott was a gifted mimic who made a career out of playing the gorilla underneath Rick Baker's fantastic gorilla suits in *King Kong Lives*, *Greystoke: The Legend of Tarzan, Lord of the Jungle*, and *Gorillas in the Mist*. Elliott brought natural, realistic moves to his performances and convinced millions of moviegoers that the actors were working alongside real apes.

Baker may indeed be the last of his kind, working with concrete materials such as yak hair, latex, and remote-controlled cables. As digital filmmaking and computer-generated imagery have gradually taken over the process, filmmakers have experienced a creative freedom unlike anything seen before in the history of movies. If you can imagine it, it can be built into a computer and animated. However, when it comes to certain creatures, directors have wisely concluded that you get a much better performance when you put a man into the suit—even if the suit is digital.

Andy Serkis is the latest man to wear the moniker of gorilla man. But Serkis has an advantage that no other gorilla man ever had: absolute freedom of movement because he's not in a gorilla suit. Rather, he wears a skin tight motion-capture suit, allowing the digital camera to pick up key movement points on his body. These are then scanned into a computer and the all-digital gorilla "suit" is drawn around the motion points. The result is a digital subject with incredibly lifelike movements.

This technique was used to smashing success in Peter Jackson's *Lord of the Rings* trilogy for the role of Gollum (also played by Serkis) and later re-used for Jackson's bombastic 2005 remake of *King Kong*. Serkis, wearing gorilla dentures and covered in little dots, did battle with green foam-rubber mallets and tennis balls that became the dinosaurs and other creatures plaguing Kong on Skull Island. His performance was so inspired that when the *Planet of the Apes* franchise was relaunched in 2011, Serkis was the first person who came to mind to play the super-intelligent Caesar. Now armed with a facial capture system that tracked every twitch of his eyelid, Serkis was able to portray a hyper-realistic chimpanzee, incapable of speech, but telling the audience everything they needed to know with his eyes, his facial expressions, and his body language. He is the gorilla man for the twenty-first century.

It seems incongruous that it would take millions of dollars in technology, computers, and high-definition camera rigging to effectively replicate what Charles Gemora did while wearing a homemade costume. As the movies have matured, so have the movie-making techniques. But one thing has remained unchanged: the audience's eternal fascination with our closest living relative in the animal world. Our notions of primates and primate behavior have changed dramatically in just a few decades, thanks to the popularity of nature documentaries and a cadre of dedicated professionals in both academic and entertainment circles who have raised awareness for the real and tenuous situation of the Mountain gorilla and other species. And yet, despite all of that, *Rise of the Planet of the Apes* was one of the top-grossing fantasy movies of 2011. Maybe it's because we recognize ourselves in these creatures—both our similarities and our differences. The gorilla men of Hollywood serve as a very real metaphor for that concept, and their performances will continue to thrill and delight and always plant the seed of doubt within us as to just how far up the evolutionary ladder we've really climbed.

DR. HUDSON'S SECRET GORILLA

Howard Waldrop

After a devastating car accident, an actor awakens in an unfamiliar body. The Mad Scientist, the Evil Assistant, and the Beautiful Woman introduce the man-beast to his fresh identity and usher him into his new life. Fueled by his obsession of bad ape movies, Waldrop masterfully explores what it means to be human.

I do not remember anything, after the wreck, until I put my finger to my ear.

And felt the fur scratch against my hairy neck.

The fur from the back of my hand.

Later, after I had tried to rip the bandages from my head, and from somewhere behind me a needle had descended and pricked me, and I passed out; later, I awoke.

I lay still. I was on my back and watched the rise and fall of my smooth chest. My head was ringing from the drug used on me. Little blue circles swirled like a gnat swarm in my eyes. Slowly I raised my hand into my line of sight and saw its hairy back, like a glove made from a shag rug.

I pulled it to my head, found the edges of the bandages which started just above my brow. The brow was thick and long as a bicycle handlebar.

I lay back. Even that small movement caused my head to scream and slip sideways, and I went over.

Late for showtime. Critic's screening of new, solid blockbuster movie, seventeen stars, studio hype. Wet night, slick streets. Down the Canyon road, around the turn, headlights catch a dog or a cat or a small child, stomp the brake, good Michelin tires grab the road, Triumph says good-bye highway, sailing, sailing the lights of LA look nice tonight and are they getting close no time to scream now...

I come up from the memory and shiver to find I have awakened myself groaning.

The groan is a hurricane inside an echo chamber, long, low, wet, with lungs and strength, hurt strength behind it.

The head pain is gone. Again, I look down my body at the hugeness, the shagginess, the alienness. My body.

I need to take a dump. I cannot move well enough to get—where? To the corner of the cage. For I am barred in. It is ten body lengths long, five wide. Through one corner is a slanted running trough of water. Through the other, a fountain with a steel foot pedal. Outside the cage is dark. It is night, or the lights are off.

I am hurt. I do not understand what has happened. I do not think I am still dreaming. So this is what it is like to begin to lose the mind. I am afraid. I try to cry.

I see him staring at me while I open my eyes. The place is bright again and the light hurts.

He looks like Albert Einstein. He looks like a thousand mad

scientists. He looks like...he has a large nose, unkempt white mustache, a fringe of hair from the temples around his head. His eyes are grey and quite gone. I have seen those tombstone eyes on the Strip, asking for change to support a habit. I saw them once in the Army, in Nam, on a guy who'd lived through an ambush when no one else had. He was over the edge. He was gone. His eyes looked like those in photographs of factory workers from the 1890s, all shiny like little steel balls.

Little steel balls with lights burning inside them.

"Tuleg! Tuleg!" he yells. "He is awake."

I twitched from the loudness of his voice. The blue gnats threaten my sight, then subside.

I try to move.

He watches me. He does not say anything. He studies the way I try to use my fingers. I cannot place them flat so I can push myself up. I realize I am trying to use them as my own hands. And that will not work. These are twice as large.

A door opens somewhere. My vision is still fuzzy. Beyond the bars of the cage is a blur. Light comes from somewhere, then goes.

And before me stands the Evil Assistant.

He is huge, he must be huge. He looks like an oak stump stretched out by chains. He is bald, a muscular Erich von Stroheim, and he moves like an acrobat. He is wearing khaki pants (I can only see the waistband. The cage is raised about a meter off the flooring of the—room?—the cage is in) and a real undershirt, the kind with thin shoulder straps and no sleeves. He is rubbing pizza sauce from his mouth as he walks in. He looks at me and scratches his chest with his right hand.

"So?" he says to the madman.

"So!?" says the other. "I have succeeded. You helped with the operation, you saw! A man's brain in the body of a gorilla. He lives! He will live, of that I'm sure."

"Mmm," grunted the man. He turned to leave. "Call me if you *really* need me."

I listened to them talk. I could not believe it. Was I making up this dialogue? Was I still asleep?

I looked at the Mad Scientist. He stared back as if I were golden, silver, a flying saucer, the Loch Ness monster.

The Evil Assistant went out the door. There was something about him I did not like. He seemed familiar.

Rondo Hatton. He reminded me of Rondo Hatton, the Creeper. He did not need acromegaly. He was an ugly man.

The Mad Scientist leaned on the cage and stared at me.

Time passed and the scientist was gone. I managed to get up and hobble my way to the trough. I took a dump.

Gorilla shit is dry, almost all the liquid is gone from it. What I had eaten, or rather what the former owner of the body had last eaten, I do not know.

When I finished I lay back down. My head hurt. My body hurt. I sank into slumbers.

Sometime later I felt another needle go into my skin. I was too weak to fight back. My sleep was filled with dim nightmares.

I saw beyond the cage a hospital stand with an empty IV bottle attached. Intravenous feeding, saves time, saves trouble.

I stood, went to the latrine, shuffled my weight across to the water fountain, stepped on the pedal and doused my face with water.

It did not feel the same as it did when I had done it...when I was a man. It felt as if the skin there was made of leather sewn on the outside of my normal face. I pushed on it, pulled at it with my clumsy hands. I pulled my fingers and tried my toes.

I stepped on the pedal, ran water into the fountain. I held my hairy, notebook-sized hand over the drain. There was light, from an indirect source, in the room.

I watched the drain fill, the water rise over my hand like a river flood covering a forest. Then I took my foot away from the handle.

I stared into the basin.

Gorilla eyes. Tiny. Brow swept back to a sagittal crest. Head like a cinderblock. Thick. Ugly.

I sat on the floor, my toes curled in. I could not believe it. I sat that way until I realized how I must look. Like a gorilla. A gorilla trying to solve the mysteries of the universe. I got up and began to pace the cage, slowly. Then I stood with my hands through the bars. Gorillas don't do that. Humans do that.

gorilla gorilla

The most nearly human, the most frightening primate. No one believed the stories the natives told. Old men of the woods. They live there, they beat their chests, they drive you off. They kill. They have teeth the size of knives. Pliny wrote about them. The Romans knew them, and later the Spanish and the Portugee. And they did not believe, either.

Two gorillas. The lowland, first, the one of the rain forest, and the mountain gorilla, he of the open hillsides. Dying, now, the bands breaking down, to the bulldozer, the city, the poachers.

Huge, the gorilla. Fierce-looking. Bestial, perhaps because he is so close to man, yet so far away. So strong, so heavy. Men twisted by nightmares.

The gorilla will fight, is shy. The beating of the chest is liable to be replaced by some other harmless activity. The males will protect the young and the females. They usually run and do not charge.

See the gorilla. Terror of the jungle. Killer of the Congo. King of the Apes. gorilla gorilla.

The Mad Scientist was named Hudson.

The Evil Assistant called him that the next day.

I watched them come into the room while they talked.

Then I stood.

"You see?" said Hudson. "He stands on two legs."

I walked to the bars. I motioned with my hands. I wanted to know *why?*

Hudson watched me.

"You see?" he said to Tuleg. "He understands. He is still a man."

I was clumsy. I couldn't walk so well on two legs. I didn't know *how* to walk on all fours. You can't walk on four legs like a man would. I couldn't do anything right. I sat down.

"He is uncoordinated," said Hudson. "He can learn, though."

"So, who's gonna teach him?" asked Tuleg.

"We are," said Hudson.

For the first time, there was authority in his voice.

The days passed. At first, they still gave me intravenous feedings and kept me groggy with drugs.

Then Hudson began to speak to me, like a child.

I tried to talk. What came out was *nnngmnnnnnnnng*.

I wanted to write. I moved my hands like writing.

Hudson handed me a pen and paper, happy as a child.

My fingers were like tree limbs. My thumb was like a sledge-hammer. One letter took up most of the page. I tried.

"You will get better with it," said the Mad Scientist. "Don't worry."

I threw the pen down, tore the paper, clumsily, in half. I couldn't even do that well.

"Nod if you understand me," he said.

I nodded.

Hudson laughed and clapped his hands. "You do!" he said, dancing in little steps. "You do!"

I nodded again, my insides were turning with joy.

"Wait until I tell Tuleg!" he said, and ran from the room. I stood dumbfounded. We had been communicating, no matter how crudely. And he left. He left.

I did not want to be alone. I roared. I yelled, I shook the bars until my head began to spin and I had to sit, I sank to the floor and shivered.

I found that gorillas can cry.

I held the ballpoint pen in my hand and rocked myself to sleep.

The next morning, I realized what was wrong. Dr. Hudson was crazy, really mad. I had never thought of the meaning of the words "mad scientist" before. He must be mad to experiment so. But his madness did not end there. No. He is *mad*. He walked away when we were ready to communicate. He works to make me a gorilla, then he works to bring the man back out. And at the instant he does, he forgets me. He is *mad*.

Tuleg walked in by himself and shut the door.

I sat with the ballpoint pen in my hand, toes curled in, my knuckles flat on the floor. I stared back at him.

He stood with his arms akimbo. With his bald head, in the daylight, he reminded me of Boris Karloff in *Tower of London*. Mord, the Executioner.

He said nothing. Then he went to the cabinet in the far corner and drew out a long, thin stick.

I jumped. I had seen one like it before.

"Ha ha ha," he said. His eyes said, "So you recognize the cattle prod, eh?"

He came toward me, moving his head to always keep eye contact with me through the bars. He reached the prod in and the sharp spark leapt like a knife. I felt as if I had been stabbed and clubbed at the same time. Smoke curled, and there was the smell of burnt hair in the air. I roared and leapt away from him.

But he moved far faster than I, and the prod touched again
and again
and again
and

I wrote with the pen, though he shocked me each second or so, and laughed as he did. I was quivering.

NO, I wrote, and he saw it, and knocked the pen from my hand. I reached for it, and he struck at me. The spark made my hand go numb. I watched the hair burn. I looked into his eyes.

"Fight me," he said. "Why don't you fight me?" He stuck the prod at my face. I tried to push it away.

Its touch blasted through my elbows to my teeth. I was crying, whimpering now. I lay down and curled up as best I could. He kept jabbing me, sending pain into me. I almost let go at each jolt. I bit my tongue in pain, felt blood run under my teeth.

The pain stopped.

"Damn you," he said, throwing the prod on the cabinet shelf. "Damn you to hell, why don't you fight me?"

He left. His words ran through my head. *Why don't you fight me?*

Because I am a man. Because. Because...

The Evil Assistant was evil. Evil with all its connotations. Evil has motive. Evil strikes without warning. Sadism is an evil which needs no motivation. To give pain is human. Perhaps Tuleg gets sexual release in giving pain? I couldn't tell. I did not give him whatever he needed. I will not. Not ever.

I have learned the meaning of the word evil. I do not like it.

There were hands on me.

Tiny hands.

I opened my eyes and winced where one of the prod burns had seared the flesh of my brow. I moaned and rolled to my side.

"You poor thing," she said. "You frightened thing."

Why, why, why when there is a gorilla, and a mad scientist, and an evil assistant, why...

Why must there be a beautiful woman?

I have seen all this before, I tell myself, as the doctor and the beautiful woman tend my wounds. I am so hurt, so stunned I can do nothing but lie and shiver. I am running a fever. My eyes feel made of grit and sand. I shake. Inside, I cry. They cover me with a blanket. I become dank, and cold by turns, and then burn for hours. I pass in and out of fever dreams. I see a jungle.

It is later, and I hear the Mad Doctor talk to the Beautiful Woman.

"I wouldn't have brought you here if I didn't want you to see it," he said. "I wouldn't have, if I had known what Tuleg was going to do. The brute! I hope he fries in hell. I'm going to send him away the moment he returns."

"I told you when he came to work for you that he was a terrible man," she said, her voice soft like an unswept floor.

"Well, he was a great help."

"I'm sure." Her voice sounded as if she had turned her back on him. "He helped you. Oh, Father," her voice quavered, then she continued. "Why?" she asked. "Why do something as stupid, as pointless as this? What use is it? What can you prove by it? What?"

"But, Blanche," he said. "If you could have known the heartache, the toil, the hours..."

"Can you imagine," she asked, turning toward him sharply, "what that poor man is going through? Can you?"

"He will make me immortal, Blanche."

"Oh Father, Father," she said. I heard her footsteps and the door open and close, hard.

"She doesn't understand. She just doesn't understand," said the old man, and moved some apparatus (the tinkling of glass and metal) around on the workbench.

I slept.

Tuleg must have come back sometime during the night. I opened my eyes and he was walking around the room, preparing food and tasting it as he put it in a bowl.

He brought it over to the cage.

"Here," he said, putting it in through the bars. "Eat."

He went back to the workbench. He took down, and began to clean, a Thompson submachine gun. He looked at me from time to time as he worked with it. "Eat, I said."

I went to the bowl. It was filled with rolled oats, raisins, bits of celery and apple, sugar. I tried it and found it good. I was still running a fever, but I put the food in my mouth anyway.

My hand brushed my incisors. I felt them both. Long, curved, they were really there. They could crunch through meat as easily as a pair of pruning shears. They could punch open a tin can. They could kill a man. I shook my head.

I finished eating

Hudson came in. He and Tuleg must have talked before, because the scientist was not surprised to see him.

"Today," he said to me, "we begin to teach you."

"You were Roger Ildell," said Dr. Hudson.

I nodded.

"You were killed in a wreck just beyond my home," he said.

"At least, your body was. I was able to remove your brain before deterioration set in. I saved it. I saved your conscious mind."

I nodded again.

"I used to read your reviews," said Blanche, who was sitting at her father's side. "The police are still looking for your body. My father and Tuleg removed all traces. They were very thorough. They were very methodical," she said.

"We have to begin all over with you," said her father. "She tells me you were an intelligent man. There should be no problem. You'll be able to write again, though you'll never be able to talk. I regret that," he said. Then quietly, "I regret that."

I opened my hands wide, held them out toward the scientist. And his daughter. *Why? Why?*

Hudson was puzzled.

Tuleg snorted and left the room. He still wore the stained undershirt he'd had on the first time I'd seen him.

I made motions of writing. The gorilla body I wore was struggling with itself. I wanted to tell them, I wanted to ask them. What was wrong? Was my mind crippled in the wreck? Why couldn't I speak? Why couldn't I write?

Blanche handed me a large pencil and a piece of paper the size of a tabloid. I wrote as best I could, taking up most of the sheet, slipping, straining to make myself understood.

WHY ME? WHY DO THIS TO ME?

Blanche read it and looked deep into my piggy anthropoid eyes.

"Oh, Father!" she said, and turned to the Mad Scientist.

He stared at me with his Einstein looks, his fringe of hair.

"I did it to save your life! Don't you understand? You would have died out there!" He began to shout. Lines of saliva hung inside his mouth as it opened and closed. "I have to teach you! I have to! You have lived so I could carry on my research! Yarr!" he screamed, and fell to the floor in a convulsion.

I watched. Blanche screamed for Tuleg. Together, they got the madman up off the floor and out the doorway of the laboratory. After a while, Blanche came back.

"You poor man, you," she said. She came to the bars of the cage. She put her hand through and touched my hairy fingers.

I jerked as if with the shock from the cattle prod.

"No!" she said. "Don't. I'll help you all I can."

She leaned closer, still holding my hand.

"My father is not well," she said, staring at my eyes. "He is a sick man in many ways."

She kissed my fingers just above the nails, and licked the hair between the thumb and index finger.

Mad. She, too, is mad.

I sit in the corner of the cage, my back against the bars, my feet and legs sticking out before me. I look at my bent legs, at my hairy knees, the flat pad where the bottoms of my feet begin.

I think.

First, there are the movies. I saw them all, in that other life. The gorilla is the image of terror, the anthropoid killer of men and children, the despoiler of women.

(The penis of the male adult gorilla is only a couple of inches long. Ask me.)

Gorilla at Large. White Pongo. Nabongo. Killer Gorilla. In Poe's "Murders in the Rue Morgue," I was Old Man Pong, the orangutan. In the film, I was gorilla. Bela Lugosi. Poor, tired old Bela, shambling through role after role in which he had nothing to do but menace and laugh. *The Ape. Return of the Ape Man. The Ape Girl. Captive Wild Woman.* They put a horn on my head for *Flash Gordon. Konga. Unknown Island. Mighty Joe Young.*

King Kong.

I think of Blanche and I dream of Fay Wray. She does not look anything like her. I see Skull Island. I fight *Tyrannosaurus* for her. Through the dim eyes of the beast I pull the wings off the pterodactyl. I throw men from the log over the ravine to the waiting spiders. I roar my challenge from the Empire State Building.

I fall to the streets below.

Why does the gorilla always lust after the beautiful girl?

Why?

Why?

Tuleg has hurt me again.

Blanche found me quivering and shaking.

She came into the cage with me, opening it with a key from the workbench. I lay moaning.

"Oh, Roger, Roger," she said, cradling my head in her lap. "I'll kill him. I'll kill him if he hurts you again! My father will get rid of him."

She washes away the scored and scorched places, soothes me, rubs my chest where the prod has not bitten.

I DIDN'T FIGHT, I write.

"I know," she says, rocking me, "I know. It'll be all right."

But it is not all right. Tuleg comes into the room.

He stops dead still when he sees her in the cage with me.

"Get out of there!" he yells, and runs into the cage, pulling her away from me. He slams the door. The key falls to the floor and he kicks it away. I try to get up. I hurt too much. I struggle up.

"Your father is dead," says Tuleg. "He went crazy and died."

"Oh no," she said, and ran up the stairs.

Tuleg followed her.

In a few moments, there is a scream, a woman's scream, and then another and another.

"No no!" yells Blanche as she falls through the door, her clothes torn from her. I hear Tuleg laughing outside, and he comes in the room, still holding part of her dress.

I shamble to my feet and roar. I slam against the cage, Tuleg laughs, then grabs Blanche by the hair and pulls her backward behind the workbench.

I mash my fist to paste against the door as I catch it between my shoulder and the bars. And still I push against it.

And still.

And still.

I have to watch the murder. And then the rape.

Then, only then, do I see the keys. I can't reach them. I try. Tuleg is not through with Blanche, though Blanche is finished with everything.

He is groaning.

The ballpoint pen. I find it with my hand. I stick it through the bars. Tuleg surely hears the jingle as I spear the brass ring. But he is busy, and finishing up.

I have the keys now, and I put them inside the cage lock.

I turn the key. The lock grates. "No," says Tuleg, as he looks up from behind the bench, his face twisted in release. He jerks from the body.

He is going for the submachine gun.

I am there first, cutting him off. He is half-naked. He bolts for the door. He slams it shut. His feet run up the stairs.

The doors part for me like a curtain, flinders flying each way.

It is a beautiful house, and Tuleg has made it to a phone. He is screaming an address into it. He turns, and his eyes go strange as he tries to stick a knife in me.

I do not feel it. I grab him by the ankle and pull him down. I am four hundred pounds of muscle and sinew, and he is a paper doll. The phone smashes against the bannister; Tuleg tries to scream.

I use him like a pogo stick, my foot and weight on his neck, while I hold to his kicking feet. One jump, two. *Snap crunch snap.* I like the sound as his neck goes soft like a pair of socks. Then I smash his head, and use the knife like a hoe in his stomach.

I carry the body of Blanche Hudson, and the air is filled with sirens, all coming toward us.

I carry her into the garden, where there is a gazebo. It looks out over the rest of the Canyon, and above me, that must be where my car plunged over.

I also carry the Thompson submachine gun in my hand.

I place the body of Blanche on the floor of the grape arbor, and lay her dress over her as neatly possible. She is sweet in death, if you ignore the blood.

The house is beginning to burn. Tuleg's smoke will rise up to Hell forever, like the doctor said.

Fire trucks, police cars, spectators drive around front.

Ah.

Two policemen run toward me, yelling.

It is night, and they could not have seen me. One turns the corner of the garden house and sees Blanche's body (the beautiful daughter of the Mad Scientist) and stops. His eyes go wide as I bite through his throat, my hand on his face in a grip like a vise.

One banana, two banana, three banana, four.

The second cop sees me and draws his pistol.

I break his arm and knock in his head with the butt of the Thompson.

There is a stinging on my cheek, and the sound of a bee going by. Bullets. Oh so many of them. *Pop pop pop.*

I turn and say my name, but it must sound like a roar to them.

I turn the selector switch on automatic and open fire.

The Thompson says *its* name.

(A: A gorilla with a submachine gun.)

There is the sound of glass exploding and brick dust powdering wherever I point. *Tinkle tinkle crash.*

Little points of light wink, and the air fills with whines and screams. I fire again, and run into the bushes where the yard ends.

They are after me. I show them, they are afraid for what I am. I'll show them how near they are to me. I show them my teeth, up close.

Someone gets in the way and I kill him as I run.

I have the machine gun. They will not take me alive. You have sent me after the Three Stooges. You have visited my nightmare form on Abbott and Costello. You have run me across a footbridge where I snarled at Laurel and Hardy.

I am funny. Gorillas are funny.

I will show you funny.

This ape can think. It can pick locks and plant dynamite charges and use an M16. Oh, there will be deaths! Run, Kong, shamble away before they catch you.

Careful, there. Almost crouched as I ran. Have to watch it.

Not to go on all fours. That is the Law.

THE APES AND THE TWO TRAVELERS

Aesop

From the father of the fable comes a tale of two men who encounter the Land of the Apes.

Two men, one who always spoke the truth and the other who told nothing but lies, were traveling together and by chance came to the land of Apes. One of the Apes, who had raised himself to be king, commanded them to be seized and brought before him, that he might know what was said of him among men. He ordered at the same time that all the Apes be arranged in a long row on his right hand and on his left, and that a throne be placed for him, as was the custom among men. After these preparations he signified that the two men should be brought before him, and greeted them with this salutation: "What sort of a king do I seem to you to be, O strangers?" The Lying Traveler replied, "You seem to me a most mighty king." "And what is your estimate of those you see around me?" "These," he made answer, "are worthy companions of yourself, fit at least to be ambassadors and leaders of armies." The Ape and all his court, gratified with the lie, commanded that a handsome present be given to the flatterer. On this the truthful Traveler thought to himself, "If so great a reward be given for a lie, with what gift may not I be rewarded, if, according to my custom, I tell the truth?" The Ape quickly turned to him. "And pray how do I and these my friends around me seem to you?' "Thou art," he said, "a most excellent Ape, and all these thy companions after thy example are excellent Apes too." The King of the Apes, enraged at hearing these truths, gave him over to the teeth and claws of his companions.

A REPORT TO AN ACADEMY

Franz Kafka

Translated by Gio Clairval

An ape named Red Peter, who has learned to behave like a human, presents to an academy the story of how he effected his transformation. Often seen as satirization of Jews' assimilation into Western culture and a metaphor for the Jewish Diaspora, Kafka's powerful 1917 story of internal identity first appeared in the German Zionist magazine *Der Jude*.

Esteemed Gentlemen of the Academy!

You do me great honor by inviting me to report to your academy about my past life as an ape.

Unfortunately, I cannot comply with your request as you have phrased it. Almost five years have passed since my simian existence: a period that, measured by the calendar, might seem brief to you, yet one that is infinitely long when spent galloping here and there as I did, at times in the company of excellent people, advice, approval and orchestral music, yet fundamentally alone, as every accompaniment played in the background or, just to remain in the metaphor, away from the limelight.

I would never have succeeded, had I stubbornly clung to my origins and the memories of my youth.

The primary commandment I gave myself was to renounce all kind of obstinacy: I, free ape, accepted this yoke, but precisely for this reason I progressively closed the door to the world of memory.

At first—had men allowed me—I could have freely gone back through the huge door the sky draws above the earth, but as I was whipped through my training, the door grew lower and narrower. Gradually, I felt more comfortable and adapted in the world of men; the hurricane that had roared behind me was abating: today it is no more than a breeze cooling my heels, and the distant breach on the horizon from which that breeze blows (and through which I myself once came) has become so small a hole that, even assuming that I had the strength and the willpower to return to it, I would scrape my hide off my bones if I attempted to cross back over.

Playing an unambiguous tune—though for some topics, I prefer to use images rather than musical metaphors—speaking candidly, then, gentlemen, your own simian phase, inasmuch as there is something similar in your past, cannot be more distant to you than mine is to me. Yet anyone who walks the earth can feel that tickling on the heels, the little chimp as well as the great Achilles.

To a lesser extent, however, I am able to answer your question and will do so happily. The first thing I learned was to shake hands. The handshake indicates frankness, and now that I am at the peak of my career, I hope that I may now add frank words to that initial gesture. My frankness will not bring anything substantially new to the academy, and will fall short of what you have asked me, considering that, despite my eagerness to please you, there are so many details I am unable to communicate. Still, my words will describe the process by which I, an erstwhile monkey, entered the human world, and settled therein. Nevertheless I would not even say what little I remember, if I were not completely sure of myself and if my reputation on music-hall stages throughout the civilized world were not already firmly established.

I come from the Gold Coast. How was I captured? On this point, I must rely on the reports of strangers. One evening one of the Hagenbeck firm's hunting expedition—with whose leader I have since drained several bottles of an excellent red wine—was hiding in the bushes by the riverbank when, with a group of other apes, I came down for a drink. The hunters fired shotguns, and I was the only one struck: I received two hits.

The first bullet struck me in the cheek: nothing serious, but it left a large and perfectly hairless red scar, which earned me the horrible nickname Red Peter—a revolting name, entirely undeserved, and a name that, oddly enough, was invented by another ape, as if that scar on my cheek were the only difference between myself and the trained ape named Peter, who had died recently after enjoying a certain notoriety. But I digress.

The second shot struck me below the hip. That was a more serious wound, and it is the reason I limp slightly even now.

Recently, I read in an article written by one of those ten thousand muckrackers who mock me in the newspapers that my ape nature is not yet entirely repressed; the best proof is that I take off my pants so easily in front of the visitors, to show the mark left by that shot.

I would love to watch while someone shoots all the fingers off that writer's little hand. As for me, I have the right to pull down my pants in front of whomever I like. All anyone will see is well-groomed fur and the scar from—let's pick the appropriate word for this particular purpose, so as to avoid any misunderstanding—the scar from a wicked shot. Everything is perfectly visible; nothing is hidden. When it is a question of truth, great minds disdain polite pretentions. Now, if the gentleman that wrote that article were to take off his pants whenever he gets visitors, his action would certainly produce a different spectacle and the fellow's reluctance to disclose what lurks under his trousers seems perfectly reasonable to me. But he will kindly keep his delicate sensibilities to himself!

After those wounds I woke up (and here my own memories begin to emerge) locked in a cage below the Hagenbeck steamship's deck. It was not a four-sided iron cage. They had contented themselves with fitting bars to three of the sides of a crate, so that the fourth wall was made of solid wooden boards. The cage was too low for me to stand upright and too narrow for me to sit properly: so I had to squat, my bent knees constantly trembling. Initially, I probably did not wish to see anyone, preferring to remain in the dark; therefore I turned towards the crate wall, causing the bars to cut into the flesh on my back. This method of confining wild beasts after capture is considered effective, and based on my experience I cannot deny that, from the human point of view, indeed it is.

But at that time I did not think about that. For the first time in my life I had no way to escape, or if such a way out existed, it was not in front of me. In front of me was the crate wall, wooden boards closely fitted together. True, a crack ran through the boards, and when I discovered it, I howled with illogical happiness, but the crack wasn't even large enough to stick my tail through, and despite all my apish strength I could not widen it.

Later I was told that I was extraordinarily quiet, from which my captors deduced that, I would either quickly die, or, if I managed to survive this initial critical period, I would be particularly suited to training. I survived. Muffled sobs, painful flea-hunts, half-hearted licking at a coconut, banging my head against the case and pulling my tongue at those who approached: these were the first occupations of my new life. Above everything else, a constant feeling: I had no escape. What I felt then as an ape I cannot properly describe, for human words necessarily misrepresent the experience. Still, though I cannot recapture that old simian truth, I have no doubts it lies along those lines.

Up until then so many ways had opened before me: and now nothing! I was trapped. Had I been nailed down, my freedom would have been no less. How so? Scratch yourself between your toes, until they bleed or press your ass against the bars until it's almost sliced in two: you will not find the answer. I had no way out, but I had to find one. I could not live without an escape. Crushed in that coffin, I would surely die. But because an ape in the Hagenbeck company is supposed to squat, facing a crate, then I would cease being an ape. Somehow, this clear and obvious deduction must have brewed inside my belly, since apes think with their belly.

Don't misunderstand what I mean by "escape." I use the word in its most common and general sense. I am deliberately not talking about freedom: I don't mean the perception of open space; as an ape, perhaps I have experienced that feeling, and I have known men who yearned to experience it. But, as far as I am concerned, neither then nor now did I ever aspire to freedom. Incidentally: too often freedom is a way of deceiving men. Since freedom is deemed one of the noblest sentiments, the illusion of freedom is considered noble, too. Several times, before going on stage, I happened to see a pair of acrobats twirl up to the ceiling, leaping, swinging, doing jumps, flying into each other's arms, one suspending the other by the hair with his teeth. "This, too," I thought, "men call freedom: mastery of movement." What a mockery of sacred nature! The laughter of the simian race, seeing this spectacle, would be likely to bring down the most solid building.

No, I did not want freedom. I only wanted escape: to the right, to the left, anywhere. I aspired to nothing else, and if escape was illusion, my need being small, the illusion would have been small, too. Moving, walking: it was all I wanted; not to be forced to keep my arms raised, not to be glued to the wall of a crate.

Today I realize that, without the greatest inner calm, I would never have been able to escape my condition of prisoner. And, perhaps, all that I have since become I owe to the calm that penetrated me after the first few days on the ship. That calm, in turn, I owe to the crew.

They were good people, despite everything. I still remember the heavy clang of their footsteps echoing through my slumber. They were accustomed to doing everything very slowly: if one wanted to rub his eyes, he lifted one hand like a counterweight. Their jokes were coarse but jovial, and their laughter always mingled with a cough that sounded threatening but meant nothing. They always kept something in their mouth to spit, and they spat just about anywhere. They complained that they got fleas from me, but in reality they harbored no bitterness; knowing that my fur was a feast for fleas, and fleas jump, they were patient. When they were off duty, sometimes they sat in a circle around my cage and, lounging on the crates, they grunted to each other instead of talking, and smoked their pipes. Whenever I shifted position, they slapped their knees, and invariably someone grabbed a stick and tickled my favorite spots. If I were invited to make a journey on that ship today, I would certainly decline, but it is equally certain that my memories of life below deck, are not all painful.

The serenity I gained in the company of those men prevented me from trying to escape. Looking back now, I believe I had a dim presentiment that I would need a way out if I wanted to live, yet that I could not find that way through escape. I am not certain, but I expect that fleeing would have been possible for an ape. With the human teeth I have now, I must be careful even when cracking a nut, but back then surely I would have been able, with time, to chew my way through the lock. But I did not. What would I have accomplished by doing so? No sooner would I have stuck my head out, than I would have been captured again, and locked in an even worse cage. Or I could have snuck away to hide among other wild animals, such as the boa constrictors opposite, and breathed my last in their embrace. Or maybe I could have been able to run up to the deck and throw myself overboard: I would have floated on the waves briefly, then sunk to the bottom of the ocean. Desperate acts, all of them. I did not reason like a man, but, under the influence of the environment, I behaved as if I were able to ponder my choices.

I did not think things through, but I watched quietly. I saw men go back and forth, always the same faces, the same movements. Sometimes I thought there was only a single man. Those men, or man, went about unrestrained! Then a grand idea struck me. No one had promised me that, if I became like them, my cage would be opened. No one makes promises about seeming impossibilities. But when these impossibilities are achieved, then the absent promises appear, and in the very place where we had first tried to find them. I found nothing particularly attractive in these men. If I had yearned for the freedom mentioned above, I would certainly have preferred the ocean to the kind of escape I could perceive in their dull eyes. Nevertheless, I watched them for a long time before obtaining this insight; indeed, it was my observations which first inspired it.

Imitating men was easy enough. I learned to spit on the first day, and we would spit in each other's face—the only difference being that I licked my face clean while they did not. Soon I could smoke a pipe like an old hand, and if I pressed my thumb down the bowl, the whole deck rang with laughter, only because for a long time I did not understand the difference between an empty and a full, lit pipe.

I had the most trouble when I tried to tackle the bottle of aquavit. The smell was torture. I forced myself as much as possible, but it took weeks before I could overcome my revulsion. Strange to say, my inner struggles produced more impression on the men than any other efforts I would display. I cannot distinguish individuals in my memory, but I know there was one who watched me, alone or with others, at all times of day or night. He would stand with the bottle in front of my cage and give me lessons. He didn't understand me, and strove to figure out my nature. He would slowly uncork the bottle, and then stare at me, to make sure I had understood. I always watched him, I must admit, with a morbid, anxious attention, and no human teacher in the world could find a better student of human nature than myself. Having uncorked the bottle, he would raise it to his mouth. My eye followed the liquid right down his throat, so to speak. Here he was: winking at me, he brought the bottle to his lips, and I, excited by the gradual illumination, squealed and scratched myself all over. He, happy, curled his lips around the bottle's mouth and took a swallow. My impatience to imitate him peaked, and I defecated, making a mess of myself and my cage, and this filled him with satisfaction, and then he held the bottle at arm's length, swung it back to his mouth and gulped it down in one go, throwing his head backwards in an exaggerated movement meant to illustrate the procedure. I, exhausted by the intensity of my frenzy, I could no longer keep up with him and I weakly clung to the bars, as he finished the theoretical demonstration by rubbing his belly and grinning beatifically.

At this point would begin the practical exercise. Didn't the theoretical part already exhaust me? Yes, certainly, but this was my fate. So I caught the proffered bottle, uncorked it, trembling with joy because I could do it, and, encouraged, I felt my strength building up again, little by little. I lifted the bottle, with a gesture that seemed to me only slightly different from the example. I brought it to my mouth...and hurled it onto the floor, disgusted—even if it was empty and contained no more than the stench of alcohol. I hurled the horrible thing onto the floor, much to my teacher's dismay. I was sad, too, and my next gesture, which I have not forgotten, would console neither myself nor the teacher; still, I rubbed my belly, and offered the most perfect grin.

All too often the lesson ended this way. And to my teacher's credit—he was not mad at me. Well, sometimes, indeed, he'd hold his lit pipe against my fur and set it alight some place I could barely reach, but then he'd quickly extinguish the flames with his kind big hand; he was not angry with me, he understood that we were fighting together against my simian nature, and that in that fight I had the more difficult part.

Thus it was a great triumph, for him and for me, when one evening, in front of a crowd of onlookers—there must have been a party, for a gramophone was playing, and an officer was chatting with the men—when on this evening, I was saying, at a moment when nobody was watching, I grabbed a bottle of aquavit accidentally placed in front of my cage, uncorked it, as I'd been taught, and amid the rising attention, I brought it unhesitantly to my lips, without grimacing, instead rolling my eyes like a seasoned drinker, and drained it to the last drop! Then I tossed the bottle aside, not in despair, but with the precise gesture of an artist. I forgot, it is true, to rub my belly, but on the other hand, impelled by an irresistible force, all my senses roaring, I could not help uttering a clear and articulate "Hello," thus breaking into human speech. With that cry

I sprang into the human community, and the cry that echoed mine: "Listen! It's talking," felt like a kiss on my entire sweat-soaked body.

I shall say it again: I didn't enjoy imitating men. I imitated them because I was trying to escape my condition—I did it for no other reason. Moreover, even this victory did not yield great results: I immediately lost my voice and did not regain it for several months. My distaste for the bottle returned stronger than ever. Yet, despite everything, now I knew in which direction I had to move.

When I was handed over to my first instructor in Hamburg, I quickly recognized the two opportunities open to me: the zoo or the music hall. I did not hesitate a second. Put all your energy, I said to myself, into training for the music hall. It is the way out. The zoo is just another cage. If you end up there, you're lost.

And I learned, gentlemen. When necessary, when you must find a way out, you study, let me tell you, you study frantically. You monitor yourself with a whip, you flay yourself bloody at the smallest obstacle. The simian nature rushed out of me head over heels and abandoned me, so that my first instructor became almost an ape in the process of training me. He gave up training and had to be carried off to a mental institution. Luckily for him, he was soon released.

But I went through many teachers, indeed, even several teachers at once. As I grew more confident of my ability, and as the public began to follow my progress (bringing the prospect of a brighter future), I began to hire my own instructors, had them sit in five connecting rooms and studied with them all simultaneously, ceaselessly leaping from room to room.

And such progress! Such wonderful effects of the rays of knowledge penetrating my brain from all sides! I do not deny that such feelings made me happy. But I should also point out that even then I did not overestimate it, even less so today. With an effort so far unparalleled on earth, I attained the education of an average European. It may seem an irrelevant fact in itself. It is something nevertheless, as it helped in getting me out of the cage, granting me this particular way out, this escape into humanity. There is a German expression: to take to the bush. That is what I did, I have gone into hiding. I had no other way, always assuming that I discarded the choice of freedom.

If I survey my development and its goal up to this point, I neither rejoyce nor complain. Hands in my trouser pockets, a bottle of wine on the table, I half-lie, half-sit in my rocking chair and gaze out of the window. If visitors come, I welcome them appropriately. My manager is stationed in the anteroom. When I ring the bell, he rushes in and listens to my instructions. Almost every night I have a recital, and my success could not be greater. And when, late at night, upon returning from some banquet or scientific symposium, or pleasant social gathering, I find a little half-trained chimpanzee waiting for me at home and I delight in her company in simian fashion. By day I do not want to see her, for in her eyes there is the blurred madness of a tamed beast. Only I can recognize it, and I cannot bear it.

All in all, I have achieved what I wished to achieve. I would not say the result was not worth the trouble, and, any way, I reject the judgment of men. I present my account merely intend to advance science. I am only reporting, and even to you, esteemed gentlemen of the Academy, I am only making a report.

FADED ROSES

Karen Joy Fowler

Anders introduces a class of sixth graders to some famous apes. The acclaimed Fowler's bittersweet tour surprises with some sobering reality checks.

Thirty-two sixth graders from Holmes Elementary lined the rails that protected the glass of the Gorilla Room from fingerprints. Two of them were eating their lunches. Sixteen had removed some item from their lunch bags and were throwing them instead of eating them: their teacher paid no attention. Five were whispering about a sixth who fiddled with the locked knob on the workroom as if she didn't hear. Five were discussing the fabulous Michael K's eighty-two-point game last night, and three were looking at the gorillas. Anders approached one of these three. It was part of his job. He was better at the other parts.

"We have a mixture of lowland and mountain gorillas," he told the boy in the baseball cap. The boy did not respond. That suited Anders fine. "I know which is which," he continued, "because they're my gorillas. Now, some experts argue the noses are different or the mountain gorilla's hair is longer; but I've studied the matter and never seen that."

There were thirteen gorillas inside the exhibit. Five sat on rocks at the back. One baby played with a tire swing, batting it with her feet and turning an occasional somersault through the center. One stared in contemplative concentration at nothing. Four alternated through a variety of grooming arrangements. One nibbled on the peeled end of a stick. One surveyed all the others. It was a dignified scene. *Sullen. Reserved. Moody. Shy.* These were some of the words commonly applied over the years to gorillas. They had none of the joie de vivre of chimps. Gorillas were not clowns. It took a dignified, reserved person to appreciate them. Perhaps it took a little loneliness. And Anders had that.

The boy pointed over the rail. "That one looks really mean." Anders did not have to follow the finger to know which gorilla the boy meant.

A lowland gorilla. Gargantua the Great. "Paul du Chaillu was probably the first white man to see gorillas," Anders told the boy. "He tracked them and shot them and came back to France and told stories about their ferocity. Made him look brave. Made his books sell. Barnum did the same thing with his circus gorillas. He knew people would pay more to be scared than to be moved." Beyond the glass, Gargantua swiveled his huge head. The teeth were permanently exposed, but the eyes, directed obliquely left, said something else. Anders was proud of those eyes.

"That gorilla there, well, an angry sailor poured nitric acid on him. The sailor'd lost his job and wanted to get even with the importer. The acid damaged the muscles on the gorilla's face, so he always looks like he's snarling. It's the only expression he can make."

A storm of peanut shells hit the glass. Anders identified the culprit and took him by the arm. Anders did not raise his voice. "I was telling a story about the big gorilla in the corner," he said to the second boy. "This will interest you. He was raised by Mrs. Lintz, an Englishwoman, and he lived in her house in Brooklyn until he got too big. He may look fierce, but he was always terrified of thunder. One night there was a thunderstorm. Mrs. Lintz woke up to find a four-hundred-pound gorilla huddled on the foot of her bed, sobbing."

There were perhaps six children paying attention to Anders now. Somewhere an elephant trumpeted. "They don't look at us," one boy complained, and a girl in a plaid shirt asked if they had names.

"Actually we have three gorillas who were raised as pets by Englishwomen," Anders said. "John Daniel. And Toto, too, the fat one there looking for fleas. And Gargantua, whose real name is Buddy. Gorillas don't look at anyone directly and they don't like to be stared at themselves. Very unsuited to zoo life. The first gorillas brought to this country died within weeks. The gorillas who lived in private homes with mothers instead of keepers did better."

Toto yawned. Her eyes closed as her mouth opened. She smacked her lips when the yawn was over. She was the newest of the gorillas. Anders had added her last year. It was harder to love Toto, but Anders did. Anders had learned everything he could about his gorillas and he knew that Toto was used to being loved. Spoiled and prone to five-hundred-pound tantrums, Toto had terrorized her way out of her first home. When her mother, a Mrs. Hoyt, saw that she could no longer control Toto, Toto was sold to a zoo, but Mrs. Hoyt came along also. "Toto was bought as a bride for Buddy," Anders said. "She was raised in Cuba, where she had her own pet. A cat."

Anders had ten children listening now. Did any of them have cats? Anders doubted it. And there were other indulgences. "When Toto came to the U.S. she brought along a trousseau. Sweaters, dresses, and socks," Anders said, "all with the name *Totito* in embroidery. The papers loved it. *The future Mrs. Gargantua.* But Toto threw her bed at Buddy when they first met, and her attitude never softened."

The prospective mother-in-law had done much to sabotage the union. "She's only a nine-year-old child," Mrs. Hoyt had said. "What do you expect?"

John Daniel moved along the back of the exhibit. His steps were slow and fluid; muscles rippled on his back. He was Anders's favorite. "John Daniel was purchased from Harrod's by Major Rupert Penny of the Royal Air Force as a present for his aunt. John Daniel had a variety of ailments, including rickets, but the aunt, a Mrs.

Cunningham, fixed that. She raised him as she would have raised a small boy. A certain amount of indulgence. A certain amount of no nonsense. He ate at the table with them and was expected to get his own glass of water and to clear his own dishes. He was taught to use the toilet and, since he cried when he slept alone, was given a room next to the major's. Mrs. Cunningham consulted no experts but used her own judgment in devising his diet, which included fruit, vegetables, and raw hamburger. And roses. He loved to eat roses, but only if they were fresh. He wouldn't eat a faded rose."

When he became too big to keep, Mrs. Cunningham sold him to a private park she believed would be ideal. Tragically, he ended up in the circus instead. Anders had lost his own indulgent mother at the age of eight. He thought he had some insight into John Daniel. He knew what it was like to suddenly, inexplicably, exchange one home for another far less happy one. John Daniel's expression was intelligent but bewildered and bereaved.

Too subtle for sixth graders. Anders was down to an audience of four. "So interesting," the teacher said brightly, although Anders did not think he had been listening. Probably he had been there with a different class last year and perhaps the year before that. Probably he had heard it before. Probably he had never listened. "Can you all thank Mr. Anders for showing us his gorillas?" the teacher suggested, and then, without pausing for thanks, "We won't see the giraffes if we don't press on."

No one else was scheduled until three. Anders opened the workroom to get his own lunch and a book. He was studying Koko now, a gorilla raised by a Stanford graduate student and taught to sign. He planned to eat inside with his gorillas, but Miss Elliot arrived instead. "Have lunch with me," she said. "I made cookies. It's a beautiful day."

Miss Elliot often came at lunchtime. She had no real interest in Anders, or so Anders thought. Her own upbringing as the baby of a large, loving family had left her with a certain amount of affection to spare. She regarded Anders as a project. No healthy young man could be allowed to molder among the exhibits. Get him out. Give him a bit of medicinal companionship. Miss Elliot wore a uniform with an elephant on the sleeve and below that the black circle. Miss Elliot showed the elephants, but they weren't her elephants and Anders doubted she even understood the distinction.

If he refused her offer: he would face her brand of implacable, perky determination. He found it unendurable. So he nodded instead and put the book back beside his tools and his sketches. He joined her at the exit, opening the door.

Miss Elliot shook her head. "You always forget," she said. Her tone was indulgent but firm. She reached back past him, brushing across the black circle on his sleeve, and threw the switch that turned the gorillas off. They ate lunch on the grass outside the Hall of Extinction. The cookies were stale. The flowers were in bloom.

AUTHOR BIOGRAPHIES

Greek slave **Aesop** (620–560 BC) became legendary for his series of morality tales.

World Fantasy Award-winning author **James P. Blaylock**, one of the pioneers of the steampunk genre, has written eighteen novels as well as scores of short stories, essays, and articles. His steampunk novel *Homunculus* won the Philip K. Dick Memorial Award, and his short story "The Ape-Box Affair," published in *Unearth* magazine, was the first contemporary steampunk story. Recent publications include *The Knights of the Cornerstone*, *The Ebb Tide*, and *The Affair of the Chalk Cliffs*. He has recently finished a new steampunk novel titled *The Aylesford Skull*, to be published by Titan Books.

Best remembered as the creator of Tarzan, **Edgar Rice Burroughs** (1875–1950) worked in many genres during his prolific career. He introduced the popular characters John Carter and David Innes and their unique worlds: Barsoom, a savage Mars, and Pellucidar, a hollow Earth civilization. Burroughs revolutionized publishing when he incorporated (one of the first authors to do so) as Edgar

Rice Burroughs, Inc. to produce his books and manage his many properties. His far-reaching influence can still be witnessed today in the *Star Wars* series and successful films such as *Avatar*.

Hugh B. Cave (1910–2004) was born in England and grew up in Boston, Massachusetts. His prolific writing career began in 1929 when he published the first of more than 800 pulp fiction stories. With the demise of pulps, he moved on to slick magazines and books, writing 350 short stories and novelettes and forty-nine books. Cave was published more than 2,400 times during his life. He received the 1978 World Fantasy Award for Best Collection (*Murgunstrumm and Others*), and Lifetime Achievement awards from the Horror Writers Association (1991), International Horror Guild (1998) and the World Fantasy Association (1999). (source: Milt Thomas)

Gio Clairval, an Italian-born writer of speculative fiction who lives in Paris, translates classics from French, Italian, Spanish, and German into English. Her latest translations can be found in Ann and Jeff VanderMeer's anthologies *The Weird* (2011) and *ODD?* (2011). The first English translation of acclaimed French author Claude Seignolle's collection of stories set in 1950 Paris is forthcoming in winter, 2012. Visit Gio at www.gioclairval.blogspot.com.

Scott A. Cupp is a short story writer and essayist from San Antonio, Texas. He has worked in the science fiction, fantasy, western, mystery, and comics fields. He has reviewed westerns and horror novels for *Mystery Scene Magazine* and currently does Forgotten Movies and Forgotten Books for the *Missions Unknown* blog. He has been a comic reader for more than fifty years. He became an ape fan when seeing King Kong for the first time in the early 1960s.

The author of dozens of books and even more short stories, **Philip José Farmer** (1918–2009) revolutionized science fiction with his 1952 short story (later a novel) "The Lovers," the first known science fiction tale to portray sex between a human and a non-humanoid alien. The winner of three Hugo Awards and the Grand Master Award in 2001, his best known series, Riverworld, was made into two TV movies, both for the SyFy Channel. He is also well known for his detailed biography of Tarzan and for his novel *Venus on the Half-Shell*, written under the alias of Kilgore Trout, a character created by novelist Kurt Vonnegut, Jr.

Mark Finn is an author, actor, essayist, and playwright. His biography, *Blood & Thunder: The Life & Art of Robert E. Howard*, was nominated for a World Fantasy Award in 2007 and is now in a second edition. Finn is the author of two books of fiction, *Gods New and Used* and *Year of the Hare*, as well as hundreds of articles, essays, reviews, and short stories, for The University of Texas Press, RevolutionSF.com, Greenwood Press, Dark Horse Comics, Wildside Press, MonkeyBrain Books, and others. He lives in North Texas with his long-suffering wife, too many books, and an affable pit bull named Sonya.

Frenchman **Gustave Flaubert** (1821–1880) most famously penned the "immoral" *Madame Bovary*. His scrupulously detailed and artistic works often reflected a scorn for French bourgeois society. An acknowledged master of the form, Flaubert is one of the most important forces in the development of the modern novel. Flaubert is buried at Rouen Cemetery in Normandy, France, alongside another literary giant, Marcel Duchamp.

Karen Joy Fowler is the author of six novels and three short story collections, including *Sarah Canary*, which won the California Book Award Silver Medal in 1991, and *The Jane Austen Book Club*, which was a *New York Times* bestseller. Her collection, *What I Didn't See and Other Stories*, won the 2011 World Fantasy Award. A new novel tentatively titled *We Are All Completely Beside Ourselves* is scheduled for publication in May 2013.

Robert Ervin Howard (1906–1936) was an American author who wrote pulp fiction in a diverse range of genres. He is regarded as the father of the sword and sorcery genre. Known foremost for the character Conan, Howard's characters include Kull, Solomon Kane, and Bran Mak Morn. Passionate about literature and writing from youth, Howard died at age thirty after only twelve years as an author. He wrote over 800 stories and poems, which take us to such divergent surroundings as the ancient Atlantis, the North African desert, secret opium dens, boxing arenas, and battlefields.

Having only published a few short stories in his lifetime, **Franz Kafka** (1883–1924) died largely unknown. At the end of his life, Kafka asked his lifelong friend and literary executor Max Brod to burn all his unpublished work. Thankfully, Brod overrode those wishes and began publishing the now-classic stories of alienation.

Leigh Kennedy was born in Denver, Colorado, where she began writing stories early in her teens, and later earned a degree in history. She lived in Austin, Texas, for five years, then moved to England over twenty-five years ago. Published on both sides of the Atlantic, *Faces* was her first short story collection, followed by two novels, *The Journal of Nicholas the American* and *Saint Hiroshima*. Recently, a second collection, *Wind Angels*, was published. Another novel is in progress. Some of her survival strategies have involved deciphering doctors' handwriting, answering phones, and alphabetizing things. She has two grown children and is at home in Hastings.

Mary Robinette Kowal is the author of *Shades of Milk and Honey* (Tor, 2010), *Glamour in Glass* (Tor, 2012), and the 2011 Hugo Award-winning short story "For Want of a Nail." Her short fiction has appeared in *Clarkesworld*, *Cosmos*, and *Asimov's Science Fiction*. Mary, a professional puppeteer, lives in Chicago, Illinois. Visit her online at maryrobinettekowal.com.

Joe R. Lansdale is the author of over thirty novels and numerous short stories and articles. He has written screenplays and comic scripts and for animation. He has been awarded numerous recognitions for his work, including an Edgar Award, eight Bram Stoker Awards, a World Horror Convention Grand Master Award, and has just received the Lifetime Achievement Award from the Horror Writers Association. He lives in Nacogdoches, Texas, with his wife Karen.

Pat Murphy is a writer, a scientist, and a toy maker. She has written a handful of novels, including *The Wild Girls*, *Adventures in Time and Space with Max Merriwell*, and *The Falling Woman*. Her fiction has won the Nebula, Philip K. Dick, and World Fantasy awards, as well as the 2002 Seiun Award. Currently, Pat works for Klutz, a publisher of kids' how-to books that come with cool stuff. Her most recent book with Klutz is *Paper Flying Dragons*, which comes with twelve dragons that really fly.

Jess Nevins is the author of seven books and roleplaying games, including *The Encyclopedia of Fantastic Victoriana* (MonkeyBrain, 2005), a guide to the characters and concepts of fantastic nineteenth-century literature, and *The Encyclopedia of Pulp Heroes* (PS Publishing, 2012). He has written numerous essays and articles on popular culture, and thinks primates are cool, pulp primates cooler, and talking pulp primates the coolest of all. He is a librarian at Lone Star College in Tomball, Texas.

Though he published his first book of poems, *Tamerlane and Other Poems*, in 1827, followed by *Tales of the Grotesque and Arabesque* in 1839, **Edgar Allan Poe** (1809–1849) did not achieve recognition until the publication of "The Raven" in 1845. A seminal figure in the development of science fiction, horror, and the detective story, Poe's works influenced the writings of Dostoyevsky, Arthur Conan Doyle, Jules Verne, and countless others.

A member of the legendary Lovecraft Circle, **Clark Ashton Smith** (1893–1961), wrote over 100 highly ornate and poetic short stories, primarily for the pulp magazines. Alongside Robert E. Howard and H. P. Lovecraft, he formed the great triumvirate of *Weird Tales* contributors.

Steven Utley, a founding member of the Turkey City Writer's Workshop that emerged in Texas during the 1970s, has published hundreds of stories, essays, and poems. Gardner Dozois, who published most of Utley's output during the 1990s in *Asimov's Science Fiction*, declares that he "may be the most underrated science fiction writer alive...able to turn his hand to almost any subject matter, mood, or type of story imaginable." Since 1997, Utley has lived in Tennessee.

A bizarre cross-pollination of Cyril Kornbluth and Philip José Farmer, **Howard Waldrop**'s writings incorporate a wide range of subjects including alternate history, American popular culture, the American South, old movies, classical mythology, and rock 'n' roll music. He has been nominated for numerous awards, and "The Ugly Chickens" won both a Nebula Award and a World Fantasy Award. Waldrop's most recent book is his tenth short story collection, *Other Worlds, Better Lives: Selected Long Fiction 1989–2003* (Old Earth Books, 2008). He lives in Austin, Texas.

Director of *Rise of the Planet of the Apes*, **Rupert Wyatt** co-founded Picture Farm, the award-winning London and New York-based production collective. His first film, *The Escapist*, was nominated for a British Independent Film Award, Evening Standard British Film Award, and London Critics' Circle Film Award. Wyatt lives in Los Angeles with his wife, screenwriter Erica Beeney, and their son Theodore.

ABOUT THE EDITOR

Professional reviewer, geek maven, and optimistic curmudgeon, **Richard "Rick" Klaw** is the co-editor of the groundbreaking original anthology of short fiction in graphic form, *Weird Business*, the editor of *The Big Bigfoot Book*, and the co-founder of Mojo Press, one of the first publishers to produce both graphic and prose novels. He also served as the initial fiction editor for *RevolutionSF*. Klaw has written countless reviews, essays, and fiction for a variety of publications including *The Austin Chronicle*, *Blastr*, *Moving Pictures Magazine*, *San Antonio Current*, *GeekDad*, *Conversations with Texas Writers* (University of Texas Press), *The Greenwood Encyclopedia of Science Fiction and Fantasy* (Greenwood Press), *King Kong Is Back!* (BenBella Books), *Farscape Forever* (BenBella Books), *SF Site*, *Science Fiction Weekly*, *Nova Express*, *Steampunk* (Tachyon Publications), *Electric Velocipede*, *Cross Plains Universe* (MonkeyBrain/FACT), and *The Steampunk Bible* (Abrahams). Many of Klaw's essays and observations are collected behind a magnificent ape cover in *Geek Confidential: Echoes from the 21st Century* (MonkeyBrain).

He can often be found pontificating on Twitter (@rickklaw) and his acclaimed genre blog *The Geek Curmudgeon* (revolutionsf.com/

revblogs/geekcurmudgeon). Klaw lives in Austin, TX, with his wife Brandy, a dog, a cat, and lots of ape memorabilia.